Praise for Marie-Nicole Ryan's
ONE TOO MANY

"...a well written whodunit that ranks right up there for me with many of the well known mystery writers." Madame Butterfly's Blog

"A spunky, totally likable heroine, four murders and a truly hair-raising climax make this a great read. Ryan has a talent for character development, and you will rarely meet such an arrogant mad man. This builds on the earlier book, but takes it to a higher level. Recommended." The Romance Studio

"David and Miranda are well-written characters that anyone can easily relate to. I hung on every page trying to figure out who the killer was. This is another one of Ms. Ryan's fantastic books and I would recommend it to any reader!" Fallen Angel Reviews

"...reminiscent of the old whodunits, like Dashiell Hammett or Raymond Chandler novels: a great mystery to be solved, some intense action and a little romance. One Too *Many* is a real page turner and will keep you guessing until the very end." Joyfully Reviewed

"Author Marie-Nicole Ryan pens a novel that seizes the reader, and does not let go until the last harrowing moment. I adored this book." Manic Readers

"Ryan did a great job unraveling this complex tale just a bit at a time to keep the reader fully involved. The climax is fast-paced and harrowing. It's a great action-packed suspense novel." Literary Nymphs

Other Books by Marie-Nicole Ryan

ONE TOO MANY

A David and Miranda French Mystery

by Marie-Nicole Ryan

RYANDALE PUBLISHING

Copyright

Copyright © 2008 by Mary Varble
Cover design by Mary Varble
Cover photo © Andrew Roland/Dreamstime.com

First Ryandale Publishing Print Publication: 2015
Second Ryandale Publishing Print Publication: 2019
All rights reserved. Ryandale Publishing
ISBN: 9781393665069

Previous electronic publication, Samhain Publishing, Ltd, 2008
Previous print publication, Samhain Publishing, Ltd, 2009

Library of Congress Registration Number: TX 6-975-148

Dedication

To Angela Britnell, fellow author and British-born MCRW member, who graciously read this manuscript and applied her eye to my use of Britishisms.

Acknowledgments

First, I owe a deep debt of gratitude to British author, Kate Johnson, for all her info about East Anglia from winter weather conditions to the Royal Mail and for her endless patience overall.

Second, I would like to thank Sergeant Mark Puglsey of the Firearms Policy Unit of the Metropolitan Police at New Scotland Yard. His input about which members of the police force are armed and which ones aren't was of great value.

Obviously any mistakes are mine alone.

Chapter One

My honeymoon started off like most honeymoons—with a lot of lovemaking, a lot of fantastic food, and a lot more lovemaking—and ended pretty quickly with a murder.

No, don't jump to conclusions. I didn't kill my beloved David. Although I'm sure he just might have considered wringing my neck at least once or twice before it was over not literally, of course.

I suppose I should start at the beginning. I'm Randi Raines, an American and newlywed to the most wonderful man in the world, David French. How this ordinary gal from Nashville, Tennessee met and married a Detective Chief Inspector from Scotland Yard *and* the Earl of Middlebury is another story.

Maybe later.

Not that I think our love story is boring, but I figure falling in love is a heck of a lot more exciting actually doing it rather than telling about it. It loses something in the translation or maybe it's just the fault of the translator.

First, Picture the English countryside. Anyone who's watched their local PBS station or BBC America knows what the English countryside looks like. Anyway, I wanted to see more of it. I had my fill of Europe when David, Jamie and I were on the run. By the way, Jamie is my son by my first mistake—marriage, I mean. Jamie wasn't the mistake, but marrying my first husband, Stefan, was. Thankfully, he's rotting in a UK prison for the second time in his most miserable life.

I picked Kinsey Green in East Anglia for our honeymoon over David's more glamorous suggestions of Paris or Bali. And he, still being inexplicably besotted with me, agreed. The Green, as I quickly found out it was called the locals, had won the singular distinction of being named the UK's most beautiful village by a poll conducted in the London Daily Record in the millennium year.

I know this not from any vast research of mine, but from the quaint sign I noticed on entering the village. Of course, I know the real reason David agreed so quickly. After all, the Green is forty kilometers from his country estate in Middlebury County. They say Balmoral Castle is where the queen feels at home. For David, home would be Wyndswept, the family estate in Middlebury where he was reared by his nanny, Mina Griswold, until he was packed off to school at the tender age of eight.

The third morning of our blissful and energetic honeymoon, I dragged myself out of bed. If I hurried, I could brush my teeth before David woke up. I have this horrid fear of morning mouth and turning off my sexy husband forever.

Really.

He's done his best to convince me of his undying passion...and I have to say without reservation I've enjoyed every blissful minute of it.

Today, we had plans. You know what they say about the best laid plans? Good. I don't have to repeat the old cliché then.

"Where are you going?" My husband's sleepy voice sent all sorts of warm sensations to places best not discussed right now.

"The loo." Okay, yes, I'm an American, but I've been in the UK so long I've picked up some of the slang.

"Come back to bed." He patted the bed next to him. "I'm cold, luv. I need you." His warm gray gaze settled on me and weakened my knees, but not my will. My teeth would be brushed first.

"Can't. We have stuff to do today."

"Like what? Other than the obvious..." He grinned and

stretched. His lean, muscular body was awfully inspiring, but I was determined.

"I saw this antique shop across the street," I said, "several in fact, and I'd love to check them out." Not quite the truth but close enough. My mom's an antique dealer and often comes to this side of the pond on shopping trips. The truth is, I had a plan, a sort of half-baked one, but I hadn't shared it with David yet.

More about that later.

He sat up, his long legs bare, as was the rest of him. Disbelief pulled his handsome features into a scowl. "It's our honeymoon and you want to *shop*?" He clasped his hands behind his head and leaned back against the ornately carved Elizabethan headboard, a wry smile pulling at the corner of his mouth. "I'm sure I don't know what the state of matrimony is coming to when, after only a few days of lovemaking, you're ready to leave our bed and chase after another sideboard."

"Come with me." I batted my lashes at him like a femme fatale which I'm anything but.

Determined to claim the bathroom, I turned. Quickly and without warning, David was on his feet. His strong arms surrounded me and pulled me close to his chest, and his morning woody nudged me in the small of my back. "Listen here, fella," I managed to gasp.

He whirled me around so I faced his muscled chest. Okay, I'm on the shy side of five-two. I looked up into his handsome face— okay, I'm so utterly besotted by this man with the pillowcase crease on his left cheek—his gaze was warm and the word *no* wasn't in his vocabulary...not that morning.

"The shops aren't open this early," he said, and winked.

Too true. I nodded and let him lead me back to bed.

Sometime later, after we shared a lengthy shower and a late full English breakfast, David and I found ourselves on the Green's main drag. Across the street from the inn, the picturesque store awnings were rimmed with a frosting of snow as a dull winter sun rose higher in a pale sky. "There it is. That one." I nudged him in the direction of my target, Greenway Antiques.

His dark eyebrow arched in my direction. "The one with the *For Sale* sign?"

Damn. I should've known he'd pick up on that. That was the downside to being married to a detective—he noticed every little detail.

"Yes, that one."

He groaned, but then his expression brightened. "Why don't I check out golfing equipment? Would you care for a set of clubs? Golf's wonderful exercise and relaxing as well."

Like the excellent detective he was, he'd also spotted the sporting goods store two doors down from the antiques store.

"In the snow?" See, I noticed things, too. "Well, if you can tear yourself away from your bride's side after only three days..." I grinned and batted my lashes at him—just to let him know I really didn't mind. It was all part of my plan.

He walked with me to the door of the antiques shop. Arms folded across his chest, he peered at me. "Now don't go running off with any handsome antique dealers, like that Lovejoy fellow you're so fond of."

"Not a chance, big boy." After an oh-so-proper forehead kiss, he opened the door for me—I know I'm setting back women's lib a generation or two, but I liked that about him.

"Go on, now." I waggled my fingers at him and watched until he was safely inside the sporting goods store.

I entered the shop; the bell over the door jingled as I shut the door behind me. The interior was dark, and the shop smelled of things musty and old, like most antiques shops, although someone had set a fresh bowl of lavender-scented potpourri at the cash register.

"Hello?"

The aroma of fresh coffee lured me farther into the depths of the store. In other words, I followed my nose into the next showroom. "There you are." I saw a man sitting in a high-backed Queen Anne wing chair. Actually all I could see were his elbows as they rested on the chair arms. He didn't respond. Maybe he'd dozed off?

I eased between a pair of Hepplewhite side chairs and faced him. And wished I'd checked out the golf equipment instead.

He was dead. Horribly dead.

The man's penis...protruded from his mouth. My gaze traveled to his crotch—yeah, oh, yeah. My breakfast threatened to make a reappearance. I gagged, then swallowed hard. My hands shook as I dug around in my purse for my cell phone. I yanked it out and punched the speed dial for David's cell.

Thank heavens, he answered quickly. "Miss me already?"

I tried to speak, really. But I couldn't get much more out than gasping puppy-like sounds.

"Miranda? What's wrong?" By the way, only David and my mother call me Miranda. I'm always Randi to everyone else.

"H-hurry."

Through the phone, the sound of his rapid breathing and footsteps told me he was on the way.

I glanced around me. Was the killer still here? I literally felt the adrenaline surging throughout my body. My heart hammered and thrummed like the roll of tympani. Have I mentioned that I'm also a musician?

The blood was still red...fresh. I eased away from the body. Had I touched anything?

The doorbell jingled. Thank God. I closed the phone and shoved it into my pocket.

"Miranda!"

"Back here." It came out as a whisper. I tried again. "H-here."

He followed the sound of my voice and found me. I rushed into his arms and shook until I could breathe. "He's d-dead."

He looked over my shoulder. "So I see. Touch anything?"

I shook my head. "Just the splat of the Hepplewhite. I assure you I had no desire to touch anything else." Good grief, I was starting to talk like my husband, too.

David took his cell and punched in nine-nine-nine. "DCI French from the Metropolitan Police C.I.D. here. My wife and I have come upon a homicide in Greenway Antiques. Male, forties, mutilated. Of course, we'll wait."

He held me tight, and I clung to him as if I were drowning. "It'll be all right." His tone was calm and reassuring. With his strong arms around me, nothing bad would ever happen. I believed it with all my heart.

"But what if—?"

"You won't be considered a suspect. You've only been in the shop a couple of minutes. Whoever did this is covered in blood."

I shivered. "Thanks. That's an image I can do without."

Within less than two minutes of his call, three local police cars came to squealing stops in front of the shop. Two uniformed constables and a plainclothes detective entered. "DCI French?" asked the detective.

"Yes. My identification." David slowly reached into his pocket and pulled out his warrant card. No surprise there. He's an absolute pro through and through—of course, he'd have it with him...even on our honeymoon.

"Detective Sergeant Tower," he said by way of introduction. "This is your wife, sir?" He nodded toward me.

"Yes, Sergeant, Miranda Raines—uh, French," I said, now that I was able to breathe more or less regularly. I had to crane my neck at the good sergeant. He was even taller than my David, who is six-two on a good day.

"Touch anything?"

I held up my hands and showed him the front and back. "Just the Hepplewhite. That's all, I think. I certainly didn't touch him."

"The victim, Sergeant—who was he?" David asked.

"Fellow by the name of James Riley Stubbs, proprietor of this shop, and quite well +known for spreading his charm around with the local ladies."

"Must've spread it times," muttered the older of the constables, his long face twisted into a sneer. "Hmph. Stubbs, he weren't so stubby."

David arched an eyebrow. "If you'll note, gentlemen, the two body parts have been amputated and reversed, along with multiple stab wounds. A very personal attack."

"You examined the body?"

"No, only what I observed, Sergeant."

The sergeant spoke into his walkie-talkie. "Coroner will be here shortly."

They seemed to have forgotten me. "Excuse me. If you'd like to question me somewhere—anywhere but here—I'd appreciate some fresh air."

The DS nodded. "Of course, Ms. Raines—uh, French?"

"French." I smiled at David. "We're newlyweds, Detective Sergeant. I'm not quite used to my married name yet."

"We're on our honeymoon. Staying at the inn," David said. I guessed he was trying to hurry the good sergeant along and get me away from the scene, and I was very much in favor of that scenario.

"Right, sir." The detective sergeant turned to the younger of the constables. "See Mrs. French to the station. Get her set up with some tea or coffee. She looks pretty shaken."

"Thank you, Sergeant." I swallowed. "I'll be more than happy to answer any questions you have."

David turned to me. "Are you sure?"

I nodded. I knew what was coming next. "Yes, maybe you should call your office and stick around to see if they need your help," I suggested.

A wry grin kicked up the corner of his mouth. "You know me entirely too well, don't you?" His words came soft as a whisper. "Sorry, luv."

"You're a detective, so go on and detect." I shrugged to let him know it was okay our honeymoon was probably over. After all, he was mine for life.

Eyes shining with love, he rewarded me with a grateful smile. "Sergeant? With your permission?"

"Happy to oblige, Chief Inspector. A simple matter of courtesy." With that, the constable nodded. "Ready, Mrs. French?"

"More than ready."

*

On the short and somewhat bumpy ride to the police station, I decided to try my hand at a little interrogation. "Your partner said something about the victim's spreading his charm around? I'm not a detective, but that sounds like maybe a jealous husband or another woman didn't like it?"

The constable was in his early twenties or close enough. Cute too, with reddish-blond hair cut short and bright blue eyes. But of course, he couldn't compare with my husband.

"My partner spoke out of turn earlier," he said. "Should've watched his words. Sergeant will have someone's head before it's over."

"Oh, I don't want to get you in trouble, but with the—uh, mutilations, it was difficult to tell what he looked like before. Was he handsome?"

He kept his eyes on the road, but he was in the mood to talk. "Pardon me for saying so, but the bloody fellow thought he was a gift to the women around here. Not a bad looking bloke, I guess." He shrugged.

"Had he lived in the Green all his life?"

"Not by half. They say he used to have a posh store on Portobello Road in London. Moved here about five years ago. Bought the shop from old Mrs. Lovelace's son after she died."

"Now why would he have left his posh shop and moved here? Not that the Green isn't a perfectly lovely village... It is."

"Haven't a clue. I leave the detective stuff like that up to the detective sergeant."

"I try to leave it to my husband, too, but I don't always succeed."

The constable signaled and turned left off the cobbles onto a road with a smoother surface. "Newlyweds, I understand?"

"Yes. We're on our honeymoon." I watched a red flush creep up the constable's neck.

I wanted to giggle, but I coughed instead. "Are you married, Constable?"

"No, ma'am." He flushed even redder.

We pulled up in front of the local police station, ending his embarrassment and my interrogation. The station was brick, a long two-story building without any real charm, but then police stations aren't necessarily known for their charm, are they?

Chapter Two

David knelt carefully by the body and inspected the floor beneath the chair. There were several yellow particles he couldn't identify. "Will your Scene of Crime Officers be here soon?" he asked Tower.

Before Tower could respond, a newcomer stormed into the showroom. "What the bloody hell difference does it make to you, mate? Who the hell are you? This is my crime scene." He was red-faced and huffing, as well as a good ten centimeters shorter. "What're you doing messing about my crime scene?" the newcomer asked again, still not offering any identification.

David stopped short and straightened to his full height. "DCI French from the Met. CID. My wife discovered the body. I was at the sports store down the street when she called me." He paused. "And you are?"

"Detective Chief Inspector Beecham, Kinsey Green constabulary. My jurisdiction." DS Tower stepped forward. "Hold on, sir. I told him it was all right for him to stay." "You had no business authorizing his presence, Sergeant."

"Sorry, sir." Tower stepped back, his face turning a dull red.

"No problem," David assured the sergeant. "My wife is already at the station. I'll join her."

"Keep yourself available. I've a lot of questions for you." Beecham sniffed.

David folded his arms. DCI Beecham wouldn't win any personality polls, but the man was certainly within his rights. It was his turf, after all. "Of course."

"Uh, Chief Inspector Beecham," the sergeant began, "do you know who DCI French is?"

"Tower, you ask the stupidest questions of any detective sergeant I've ever had. He's DCI French from the Met. Big eff-ing deal."

"Well, yes, sir, he is, but—you're not a local. He's the Earl of Middlebury, too."

Beecham gave David a long, appraising look and curled his upper lip. "I'd heard his lordship was a copper. See here, I don't give a brass pence about your title or your position in the Met. At best, you're just another interfering witness or at worst, a suspect."

"Fine. I'll step back, but you might want your SOCOs to check out the trace under your victim's chair."

"Yeah, yeah. They'll get to it soon enough." He turned to the sergeant. "Where are those buggers anyway?"

The long-suffering sergeant rolled his eyes. "They were called out to the new crop circle—"

"Bloody hell! Crop circles don't require a forensics team. Get their arses here where we've got a real crime."

DS Tower nodded at Beecham and David. "Excuse me for a moment." He walked away from the group. From the jerking movements of the sergeant's head and shoulders as he spoke into his walkie-talkie, the sergeant was laying into someone. No doubt ordering the SOCOs to abandon the crop circles and be damned quick about it.

David cleared his throat. "Chief Inspector, any idea who might've done this?"

"And if I have, why should I tell you? I've a mind to interrogate that little wife of yours, French. I don't have to tell you how many times the person who discovers the body is the guilty party."

"I hardly think my wife had time to overcome a man nearly twice her size, rearrange his body parts and call me...all in less than two minutes. Mind you, she doesn't have a drop of blood on her."

"Forensics will determine that."

"Fine. My wife and I will cooperate fully in your investigation."

"Long as that includes you keeping your nose out of it."

DS Tower rejoined them with a peculiar glint in his eye. What did it mean? "Spoke with the captain," Tower said.

"Heard about the murder already, has he?" Beecham stretched his neck and ran his forefinger around one side of his collar, as if it were too tight.

Tower cleared his throat. "Captain Willis said to offer DCI French every courtesy and asked if he would give us a hand."

To the sergeant's credit, he kept his expression blank.

A dull red flush crept up Beecham's round face. Guess his anger was unavoidable. Not that David blamed Beecham for being upset. No copper liked having his turf invaded.

"As it happens, I'm on my honeymoon...but I'm happy to oblige Captain Willis's request."

Miranda would understand...of course she would. "If you wish to interview my wife, I'll stay here with Tower and wait for forensics."

"Well, I do need to get her statement, officially that is." Beecham's jaw was clenched so tightly, it was a bloody miracle the man managed to speak.

I hopped from the patrol car and followed the constable into the police station. To be perfectly frank, this was my third visit to a police station. The second had been to David's office at New Scotland Yard when he'd introduced me to his fellow detectives as his fiancée. Believe me, that was one rowdy group of guys.

I sort of skipped the first time, didn't I? Well, my first visit to a police station was traumatic in the worst way. Six years ago, my flat mate, Cassie Wheeler, was killed by a car bomb—a car bomb set by my ex-husband, Stefan Kristoforus, intended for her fiancé, then Detective Inspector David French.

But this third visit was somewhat different. I was there to answer questions about a murder—true enough—but I was more of an innocent bystander and not the inciting incident.

The young constable smiled apologetically and said, "I hope you don't mind waiting in the interview room. I can get you a cup of tea or coffee."

I shook my head. "I've heard all about stationhouse coffee. I think I'd like a cup of tea, please."

"Very wise, Lady Middlebury. I can't recommend the coffee either."

"Wh-what? Oh, I'm Lady Middlebury, right." Okay, I wasn't used to that title business yet. When members of the inn's staff first addressed me in that manner, I looked around to see who they meant.

The constable's expression grew puzzled. "What would you prefer?"

"Well, I guess I ought to get used to it, but honestly it's a bit much for a fiddle player from Nashville, Tennessee."

"Understood. My family farmed the Middlebury estate for generations, so it's natural. I heard his lordship had married an American," The constable said and favored me with a smile.

"Constable Dean, you have lovely manners, but if you want to call me Mrs. French, it would suit me just fine."

"Mrs. French it is then. And I'll fetch that cuppa for you." I smiled and nodded my appreciation.

He left the room and I glanced around. Now if I were a felon of some sort, I suppose the interview room might seem like an ominous place. But really, it was quite plain and ordinary. Gray walls, freshly painted ones at that, if my nose wasn't mistaken. There was a large mirror on the wall to my left—no doubt that was a two-way deal for observing interrogations. A table, two chairs in addition to the one where I sat, plus a tape recorder on the table and a video camera highly placed in one corner.

The constable brought my tea and left me alone again.

I sipped on the tea and boredom set in pretty quickly. I was anxious to know what the hay was going on with my beloved husband. He was in his element with an investigation brewing, but sitting alone in an interview room without so much as an out-of-date magazine to read was the pits.

The fingers of my left hand started moving nervously through the fingerings of the last classical piece I'd played. Another minute of boredom and I would be playing an imaginary violin and someone would haul me off to a loony bin.

The door opened like a crash of cymbals, and I jumped.

"I'm Chief Inspector Beecham. You're French's wife?"

"Yes."

"I'm in charge of this investigation, and I'd like to ask you a few questions." He turned on the recording equipment, stated the date and time.

"Certainly." My heart settled back into a reasonable four-quarter time. DCI Beecham was five to six inches shorter than David, red-faced, and already had Dunlap's disease—the belly done lapped over his belt syndrome. The dark gray suit he wore was wrinkled and creased. His bright red tie had seen a few too many roast beef and gravy dinners.

He walked around the room as if sizing me up. "Stand up."

I did as I was told. I'm not quite five-two and small-boned. I hoped it was readily apparent I couldn't have done anything like what had been done to the antiques dealer. I smoothed my dark brown slacks and held out my hands and arms for his viewing. "No blood, Chief Inspector."

"I'll have the forensics check you over. Could be hiding something on those dark trousers or that suede jacket."

"Whatever you say. I'm only too happy to oblige."

He walked back around to the opposite side of the table and motioned for me to sit down. I did. "American?"

"Yes, but I've been in the UK for almost seven years."

He leveled his gaze on me. I think I was supposed to be intimidated, but I've been interviewed by the police before.

"I've been checking you out." He scowled. "Found some interesting things in your file."

"I don't think I've been in the arca long enough to have a local file, but if you're referring to what happened in London six years ago, then yes, I do have a file with the Yard. Not that any of that has anything to do with today's events."

"Got yourself involved with an arms dealer." He pulled at his collar.

"I guess you could say that since I was married to him...briefly."

"And you were involved in a murder investigation."

"Yes, it's all a matter of public record, Chief Inspector." Why the man wanted to hash over my painful past, I didn't know. Maybe it was just his not-so-charming way of being sociable.

"Okay," I said. "Here's the quick version. I met Stefan Kristoforus. He swept me off my feet and we married. In spite of my mother's warnings it was happening too quickly, I plunged ahead. All I knew was he was totally besotted with me—or so I thought at the time. He turned out to be an abusive and seriously twisted man. I was a prisoner on the family estate for several months before I managed to escape to London where I found a job in Cassie Wheeler's bookstore. She felt sorry for me and offered to let me move into her flat."

"Didn't turn out too well for her, did it?"

"No, it didn't. But you know that already." I swallowed before I could bring myself to tell the rest of the story. "That's where I met her fiancé, David, DI French he was then. He was so lovely to her and polite to me. Then Stefan found me. He came to the flat and made threats. David warned him off and threatened to take him in if he didn't leave me alone."

Never has an act of generosity been so cruelly rewarded.

DCI Beecham frowned, but gestured I should continue.

"Stefan didn't take kindly to anyone's interfering with his wife, so he rigged a bomb in -David's Rover. But it was Cassie who was killed." I could just imagine what he was thinking. I'd turned my flat mate's tragic death into a bonus for myself. But it didn't happen like that.

"During Stefan's trial, I managed to keep the fact I was pregnant from everyone, including him and his family of arms dealers. MI5 placed me in Oxford, their version of witness protection."

Beecham pulled at his collar again—nervous tic? "Now why are you here in Kinsey Green?"

"My husband and I are here our honeymoon. Do you know him—DCI French?"

"Yeah, Yeah. I met him at the crime scene. You married your flat mate's fiancé?"

"I know how it sounds, but we didn't see each other after Cassie died, except once at the hospital. David was burned trying to free Cassie from the burning car. After that I was in Oxford. My son, Jamie, was born and we lived a quiet life. He was five last fall when David showed up one night to tell me that Stefan had escaped from prison."

"Your ex—that must've given you a turn."

I shivered at the memory. "You have no idea. Anyway, David said he was assigned to take us to a safe house until Stefan was recaptured. Somehow, Stefan had inside information and followed. He attacked us at the safe house. David took Jamie and me zigzagging across Europe with Stefan and his brothers not far behind." I smiled at the next memory. "Along the way, David and I fell in love, and here we are today in a state of honeymoon interruptus."

DCI Beecham shook his head. "Quite a story."

"But, surely you must realize I didn't have anything to do with the antiques dealer's death."

"Wouldn't be the first time the person reporting the crime did the deed."

"Now that may be true in a lot of cases, but I assure you *I* didn't."

"All right, suppose you tell me how you happened to find Mr. Stubbs's body."

"First of all, my mother is an antiques dealer, so I have an interest in antiques myself. I spied the shop—we're staying just across the street at the inn—so I suggested we take a look. My husband—he likes golf better than antiques—decided to check out at the sporting goods store down the street instead."

"Go on."

"We separated. I went inside the store and didn't see anyone. I smelled fresh coffee so I followed my nose and saw someone sitting in a Queen Anne wingback chair."

"That's the high-backed chair with the back toward you as you entered," he said, then pursed his lips. "How could you see someone sitting in it?"

"I saw his elbows resting on the chair arms. I called out, but he didn't answer. When I walked around to face him...I saw the blood. He was dead."

"How did you know he was dead? Did you touch him?"

"Because he wasn't moving. Blood was everywhere and while it appeared fresh, it wasn't pumping from any of the...orifices." I couldn't help but shudder at the memory.

"Not a pleasant sight, by any means, for someone on her honeymoon."

Thankfully, over the course of the interview his tone had mellowed and was less accusatory.

"No, it wasn't."

"Session ended at eleven-oh-one," DCI Beecham said and turned off the recorder. "I'll send in a technician to check your clothing. Just a formality."

"I understand," I said, beginning to warm to his kinder and gentler attitude. Maybe he wasn't so bad after all.

Chapter Three

The SOCOs had taken over the crime scene. David went back to their hotel suite to see if Miranda had returned. She hadn't. Apparently Beecham was still interviewing her. David put in a call to his superintendent and updated him. He clenched the mobile in his fist and listened. "But see here, guv—"

"My mind's made up. Eric Stafford's your new sergeant, and I'm sending him over to assist you in this enquiry."

"But surely I have a choice—"

"Normally I'd have consulted you, but you were on your honeymoon, old man. Stafford excelled on his examinations. The decision needed making. I made it."

"And the fact that his father is the commissioner has nothing to do with it?"

"Don't be unreasonable, French."

"Stafford may be book smart, but he's lacking investigative field experience."

"Well then, he'll have some before long, won't he? Never known you to balk at a challenge."

David growled. Bloody hell. He was supposed to be on his honeymoon—not playing nursemaid to a new sergeant. "Send him on, then."

"He should be in the village by now. Might even be walking into your lobby as we speak."

"Guv, this is a dirty trick. You haven't given me a choice. But know this. You owe me."

A low chuckle came over the mobile. "I know. Sorry about the honeymoon business."

"Right." At that moment, the room phone rang. Bloody hell. The front desk, no doubt.

DS Stafford stood as soon as David entered the lobby. The fellow was homely with a long face and sad brown eyes, but his forlorn expression didn't matter, as long as his brain and observational skills were up to snuff.

"Sir!"

Damn it all if the kid didn't salute.

"This isn't the military, Sergeant. Congratulations on the promotion." David smiled and offered his hand in greeting.

Stafford fumbled, and his face flushed, but the fellow managed a decent handshake. "Thank you sir—your lordship—what should I call you?"

"Forget the lordship crap. On the job, call me French or Chief, and if we're at the pub having a beer, call me David."

"Yes, sir."

"Come along, Stafford." David led the sergeant down the hall to his and Miranda's suite. After unlocking the door, he motioned for the younger man to enter and be seated. David crossed the room and sat in a comfortable wing chair. "We've a homicide. Antiques dealer. It's a delicate situation. The local DCI, by the name of Beecham, isn't happy we've been asked to look into the affair. His subordinate, DS Tower, is a good copper and cooperative. If we can manage to keep out of Beecham's way and him out of ours, we've a number of suspects to interview."

"Not popular with the locals, our vic?"

David grimaced. "Popular with too many of the locals—female variety. In addition to his antiques business, he specialized in charming married woman."

"So we have jealous husbands and the women as well."

"Precisely." Good observation. Stafford might work after all.

David pulled out a notepad from a bureau drawer. "After Beecham left to interview my wife, Sergeant Tower shared the names of two married women and their husbands, as well as

Riley's business partner. We may come across more as we interview them."

"Split the list, sir?"

David shook his head. The fellow was a go-getter, but could he trust him?

"Stick with me for a bit. We'll split up later as we come across more...and we surely will."

Stafford gave a brisk nod. "Perfectly understandable, sir. You need to take my measure first."

"Exactly." David smiled. His new sergeant was no fool. Fellow might just work out after all.

"So with whom do we start?" Stafford's university education showed.

David flipped a page in his notebook. "First is Moira Delaney. She's the business partner, divorced, but reputedly his longtime mistress as well. Next, is Evie White, a waitress at the local, Grey Fox Laughs. She has a husband, Jack, who's known for restoring Harleys and for his short temper. One arrest for assault. Seems Jack felt a customer was a little too bold when the wife served the customer his pint."

Stafford grinned. "I could do with a pint myself."

"My thought as well."

David and DS Stafford walked to the end of the main village street. The pub sign was dark green and featured a rakish, laughing gray fox, established. Nothing of note in the surroundings. It occupied a corner location on the main village thoroughfare. Typical of local public houses found in any village in the UK.

"I'll get our pints, suss out our suspect, sir."

The smell of hops and tobacco over two centuries in the making was imbued in the very air, not to mention the black oak paneling. David nodded to the corner. "Over there. Empty one."

He watched the sergeant amble up to the bar. A pretty blonde about Miranda's height flashed a pair of big blue eyes. Stafford chatted her up a bit and then brought the two pints over and sat across from David. He leaned forward. "Well? First impression?" He took a long pull on his pint and waited for the sergeant to answer.

"A definite looker. I like a taller woman myself—"

"Don't care about your preferences in female companions, Stafford."

"I'm getting to that, sir. She's friendly, not overly so, but I get the impression she's no better than she ought to be. Has a way of sizing a bloke up with a long, slow glance." Stafford pulled at his collar. "Is it hot in here?"

David grinned. "Going to get hotter if you don't keep on task."

The sounds of a motorcycle roaring up intruded on their banter. The pub door opened and a blast of frigid air entered along with a tow-haired, stocky young man. He strode with a stiff-legged gait to the bar and banged it with his fist so hard, the nearby pints clattered. "Bloody bitch! Where the 'ell 'ave you been?"

The barmaid flushed a deep red. "Shut your cake hole. Why d'you have to come in here and embarrass me in front of my mates?"

Even though David didn't see anyone but the bartender, he didn't blame Evie White for blasting the man who was apparently her husband.

"Where did you sneak off to? Your shift doesn't start at six in the eff-ing morning." "Jacko, please..."

Unable to stand by and watch any woman being abused, David sprang to his feet and clapped a hand on the younger man's shoulder. "Here now, that's enough!"

"Sod off!" Apparently anxious to brawl anytime, anywhere, he swung around, ready to let go with a roundhouse punch.

David blocked the punch and grabbed White's wrist and twisted it behind his back. "I'm DCI French of the Metropolitan Police and this is Detective Sergeant Stafford. I don't advise further resistance."

"Bugger you! This is a private matter between me and my wife."

"Sit down, or I'll be forced to arrest you for assault on a police officer."

"Fine." The young man quit struggling, but scowled at his wife. "I'll see you at 'ome."

Not willing to let the opportunity pass, David asked, "And where were you this morning?"

"Me? Riding around, freezing my arse off, trying to find my stupid wife. Wot's it to you?"

"I understand you had a recent bust up with the local antiques dealer?"

"Not this morning, not by 'alf." White's scowl deepened. "Wot? Did he accuse me of somethin'?"

"Not at all. You say you were riding around. Did anyone see you? Anyone at all?"

"Wot's going on 'ere? Am I under arrest?" White started to stand, but Stafford placed a hand on his shoulder.

"Not so fast. We've more questions."

"Bugger your questions!" Jacko sprang from his seat and lurched towards the door. "I've got to get back to me shop. Customers waiting like."

"Settle down, Jacko," Stafford warned, shoving White down into a chair, "or I'll have to—"

"Now, now, Sergeant." Might as well play good copper to Stafford's bad. "See here, White, you're not under arrest. We'd like to clear you for our inquiry. Just a few simple questions and you may be on your way."

"I'm a respected businessman. You can't just shove me 'round." White straightened the collar of his leather jacket and glared cockily at David. "I'll cooperate...long as I'm treated like a 'uman being."

David nodded. "Let's go then. We'll complete the interview at the stationhouse." If White had been riding around all morning, his cheeks were certainly red enough from the cold. Plus, there wasn't any obvious blood spatter on his clothes, but he'd have a forensic tech examine the man's clothes anyway.

*

After a brisk five block walk in the brisk winter air, David, Stafford, and suspect number one, Jacko White, reached the local stationhouse. It was a long, two-story affair, brick, with pretensions of being a half-timbered Tudor, meaning a bit of stucco and some manufactured timbers had been applied to the upper story at some point in the last twenty or thirty years.

Inside, it smelled of stale coffee and sweat. The dry heat was stifling and close.

He produced his warrant card and showed it to the desk sergeant. "DCI French." He nodded at his partner. "And this is DS Stafford. DCI Beecham is expecting us."

The desk sergeant was a hunched, gaunt figure with gray hair, gray eyes and a pasty gray pallor which hinted of ill-health. But his grizzled face came alive as he smirked. "Oy, that 'e is. Go through— then to the left. You'll 'ear 'im first."

"Come on, White. Let's go." David followed the desk sergeant's directions and sure enough he heard DCI Beecham, but damned if the fellow wasn't laughing.

He peered through the two-way mirror. Sure enough, Beecham was leaned back guffawing and slapping his knee. Miranda was gesticulating like a mad woman and regaling the detective with the details of David's proposal in the middle of Heathrow.

Leave it to his wife to charm even gruff, self-important DCI Beecham.

David tapped on the door. Beecham excused himself and opened the door.

"Good show, French. You've picked a winner with this wife of yours."

"Thank you. I'm well aware of her wonderful qualities." A sense of irritation nagged at him. Jealous? Yes, he was, although it surprised him. It wasn't that he didn't trust his wife, but this fellow was too forward by far.

Miranda rose from her chair and slipped her arms around his neck, easing for the moment his fit of jealousy. The warmth of her body...made him want to rush her back to their suite at the inn and engage in some afternoon lovemaking.

Not now. "Darling, it appears the interrogation went well?"

"Of course. Don't be silly. DCI Beecham was very businesslike and professional. He asked me a ton of questions and he already knew a lot about—well, you know all that business with Stefan—but anyone who's as intelligent as the Chief Inspector here could see I'm not a murderer. We just had the nicest conversation while the CSIs checked my jacket and slacks for trace evidence."

"I'm sure you have. Now, with your approval Beecham, I'd like to send my wife back to our rooms, while I go over some information with Jacko White here."

DCI Beecham nodded and smiled. "It's been a trying day and it's only eleven.

Honeymooners need their rest. I'll send a constable over to the inn with her. See she arrives there safely." He paused. "No, I'll take the little lady back to the inn myself."

Miranda's eyebrows rose and she wore a smug little smile. The minx. She knew damned well she'd made a conquest.

"Oh, Inspector Beecham, I'm sure you're much too busy and important to do any such thing," she gushed in a most obvious southern belle tone which only served to make Beecham's face flush a ripe red.

Enough. David cleared his throat. "That's very gracious of you, but a constable should be sufficient to escort my wife back to the inn. I really would like to go over some of the evidence with you, Beecham."

Beecham's face flushed even redder; he huffed, and then ran his finger around his collar. "Right."

Miranda tiptoed and kissed David on the cheek. "Play nice," she whispered in his ear.

"Always," he mumbled.

Miranda left. DS Stafford and Jacko White, who'd waited outside the interrogation room, entered.

"Well, well, well, Jacko White. Have a seat. Why am I not surprise to see your mug in here?" DCI Beecham turned to David. "What're we talking to him about?"

"Seems Jacko and his missus had a war of words in the pub this morning. Came very close to abuse. He seems to think his wife was somewhere she oughtn't."

Beecham turned on the tape recorder, stating the time and the individuals in the room. "Okay, Jacko, tell us what happened. Did you catch Evie with Riley Stubbs this morning?"

"No, couldn't find 'er. Didn't think of checking with old Riley. But 'e's been playing rumpy-pumpy with 'alf the women in the village—don't care if they're married or not."

Jacko jumped to his feet. "I'll kill that bitch if she's been 'aving it off with that old fart."

"Sit down!" Beecham bellowed.

White sat, but kept grumbling under his breath. "Just wait. Just wait."

David leaned forward. "So you didn't see Riley Stubbs this morning?"

"No. I was riding 'round on me 'arley. Evie left early like this morning, and I was trying to find 'er. Thought she might be up to no good, y'know?"

"What route did you take on your early morning ride?"

"Went far as Richmond's Nursery, no one there. Nan already out working somewheres, I guess. Then I come back slow like, up and down the village byways. Nothing. Went to my shop, worked on Charlie Jarvis's 'arley for a couple of hours, then I did another round—same route. Ended up at the pub. There my Evie were, like butter wouldn't melt in her mouth."

"That's it then?" Beecham scowled and fiddled with a ball point pen.

Jacko leaned forward and banged his fist on the desk. "No! Tell you one thing more, if she's been doin' Stubbs, I'll kill him, too."

"Someone's already beat you to it, and your alibi leaves a lot to be desired, White," David said.

"Wot you mean?" White stood, somewhat shakily. His face paled. "Wot's going on 'ere? You lot trying to trick me?"

"Just trying to get the straight of the story."

"I got nothing to do with this business. Lost my temper, said some rash things, but I'm no killer."

David shook his head. "White, in the space of ten minutes, you've threatened to kill both your wife and Riley Stubbs. You have to realize this makes you our number one suspect."

White's gaze narrowed. He glared from David to DCI Beecham and back again. "I'm not the only bloke 'as been taken advantage of. I can give you plenty of names. Folks talk to me. I see things, too."

"Stop wasting police time. Spill it," Beecham ordered, his voice a gravelly rasp.

"I know at least three other women wot were gettin' it from Stubbs." He held up his forefinger. "One is Nicola Denton. Her 'usband's in real estate—got a quick temper 'e does." Two fingers held up. "Two is Stubbs's partner Moira Delaney. Word around the village is they were caught doing it during their lunch break right on one of the antique couches—forgot to lock the door they did."

He held up a third finger. "And number three would be 'er 'igh and mighty ladyship, the Lady Jane 'Utton. She does the lady bountiful routine when she's not attending auctions and 'umping Stubbs. I 'ear she likes a bit of rough—if y'know wot I mean."

DS Stafford penned the names and sketchy info while David mentally went down the list. Three women named, two with husbands—five suspects, not counting the obliging Jacko White and his wife.

Just what he needed on his honeymoon—a murder investigation with a list of suspects which could possibly end up comprising half the village residents.

DCI Beecham leaned back, rolled his eyes and groaned. "Cor! Is that all?"

"So am I under arrest or not?" White leaned back in his chair and let his arms dangle.

"You're free to go...for the time being." A scowling Beecham stood and folded his arms across his chest. "Don't leave the vicinity."

White grinned and shrugged. "Born and bred in this county—now, where would I go?"

"Just see you don't. And leave that wife of yours alone."

White ducked his head and glared. "That's a family matter."

"Well, it'll be a police matter if she comes up with any more bruises," Beecham said. David watched the interchange between Beecham and White with a growing rage burning his gut. During the short time Miranda was married to her first husband, she'd been abominably abused before running away. His own mother had suffered emotional abuse and ended her life at the bottom of a wine bottle.

How any man could profess to love someone and mistreat them was beyond his understanding. Jacko White was a working class bloke, but David's own father had been university educated, and while his abuse was more subtle, it was just as damaging.

Damn, but he would rather die than lay a hand on a woman or destroy her emotionally with words.

He followed White out of the interview room. "Wait up. I need another word with you."

White stopped short and whirled around. "Yeah? A word is about all I got time for."

David leaned close. White's breath already reeked of drink. "Don't hit your wife or any other woman again," he warned. "It would please me greatly to put your arse in the nick for abuse."

White's chin went up. "Bugger off, mate. That's nothin' to me." He strode off as if he hadn't a care in the world.

The man would bear watching. He was entirely too ready to shift the blame toward others in the village.

David walked back into the interview room. "Is he good for it?"

Beecham shrugged. "As good as anyone he named. I wouldn't rule him out at this stage."

"Stafford? Your impressions?"

The sergeant rubbed his chin. "Hot temper. No alibi. And quick to point the finger at others. Not that we shouldn't check them out—we should."

David nodded. "Village like this—we'll likely come up with several more suspects. Stafford, why don't you check out the Richmond Nursery. See if anyone saw him out that way and what time."

"Sure thing, guv." Stafford glanced around and grinned. "That is, if someone will point me in the right direction?"

Beecham chuckled. "Right. You're a stranger here. I'll assign one of my constables to guide you."

David found it difficult to believe the one-hundred-eighty-degree change in Beecham's attitude. All Miranda's doing. "Very kind of you, Beecham, but it won't be necessary. I'll ride along with my sergeant. After all, I spent most of my summers in Middlebury."

"Right." Beecham's face flushed, but then a slow grin found its way to his face. "Should I be bowing or scraping—?"

"Nothing like that. I'm on the force. Same rank as you."

Beecham laughed. "Your wife said that 'bout you. Decided to cut you some slack, I did."

There the man was, harping about Miranda again. David tamped down an unreasonable flash of jealousy and managed to mutter a quick, "Thanks."

His Miranda had the ability to charm just about anyone she met. Instead of acting like a territorial hound, he should be grateful Beecham had decided to cooperate.

Who was being territorial now?

Chapter Four

I rushed through the nippy air from the police constable's car into the warmth of the inn, where a cheery fire roared in the fireplace. I sat in one of the overstuffed chintz chairs. More than anything, I needed to clear my head and figure out just what I would do about the plan I'd kept from David. Not that it was a big deal, not really. But now with the murder, everything was sort of complicated.

I never planned on being the lady bountiful after marrying David. He seemed to manage to have his same career without all the complications of managing an estate.

Okay, so he had someone do that for him, but I'd always worked, and I planned to keep working.

All right, my plan was to buy an antiques shop—Greenway Antiques would certainly fit the bill, since it was close to David's— our—country estate.

My mother has had a shop down on Eighth Avenue South in Nashville for years.

And I thought it would be kind of cool to have one of my own on this side of the pond.

I'm not the expert she is, but I'd absorbed a lot during my formative years when she dragged me to estate sales. We poked around shops all over the southeast. She made annual trips to the UK and France, and it was on one of those jaunts that I met the evil ex.

So my dilemma was when should I tell David what I wanted to

do? I'd talked to Stubbs on the phone just once about the possibility, but it was bound to come out in the investigation. There'd be a phone record.

Now was the time to tell him. Every movie and every book I'd ever read which dealt with a secret warned if you kept the secret, the other party would find out at the worst possible time.

So as soon as he bopped in here, I would tell him. Not that he bopped anywhere. He was much too dignified. Bopping—much more my style.

Whew. Once that was figured out, all I had to do was decide how I could keep busy while David was tied up with his investigation.

One idea came to mind. I'd help him investigate—behind the scenes—and he'd be through sooner and back to the honey part of our honeymoon.

After all that heavy thinking, I rose and headed to our second-floor suite. I walked inside and there, the first thing I spied sitting on the dark oak bureau was a photo of my six-year-old son, Jamie. His jet black hair and dark brown eyes were inherited from his Greek-born father, the one I liked to call the evil ex. But the rest of my son, with his brilliance and his sweet nature—those were my gifts to him. Okay, so maybe his brilliance is a genetic fluke, but I'm claiming it for my side of the family tree, all the same.

I reached for my cell phone and dialed in the number for Mina and Jean-Luc Pelletier. Jamie was staying with the couple in the Provençe countryside. Mina Griswold Pelletier was David's nanny who retired to Ste-Thérèse and married a jolly farmer by the name of Jean-Luc. Jamie and I met them last fall when David took us on the run from the evil one. They fell in love with Jamie, and he with them, their farm and all their animals.

I was sure he hadn't missed me for even a second, but I'd certainly missed him. My son's a great hugger. I know he'll change someday and barely tolerate my presence, but until then I would take advantage of all those hugs.

Not that David doesn't hug well—he does everything well. Take my word for it. "Âllo," Mina answered. "How's the honeymoon?"

"It's wonderful. David's wonderful. But there's been a murder and he's all involved in the case. May I speak to Jamie? I miss my baby, but don't tell him I called him baby."

"Oh, dear. A murder. Well, that sort of thing is his lordship's cup of tea, but, Randi, Jamie isn't here. He and Jean-Luc have gone to the village on some pretext or other."

Disappointment seeped through my heart. I guess that was a little melodramatic, but I really missed that little guy of mine. "Okay. Then I'd better get busy and help David with his investigation."

I heard a giggle from Mina. "Yes, I'm sure that's exactly what you need to do."

I reminded her of my cell number and told her anytime Jamie wasn't too busy, he should just call...anytime really.

She laughed and said she'd remind him he had a mother.

Cute.

I hung up. Now I had two opinions that I should help David with his inquiries: Mina's and mine.

I gave it some thought. I wasn't a trained investigator, but I was a mother and I could usually tell when my offspring was fibbing. Plus, over my lifetime, I'd read at least a thousand murder mysteries, and I was pretty sure I could be a damn good detective if the situation called for it.

And this one did.

David gave the directions while DS Stafford drove out of Kinsey Green into the countryside of East Anglia. Gone were the picturesque green fields of spring and summer, for now those same hills were blanketed with a light layer of snow.

"This is a sweet ride, sir." Stafford caressed the steering wheel like he would a lover's shoulder.

"It belongs to the estate. I don't use it often, but I agree." David loved the old Roller, but it was an impractical choice in the city. "If my memory serves, the Richmond Nursery should be just around the next curve."

"What do you know about them, sir?" Stafford asked.

Damned fellow was apparently determined to "sir" him to death. "Nan Richmond inherited the place from her father. She married a bloke from Manchester. Don't know anything much about him. Surname of Morgan—I think."

"Can't have much business. Don't most of the toffs have their own gardeners and such?"

David let out a low chuckle. "Maybe some toffs do, but most hire out. Death duties, Inland Revenue—they take most of the estate income."

Stafford turned into the winding drive. "Not much to see, landscaping wise. Case of the cobbler's children going barefoot?"

"Dead of winter and you're right, there's not much to see."

Stafford parked in front of a comfortable two-story cottage with a thatched roof. Stone outbuildings were visible to the right and back of the dwelling. A trail of smoke issued from the chimney. "Someone's home."

David and the sergeant climbed from the Roller, then crossed the pea gravel drive, their footsteps crunching loudly in the silence. David knocked on the door and waited.

The door was opened by a balding middle-aged man, at least a head shorter than David. "No solicitations. I'm working." He reached to shut the door.

David delayed the man's action by showing his warrant card. "Mr. Morgan? I'm DCI

French and this is DS Stafford. We're making some inquiries in the neighborhood and would appreciate a few minutes of your time."

An expression of annoyance flashed across his face. "Freddie Morgan, here. Come through. I don't know how I could help. Not much going on out here, but ask away."

Morgan led the way through an entrance hall filled with a jumble of boots and coats into a cozy reception room. He sat down on a sofa in front of a wood fire blazing in the fireplace. An ancient Irish wolfhound slept and snored on a rug in front of the hearth. "Poor old fella, he's fourteen and deaf as a post," Morgan said.

"Now, what's this enquiry about?" With his left hand, he picked up a pen from the table and started running it through his fingers like a baton.

The air in the room was stifling. David unbuttoned his coat and spoke first. "Did you hear any loud noise anytime this morning, fairly early?"

"Like what kind of noise?"

"Car backfiring, or a motorcycle? Anything like that?"

"Can't say as I did. I'm up 'round six-thirty. My wife Nan's up earlier. Don't know what she wants messing around in the nursery at that hour, but she's always been an early riser." He eyed David. "You didn't say what this is all about."

"We're trying to verify an alibi in our investigation. That's all."

"Sorry, I couldn't help you chaps." Morgan rose as if anxious for them to leave. "If that's all, I've work to do."

"What is your work, Mr. Morgan?" David asked.

"I'm a computer expert. I set up business's computer systems, accounting records, networking—the like." He glanced toward a rear doorway. "Keeps me quite busy."

"Lot of call for that type work around here?" Stafford asked.

Morgan's posture straightened, turned cocky even. "You'd be surprised. Lots of local work—mostly small jobs. The majority of my business is in London. Don't have to be there to do it. That's the good thing about computers."

David motioned Stafford they should leave, then stopped. "What about the village antiques business? I imagine they could use your services to keep track of their sales and stock."

"Indeed. I almost had a deal with that bugger Riley Stubbs at Greenway Antiques. Promised me a good payoff he did."

"So he reneged?" Damn, another suspect with a possible motive.

"Yeah, after I'd already shot my mouth off about it too. Made me look a right fool.

But that's the way it goes, sometimes," Freddie said with a casual shrug.

"You say you were up at six-thirty?" Stafford whipped out his notepad. "What about after that?"

Morgan frowned, looked to the left. "Had my cuppa. Nan came in from the nursery about seven and fixed us up a bit of porridge. She left again around seven-thirty, said she had errands. Since then I've worked on setting up a new account with a car dealership in Yorkshire. One more time, what's this about?"

"Murder, Mr. Morgan," David said. "It's a murder investigation."

"Murder? Whose? I'm not under arrest, am I? You certainly didn't caution me."

"No, we just had some questions. Thank you for your assistance." David turned to leave, then stopped again. "Riley Stubbs was murdered this morning."

Morgan's eyes widened and his mouth dropped open. He grabbed the back of a chair to steady himself. "Th-that's terrible. I'm really quite shocked."

"Have a good rest of the day, Mr. Morgan." David smiled to himself. Another one with a motive, but genuinely shocked—or was he?

Since David was obviously getting on with his investigation, I decided I might as well get on with mine—and the sooner the better. It was almost lunchtime, I stopped at the registration desk and asked for directions to the nearest tea room.

"Lady Middlebury, there's one here at the inn."

"Thank you," I barely managed to say. I felt more like I should've given myself the dope-slap, but something told me Lady Middlebury wouldn't do something like that. Besotted newlywed that I was, I hadn't noticed the tea room situated just beyond the lobby. After all, we were on our honeymoon, and we'd had all our meals in our suite in front of the romantic fire.

I hoped no one would notice my red face, so I slinked into the Rosalie Tea Room and was greeted and seated quickly. The walls were painted a periwinkle blue, and white lace Priscilla curtains graced the windows. Billowy green ferns were strategically placed around the room. Bright yellow linen table cloths covered the white wicker tables.

Comfortable cushions were covered in a colorful blue and yellow dragonfly print. The effect was warm and spring-like and a definite mood enhancer. The cheery fire in the old stone fireplace helped mask the fact that the temperature outside was heading down instead of up.

"Ahem. Are you ready to order?"

"Wh—" I looked up. The waitress, a pleasant faced woman of about fifty, stood there patiently waiting for me to get my brain in gear. "Sorry, I was staring at the fire. It's almost hypnotic." Geez, what drivel had I just spouted?

I looked at the menu and ordered the first thing I saw. "Tea, Earl Grey, and the open-faced cucumber and chicken salad sandwich on the freshly baked whole wheat toast."

"Excellent choice. Anything for dessert?"

"No dessert, but I was just wondering if you heard what happened across the street this morning?"

"Oh, yes, just a dreadful business." She smacked her lips together. "They say one of the our guests stumbled on his body and even had to go down to the station to be interrogated."

Really. Randi hid a smile. "I'm new to the area, but do things like this happen often?"

"Oh, no. Never. This is the quietest village—quite boring, in fact. Most of the young ones leave and go to Keyeston or even London." Her gaze darted around the tea room. "Now that bloke, Stubbs, he were a bit of a ladies' man. That's the talk anyway."

"Was he married?" I warmed to this investigating gig. If I could just keep her talking long enough, I could find out all about him.

She leaned forward. "No. And I can tell you a thing or two about the goings-on over there. Have a real good view from here."

"Really?" I leaned forward, but I couldn't help but wonder if I should have brought a note pad or something to take down the details.

She nodded. "Lady Jane Hutton—she was in and out of there on a regular basis, and even before her was that snooty Nicola

Denton. Calls herself a supermodel or some such nonsense, but I remember when she was just a runny-nosed kid. Her daddy drank the family's income and her mother wasn't any better than she oughta be."

"I see." Boy howdy, did I ever. Small towns were the same everywhere. Everyone knew everybody's business.

"So she's a model?"

"Not anymore. She be a bit too long in the tooth now. But she come home and married a local boy, Phil—now he's an up and coming estate agent—did right well for herself, she did."

Hmm. A Lady Hutton, a supermodel and now maybe their husbands, too. Note to me: bring a pen or note pad. Real detectives didn't take notes on napkins. And even if they did, I couldn't very well abscond with one of the tea room's lovely yellow linen ones.

My source of information was called away, so I dug into my bag.

After a good rummage, I finally found a pen and a scrap of paper about one inch square. I wrote lady and supermodel and hoped like hell I'd be able to decipher it later.

I could hardly wait to share my intel with David...and I'd tell him about my idea regarding the antiques shop, too. Mustn't forget that.

While DS Stafford drove, David compared impressions with the sergeant. "We already have a list of nine possible suspects who either have a motive or no alibi for the time in question. First we have Jacko White a hot-tempered bloke who smacks his wife around. She left home too early to go to work, so where was she? And where was he? We can't confirm his alibi."

"Maybe we ought to talk to her?" Stafford suggested.

"Exactly," David agreed. "Then Jacko gives us three names of women involved with Stubbs. Moira Delaney, his business partner, Lady Jane Hutton and a Nicola Denton. We'll have to interview all of them and the two husbands as well."

"Makes my head ache, sir."

David groaned. The sergeant was right. This entire investigation was a headache, and headaches had no place on a honeymoon. "Let's head back to the pub. Coffee would be good. And a sandwich."

"And we can interview Evie White at the pub."

"Gently, Stafford. Something tells me she knows something. She was nervous this morning."

"That husband of hers threw a screaming fit. Make any bird nervous." "True enough."

At one, the Grey Fox Laughs was bustling with locals. David grabbed a table while Stafford put in their orders.

Stafford came back to the table with two cups of steaming coffee. "Not a very good time for an interview," he said with a wink.

"We can always take her down to the station later." David took a gulp of coffee and swallowed. "Damn it's hot," he gasped. He set down the cup and took a breath. "For now, I prefer a subtle approach. Don't want her to put up her guard."

"We lucked out. We're at one of her tables."

"Then we sit back and watch," David said. "When she brings our lunch, you'll engage her in conversation. Mention her husband was released. Watch her reaction. Go from there. Easy enough?"

"Right."

David leaned back and took a more cautious sip of coffee. The stuff was good for warming his insides, at least. Evie White bustled around serving her customers their lunch orders with a bright smile and a wink. As she made her way through the crowd of lunch goers, he could just make out a bruise on her neck. More of husband Jacko's handiwork, no doubt.

When she recognized them, her cheeks turned a pretty pink. "Well, here you two are again. No accounting for tastes." She set their plates down with a thunk.

As planned, Stafford spoke first. "Are you all right? We had to let your husband go.

Sorry we couldn't keep him until he cooled down."

The waitress shrugged and laughed. "Jacko? Yeah, he's got a quick temper, but he cools down pretty quick. Don't have much trouble with him. He's not such a bad bloke as husbands go."

She gave a self-conscious tug on the collar on her blouse. Perhaps she was trying to hide the bruise on her neck.

"Maybe he should be looking into some anger management therapy," David said.

Evie responded with a quick snort and an eye roll. "Yeah, I can see that happenin'. Not in my lifetime." She shook her head. "Anyways, he's not that bad."

"You don't have to put up with being smacked around. Man shouldn't treat his wife that way," Stafford said.

"And I guess you'd know?" She eyeballed Stafford. "You married?"

"No."

"I didn't think so," she said with a huff. "What goes on between a husband and wife is private. None of your business."

Hearing Evie White defend her abusive husband didn't set well with David, but women did it all the time—even took the blame for their partner's boorish behavior. He leaned in and said in an undertone. "What he did this morning wasn't private. He was in here abusing you verbally, and if we hadn't intervened, he likely would've hit you."

"Jacko—he was just blowing off steam." Her cheeks grew pinker and her eyes blinked rapidly.

"Spousal abuse is a crime. He's been warned."

"Like I said already. He likes to blow off steam, but he don't get physical like." She glanced around. "I've got other customers. If you don't have anything else, I'll tend to them." She flounced off to the bar and poured a pint for a glaring customer.

"At least we have her attention, guv."

David nodded. "Indeed we do. Let's pick her up when her shift is over and bring her down to the stationhouse."

"Sure thing, guv."

David bit into his hot roast beef sandwich. At least "guv" was better than the annoying "sir".

Stafford's brow furrowed. "What does your wife think of your getting involved in this investigation on your honeymoon?"

David wiped beef juice from his chin. "She understands."

"Come on, guv. Couldn't you have sprung for a more exotic location than Kinsey Green? It's a nice village, but..."

A smile tugged at David's lips as he recalled the circumstances of meeting Miranda again after six years and falling in love with her and her son. "We had quite a tour of the EU while we were running from Stefan Kristoforous.

"I might've heard something about that."

"Long and complicated story, Eric. For another time, perhaps."

"I'll wager it is."

David glanced over at Evie White. She'd just put on her coat and was headed for the door. "She's leaving."

"I know what that means," Stafford said. "Half-eaten or skipped meals are part of the job."

Chapter Five

After my first successful foray into detecting, I wrote up my conversation with the waitress...as much as I could remember. This detecting was a little more difficult than I'd imagined. So I gave it some thought. The first time, I'd gone off unprepared. The next time I'd have a tape recorder in my bag.

Now where was the best place for small town gossip? The hairdresser—for sure. The women in there would know everything.

After I popped down to what passed for the village electronics store and picked up a tape recorder, I headed to the Shear Haven. They weren't all that busy and worked me in for a wash, cut, and blow dry. I was given to a young hairstylist or beautician who had a bumblebee tattooed on her neck, a nose ring, and six—I counted them—piercings in her left ear and two in her right. Oh yeah, she appeared almost old enough to wear her mom's high heels.

How bad could she be? Besides, my hair grew quickly.

"I'm Daisy," she said. Daisy was about my height and still carried some baby fat in her cheeks and tummy.

"I'm Randi French."

After I told her how I wanted my hair cut, I reached inside my purse and surreptitiously turned on the little recorder. I waited until after she finished shampooing and asked my first question. "Lot of excitement this morning, wasn't there?"

Daisy combed my damp hair and then snipped away a few strands. I looked down at the floor. Heavens! I had no idea my hair was that long.

Then she leaned over my shoulder. "Yes, that antiques fella. Someone whacked him right proper, they did. Had to be someone's husband. Stubbs were a right dog when it come to women."

"Really?" Her scissors went snickety-snick, and more of my hair hit the black and white tile floor. I had to wonder if David would be aroused by a bald woman— specifically me.

"The tales I could tell..." she said, and I waited. And waited.

Most of my hair was already on the floor. Was that it? How could I get her to elaborate? Now, in detective movies and books, sometimes a little bribe helps the information flow a little freer. "You know, I think I'd like to change the color, too?"

"Really? Now your hair is thick and a nice shade of dark blond, but I could jazz it up a bit."

"Sure. That's it. Jazz it up." Heaven only knew what "jazz it up" meant to a young woman with a tattoo and body piercings. David would just have to understand.

Besides, it couldn't turn out any worse than what I'd done to it myself when David, Jamie and I were on the run last fall.

Daisy hummed and started wrapping the little hair I had left in strips of foil. "We'll give you some lowlights and some highlights, and it'll create a lot of depth. You'll be smashing."

The ammonia from the hair color was strong enough to choke a cat. "Cool." Did I actually say cool?

"So tell me, who do you think did the Stubbs fellow in?" I asked, since I was desperate to get her talking again.

"Well, lately, I've seen lots of ladies in and out of his shop. Got a real good view from here."

I looked out the window. Daisy spoke the truth; the entrance to Greenway Antiques was clearly visible. "But that's only natural. We like to shop 'til we drop."

"Yeah, but with some of them he turns the 'Open' notice board around to 'Closed' and leaves it there for quite a while. In fact..." She hesitated.

"Go on. Don't stop now," I begged.

"He forgot to turn it 'round one day, and I walked in on him. He and that business— monkey business, if you ask me—partner of his were humping away on a sofa in his office. I could hear them the minute I walked into the store."

"And why were *you* there?" I asked it rather naughtily, I thought.

"Not for any of that." Daisy wrinkled her nose. "My mum's birthday was coming up, and she likes little cup and saucer things to stick in her display cabinet."

"Did you actually see them...at it?"

Daisy sniggered. "No. I headed back to his office and stood outside the door long enough to know what was going on. 'Oh, Riley, you're such a stud' and the like. That and with the heavy breathing and the furniture squeaking—"

"Okay. Okay." I held up my hand. Frankly I'd heard way more than enough. "I believe you."

"All right. Now I'm going to set you under the dryer and let the heat speed up the process."

"Wait. Please, just one more question. Who else did he turn the sign around for?"

"Evie White, she's a waitress at the pub, Nan Morgan—though what he'd want from that old cow—and Nicola Denton, but she hasn't been around much lately."

"Busy fellow." Heavens, how did he keep them all straight? Must've had a hell of a day planner. His day planner—I'd have to remind David to check it out.

"Yeah, one of those husbands did him for sure...or maybe it was one of the women."

I nodded and let her put me under the hair dryer. No matter. David would still love me—even if my hair was on the far side of jazzed up.

Through the observation glass, David and Stafford watched Evie White fidget and bounce in her chair as if some pop tune was playing inside her head.

David and Stafford entered the room. The recording and video devices were activated. "DCI French and DS Stafford have entered the room at three twenty-two for interview of Mrs. Evie White," David said for the recorder. "Please state your full name."

"Evie—Evalina—White. I just want you to know I really resent you making me come down here like this. I'll be late for tea. My Jacko really likes his tea on time."

"Mrs. White, we appreciate your time and we won't take long. The sergeant and I have a few questions."

She tossed her hair. "Ask away. I got nothing to hide."

David leaned back in the chair. "Where were you this morning between six and ten?"

"This about that Stubbs fellow's murder? What makes you think I would know anything about that?" She rocked back and forth in the chair. She glared at David and then gave Stafford a little smile. Stafford smiled reassuringly back at her. Good. He was paying attention.

"Yes, we'd like to clear you as quickly as possible," Stafford said softly. "So just tell us where you were and then you'll be eliminated as a suspect."

The White woman's posture relaxed a bit and her shoulders moved from side to side as she started to squirm suggestively in her chair.

"I woke up early. Jacko was still dead to the world, so I got up and put some coffee on. Then...I dressed and went out and...I took a walk on the heath."

"In this weather?" David asked. "It's awfully cold out, especially this morning."

"I'm used to the weather, Chief Inspector. I was brought up on a farm, and we always got up early to care for the animals before going off to school."

"And did you see anyone on your early morning walk?"

"No." She looked down at her hands as if studying the backs of them.

"How long were you on the heath, Evie?" Stafford asked.

"Don't rightly know. Wasn't wearing me watch."

"After your walk, what did you do?"

"Went back to our flat, but Jacko was already gone. Guess the prat was chasing all over trying to find me."

"Anyone see you come back to your flat?" Stafford managed to keep his tone easy and non-threatening.

"Not that I remember. Anyway I took me a shower and changed for work. Got to work at my usual time of ten."

"So basically what you're saying is that between six and ten you don't have an alibi."

She glared back at David and folded her arms across her chest. "Why do I need an alibi? Riley Stubbs is—was—nothing to me."

"That remains to be seen. Interview ended at three forty-five." David turned off the recorder.

She rose slowly as if uncertain. "That's it?"

"For now," David said. "As the investigation progresses, we may have more questions."

David waited until Evie had left, then turned to Stafford. "Impressions?"

"She's hiding something. And she likes me better than you," he added with a grin. "Yes, she is. You played her well during the interview. We can use that."

"Who do we go after next?"

Before David could respond, DCI Beecham entered the interrogation room. "Got some news. Medical Examiner says according to the liver temp, the time of death is eight—give or take an hour.

"That helps narrow it a bit, but we have more people to interview."

"How 'bout an update? Who've you seen so far?" Beecham settled down in the vacant chair.

Stafford pulled out his note pad. "Jacko White and his wife—neither of them have a solid alibi for the time, but as yet no real motives either. We attempted to verify that White was out by Richmond's Nursery, but Freddie Morgan says he didn't hear a motorcycle at any time that morning. And his wife was out during the time in question. Evie White was out early. Walking on the heath, she says, but no one saw her either."

Stafford closed his note pad and stuck it back in his pocket. "That's it. We still have Stubbs's partner, the Huttons and the Dentons to interview."

"Old Jacko was quick to point the blame away from himself."

Beecham nodded vigorously. "Wonder if his missus wasn't one of Stubbs's conquests?"

David agreed. "The women may all have motives, but his manner of death says jealous husband to me. We have two of them who are known for their short fuses White and Denton."

"You might as well add Freddie Morgan to that list of hot tempered husbands," Beecham said. "We got a call on the tip line saying Morgan and Stubbs were yelling and screaming at each other not two days ago. Something 'bout a business deal."

"Yes, Morgan mentioned something about a deal that didn't work out. He brushed it off, downplayed it even."

"Yeah, he would. Caller said Freddie was red-faced and huffing when he left the place. I'd have another chat with him."

"Now that the M.E. has given us a tighter timeline on which to focus, we'll do the rest of the interviews with that in mind. Someone in this village is bound to know something. Something which will lead us to the killer," Stafford said.

David leaned forward. "Well, if someone does know, we'd better find them before the killer does."

Chapter Six

The air was cold and crisp, and Lady Jane Hutton breathed in a deep lungful. She walked briskly every morning through the back garden at Newstone Manor. Granted, it was winter and, other than the evergreens, there wasn't much to see. Still, the daily walk suited her need for solitude and exercise. Her body was trim and elegant. She didn't look a day over thirty, in spite of having spent forty-seven years on this good earth.

She was late for her walk today, having been delayed by discussing preparations for a light luncheon with Cook and the dinner party for twenty of husband Edward's business associates planned for that same evening.

Very few of the nobility could avoid having business associates, and her husband was no exception. Still she dreaded the prospect of rubbing shoulders with the commoners. They were so...well, common.

She did make exceptions, of course. One did frequently make friends in one's youth when one had a tendency to rebel against such class restrictions. Her gardener was one such exception. Strong, handsome and so talented in the garden and in bed. They'd connected when only children, but they'd become even closer one glorious summer when she'd come home on holiday from school.

No one since had ever touched her soul or loved her as deeply—certainly not Edward. He was an arrogant fool who couldn't comprehend her desiring anyone but him.

No, there was no one like her Nan.

The crunch of footsteps on the gravel walkway. She turned and reached for her lover's hand. "Nan, darling. We need to talk."

Nan nodded and kept hold of Jane's hand. "Yes, we do. Have you heard about Riley?" Shielded by the tall evergreens, they continued to walk hand in hand.

"Yes, from one of the cleaners this morning. Tell me, what do you know?"

"The village is all abuzz. Someone cut off his most beloved body part. Quite a mess,

I hear."

"Good Lord. How gruesome." Jane cast a sharp glance at Nan. "You didn't do it, did you? I mean, what he did—I wouldn't blame you."

"Wish I'd thought of it. Wouldn't mind a little blood on my hands after that sleaze sold me fake Staffordshire dogs and charged me a month's income for them."

"Yes, darling." Lady Jane sighed. She'd heard it all before. Sometimes Nan could go on a bit. "Now then, what time did he meet his untimely but well-deserved demise? Do we need alibis?"

"Don't know about you, but I might. I was in the nursery almost all morning, didn't even see Freddie. Don't know where he'd got to, but he can't alibi me."

While they walked along the frozen footpath, Jane thought for a moment. "Well, darling, I'm afraid I was embroiled with Cook most of the morning. So I have an alibi, and honestly I'd give you one, but...dear, let me think." She ran a hand back through her hair. "I have it. You can say you were working here in the back garden and that I saw you through the window from Cook's office."

"Jane," Nan said in a very aggravated tone. "You couldn't see me working in the garden from Cook's office. The evergreens shield the rear garden from that level."

"All right. You don't have to get out of sorts with me." She stopped and faced her dear Nan. "I'll say that I had asked you to check on the vegetation and the mulching and saw you working from the window in my room."

Nan removed her billed cap, pulled out an old handkerchief from her pocket and mopped the perspiration from her forehead, then put the cap back on and settled it on her head.

"Nan, darling, are you sure you didn't do it? Not that I would ever tell." "Hmph."

"All right. I believe you. I won't ask again." She pulled Nan's hand to her breast. "Now, let's go to our special place and I'll make you forget all about that nasty man."

"Will you be good to me?"

"Be good to you? I should say not. I'm going to punish you for not having killed the bloody bastard."

Nan smiled and brought Jane's hand to her lips. "I knew I could depend on you, Janie."

By afternoon, I had so much to tell David, I could hardly wait. Would he leave off detecting long enough for tea? No, of course, he wouldn't, but maybe he'd make it in time for dinner.

I looked in the mirror and shuddered. We definitely wouldn't be eating dinner in the dining room, not with this hair of mine— short, spiky and colored in alternate shades of blue, yellow, and red. Highlights and lowlights?

Jazzed up? Definitely.

More than once, as I wrote out my notes from the recorder, I wished David had brought along his laptop. Neither one of us dreamed our honeymoon would end with a murder, and naturally I would've pitched a holy fit it he'd brought it.

But that was before the murder. No matter. He had to return to the inn sometime and when he did, he'd get the loving of his life. What a wonderful lover he...

No point in thinking about all that, not until after dinner anyway.

I fingered the remaining wisps of my hair, and while the cut wasn't so bad, the color would have to go. Tomorrow morning I'd find the nearest drug store or chemist's shop—that's what they call them here in the UK—and buy the British version of L'Oreal.

*

After comparing their final impressions on Evie White's interview, David and Stafford were ready to head out for the evening. David pulled on his overcoat as did the sergeant, and they walked through the squad room. "I need to touch base with my wife, even if just for a second," David said.

"Understood, sir. It's your honeymoon." A wry grin kicked up at the corner of Stafford's mouth.

David ignored his sergeant's smirk. "Miranda understands, but I haven't seen her since this morning. Not quite cricket to leave her to her own devices."

"She's probably all comfy cozy in your suite..."

"Eating bonbons, perhaps? You don't know my wife. She has a way of finding excitement, or it finds her."

"Sounds like an interesting woman."

David smiled. "She is that. And her son Jamie, my stepson now, is quite a character in his own right."

"How old?"

"Six going on twenty-one." David laughed, then stopped.

A tall woman, well-dressed in expensive tweeds, approximately fifty, was yelling at the desk sergeant. "I want to know when my shop will be free. I have a business to—"

"See 'ere, Ms. Delaney," the desk sergeant interrupted. "That's a crime scene. It'll be released when we're good and ready to release it."

"Ms. Delaney?" David said. "I'm Detective Chief Inspector French. My partner, Detective Sergeant Stafford." He nodded at Stafford. "Why don't you come through? We have a few questions."

"This is most inconvenient." She glared from one to the other. "All right. Fine." She straightened her shoulders and thrust her chin forward. "If it'll help me get my shop back quicker, I'm more than happy to cooperate with the authorities." She scowled. "I must say, I don't know either one of you two."

"We're from London," David said. "We've been asked to assist with this enquiry." He directed her to the interview room, then said to Stafford, "Observe on this one. Her responses, body language, et cetera."

Inside the interview room, Delaney set her alligator bag down on the floor and carefully removed her gray tweed overcoat and folded it over the back of her chair.

David turned on the recorder and made the official obligatory statements.

The woman hesitated as if she expected him to pull out her chair. "Hmph." She sat and leaned forward, her elbows on the table. "Now what is it you want to know, Chief Inspector?"

"You were Riley Stubbs's business partner?" David asked.

"Yes, of course. Everyone knows that."

"And now the business is all yours, or did your partner leave his share to someone in his will?"

"It was part of our business agreement that each of us should make such an adjustment in our wills. So, yes, the shop is now mine."

"Do you know for a fact that this is the case?"

"It damned well better be. His body is hardly cold, and there's been no reading of the will as yet." Her tone was haughty as if he were some stupid shop assistant. Doubtless she was less than a pleasure to work for.

"And when will his will be read?"

"I spoke with his solicitor, Armitage, and the day after tomorrow at ten. His office." "Where were you when you heard of your partner's death?"

"When I came to the shop this morning. Police vehicles were everywhere. One of the constables told me Riley was dead. Murdered."

Great. A constable with loose lips.

"Do you have any idea who would want to harm Mr. Stubbs?"

"Riley didn't have any enemies. He was charming and still somewhat handsome." She curled her upper lip and sniffed. "Still, he wasn't too popular with some of the husbands around here...if you know what I mean?"

"He was a ladies' man."

"In every sense of the word. Not that I—I mean, our partnership was strictly business."

"Really? So you were immune to his charms?"

"Of course. It was business with us." She gave a small, self-satisfied smile and patted her well-coifed hair. "Not that he didn't give it a try."

"Only natural he would," David said, hoping an appeal to her vanity might soften her attitude.

"And where were you this morning before you came to the shop?"

"Well, I was a bit later today than usual. I slept in this morning. I had quite a good book last night and read until two. I just couldn't put it down."

"What was it?"

She blinked. "What? Oh, you mean what book?" She paused. "A mystery. Yes, it was a mystery."

"You couldn't put it down but you can't remember the name of it?"

"Yes, of course. Hanover Close—one of Anne Perry's. Are you familiar with her work, Chief Inspector?"

"As a matter of fact, I am. But I prefer her Inspector Monk series."

"Yes, well, that's quite a good series as well," she said with a shrug. "Now when will they release my shop? I've a living to make."

"I'll check with forensics. It may be another day or two."

"I need to get someone in there to have it cleaned before I can reopen. I hear it was quite...bloody?" She grimaced and gave a shiver.

He remained silent. Delaney certainly had more than her share of information about the crime scene. Small village like this. Couldn't be helped.

"Was anyone with you this morning?"

"No, I live quite alone."

Damn. Another party without an alibi.

"By the way, you should probably check the phone logs. You might find this of interest. A woman with an American accent called him once that I know of. I thought it strange since he went into his private office when she called. I don't know what it was about."

"An American?"

"Yes. Definitely a Yank with one of those syrupy sweet southern drawls like Scarlett O'Hara in that movie, *Gone with the Wind*."

David smiled. If he didn't know better, he'd think she was describing Miranda.

"Thank you for the suggestion. We're working on the phone logs."

"Excellent, then. You've really got these locals on the ball." She reached across and stroked his forearm. It took him by surprise, but he managed not to jump. "I don't suppose you'd like to have dinner with me while you're here in the Green?"

"I'm afraid that won't be possible, but thank you for the offer." He reached for the recorder, his hand pausing over the Stop button. "Interview ended at four fifteen p.m."

"We're through? Well, that was certainly painless." She rose, collected her coat and bag.

"I may have more questions later. Stay available. Stop by the desk sergeant. Tell him I need your prints taken—merely a technicality."

"My prints?" Her cheeks turned a bright pink. "Of course. As I said earlier, I'm only too happy to cooperate, and I wouldn't dream of leaving while poor Riley's murderer is still running around."

David waited until she was out of earshot and groaned.

Stafford came in with a wide smirk on his face. "Thought I was going to have to come in here to rescue you from that man-eater, guv."

"Very funny. What did you pick up from her body language?"

Stafford laughed. "That she was ready to jump your bones—sir."

"Besides that, Sergeant."

"She glanced to the left when she gave you the song and dance about reading a good book and sleeping late this morning. Also when she described their partnership as 'strictly business'."

"Agreed." He thumped Stafford on the shoulder. "Let's get out of here. I need to find that wife of mine and see what kind of trouble she's gotten herself into."

My stomach rumbled. Time for tea? I glanced at my watch. It was past time for tea and too early for dinner. I sat at the desk in the bedroom and arranged all my notes into some kind of order. I'd go over them one final time to see if anything new jumped out at me.

I heard the door to our suite open. "David?" It'd been hours since I'd seen my new husband, and I was anxious to hear the scoop on the investigation. Okay, so I was pretty anxious to see his handsome face and have his arms around me, too.

I jumped up and ran into the sitting room and stopped short. David wasn't alone. He had a tall, long-faced young man with him, whose mouth dropped open at the sight of me.

"Oh, I forgot." I ran my fingers through my colorful new hair. "Short hair. Long story."

Poor David. His mouth didn't drop open, but his eyes bugged at the sight of me. He swallowed and bravely continued as if my hair were always red, yellow and blue. "Miranda, this is my new sergeant, Eric Stafford. Eric, my wife Miranda."

"Ma'am," DS Stafford managed.

"Hi, Eric. So nice to meet you." Nervous as a long-tailed cat in a room full of rocking chairs, I ran my fingers through my hair again. "I can explain."

A low chuckle from my husband told me he was amused, not appalled. "I'm sure you can," he said with an eye roll.

"I have so much to tell you. I've been really busy—helping you." I relaxed a bit. "Come on, both of you. Take off your coats while I pour tea. I'll have the inn send up some sandwiches and petit fours." I reached for the phone.

"We can't stay long, darling. I wanted to see how you were." His gaze kept going to my hair, but his lips kept twitching. "Obviously you found something to do."

"That's not all. I've done some investigating on my own, and I'm dying to tell you everything. But first, I'm ordering some food. You have to eat. I don't want to hear another word." Ignoring David's protests, I made the call.

David shrugged out of his coat and set it aside. "Mi-ran-da." He drew out my name as if he was a mite perturbed. As for DS Stafford, he merely coughed and cleared his throat.

"Mind you, I know I'm not a professional. That's your territory, but I interviewed two people."

"*Two people*?" David's tone turned a little frosty, I thought, but I knew he'd warm up as soon as I shared all my info with him. He settled down in a Queen Anne wing chair and did the eye roll thing again.

"My notes are in the bedroom. Wait just a minute." I ran to get them, re-arranged them several times, then returned to the reception room. The sandwiches and petit fours had already been delivered. Apparently David's title prompted swift service. The sergeant had removed his coat and settled on the settee. Before launching into my tale, I poured the tea. Such a nice little hostess I was.

I picked up my notes. "My first interview was with a waitress in the tea room right here in the inn."

"Did you really interview two people?" David's tone wasn't quite what I expected. "Did you represent yourself as being part of the investigation?"

This time I did the eye roll. "Don't be silly. It was all very casual, but skillful, even if I do say so myself."

David let out a quiet groan, which frankly rather pissed me off since I was only trying to give him a hand.

"All right, now. The first interview was rather short. I found I wasn't prepared to do an in-depth interrogation. According to her badge, her name is Ruthie."

"This waitress in the tea room?"

"Yes." I flipped through my notes. "First of all, she said Stubbs was a ladies' man, and that he had been involved with a former model, a Nicola Denton, and after her, perhaps, was seeing quite a bit of a Lady Jane Hutton. I didn't get much out of Ruthie because she was called away. I had to make notes on a square of paper in my purse—like I said, I wasn't really prepared."

The sergeant leaned forward and was paying attention to everything I said.

Compared with David's glazed expression, the sergeant's interest was encouraging.

"But I came back up here and wrote my notes while it was all still fresh in my mind."

"That's very good, ma'am," the sergeant said.

"With my next interview—David, are you paying attention?" I gave him a sharp look. If I'd been sitting beside him, I would've given him a sharp elbow in the ribs.

"Yes, dear."

His jaw clenched. I ignored it because I was determined he'd soon stop being amused and take notice of my next interview. "I bought a little tape recorder thingy and put it in my purse, so that I wouldn't miss anything. I headed over to the Shear Haven. Believe me, the hairdressers always know all the latest gossip."

David glanced at his watch, then took a drink of his tea.

"Okay, I'll make it quick," I promised. "My hair dresser, Daisy—I don't know her last name either, but she's young, and has a butterfly—no a bumblebee—tattoo on her neck and six piercings in her left ear and two—"

"Come on, Miranda."

"All right," I snapped. I was immediately sorry, but I continued. "It was very clear she wanted to talk, and more and more of my hair fell on the floor, but there was no way I could stop her."

"Mi-ran-da." That tone again, the one that said he was losing patience.

"First she said it had to be a jealous husband because Stubbs was a 'right dog with the women', and the stories she could tell. So to keep her talking I told her to jazz up the color a bit."

"I see."

David's mouth tightened as if he were trying to control himself.

No matter. I continued, "She has a good view of the antiques shop from her station and she said lots of women were in and out all the time. Sometimes he turned his "Closed" notice around and left it for particular women. One day, Daisy went over to pick up a cup and saucer for her mother's birthday—she collects them—and the notice wasn't turned around. She went into the shop and heard sounds of Stubbs and his partner 'humping away'."

David coughed as if he'd choked on a bite of his sandwich, and so did the sergeant.

"Sorry for the frank language, but I'm just quoting her here. I asked her specifically who he turned the sign around for and she said there was an Evie White, a waitress from the pub, and a Nan Morgan—Daisy called her a cow—and a Nicola Denton—that's the supermodel, but Ms. Denton hasn't been around in a while. So there—what do you think?"

"You know I can't reveal anything from our investigation, but we've come across some of the same names. Good job."

Ah, finally some praise from my dear husband. It made me all warm and fuzzy inside and, if it hadn't been for the sergeant, I would've planted a big wet one on my husband.

David leveled his gray gaze on me. "Don't ever do such a thing again. This is a murder enquiry, not a game for a bored honeymooner. Someone murdered that man, and murdered him most horribly. I have half a mind to send you back to—"

I rose and put my hands on my hips. "Oh, no you don't. I'm not going anywhere. This is our honeymoon and—"

He stood and put his arms around me. "Miranda, please. I'm terrified whoever murdered Stubbs will discover you're sticking your nose into his business. Can't you see you're putting yourself at risk?"

Of course, I melted. He loved me and was afraid for me. Pretty heady stuff when you think about it.

"Okay. I'll find a good book to read. Will that make you happy?"

"Exceedingly." He kissed my forehead tenderly. "I hate to do this, but we have to return to the station. Your information was very useful, and I appreciate your wanting to help. But no more."

He left his half-eaten sandwich and headed for the door.

The sergeant scrambled to his feet, grabbed another sandwich and a couple of petit fours, and jammed them into his coat pocket. I followed them to the door like a puppy who'd just peed on the floor and been smacked with a rolled up newspaper.

"Will you be back? Tonight, I mean?" Somehow I managed to keep the whine out of my tone.

David stopped at the door, grinned at me and winked. "Yes, you may depend on that."

I chewed my bottom lip. I would definitely give him some good loving tonight.

It wasn't until I went back over my notes that I realized I hadn't mentioned my interest in the antiques shop or the one phone call I'd made.

Crap.

Chapter Seven

Back at the stationhouse and waiting for the murder squad to convene, David drummed his fingers against the desktop. Bloody hell, but Miranda's sticking her nose into the investigation wasn't something he'd foreseen. She wasn't one to sit around and do nothing, and since he'd literally abandoned her to find the murderer of the antiques shop owner, she'd occupied herself...and done a damned good job of it.

He shook his head. No. He didn't want her involved in the case. It was bad enough she'd found the body, but any further digging into the locals' affairs—business and otherwise—might prove unhealthy for his spunky wife.

DCI Beecham walked up to the desk. "Going to try out for a rock 'n' roll band?"

"What?" David looked down. His fingers were tapping out a staccato rhythm on the scarred metal desk. "Oh." He gave a self-conscious laugh. "Just anxious to see what we've come up with...all in one place."

"Let's do it," Beecham said. He walked over to the dry erase board. "All right. Oy, you there, Tower. Snap to."

"Yeah, guv. Sorry." Tower sat down, a little red-faced.

"We're fortunate to have DCI French here from the Met and his Sergeant Stafford to assist us in this case. Every cooperation will be extended to them. Now, I'll go over the forensics and the canvass, then you two can go over your interviews." He nodded at David, then continued, "Coroner says time of death around eight, give or take an hour either way, so we're looking at a timeframe from seven to nine. He says the bloke was probably unconscious when his parts were removed and switched." He waved his hands. "Yeah, I know we're all glad of that, but he was still alive because he bled like crazy. Tower, what about your canvass?"

Tower stood and walked to the front of the room and picked up a marker. "This is the shop." He sketched a crude floor plan of the scene. "There's a back door for large deliveries. More about that later. I spoke with shopkeepers all along the street and no one saw anything. It appears the killer entered and left through the back. The lock was jimmied and there was a trail of blood spatter leading from the murder scene to the back."

"Any surveillance cameras in the Green?" The Green wasn't London, where they abounded, but perhaps—

"Several, sir, but we've reviewed the footage. Everyone who came in the front exited the same way without any visible blood stains. Whoever did this was bound to be covered with the stuff. We found various prints throughout the shop, but nothing near the scene except for Lady Middlebury's prints on a chair arm. Back door was wiped clean except for some spatter imbedded in the threshold."

"What about her clothes?" David asked. "We tested them, right?"

"Yes, sir. We examined the lady's clothing and shoes with Luminol, and there was no blood trace."

David held back a deep sigh that demanded release. At least his gut could quit twisting.

DS Tower continued, "There were prints in the front of the shop, dozens, and that's to be expected since it's a business open to the public."

"Are we checking those out?" David asked.

"As much as we can. Not that many village residents are in the national data base."

David leaned forward. "What about Jacko White? Any trace on him?"

"No. Not at the time we brought him in, but he could've gone home and bathed and changed," DS Tower said with a shrug.

"True enough, Sergeant Tower. Good job," DCI Beecham said.

"What about prints on Stubbs's business partner, Moira Delaney, or White?" David asked.

"Moira Delaney's dabs were there all over the place, but with reason. None at the actual scene. As for White, his prints are already on record, but we didn't find them anywhere in the shop."

David stood and walked to the front of the room. "The sergeant and I have done some preliminary interviews. Jacko White was quite free with his information and mentioned several who might have motive to cut short Mr. Stubbs's life. He incriminated his wife and himself since neither have alibis for the time involved, Moira Delaney the business partner, a Lady Jane Hutton and therefore her husband. I know him, Lord Hutton, so I'll interview him and Lady Jane, if you don't mind."

Beecham nodded. "All right by me. You toffs speak the same language."

"Jacko also mentioned a Nicola Denton and possibly her husband Phil. We couldn't find anyone who saw him out riding his Harley this morning. He stated he rode out as far as Richmond's Nursery. We interviewed Freddie Morgan at the nursery. Before we told him Mr. Stubbs was murdered, he told us he had a business deal with the deceased go south. Could be a motive, but if Morgan were the murderer, he'd have likely kept that business to himself. He has no alibi for the time of the murder either. Through a secondary source..."

DS Stafford coughed.

"...we have been given information again that the deceased had multiple affairs. Lady Jane Hutton, Moira Delaney, Evie White, Nicola Denton and Nan Morgan—all have reportedly had affairs with him."

"Bloody hell, that's almost half the Green when you take into account their husbands," one of the detectives said.

"It does complicate things, but together we'll sort it out. It's going to take dogged police work. As far as we've been able to determine, none of these individuals has an alibi."

The room grew silent. A few frowns were scattered here and there. "It's been five years since there was a bonafide murder here in the Green," DS Tower said. "But we're up to it, sir. We won't let you and Chief Inspector Beecham down."

David smiled. He liked DS Tower. As for DCI Beecham, once he'd recovered from his bout of territorialism, he'd proved intelligent and cooperative. "Good. So far, preliminary interviews have been done with the deceased's business partner, Evie White and her husband, and Freddie Morgan. I'll take the Hutton's and Nan Morgan née Richmond—I know her as well. DS Stafford will take the Denton's. Inspector Beecham, if you and your men could do follow-ups on the Whites and Moira Delaney, and Freddie

Morgan, I'd like your impressions. Push them. Also we need to bring in a hairstylist by the name of Daisy from the Shear Haven. She volunteered a great deal of information quite informally and might actually have something more valuable to offer if pressed."

DS Tower raised a hand. "Daisy's my cousin once removed, sir. How about I take her?"

"Fine, and I'd like my sergeant to observe these interviews through the two-way. All right with you, Beecham?"

"Sure. Men, Riley Stubbs was a bit of a bounder, and any one of us might've done him if we found him messing with one of our wives, but this murder—as you say, Tower, the first in five years—reflects on our village and our police force. The murderer will be found and he or she will be brought to justice."

Bloody hell. David gave the mental equivalent of an eye roll. Surely Stubbs wasn't fooling with any of the policemen's wives.

"One more thing," DS Tower said. "We've located some likely DNA at the scene. Forensics is working on it now. It's not Stubbs's—his hair's dark. The hair found clutched in his fist is pale blond or gray, and there are root follicles attached to several, so DNA is involved."

"And if it matches one of our suspects, we have our killer," Beecham said.

"Excellent," David said. "Once the DNA results are known, we'll know on whom to center our investigation."

"What about a psychological profile?" Stafford asked.

"Right now…" Beecham stuck his hands in his pockets and paced about the front of the room. "…I'd say our killer is male. Stubbs wasn't a small man. A knife is usually a man's weapon. At any rate, whoever killed him, it was someone he knew. Have to be to get that close."

"And given the nature of mutilations, the murder was very personal," David added. "Once we have a final autopsy report, we'll have a better hold on the sequence of events. It's certain he was rendered unconscious with a blow before the mutilations. Therefore, we should learn what kind of blow and by what kind of object. Was the instrument left in the shop or taken with the killer?"

Hunger gnawed and David's stomach growled. The men had been on duty all day. "Beecham, might I suggest everyone grab a quick dinner?"

Beecham chuckled. "What's the matter, French? Anxious to see that pretty little wife of yours for a snack?" He leered, and the squad room broke out in laughter.

Although the remark was intrusive and inappropriate, squad room humor was often that way. Simpler to go along than have the entire murder squad think him prudish.

"Something along those lines," he said with a wink. "Doesn't sound like such a bad idea, at that."

Stafford got to his feet. "I believe I'll head over to the pub for a bite, then I'll head over to the Denton's if someone will point me in the right direction."

The only female in the room, a tall and slender detective constable with an English rose complexion, blue eyes and honey brown hair, rose quickly. "Sergeant, I'm DC Pettigrew. I'll be happy to show you the way, and it might be of some help, I went to school with Nicola Denton."

A wide smile wreathed the sergeant's face. "Excellent." He turned to David. "All right with you, guv?"

"Certainly." His sergeant taken care of for the evening, David couldn't resist smiling his approval. "I'll reserve you a room at the inn, if that's all right?"

"Thanks, guv."

David grabbed his coat and headed out. Heaven only knew what else Miranda had accomplished in his absence. Life with her promised to be exciting and never boring. What more could a man ask?

Click. Click. Click.

One fuzzy station after another. I considered throwing the TV remote across the room. The reception sucked. On a normal honeymoon, watching the television would rank pretty low on my list of things to do.

But this wasn't a normal honeymoon, and David wasn't just anyone. He was a copper—that's what he called it, anyway. And I knew going in that the divorce rate was high among the police force—not that I was considering divorce. It's a fact of the life. It's difficult to have a normal life when married to policeman. It didn't matter if he was a bobby on the beat or a Chief Inspector like my David. I would have to find something to do. I wasn't the lady bountiful type. I needed a job, and my dear hub had already made it clear he didn't want my help in this case.

That was why I'd inquired about the antiques shop. In addition, I already had my eye on another shop in London in the same area as our townhouse. Obviously I'd intended to tell David all this the morning after I went to the antiques shop. It was a decision we would make together, but I was sure I could talk him into it without any problems.

Big problem. A murder.

I'd ordered a proper dinner just in case David made it home— well, for now the suite was our home. Dinner was cold. I picked at the salmon, but my appetite wasn't what it normally would've been. In fact, I was starting to feel more than a little sorry for myself when the door opened. "David," I squealed, jumped up from the chaise and ran into his arms. Omigod, he felt so good.

My husband is tall and I'm at least a head shorter. Okay, a head and a half shorter. I reached up and ran my fingers through his auburn hair. He wore it cut GQ short, but longish on the top. "I've missed you."

As he smiled down at me, his gaze was warm and it set a blaze in my belly.

"Missed you too, darling. I'm so sorry about all this." He glanced over at the table where dinner had been set. "Did you eat? I hope you did."

I wrinkled my nose at him. "I wasn't very hungry." Then I batted my lashes at him. "But I'm getting hungrier now." And I was, but it wasn't for cold salmon.

"Mm, you're a wicked woman, you are. You're making me hungry, too."

He picked me up in his arms and carried me into the bedroom and set me down on the bed. His lips met mine, and he had me for dinner instead.

Somehow, I never got around to telling him about my connection to the antiques shop owner.

Chapter Eight

Tuesday

The next morning I woke up early, but my bed partner and lover extraordinaire was already gone. I felt around under the covers. Nope, not hidden there. The sheets were still warm and I could smell his scent on the pillow. Gradually my brain caught up with my eyes, and I heard the water running in the bathroom.

Ah, maybe time for more loving, I thought.

But I was wrong. David chose that moment to come out of the bathroom. He already had on a pair of slacks and a shirt; his hair was wet, but combed. "I heard the water. I thought maybe..."

He grinned. "Brushing my teeth."

Now I might be a silly goose, but the sight of my dear hubby freshly shaved and in all his manly studliness did things to my heartbeat as if the conductor shifted to cut time instead of four/four.

I admit it. I sighed.

"I could do with a good morning kiss," the dear man said. I jumped up. "Have to brush my teeth first."

"It's now or wait until tonight, Miranda. I'm running late as it is." "But..." I wrinkled my nose. "Morning breath."

He crossed the room in two long strides and grabbed me. "Bloody hell, woman. I married you for better or worse, morning breath and all."

Then he planted a big kiss on my mouth. My knees weakened

and I could've eaten him for breakfast. But no.

He pulled away and gazed down at me. "I have to go. I promise you we'll have a real honeymoon when this case is cleared."

"But I really need—" I tried to protest.

"I know. I really need you, too." He glanced down at his watch and was already walking toward the door. "I'm five minutes late already, and believe me, I'll hear it from the squad."

"I'll do something with my hair today," I said and waved.

He grinned his half grin and said, "I think it's cute. Just behave yourself and don't get involved in anymore interviews."

"All right. I'll be good."

And I meant it at the time. Honestly.

I watched David leave, and the hours of the day seemed to stretch before me like I40 between Nashville and Memphis.

Dang it. I needed some way to occupy my time, so I sat down and made a list: shower, breakfast, hair color... My pen ran dry. Okay, I could find a bookstore and buy something to read; maybe several books to read, since murder cases aren't solved overnight. I was likely to be here for a while.

My list took some time. I showered—and no, the color didn't wash out. If anything it was even brighter than before. I had coffee and toast for breakfast, then I dressed, ran out and picked up some hair color at the local chemist's shop. I was about to head into the secondhand bookstore when I met a young woman coming out—a woman who was so beautiful, it was unnerving. Doubly unnerving because she reminded me so much of David's late fiancée, Cassie Wheeler. Same ivory complexion, same long ebony hair and eyebrows arched like the wings of a raven. And eyes so blue, they reminded me of the stones set in my mother's turquoise and silver necklace.

My mouth must've dropped open.

"Are you all right?" the Cassie look-alike asked.

"Y-yes, it's just that you remind me of someone—my roommate from a long time ago. Only you're even more beautiful."

She smiled, obviously pleased by my gauche compliment. "Thank you. I'm Nicola Denton. You're new in the Green, aren't you?"

"Yes—uh, I'm Randi French. My husband and I are staying at the inn." This was the former model Daisy had told me about.

"Lovely to meet you," she said and offered me her hand. Her fingers were long and graceful, the nails perfectly manicured.

"Likewise. Would you like to have a cup of tea?" Dear heaven. Here I was again. Ready to do a little more digging into the murder case. David would kill me.

Her eyes widened. She looked down at the parcel in her arms, then frowned. "I really should be going. I have an engagement."

Determined to not let my quarry get away, I persevered. "But it's so cold. You look like you could use a hot drink. It won't take that long. We'll just pop over to the inn and we can warm up in front of the fire."

A little sigh, then the supermodel gave an elegant shrug. "I don't see why not. That would be lovely, Randi."

I smiled and gestured toward the inn. And no, I didn't have my tape recorder, but I'd discovered I had a good memory for details and the like.

Once we were comfortably situated in the tea room, our tea was served in lovely Royal Doulton china—a sunny yellow and blue pattern, Carmina, if I remembered correctly. I leaned forward and asked, "Did you hear? There was a murder yesterday...in the antiques shop across the street."

A frown quickly marred her beautiful face and turned it into a mask of hate. "Yes, he was a despicable man. The only surprise is that it didn't happen sooner."

"Oh, really?"

Her gaze downcast, Nicola sighed and folded her hands together. "I'm originally from this area, and when my husband and I settled here, I went into his antiques shop to browse and—uh, ask his advice on the best auctions. At first..." She glanced to the left. "...he was very helpful, but he became very flirtatious and wouldn't take no for an answer." She held up her left hand, demonstrating her platinum and diamond wedding ring. "As you can see I'm married, but he would call me at all hours on some pretext or other. And he would show up at various functions and make an absolute nuisance of himself."

"Gracious," I said. "What did your husband think of all this attention?"

"At first, he thought it humorous, but he soon became quite angry. He even warned the cretin to leave me alone."

"And did he?" I took a sip of the fragrant hot tea.

"No. If anything, his attentions increased. More harassing calls. Somehow, he managed to obtain my mobile number and would call me on that as well. I was at my wit's end. And then today when I heard the news, it was like an answer to a prayer."

Finally she directed her gaze directly at me. "Shameful way to feel, I know but I'm so glad he's gone."

"When exactly did you hear the news?" I asked and took another sip.

She did an eye roll—just like Cassie had done when something annoyed her. "Let me see. I'd just gotten in my car and switched the radio over to the local station for the weather report. That's when I heard it—with the yesterday's noonday report."

"So all morning you were going about your normal daily routine and didn't know anything about the murder until noon yesterday?"

"Yes. That's it exactly. Riley had called me Sunday night on my mobile and threatened to tell my husband we were actually having an affair—as if I would ever let that slimy man touch me. I told him to go right ahead. I know my husband would never believe him over me. We're very happily married."

"That's just awful."

"Truly it was. I tossed and turned all night, trying to decide what to do." "And...?"

"Finally I decided to tell my husband that Riley was harassing me again and what he'd threatened."

"And did you?"

"No, when I rose at nine yesterday, Philip was already gone for the day. He's an estate agent. He frequently goes into his office at seven and works many nights until nine."

Hmm. Having a husband who worked those hours left the former model with a lot of time on her hands. Maybe she'd had an affair with Stubbs and tried to call it off. "So what do you do with your time?"

She let out a very dignified sigh. "It was difficult at first. My former life as a model kept me quite busy. I was always on location shoots, all over Europe."

"I thought I recognized you," I offered. No, I hadn't really recognized her. She'd resembled poor Cassie too much for me to think of supermodels. I recognized the name, though. After all, that was why I'd asked her to have a cup of tea.

Nicola smiled. "Of course, one can't go around the village made up like a supermodel, but I try to keep up my appearance. To keep in shape, I go to the gym in the next county. That's where I was headed yesterday when I heard the news that horrible man was murdered." She visibly shuddered, then drained her cup of tea.

"This was such a lovely suggestion. Thank you. It was just what I needed," she said, setting her cup on the table.

"Perhaps, if you're in the area long enough, you and your husband could come for dinner."

I frowned. "That's a lovely offer, but I'm not really sure how long we'll be in the area." I wasn't sure how much to tell her, but maybe seeing her reaction to who I was and who David was might be valuable. "My husband and I are on our honeymoon. But we do have a country house here in Middlebury, Wyndswept. Do you know it?"

Her eyes widened. "You're—"

I gave a dismissive wave. "Lady Middlebury—I'm not used to all that yet. Actually my husband David is working with the local authorities on the murder investigation."

"R-really?" Her ivory complexion turned as chalky as those famous hills of Dover. She swallowed hard. "I had no idea."

"In fact, I'm the one who blundered into the antiques shop and discovered the body."

"Oh, my. H-how h-horrible for you." The ex-model's hands fluttered across the table as if she couldn't keep them still.

"I could've done without it. Basically my honeymoon is over, and my new husband is keeping the kind of hours that yours does."

She leaned back in her chair with a world weary expression. "So the question is what are you going to do with all your free time?"

I smiled. "I have a son by my first marriage, so he'll keep me plenty busy. He's not old enough to go away to school yet. I'm a musician and I have a background in antiques, so I thought I might open a shop in the Green and possibly one in London."

"Well, of course, there'll be charity work you can do as well. As Lady Middlebury, it'll be expected that you'll do certain things."

"I'm not sure about meeting all those expectations. I'm not used to all that stuff. I'd rather keep busy with a couple of antiques stores, or maybe play second fiddle with a local chamber group."

The interview hadn't gone quite like I'd expected. I'd blathered on too much about myself and forgotten Nicola was a suspect in a murder case.

Nicola glanced down at her watch. "Oh, dear. I'm late for my workout. My trainer will be furious with me."

As I watched her leave the tea room, my emotions were conflicted. I could almost identify with her loneliness. Not that I would ever cheat on David. It isn't in my nature. But I could understand the need to find something to do.

And that night, for sure, I would tell David about my interest in the antiques shop.

The road was narrow and curvy as Nicola drove through the countryside. Damn. Damn. Damn. How could she have been so stupid as to sit down and spill her guts to the wife of one of the investigating officers on that bastard's murder?

And the new Lady Middlebury to boot. Heaven knew she'd

heard all the gossip about Lord Middlebury's American wife. She was cute and petite with lovely green eyes, but she had the oddest hair Nicola had ever seen. All spiked and multicolored like a punk rocker. Otherwise she acted and spoke like a normal person, for an American.

She puffed furiously on her cigarette, sucking the smoke deep in her lungs. She hadn't had one of the dreaded things for two weeks, and now, with Riley's murder, she'd started again. Still, almost nothing else could relax her the way a good smoke could.

As soon as she'd left the tea room, she'd sent Philip a text message. But he still hadn't responded.

Bugger.

She rounded a curve and had to whip over to the right because of an oncoming truck. Yes, she'd lied to the little American about one thing. Sunday night, she'd finally come clean and told Philip about Riley's threats.

But not completely clean.

Philip would kill her if she'd come completely clean. He would never see it as partially his fault she'd been unfaithful...even if it was only twice. Riley wouldn't leave her alone afterwards—that much was true. Bloody bastard—she was glad he was dead.

He deserved it.

The mobile rang, and with one hand still steering, she grabbed the phone from the seat beside her with the other. "Philip?"

"Yeah. What's up?"

"I'm afraid I've done something rather stupid."

"Come on, luv. What's new?"

Jerk. "I met someone today. She invited me for a cup of tea, and before I knew it I was spilling my guts about how I hated Riley Stubbs."

"Do we have to do this now? I'm about to close on a deal for a nice piece of property."

"Yes! We have to do this now. It was the wife of Lord Middlebury, and he's a DCI with the Met, you know. Well, they're on their honeymoon, and he's been called into the investigation because his wife found the bloody body."

"Just calm down. I'll see you tonight, early if I can. We'll get our stories straight."

"But what if she tells her husband what I said and they call me in before we get our stories straight? Where are you? I'll meet you in thirty minutes. We have to do this now."

"Bollocks. All right. All right. I'll finish here and meet you at the gym in the car park."

"Good. That's where I'm headed now."

She disconnected. Get their stories straight? What had he done? Surely he hadn't made good on his threat to kill Riley—or had he?

David drove through the iron gates of Lord Hutton's estate. Newstone was a four-story stone structure. It loomed in the distance as he emerged from the long narrow drive formed by a double row of ancient oaks. The front garden boasted a fountain and a concrete circular drive.

He stopped in front of the somewhat Gothic entrance. After climbing the stone steps, he knocked on the massive arched door. The door opened slowly. The butler took note of David's bearing. "Sir?"

David handed the butler two cards: one of ivory heavy card stock, engraved with David L. French, Earl of Middlebury, the other of basic card stock, with again his name and rank, Detective Chief Inspector. "I'm here to see Lord Hutton."

The butler glanced at the two cards, shuffled them between his thumb and first two fingers a couple of times, his eyebrows rising with an air of dignified curiosity. "I'll see if his lordship is at home."

"I'm here on *official* business."

The butler blinked once, then gave a slow nod. "Lord Hutton is in the library. If you'll wait in the morning room, I'll advise him of your presence." The butler took David's coat and gestured to the first room on the left of the wide entry hall.

David nodded and walked into the morning room. He barely

had time to register the luxurious furnishings when Edward Norris Hutton, Lord Hutton, entered the room with a smile on his face and a carved ivory pipe in his left hand. Hutton was in his late forties, tall, silver-haired, slender and immaculately tailored, as befitted a man of his station.

"Davy. How nice to see you. Turner said it was official business. How may I help you?"

"Good morning, Edward. I've been asked to look into a murder here in the Green."

Hutton raised his eyebrows and motioned for David to be seated. "Really? That Stubbs fellow? Wonder it didn't happen before now. Apparently he was quite a bounder, or so I've heard. Turner will bring coffee and tea."

David clenched his jaw and inclined his head. "It's rather delicate. Your name, as well as Lady Jane's, has come up more than once in the investigation."

"Really?" Hutton leaned back and casually placed his arm across the sofa. "I can't imagine in what context it would. But I admit I'm curious, old fellow." He took a puff on the pipe.

"As you may imagine, the rumor mill is quite efficient in a village the size of Kinsey Green. Stubbs was indiscreet with his relationships. I don't know any other way to say this, Edward, but your wife has been named as one of his...lovers. As you can see, this certainly gives her a possible motive."

"I've no doubt that Stubbs took advantage where he could, but not with my wife, I assure you. She's an avid antiquer—that's the expression they use—but my wife would never lower herself in such a manner."

"Are you sure?"

"Good heavens, man. I know my own bloody wife!" Hutton's nose flared with indignation. "Our children are away at school, but she has charity work which keeps her busy. She and Nan Morgan are always out in the garden making plans for the next season. I can't imagine anyone less likely to have an affair with a local tradesman than my wife." He set down the pipe with a *thunk*.

There it was, the word "tradesman". Usually hidden, but now

revealed, the anger, the arrogant upper-class disdain for those in the business world, even though Hutton himself depended on business for his livelihood. This was the real Edward Norris Hutton, the one who'd belonged to the same club as David's late father.

"I'll need to speak to Lady Jane as well."

Hutton's face grew red, making a blazing contrast to his silver hair. "That's bloody absurd. I won't allow it."

"I must insist. Either here or down at the station. I know we all would prefer to avoid the latter."

"Bloody hell." Hutton shifted on the sofa, clearly uncomfortable with David's adamant attitude.

"I'll need to interview both of you."

"Really? *Both* of us?" His lordship's face grew even redder.

"Surely you see that as her husband, you would also have a motive for killing Stubbs."

The veins in Hutton's neck and forehead bulged. Was he about to have a stroke? David had been as discreet as possible, but no one was immune to investigation, not even the arrogant Hutton.

Hutton rose and rang for Turner. "See if her ladyship is available and request she join us immediately."

Turner gave a quick nod and hastened to do as Hutton requested.

"I must say you've some nerve. Your father and I go back to—"

"I'm sensitive to your feelings, but I must question you both as a matter of record."

"Edward?" The lady in question, neatly dressed in blue wool slacks and a white sweater, entered the room. She was a slender woman in her late forties with shoulder length dark hair streaked with silver at the temples.

David stood, at her entrance into the room. Still somewhat red-faced, Hutton introduced David, using both his title and reason for being there.

Lady Jane didn't flush like her angry husband. She smiled, seated herself across from her husband and David, then gestured for him to be seated. "What an extraordinary mission you're on.

My mother knew your mother quite well. In fact, they served on some of the same charities...before your mother's health declined."

Her polite way of telling him she knew all about his family and his mother's descent into alcoholism.

"I need to interview each of you separately."

She smiled again. "By all means, Chief Inspector. I've nothing to hide."

"I don't see how you can take this so blithely, Jane," Hutton said with a huff. "Someone has slandered you, and me as well."

David didn't blame Hutton for his anger and wondered why her ladyship was taking it all so calmly. Was she that good an actress? Wouldn't any married woman accused of infidelity be upset whether or not she was guilty of infidelity, much less the murder itself?

"Edward, remember your blood pressure. Darling, why don't you take a walk in the rear garden while I answer the inspector's questions? You'll feel much better."

Hutton stood, stuck his hands in his jacket pockets. "I believe I will."

After Hutton left the room, David frowned at her ladyship. "Your name has come up in our investigation—more than once, I must add—as one of the women with whom Riley Stubbs was having an ongoing affair."

"A ridiculous charge, but I understand you must investigate all leads." She stroked the arm of her chair. Was she trying to smooth things over?

"Were you having an affair with the deceased?" He needed a reaction from her. Her continued good humor was an irritation. She was hiding something. Had to be.

"No. Absolutely not." Her gracious smile never faltered.

"Then why would the deceased close the shop whenever you came in?"

"That's absurd." She paused, slowly placing a hand to her chest. "He did no such thing." She shrugged. "At least I never noticed. Perhaps he closed the shop when I came in as a courtesy."

So, lower the boom. "And by all reports, you're not the only married woman for whom he closed his shop." See how she liked that bit of news.

Her nostrils flared, respirations quickened, along with a slight quiver of her hand. Good. She might have known there were other women in Stubbs's life, but she didn't like David's mentioning it.

He reached in his jacket pocket and removed his notepad. "Where were you yesterday morning between the hours of seven and nine?"

She rose from her chair, her hand still positioned rather theatrically on her rapidly rising and falling chest. "You've some nerve." She glanced around the room. "If you must know, I—uh, was here...until early afternoon."

"You were here the entire morning?"

"I believe that's what I said." The grit in her tone was unmistakable. "Yes." She sat again, but was no longer as calm and composed as she'd been earlier.

"And your staff can verify that fact?"

"Of course, they can."

"Give me a run down on your morning activities as well as those staff members who can verify your whereabouts."

"I was with Cook most of the morning. We were having a dinner party that night for some of Edward's colleagues, and menu planning took most of the morning."

"Most of the morning?" He raised an eyebrow. "Please be more specific as to time."

She straightened her back and maintained the rigid posture. "I rose around seven. My maid brought my morning tea and the Daily News. I bathed." She brushed her hair from her shoulders. "Would you care to know which soap I prefer? Would that help your inquiry?"

He ignored her sarcastic tone. "What time did you and Cook go over the menu?"

"I finished dressing around nine, read the paper, then I went downstairs around ten."

"Was your maid with you until after you dressed?"

"No, she brought my tea around a quarter after seven. I

dismissed her. I'm a modern woman, Chief Inspector, and I'm perfectly capable of bathing and dressing on my own."

But this modern woman still required a maid to bring the morning tea and newspaper. All part of the trappings of her station.

"So you were alone from seven-fifteen until ten."

"I was alone in my room—yes." Her gaze darted to the left.

"No one saw you during this time?"

"No, Inspector. I didn't know I'd need an alibi or I'd have kept the maid up there to do my hair. Wait—I did see someone—not that it will help." She let out a theatrical sigh.

"Whom did you see?"

"I saw the landscaper, Nan Morgan, down in the back garden. I'd asked her to check on the winter vegetables and see to the mulching. I pecked on the window and waved at her." She sighed and shrugged. "But she didn't see me. I'm afraid that's the best I can do."

"Thank you. Now I'll need to speak with your maid and Cook."

Her equilibrium apparently restored, she smiled at him. "Of course, Chief Inspector. I'll ring for Turner. He'll take you to them."

David watched her ladyship leave the room. Always graceful. No, he amended— almost always graceful under fire. It didn't take a lot to shake her story. The woman was hiding something, but whether it was a murder or merely something more mundane he had yet to determine.

Chapter Nine

Detective Sergeant John Tower walked into the Shear Haven and quickly located his cousin, the flaky Daisy. True enough, her station was only fifteen feet from the window, and she had an unobstructed view of Greenway Antiques.

"Oy, there, Daisy."

She stopped snipping her current client's hair and gave him the evil eye. "What d'you want with me, Johnny Tower? Poppin' in for a trim and some highlights, are you?" She gave a snort and resumed her butchery.

"Need to ask some questions about...what happened yesterday."

"Don't know nothing." She wrinkled her nose at him. "Can't you see I'm busy, you silly bugger?"

"Just background questions. Come on your lunch break."

Daisy shook her head. "Can't. I'm booked all through lunch. Got to keep the ladies of the Green looking their best. Isn't that right, Mrs. Birdsong?"

Billie Birdsong, all of eighty-two years, looked up and nodded at him. "That's right, Johnny. Now go on with ya and let her finish my hair. I've a date for dinner with...well, never you mind."

Little old Billie Birdsong had a date for dinner. What was the world coming to?

"It's official police business. Come on, Daisy, it won't take long. It's not like you're a suspect or anything."

"Well, I should hope not!" Daisy slammed her scissors down on the counter, and Billie Birdsong gave a jump.

"Oh, my, please be careful. See here, dear, why don't you take Johnny in the back and answer his questions. I don't mind waiting."

Before his cousin could object, John quickly agreed. "Thank you, Mrs. Birdsong. You're as fresh as a blooming rose, you are."

Daisy scowled, but she led him to the back room and sat down. "Aw-right, ask me anything."

"It's come to our attention that you might have some information pertinent to our enquiry into Riley Stubbs's death."

She looked down and studied her nails. "What of it? I didn't see anyone kill him, if that's what you mean."

"No, but you've a pretty good view of the comings and goings at the antiques shop. Anything unusual?" He pulled out his notepad and pen.

"You mean like him turning his "Open" notice around to "Closed" when certain ladies of the village pop in for an antique or two?" She grinned up at him with a knowing smirk.

"Exactly."

"I was just telling one of my customers yesterday about this. Guess it won't hurt to tell you, too. First of all, he forgot to turn it round one day and I heard him in there with his business partner playin' a little game of hide the salami. Second, he turns—turned— it round for Nicola Denton, Evie White, old Nan Morgan, and don't forget her ladyship Lady Jane Hutton-smutton."

"Wide variety of ladies," he muttered.

"Ladies?" She curled her upper lip. "That's not what I calls 'em." "Anything else?" John prompted.

"Yeah, except for his business partner, all those women got husbands—that's who I'd be lookin' at."

John rose. "Thank you for your cooperation. I'll write this up, and if you'll come by the station, you can read it over and sign it."

"Aw-right. After six okay?"

John nodded and left the shop.

Bugger. The same names kept coming up in the investigation. Had to be something to it.

*

Nicola Denton whipped into the car park and stopped. She glanced around. Drat. Philip's silver Aston Martin wasn't anywhere to be seen. Her fingers tapped against the dash. Did he think she had nothing to do except wait on him to appear?

And that remark of his: "Get their stories straight?" Had he done something rash? He had a temper. Everyone knew it, too. Why, oh, why had she been unfaithful? All right, truthfully she'd been bored with life in rural Kinsey Green. It was also true she'd been born there. But when she met and married Philip in London, she never dreamed he would want to live in the country instead of the city.

She loved him...still. But he was so busy buying and developing rental property, she never saw him. He supported her—quite well, too—but it wasn't enough. Kinsey Green was Dullsville, UK.

There it was: the whine of a high performance engine. She turned. Yes, Philip had finally arrived.

He stopped, jumped from his motor, opened the door and slid into her passenger seat.

Without so much as a peck on the cheek, he launched into a tirade. "What the bloody hell did you do? Did you kill that bastard? If you did, we'll have to make an argument self-defense."

"You're no bloody barrister. Besides, I didn't kill him." "Well, where were you yesterday morning?"

"I've already been interrogated by the inspector's wife, and I'll not have you interrogating me, too."

"How the bloody hell did you come to be interrogated by the inspector's wife?" He scowled over his sunglasses.

"Coming from the bookstore, I met this nice American girl. We chatted a bit. She invited me to the inn and we had a cup of tea. We were merely having a conversation, but the more I think about it, the more I realize she was interrogating me. I told her how I hated Riley and how he was stalking me and that I was glad he was dead. So there—that's what I've done." She turned and looked out her right window. She just couldn't face his righteous indignation.

Not now.

"Now, now, doll. I'll give you an alibi," he murmured.

"You can't. I've already told her you were gone when I got up yesterday." Tears started to well in her eyes. "Now I'm a suspect. I can't go to jail."

"If you're a suspect, then so am I. We're in this together." He put his arm around her shoulders and pulled her close. "Don't cry, little one. It'll work out."

"You d-didn't do it, did you, Phil? The rumor mill says he was mutilated—you wouldn't do anything like that. I know you wouldn't." Still there was just a tiny bit of doubt.

"I could do, but someone beat me to it. Good thing I'm as busy as I am, or you might've been trekking to Keyeston on visitors' day."

Nicola shuddered. Somehow she couldn't quite imagine her husband in prison or herself visiting him there. "Swear to me you didn't do it."

"I didn't do it, swear on my mum's grave. Just keep to your same story. If he was mutilated, that's a man's modus operandi, not a woman's. Trust me on that. I've seen all the forensics shows."

"I do trust you." Comforted by his presence and his warmth, she snuggled deeper into his embrace. "I love you. I really do."

"I know, doll." He pulled away, leaving her bereft and without warmth. "Now, I've got to get back to work." He gave her a peck on the cheek and was gone.

Damn him. He couldn't wait to run out on her and back to his more lucrative pursuits. Wonder what the little American's inspector looked like? She probably received better treatment.

Bloody hell, the hounds received better treatment than she did. But she'd been a bad girl. A couple of quickies with Stubbs were the least of her sins.

After Nicola left the tea room, I became aware of some pretty pointed stares in my direction and a snigger or two. Then I remembered—my hair was still multicolored. I put my hand up to the back. Dang. It was pretty short, too.

About time I did something to the mess, so I went up to our suite and opened the box of hair color I'd purchased just that morning. I read the directions and put it on my hair, and waited anxiously for the full twenty-five minutes for the results. David, being the doting husband he is, hadn't seemed to mind the multicolor explosion, but then we were still on our honeymoon.

Twenty-five minutes was an awfully long time. I paced and gazed out the window at the street below. From my perspective on the second floor, I had a direct view of Greenway Antiques, and I could almost see the alley behind it. Now, if I'd just been looking out the window yesterday morning instead of snuggling with delicious David, I might've seen the killer.

And that made me wonder if anyone else had been looking out their window yesterday morning. But of course, the detectives would've canvassed the inn's guests. I sat down at the lovely George III desk and made myself a note to ask David about that the next time I saw him.

Finally it was time to shampoo the hair color from my hair and be normal again. Only that wasn't what happened.

My first inkling of disaster was the violet color of the gooey mess I was about to wash out. I crossed my fingers, said prayers to whomever might oversee hair color snafus, then I shampooed the devil out of it—not an easy task with crossed fingers.

I wrapped a towel around my head and took a deep breath. I removed the towel and peered at my reflection through my fingers—just like I always watched horror movies whenever I got sucked into watching one. Whatever color it was, it was dark. Very dark.

I grabbed the blow dryer and started drying the short strands of hair dippy Daisy had left me.

Except for the crown, which was cut so short it stood straight up, the rest of my black and green hair settled in a soft cap around my face.

Yes, black and green.

While the red and blue had taken the dark brown dye a little too well, the previously yellow sections were now a bright Kelly green.

Now I looked more like a Goth teenager with my pale freckled skin and black hair. My eyes are green, and the green in my hair—let's just say I looked like a Goth creature from the black lagoon with iridescent green eyes.

All I needed were a few scales and my makeover would be perfect.

Not.

After interviewing Lady Jane's maid and cook, David returned to the morning room with the butler dogging his heels. Neither interview with Lady Jane's maid or cook had produced anything of value. Lady Jane still had no alibi from approximately seven-fifteen until ten. Two hours and a quarter was certainly sufficient time to dress and drive into town, kill Stubbs, divest herself of any blood evidence along the way and return home unseen.

All right, it was possible, but damned unlikely. Stubbs was murdered by a man; David was sure of it.

"Turner, if you will tell his lordship I'm ready for him?"

"Certainly, Inspector." Turner bowed and left the room.

He didn't have long to wait. Hutton entered the morning room. He carried his pipe in one hand and seated himself comfortably in an overstuffed chair. By all appearances, Hutton's walk in the garden had done him good. His color had returned to normal and his body language was more relaxed.

"All right. Let's get this over with, Inspector." Hutton's tone was calm and it was time to see how deeply the calm exterior went.

"Were you aware of your wife's affair with the deceased?"

"Back to that again are we?" He stopped and took a deep breath. "I really have to watch my blood pressure. My physician recommends deep breathing whenever I'm upset. And don't get me wrong—I'm very upset."

"Then try a few more deep breaths," David suggested. Hutton's deep breathing could be a delaying tactic while he thought up a response.

Hutton lifted his chin a defiant notch. "My wife wasn't having an affair with anyone." He stopped to take another deep breath. "We're devoted to each other."

"And where were you yesterday morning?"

"Walking with my dogs."

"From when to when. Details please."

Hutton scowled, but continued. "I rose at six-thirty. Showered, shaved. Dressed. Breakfasted at seven. At seven-thirty after my second cup of tea, I took the dogs—four English Spaniels and one Jack Russell—outside."

"Surely you have staff who could take the dogs for their morning walk?"

"I prefer to walk the land and I prefer their company when I do."

Behind Hutton's arrogant attitude was a lie. Everyone lied to the police, even when they didn't have anything to be guilty about. It was a given.

"Did you go into town at all yesterday?"

Hutton leaned back and appeared to be mulling over his reply. His fingers tapped on the armchair. Then he reached for his pipe and began the fiddly process of lighting it. Another stalling tactic. Why?

"Not at all. I went to Keyeston, had an appointment with my solicitor—business deal actually." His cheeks twitched as he struggled to keep the pipe lit. The sweet scent of the pipe tobacco filled the air.

So Hutton consulted his solicitor the same day Stubbs was murdered. "What time did you leave for your appointment?"

"Around noon."

"So you were wandering around your estate from seven-thirty until noon? Anyone see you?"

"No. As I said, I prefer solitude. And I returned around eleven-thirty, changed to business attire and left for my appointment."

"Good God, man, it was zero degrees Celsius most of the morning. You expect me to believe you were tramping the hills all this time?"

"I was dressed for the weather—tweeds, wellies and so on. Walking is good exercise, Chief Inspector. You should try it sometime."

David ignored the jibe. "I need the name of your solicitor in Keyeston."

Hutton took a deep puff on his pipe. "He can't reveal anything about our business dealings."

"No, but he can verify the time you were in his office."

"Very well. His name is Reston. Harwell Reston." Hutton stood and inclined his head. "Is that all?"

"One more thing. I'll need to talk to your driver or whoever looks after your motors." "I drove myself. My driver's on leave. His mother's ill."

"When did he leave?"

Hutton smiled. "Day before yesterday, I believe."

Convenient. "That'll be all then." David turned to walk away, then stopped in the doorway of the morning room. "Just in case, I need your driver's address and number if you have it."

Hutton's jaw clenched on the pipe stem. "Turner will have it."

More and more certain that Hutton was hiding or withholding information, David nodded and walked into the hall to wait for the butler.

Back in the stationhouse, David found DS Stafford and the pretty DC Pettigrew huddled together. "Well, how did the interview with the Dentons go?"

Stafford and Pettigrew both jumped as if they'd been caught cheating on an exam.

"Sir." Stafford stretched his neck and ran his finger around the collar of his shirt as if it were choking him. "The Dentons weren't home last night. Lights were all off. W-we went there—uh, after we had dinner at the pub, the Grey Fox Laughs."

"Yes, Stafford, I know the pub," he said somewhat testily. "What's going on?"

DC Pettigrew's cheeks turned a deep pink. "The time sort of got away with us—at dinner. They might've already gone to bed, sir."

"What time was it, Stafford?"

"About eleven, sir," Stafford said, unable to meet David's gaze.

David turned to Pettigrew. "Thank you for entertaining my sergeant last night and for showing him the way to the Dentons." Under his direct gaze, Pettigrew swallowed and made a quick excuse to leave.

"Stafford, I don't know what the two of you were up to last night, but it better never happen again. When you're given an assignment, you'll do as you're told, no matter how distracting your partner might be."

The sergeant nodded vigorously. "Yes, boss. I'm sorry. Lost my head."

"I'm not being harsh. I do understand. I was young and unmarried once, but getting involved on the job is unwise."

"Yes. Don't know what I was thinking."

"You bloody well weren't thinking."

"No, sir. I wasn't."

Poor Stafford—he was pale and looked as if he might need to vomit. "Now I want the Dentons interviewed, separately and thoroughly. Why don't you and DC Pettigrew try again...and this time, no funny stuff."

"Yes, sir. I mean, no, sir."

"Today, Sergeant."

"Yes, sir!"

David nodded. "Fine." He glanced around the desk. "Is there anything new from the medical examiner?"

"Yes, Beecham's convened at meeting at four to go over all the findings."

"And I'm just hearing about it now?" Was Beecham trying to sandbag him?

"Just got the call right before you came in. I was going to call your mobile, but you came back, and then we were distracted."

"Distraction seems to be an ongoing problem with you, Sergeant."

"Sorry," Stafford mumbled.

David glanced at his watch. It was two-thirty. Maybe he should run over to the inn and check on Miranda and make certain she hadn't done any additional investigating.

What an abysmal showing as a honeymoon. True they had the rest of their lives, but several years ago, he'd learned one tough lesson and that was there were no guarantees in life. His mother had died while he was at school. His young fiancée, Cassie Wheeler, had died in a car bomb. So had his father. Also critically injured in the same explosion was his older brother Terrence, who inherited the title, but died shortly thereafter from his injuries. All of which made it extremely important for Miranda to stay as far away from the case as he could keep her.

But his new wife had a mind of her own.

Chapter Ten

I stood in front of the mirror and wondered what I should do. Shave my head completely?

No way.

As short as my hair was, I couldn't face being bald, even if it would be temporary. Now if David grew bald over the years of our marriage, it would be gradual and it wouldn't bother me because...anyway, because I just loved him so much.

Actually it was only when I stood in the bright light from the window that the Kelly green was so noticeable.

No way.

I was just trying to fool myself. Better go back to the tattooed Daisy and have her try to take it back to something resembling my natural color which, if I remember correctly, was dark ash blonde.

Yes.

That was exactly what I needed to do. So, I phoned Shear Haven and was told Daisy could work me in at three. I gathered up my brown suede jacket, headed for the door and opened it.

There stood my dear hub with his key card in hand. I smiled and gave him a hug. "Honey, I'm so happy to see you. I was just going out."

He grinned down at me from his great height of six two and ruffled my hair. "Life with you will never be boring." He picked me up and swung me around, and I gave an obligatory squeal.

"I've missed you so much," I said when he set me down. "Tell me all about the case."

He wagged his finger in my face and shook his head. "Ah, ah. No can do, feisty one. I'm here to make sure you aren't going out detecting."

"No, I'm off to the Shear Haven. Daisy's going to work me in at three." I patted my hair and tried pulling at the wisps to make them longer.

"You don't think she did enough damage the first time and you wanted to give her another go? Is that it?"

I put on my most charming southern belle persona. "I tried to fix it earlier, but as you can see..." I preened for him. "...the color didn't take evenly. Not that I mind looking like a green-haired, green-eyed monster—honestly I don't. But I thought you might prefer your Lady Middlebury to look a little more normal."

He stood with his arms folded across his chest, sort of tilting his head from side to side. "I'm trying to decide. Perhaps this Daisy person could make it all green. It really would suit you."

I did a double-take. "What?"

Then I heard it, the delicious sound of my husband's laughter. "Oh, you." I poked his chest. "You're such a tease."

"No, I'm a strict husband. No more detecting. I'm here to check up on you."

"Well, the tattooed Daisy is just going to do something with the color. I promise." I chewed on my bottom lip because I know it turns him on and might distract him just a little. "If you give me a daily update, I wouldn't be tempted to investigate on my own."

"Miranda—"

"Oh, wait." I grabbed his arm. "Guess who I ran into this morning as I was going into the bookstore?"

"Whom?"

"Nicola Denton. We had tea...right here in the tea room."

Uh-oh. My dear hub groaned, sat down and leaned back in a wing chair with his hand to his forehead. "Tell me. Go ahead. I can take it."

I sat on the sofa across from him. "Well, there's no love lost. She called Stubbs a despicable man and said she was glad he was dead. He stalked her, threatened to tell her husband they were having an affair."

"Was she?" His eyes brightened. This time I definitely had his interest.

"She'd hardly tell me something like that, but my woman's intuition tells me maybe that's what started it. She's a former model and was used to a hectic social life and lots of attention. Now she's buried in the country with a husband who works all the time. I think she loves him, but she got bored, had a little fling with the antiques dealer."

David straightened his shoulders and gave me a sideways glance. "A little fling—is that what you'd call adultery?"

"No, of course not. But that's how she probably saw it. Afterwards, wifely remorse set in and she tried to end it. Only Stubbs wouldn't let her go."

"Does her husband know?"

"She says he knew about the stalking, but not about the threats. Supposedly she tossed and turned all night and made up her mind to tell him, but he left early for work the next morning—same day the dealer was murdered."

"Is that it?"

I nodded and resisted the urge to cringe. As proud as I was of myself for getting the scoop, I waited for David to read me the riot act. I'd done the opposite of what I'd promised.

He rubbed his chin. Oh no. He always did that when he had a difficult choice to make.

"See here. Someone murdered and mutilated a man here in the Green. That someone isn't going to take it lightly when someone else goes poking her cute little nose into his or her business."

"I'll be careful."

Worry creased his forehead. "Being careful isn't enough, darling. Without know it, you may have already spoken to the killer."

"Oh, I don't think so. I've talked with one person—well, one person involved, that is. The rest was just gossip."

"Gossip. Rumor mill. Grapevine." David shook his head. "In a small village like this, it gets around very quickly when someone is a nosy Parker. Someone you've spoken with could easily speak to someone else, who could be our killer."

I wrinkled my nose. I might not like what David said, but I knew he was right.

"We have a son." He leaned forward, his expression earnest. "And I don't fancy having to explain to Jamie how his mother thought so little of herself she ended up dead just because she was bored and wanted to play private detective."

His words cut deep. My son was a part of my soul. No way would I risk David's having to tell Jamie I was dead. "You're right."

"Having you at the inn is wonderful for me, but..." He shook his head. "I've half a mind to—"

"Please, David. I'll get down on my knees and beg... Whatever it takes. Please don't send me back to London." Then my modern-woman gumption emerged. I stood and put my hands on my hips. "I won't go."

He grinned. "London's my preference, but I'm open to compromise. Make me a counter offer."

"What about my going to the estate? I'll call Mina and ask her to bring Jamie home. Riding herd on him will keep me out of your hair."

He rubbed his chin again. "All right, as long as you agree not to mingle with anyone in the village until this case is cleared."

I stuck out my hand. "Deal."

"It's either that or back to London." He leveled his steel gray gaze on me, and I knew he was deadly serious.

"Okay. I love you," I said.

He gave me his hand and pulled me down onto his lap. I put my arms around his neck and we kissed a long time, long sensual kisses that left me breathless for more.

He pulled away finally. "I have to go back. M.E.'s report's in."

"Do I have to leave today? And you'll keep the suite?"

He nodded. "I'll keep a room here. No need for a suite. Will you arrange it?"

"Sure," I said, sunk deep in a momentary depression. At least Jamie would be coming home. I love my son with all my heart and

I'd really missed him, so the depression didn't last long.

"It's only forty kilometers away," David said, "but I'm going to miss you like the devil."

"Ditto."

Another good-bye kiss and he was out the door. I looked around at our honeymoon suite and sighed. We'd had three wonderful days and nights together. If I just hadn't wanted to see the antiques shop...

Sheesh. I still hadn't mentioned my interest in it.

Under a bright winter sun, David walked from the inn to the stationhouse. The afternoon was clear without even a hint of the early morning mist. The smell of wood smoke in the air reminded him of the cozy fireplace in their room and making love to Miranda.

Under her spunky personality, his wife was a very passionate woman. What made it all the more surprising was she'd been abused by her first husband. Fortunately she'd had the good sense to escape from the bastard before he'd ruined her spirit...or worse.

Whether or not he deserved the good fortune of being the recipient of her love and that of her son's, he loved her deeply and would protect her at any cost...even if it meant sending her to the estate instead of having her nearby at the inn where he could hold her close every night.

From the bright sunlight, he entered the dark gloom of the stationhouse. He nodded to the desk sergeant and headed back to the murder squad. Formal autopsy and forensics reports were ready, and he for one couldn't wait to clear this case.

He surveyed the squad room and didn't see DS Stafford or DC Pettigrew. Just thinking about the possibilities was staggering. Plus, he was anxious to hear Stafford's impressions of the Dentons so he could compare them with Miranda's.

"Sorry." A harried Stafford entered the squad room with a smiling DC Pettigrew trailing behind him. "Had a devil of a time chasing down the Dentons," he said.

"Good," David said, grateful that Stafford's momentary lapse of common sense was

momentary.

DCI Beecham strode in with the M.E., Raymond Ballard, RCP, PABFP, BAFS in tow. "Aw-right. Mr. Ballard will start with his findings."

Ballard stood in front of the dry-erase board which was already covered with photos of the body and the crime scene. "Cause of death is exsanguination due to amputations of his penis and tongue. It appears he was immobilized by a blow to the left occipital region by a blunt object. Said object isn't in evidence as yet. Time of death determined to have occurred between the hours of seven and nine, but closest to eight.

"In addition, there were several long gray and blonde hairs found in the drying blood. DNA analysis has determined they are from a woman."

DCI Beecham frowned at that bit of news. "Not a man? Is there any possibility they're incidental trace?"

"Not since they were matted in the blood spatter and clutched in the victim's hand. One can only conclude they were shed at the time of the murder."

"Or planted there," David suggested since he was still of the opinion the murderer was male. Bloody hell, but he'd hate to meet a woman capable of such atrocity.

"Yes, that's one possibility, but it's more likely the hair was lost in the commission of the murder," the medical examiner said.

"DS Tower, what have you to share with us?" Beecham prompted.

Tower made his way to the board. "My areas of enquiry were two-fold. I interviewed one Daisy Mellon, hair stylist at the Shear Haven, and I also examined the antiques shop's books and computer.

"According to Miss Mellon, she verified that the deceased did indeed close his shop for a specific group of ladies: Nicola Denton, Evie White, Nan Morgan, and Lady Jane Hutton. Same names keep poppin' up. Has to mean something." He gave an emphatic nod and flipped over a page of his notebook.

"Now for the computer files. There was a disgusting amount of personal correspondence in his e-mail folders. I'm still reading through a lot of it. Haven't come across any hate mail. In his business files was a letter expressing interest in the possibility of selling of his shop from a Miranda Raines as well as record of a single phone call from Miss Raines a week before the murder—none the day of the murder though."

"What?" Bewildered by suddenly hearing his wife's maiden name bandied about during a discussion of evidence in the squad room, David stood and stretched out his hand. "May I see that letter?"

What the devil was she about? Making an offer on an antiques shop, the very shop where she'd stumbled over a body.

"Here you go, guv. Here's a copy." Tower brandished the letter as if he were a towel boy in an auto wash. David scanned the letter. It was very straightforward, expressing an interest in the possibility of purchasing Greenway Antiques. And signed with his wife's flowing scrawl.

Bloody hell.

He sat down. Every face in the squad room turned in his direction. Expressions of amusement, surprise, and no doubt his was the most shocked of all.

"Ahem," he began uncomfortably. "My wife's mother is a dealer, and Miranda has always had an interest as well. Nothing like a firm offer," he finished rather lamely.

DCI Beecham chuckled. "Yeah, she did at that. Maybe we ought to bring her back in for another go in the interrogation room."

David tamped down his anger and the rash reply on the tip of his tongue. "You know very well that my wife had no blood spatter on her at the scene."

"Oh, come on. I'm just pulling your leg, French. I know your pretty little wife didn't have anything to do with the murder."

"For formality's sake, I'll call her now and see that she comes in for a DNA swab. And you should know that since I have no idea how long it'll take to clear this case, she's leaving for our estate this afternoon."

"Don't blame you for getting her out of the area, French," Beecham said.

David pulled out his mobile and hit the speed dial for Miranda's.

As soon as she answered, he barked, "I need to see you at the stationhouse now." Without another word, he broke the connection.

"That wasn't a very nice tone you used with her," Beecham offered with a grin.

Business was business, and the sooner she left the Green the better. He turned to DS Tower. "What about the phone calls? I want a copy of the log. And Stafford, how about your interview with the Dentons?"

"Sure. DC Pettigrew and I..." Stafford looked across the room and smiled at Pettigrew. "...Nicola Denton says she was at home most of the morning and didn't hear about the murder until the noon news. Her husband had already left for work. Basically no alibi."

"Go on." David's tone was terse and pointed.

DS Stafford swallowed. "Philip Denton said he was checking out some properties for purchase. He gave me the names of his business associates, and we're in the process of substantiating his alibi."

David nodded.

Bloody hell, but the entire case was a mish-mash of suspects without a single verifiable alibi. His new wife had played detective, and to make things worse, she'd kept a secret from him. DS Stafford and DC Pettigrew were up to more than interviewing suspects, and that was certainly a smudge of pink lipstick on Stafford's collar.

What was the eff-ing world coming to?

I barely made it to the Shear Haven in time for my appointment. I slid into the chair, and tattooed Daisy gave me a frown. "Now, what've you been doin' to your hair? Tried to change the color again? You should've told me it didn't suit. I could've fixed it then."

I wrinkled my nose and grinned. "I didn't want to hurt your feelings, and I thought I could fix it on my own."

"And you didn't want to give me another go at it? 'Fraid I'd make a bigger hash of it?"

Her tone was playful, so I didn't think I'd hurt her feelings at all. "Sort of. But I'm here now."

"Aw-right, I'll set this mess to rights in short order."

I let out a sigh of relief. "My husband thought it was—"

"What? Did he give you what for?" Daisy asked, already glopping another thick concoction of chemicals on my hair.

"No, he's very understanding. In fact, he said it was interesting."

"Well, you're lucky then. Most men either don't give a toss or try to control every little thing. Believe me, I know."

"Do you have a boyfriend? What's he like?" Since talking about the murder was off the books, I figured I'd better make an effort to talk about something else.

"Nothin' special. Bad temper, jealous and a jerk most of the time. Typical of the blokes around here."

"Well, you're too young to settle down with just one guy. You should play the field. You've plenty of time."

"Easier said than done. If it weren't for me mum, I'd head to Keyeston or London. Man, I'd love London. Big city like that—there'd be lots of blokes."

"Is your mum ill?"

"No, but I'm her only, y'know? I'd hate to leave her. Since me dad died, she just goes to work and comes home and falls asleep in front of the telly. That's no kind of life I told her, but she doesn't care. So I'm stuck for now."

She added a final glop and worked it through my hair. "There now. Didn't take long at all." She set the timer on her counter. "Twenty-five minutes and you'll be a new woman..." She giggled. "...or at least one your husband will recognize."

While I waited, Daisy received a call on her cell phone. She took it into a corner. I couldn't hear a word, but she was very pale by the time the call ended.

I had to admit my curiosity radar was on alert. Was it her boyfriend? I didn't think so. She didn't have that squirmy body language some girls exhibit when they're talking to their fellows.

No, her body language was more guarded. She sat all tense in a chair in the reception area. Her hand gripped the cell gingerly as if it were a snake about to strike. Mostly she appeared to listen. Once the conversation was over, she came back to where I waited. The usually animated Daisy was very subdued.

"I think it's been on long enough," she said without inflection. "Let's get this stuff washed out."

I followed her back to the shampoo chair. She reached for a bottle of shampoo. "I couldn't help but see you on the phone. Was that your boyfriend?"

The shampoo bottle slipped from her hand. "N-no. What makes you ask that?"

"I just thought you might be having an argument with him."

"Wot are you—a bloody detective?" Her fingers dug into my head as she worked the shampoo through my hair.

"No, sorry."

Daisy rinsed the shampoo from my hair and thankfully didn't soak me too much. She wrapped the thick white towel around my head and leaned forward with a whisper. "Sometimes things aren't what they seem. And sometimes, I see more than I should. It'd be better if I kept me trap shut."

As soon as we were back at her station, she picked up a dryer and blew my hair dry without another word. I was on the verge of paying her when my cell phone rang.

All the way from the Shear Haven over to the stationhouse, I ran the short scenario through my head. David called me and ordered me down to the stationhouse, then without another word he hung up. Such rude behavior could mean only one thing. He'd found out about my one measly little phone call to Stubbs, and he was really angry.

He was probably going to—what could he do? Bawl me out in front of his fellow detectives. No, he'd be more subtle. He'd make me feel guilty, as if I'd betrayed him, no doubt.

By the time I reached the stationhouse, the sun was low in the sky and the chill in the air gave me the shivers. Well, no matter. I'd screwed up and I would take my medicine like a good girl.

But I wasn't taken straight to David. DS Tower put me in a room all by myself. Yes, two-way mirror and all. Okay, so David wasn't going to play nicey-nice. It would be the hard-nosed inspector.

Instead a forensics tech came in and asked my permission to take a DNA swab from my inner cheek. So now I was a suspect? Naturally I agreed and it was over in a second. The tech left and I looked around.

All right. All right. Where was he? Was he behind the two-way mirror watching me squirm? I leaned back in the chair and waited. Finally after a full ten minutes, my unsmiling husband came in and quietly placed a file on the desk. I raised my eyebrows.

"Well?"

Oh, yeah, he knew something. And he was totally pissed off, if the flat expression and the tension in the muscles around his eyes were indicators. "I'm waiting for an explanation," he said. "In going through the victim's correspondence..."

I bit my bottom lip for a second. "I can explain."

"I'm not stopping you." His lips formed a taut line and the muscles in his jaw jumped. Never a good sign.

"I was trying to find the right time to mention I'd contacted Stubbs. Just a letter of inquiry and a single phone call. Every time I was ready to tell you, something got in the way."

"For example...?"

"Finding Stubbs's body. I was going to ask for your input that morning. Honestly I wouldn't have proceeded or finalized anything without consulting you."

"Ask for my input?" He picked up the letter and waved it in my face. "It appears that you'd already made up your mind to buy the shop."

"Well...I had the money from the sale of my cottage, and I thought I could buy a couple of antique shops—"

"A couple?" His eyes widened.

I shook my head. "I thought maybe one here and another in London. Look, David, I'm used to working. I just wanted my own thing to keep busy."

"We're married, Miranda. We're supposed to discuss things like this together before any decisions are made."

"We would have, but you hared off to the sporting goods store, and then I found the body."

He took a deep breath as if trying to calm down and avoid grievous bodily harm. "You certainly did."

"I'm sorry...really."

"I had to hear about it in the squad room full of detectives. Looked a right prat, I did."

I shook my head. "No, you could never look like a 'right prat'."

"What about the last thirty hours. You've had the opportunity to tell me more than once." He tapped on the table top with a pin. Still mad—yes, he was.

"And I meant to, honestly. Things just kept interfering." Then I remembered the DNA swab. "Why did they take a DNA swab? Do you really consider me a suspect?"

"Some trace evidence showed a woman was there at the time of the murder. You're a woman," he added, somewhat unnecessarily, I thought.

"Well, I have an alibi: I was with you," I said with some heat. "That's more than I can say for anyone else in this case."

His face softened and his mouth curved into a smile, as well it should've because we were making love during the time of the murder.

"I remember."

"Am I forgiven?" I reached for his hand. "Or are you going to divorce me while we're still on our honeymoon?"

"Don't be silly. But you're still going to the estate. You're well out of this mess." He pulled me up from the chair and into his arms. "Life with you is never boring." Then he kissed my forehead. "I never want to lose you."

"You won't. I promise." My husband had already had too many losses. My recklessness disturbed him on several levels. Regretfully I pulled away. "By the way, I cleared our things from the suite. They don't have another room for you, but DS Stafford has a double, so they'll put you up with him...or you could come home every night," I added, knowing he'd prefer to stay closer to the scene.

David burst out laughing. "I'm sure Stafford will be pleased."

"What's so funny?" I asked, but he just shook his head and wouldn't spill the beans. I patted my newly ash blond hair. "You haven't mentioned my new color."

He grinned. "It's an improvement."

"Well, I could've come to the stationhouse with my black and green. How would you have liked that?"

His mouth twitched. "I'm sure the detective squad would have found it amusing.

Now is that your true color? I've quite forgotten how many times you've managed to change it."

I stopped long enough to consider. "Hm. I think it's pretty close." He only teased because when he, Jamie and I were on the run from Stefan, I changed my hair color at least twice—once to platinum blond and later to blazing red. "Of course, I've never disguised myself as the opposite sex as you did."

An expression of absolute horror crossed his face. "You said you would never refer to that incident. We *agreed*."

"But you were *so* striking as a woman."

"Mi-ran-da."

I let the issue drop. Besides, it never hurt to hold something back for future negotiations.

I gazed up at him and batted my lashes. "I have to tell you I'm not looking forward to spending tonight alone."

He pulled me tighter into his arms. "Neither am I, little one."

I giggled. "But you won't be alone. You'll have Sergeant

Stafford."

"Hardly the same."

"I should hope not."

"Are you ready to leave—to go home?" he asked, still embracing me.

"Yes. They're keeping my bags at the registration desk. Shall I take the car or—?"

David shook his head. "No, I'll need the Roller. The estate manager, Robbie, will pick you up in the Rover." He glanced at his watch. "In fact, he should be here any moment."

By now, he was walking me through the stationhouse to the entrance, and with each step, my heart grew lonelier. This husband of mine meant more to me than I could've ever dreamed any man would. His wanting to protect me was only natural, and I loved him for it, even if I chafed at being "sent home to the country" like some misbehaving medieval wife.

Chapter Eleven

By the time Robbie and I reached Wyndswept House, the sky was dark and wisps of fog were threading through the trees. I feared my welcome would be cold and the house empty without David, but as we pulled up and stopped in the front of the house, I was amazed to see the house lit up like a party and all the house staff lined up to greet me as if greeting the queen.

Robbie went around and let me out of the Rover. "Robbie? All this isn't necessary. It's cold. Everyone should come inside right now."

"Not before we welcome your ladyship as you should be."

"But—"

"No buts, your ladyship. This is your new home, and we are here to serve."

Tears welled in my eyes. I knew it was silly of me, but I was so touched by the gesture. "Well, then I'd better get a move on, so everyone can get back in the house and get warm."

I was quickly greeted by Fields, the butler, Madison, the housekeeper, Shirley Havers who was normally just called Cook and the rest of the house staff.

Madison, a tall woman with iron-gray hair, said, "This house has been too long without its lady. Welcome to your new home, Lady Middlebury."

In spite of my sniffing, I managed to greet everyone and remember most of their names. "First of all, I can't tell you how much your warm welcome means to me. David would be so pleased. Now, let's all go inside before half of you come down with pneumonia."

At that, everyone trooped inside the enormous house which was now my home. I can't say I didn't feel like a pretender or the heroine of one of Victoria Holt's gothic romances. I could almost see David and his older brother romping through the long halls and raising hell in general. I could see Jamie doing the same and soon, too.

This wasn't my first visit to the estate. The first visit didn't end very well. Like an idiot I'd let one of David's cousins convince me I wasn't right or good enough for David. I rushed out that night without even saying good-bye to the man I loved.

But this time, I belonged—no matter what anyone said or thought. David was the only one who counted now and forever.

Following the housekeeper Madison, I walked up the stone stairway past the portraits of seven earls of Middlebury and their ladies. I stopped at the last one...the one of David's mother. It showed her to have his auburn hair and gray eyes. She'd sat for the portrait while quite young and wore a black lace and silk gown. The brush strokes were so skillful it was easy to tell her gown was silk and not velvet. I gazed into her eyes and fancied I could see her gentle heart full of hope for the future.

Someday maybe our portraits would grace these walls. In the future, perhaps, a new lady would look into the eyes of my portrait and what would she see?

Oh, well, I was letting the history of the house and its former inhabitants overwhelm me. One reason for my melancholy frame of mind was I would never meet his gentle mother and win her approval, and the fact David wasn't here to carry me over the threshold merely added to it.

"Here we are, your ladyship. I hope you find your rooms satisfactory."

I walked into a room large enough to have held the entire little cottage where Jamie and I had lived. A massive Tudor four-poster oak bed occupied the far end of the room. The window and bed hangings were a pale sage green silk which pooled on the floor.

Fresh flowers—where on earth had they found them on such short notice in winter—were placed in lovely cut glass vases around the room.

The floors were stone, but covered with two large thick antique Axminster rugs in Savonnerie style designs. One was placed under the bed and the other horizontal to the Tudor arched fireplace, where a settee and side table had been arranged.

"The room was redecorated just for you, according to his lordship's instructions."

"It's beautiful. You did a wonderful job. I had no idea. It's a wonderful surprise." And it was. I had no idea David knew me so well. It was warm, comfortable and more luxurious than anything I'd ever known.

Don't get me wrong. My parents were well off, but educating my brothers and me took precedence over elegant furnishings.

"Summers will unpack for you. Cook is preparing dinner. Do you have any special requests?"

"Nothing fancy. And since it's just me, I'd love to have it here before the fire."

"Certainly."

Madison left and I whirled around and hugged myself. This was a dream and I'd have to wake up any minute. Once the case was solved, David and I would actually live most of the time in the London townhouse. Coming to the estate would be more along the lines of a vacation. But I would enjoy the pampering while I could.

If only my David were here to share that big bed with me.

After Robbie drove away with Miranda, David told himself it was for the best. He turned to go back inside the stationhouse when Stafford met him at the entrance.

"Know it's none of my business, but is everything all right with you two?"

"Of course." David glanced at his watch. "By the way, I'm bunking with you tonight. All right with you?"

Stafford's mouth dropped open. "I-I thought you said—"

He grinned at the sergeant. "It is, but I've sent her to our house in the country. We've given up our suite at the inn and nothing else is available."

An expression of utter dismay crossed the sergeant's face.

"What's the matter, Eric? Did DC Pettigrew forget her knickers?"

"God, I hope not."

"True love, is it?" David asked with a wry expression.

Stafford's cheeks turned pink cither from the cold or embarrassment. "More like true lust, sir. She's wild—"

"Enough!" David raised his hands in surrender. "Let's have some dinner—if you don't already have plans?"

"No, sir...she's having dinner with her folks tonight."

"Good, then we can go back out to the nursery. You can have another go at Freddie and I'll talk to Nan."

"You sound like you know her?"

"From way back. Her father did a lot of work on my father's estate, and she was always around to give him a hand. Her father's gone now, but she's kept the business going. The actual estate isn't that big anymore. My father sold off quite a bit of land to the local council. The estate now consists of a manor house on twenty acres abutted on either side by mini-mansions. Shame really, but I suppose it made sense financially."

"Kept the family coffers happy." Stafford's tone was ironic. "My family used to have a large house and farmland, but my grandfather gambled it away long before I was born. My father turned to the law."

"And now he's the commissioner of the Metropolitan Police. He did well, and you've followed in his footsteps and done well by all reports."

By now they were at the pub where the locals had started to gather. Eric headed for the bar to give their orders and David found them a table in a corner.

While he waited, he stared at a container of mustard. Then it hit him he'd forgotten something.

"Here's your pint." Stafford set it in front of David, then sat himself down and took a long drink.

"What about the yellow powder found at the crime scene?" David asked. "I let the business with my wife distract me."

Stafford leaned forward. "Very interesting detail, it was, too. Ground mustard seed." "Mustard seed?" A link to the Nan Morgan?

"Yes, sir. Ground up into a fine powder."

"Was it pure or mixed with any other trace?"

"It was pure. Never seen anything like it." Stafford leaned even closer. "Get this. Inspector Beecham is calling in the rest of the women involved with Stubbs for a DNA swab. Likely he'll solve the case."

"Hmm." DNA or not, David didn't believe a woman committed the murder. "DNA results might actually tell us who the killer wants us to think killed Stubbs, and that might tell us something about the murderer."

"You still think the killer's a man?"

"Yes, The mutilations were a personal attack on the man after he was already unconscious from a severe blow which would've lead to his death had he not been hacked apart."

"Yeah, a psycho—that's my guess." Stafford took another long drink.

David shook his head. "No. Our killer is cold, calculating, very intelligent and organized. It was a crime of anger by someone who didn't care it was wrong, but who believed he was exacting revenge and planted evidence to implicate someone else."

"Just so he wouldn't be blamed, you mean?"

"More than that. He has his own reason for implicating this particular person. Once we discover who he really meant to get rid of, then we'll know who killed Stubbs."

"Hold on. Let me get this straight. He's really mad at someone else, so he killed Stubbs and made it look like this person was the killer?" Stafford frowned and scratched his head. "Why didn't he just kill the person he's trying to frame and be done with it?"

"Too direct a connection, perhaps. If we knew, we'd have our killer, and I could go home to my wife."

David took another drink. Miranda must've reached home by now. He hoped she liked their new bedroom furnishings. When he planned the surprise, he'd asked the designer to use green to match Miranda's eyes, and he hated the thought of her spending the night alone in that big old bed.

Nor was he looking forward to sleeping in the same room with his sergeant.

I picked at my solo dinner before the warm fire which reminded me of the one in our suite at the inn. We made love all night long the first night we spent as man and wife. It wasn't our first time to make love, oh no. But there really was something special about making love as a married couple.

Enough of that, I told myself. I could still call my son. I reached for my cell phone and punched in Mina and Jean-Luc Pelletier's number at their farm.

"*Âllo*," Mina answered, and I quickly explained the situation.

"I see," she said. "His lordship's still involved in the case and left you to your own devices."

"That's it in a nutshell."

"I'm sure Jean-Luc can do without me for a while. I'm sure Master James would enjoy another trip on the Eurostar."

"You're a life saver, Mina...in more ways than one."

"Oh, my. What have you been up to?"

"I'm afraid I did a little too much investigating on my own and David's upset. That's why he's banished me to the country."

"I can't say that I blame him, Randi. Solving murder is a serious business and best left to the professionals."

"I know, I know. Don't you get on my case, too. I know it's for my own good, but the upshot of it all is that I'm not used to being a lady of leisure or a ladyship either."

"I think it's very wise of you to have Master James at your side."

"Right. Keeping up with him will keep me out of trouble."

"As you said earlier, dear, 'that's it in a nutshell'."

We decided that Mina would leave the next morning and bring

Jamie all the way to Wyndswept and I would make all their reservations.

"Is Jamie still up?"

"Yes, he's standing right by me, dancing up and down with anticipation. I'll put him on."

"Hi, Mummy, how's the honeymoon?"

"It's great, sweetie, but David's busy with a case, and the honeymoon is on hold. So tomorrow morning, Mina is going to bring you home…to our new home in the country."

"David's castle?" I heard the rising excitement in his voice and it hit me hard how much I missed my little guy.

"It's not really a castle, sweetie, but it's a lot bigger than our cottage. You'll love it."

"I'll see you, Mummy. Kisses."

"Yes, baby, I got them. Bye-bye."

I put down the phone and excitement bubbled up. Jamie was coming home tomorrow, and I could hardly wait to give him a big bear hug. And the sooner I went to bed the sooner tomorrow would come.

It was quite dark and the air had a definite winter nip when David and DS Stafford pulled up in front of Richmond's Nursery. From the ground level windows, the light cast a cheerful glow on the snow in the front garden.

Nan Richmond Morgan admitted them without protest. She was five-ten and solid from all the years of hard outdoor work. Her hair, a mixture of blond and gray, was pulled back with a plastic headband. Her clothes were clean and serviceable, probably purchased in the men's department.

While Stafford left the room to re-interview Freddie in another, David remained in the comfortable and cluttered living room with Nan. "Hope you've had your dinner," he said.

"We just finished. It's been a long time hasn't it, David?"

"Yes, it has. We're looking into the death of Riley Stubbs."

"I've heard about it in the village," she said with no affect.

"I hate to mention this, Nan, but your name has come up a couple of times in our investigation." He watched for her response.

She took a deep breath and clenched her jaw. "In what respect, Chief Inspector?" No more friendly "David", but the more formal address "Chief Inspector".

"Were you or have you seen Riley Stubbs...intimately?"

She jumped up, her large meaty fists clenched at her sides. "That bugger? Someone said I was having an affair with him?"

"That's what a couple of people have told us, yes. He was reported to have closed his shop whenever you came in."

"That's because he didn't want his other customers to know what a foul, cheating, lying piece of shit of a dealer he was. Bastard sold me fake Staffordshire dogs. I paid a month's wages for them, too."

"You never had an affair with him?"

"No, I'd rather take a bath in sheep shit than let that sod touch me."

"This was seen to happen more than once."

"And well it should." Her face grew red. "I went there more than once to reason with him. First, I thought he'd been fooled and would reimburse me. 'Buyer beware' is what the bugger said to me. Buyer beware! I told him 'seller beware' because I'd see him in court."

"Did this have any effect on him?"

"Bugger laughed and said...never mind. Doesn't matter, now. He's dead."

"What did he say?"

"Just some rubbish about he knew my secret and I'd better be careful or he'd tell everyone."

Interesting. "What did he know?"

"How should I know?" Nan scowled and her posture remained tense. "He was full of it, that's all. I got no secrets."

"Everyone has secrets, Nan."

"Well, I got none I care for anyone knowing," she huffed and averted her gaze. "It's getting late. And I'm an early riser."

"I understand, but one more thing. Where were you yesterday

morning?"

"Alibi? You want me to give you my alibi? Aw-right, I was working at Lord Hutton's place. That's where I was yesterday morning."

"Can anyone verify that?"

"Dunno. Lady Jane asked me to look over the winter veg beds and renew the mulch if it needed it. I works alone most of the time. That's the nature of my days."

Stafford came back into the room. He tugged at his ear which was their prearranged signal he'd learned nothing new from Freddie.

"All right. We'll leave you for the time being, but we need you to come down to the stationhouse for a DNA swab. Just on a voluntary basis as a way of eliminating suspects."

"I'm a suspect?" Her voice rose an octave, and again those meaty hands of hers were balled into fists.

"We just need to clear you, Nan. That's all."

"Yeah, I'll come down and let you swab anything you're a mind to. I got nothing to hide."

"As you said." David nodded. "That's it then. Sergeant Stafford and I thank both of you for your cooperation."

Outside, Stafford chuckled. "I thought she was going to pop you one, sir." "So did I, Eric. So did I."

It was after ten when David and Stafford returned to the Green. David pulled up in front of the inn. "See here, Eric. I'm not bunking with you tonight after all. I'm going to make sure Miranda's settled at the country house."

"Of course, sir. I mean, it stands to reason that with all those servants, her ladyship's likely to get lost in the shuffle."

David noted the smirk on his sergeant's face. "All right. I admit it. I just want to see my wife."

"And no one blames you, sir. She's a charming lady." "Thank you. I'm rather fond of her."

Eric hoisted his bulk from the vehicle, turned around and

snapped a salute in David's direction.

He shook his head and gunned the motor. He was headed home to his wife.

Home. Wife. A year ago those words brought up only painful memories, and now they brought warmth to the very depths of his being.

After the travel arrangements were made and called back to Mina, I had a cup of hot cocoa, then went to bed at nine. Strange house, strange bed, and no husband to keep me warm. It's no wonder I had trouble going to sleep. Right after dropping off, something, a bump in the night, woke me. I looked over at the clock and the red LED read ten minutes after eleven. I lay still for a moment and listened.

Thump.

There it was again. I wasn't imagining anything. Surely all the servants had gone to bed. That could only mean someone was sneaking around the house and outside my room at that.

My heart pounding, I slid over to the far side of the bed onto the floor, then peeked over the edge of the mattress. I glanced around, but in the darkened room, I couldn't see anything I could use as a weapon. I felt around the table top beside the bed. A lamp. And a heavy one at that.

I picked it up and scurried across the room to hide behind the door. I held it high over my head ready to bash whoever it was on the other side. My skin tingled and grew cold with the fear racing through my body.

The door opened. I took a deep breath—

A soft whisper. "Miranda. Are you asleep?"

Deflated and thrilled to pieces at the same time, I put down the lamp and sprang from behind the door. "Boo!"

David jumped. "Miranda, what on earth are you doing? You startled me." He reached for the light switch and flipped it.

I blinked and rubbed my eyes. "Well, you scared me to death. I thought we had a burglar."

He grinned down at me and took me in his arms. "No burglar, just a lonely husband." He picked me up and carried me to the bed. "Do you like my surprise?"

"Which one? The beautiful new room furnishings or the sneak attack on my boudoir?" I snuggled against him. The warmth of his body melted away the loneliness I'd felt ever since leaving the Green.

"Both." He nibbled down my neck to my breasts.

"Mm. You're going to have to stop that if you want a coherent answer." "Tell me in the morning because I have no intention of stopping."

And bless him, he didn't stop all night.

Chapter Twelve

Wednesday

The next morning, David woke me up with a kiss. "Mmm." I reached for him. "Love you." He reached under the 500-count Egyptian cotton sheets and tweaked my nipples which were on the tender side from all his attentions last night.

"Love you, too." He turned to the dresser and adjusted his tie. "Have to go back to the village this morning." Once his tie was perfect, he came back and sat on the side of the bed. "Did you speak with Mina last evening or will you call her this morning?"

I nodded. "Last night. I offered to meet them in Waterloo station, but she said she'd be happy to bring him directly here. So I've made all the reservations from Aix to Paris and the Eurostar to Waterloo, then to the local station. Robbie and I will meet them there."

"Sounds perfect." He kissed me on my forehead. "I miss that little fellow, but I'll trust you to keep him occupied and away from the Green."

I pretended to pout, but he saw through me.

"Good girl." He glanced at his watch. "Have to run. Stafford's going to give me a difficult time about running home for the night after I'd already decided to stay in town." He said this in all seriousness, but with a devilish glint in his eyes.

"He'll give you an even harder time if you're late, too, especially since you had so little sleep. You'll have to be careful not to yawn all day." I winked at him, even though I wished he could stay and spend the rest of the morning in bed with me.

"Grr." He wrapped his arms around me and the low growl sent a shiver through my entire body.

"If DS Stafford knew what a lusty wench you truly are, he'd die of jealousy."

"And he'd better not hear what a wench I am, or I'd be forced to tell him that you're insatiable."

"A gentleman never tells."

"Then you're safe because neither does a lady."

After another nibble and a pat on my behind, he stood, adjusted his tie again. "I really must leave."

I swung my legs over the side of the bed. "Wait. You need some breakfast or coffee at least."

He stopped and smiled. "Cook will have a thermos for me and breakfast for you whenever you want it."

I pulled on a pale green silk robe, one from my honeymoon trousseau. "I'm going down now," I said as I tied the sash loosely around my waist. "I want to walk you to the door." Then I stopped. What if it wasn't...? "Is it all right if I go down in my robe to see you to the door?"

"Guess what, darling? This is your home, and you're perfectly decently attired...and extremely lovely, too."

"Keep up with all these compliments and I'll never let you leave the room."

He swatted my butt and put his arm around me. "Come on, let's go."

Downstairs I kissed him good-bye at the front door and let out a big sigh. I still have a hard time believing this wonderful man married me...me with all my problems and insecurities.

I may have a few insecurities left over from the first marriage from hell, but this time I married my soul mate—a man who recognizes my value in his life, wants to protect me and adores my son.

I must not be so bad, after all.

*

Daisy Mellon sat in her old Rover listening to the Acid Rain Checks' latest tune on her iPod. It was way past time for her bugger of a boyfriend to show. Her head bobbed and she beat out the heavy metal rhythm on the steering wheel.

If he didn't put in an appearance soon, she'd have to duck out and get to work. The ladies of the Green depended on her skillful hands to keep them beautiful, and she couldn't disappointment them, not even for a quick snog with Jacko White.

She'd offered to alibi him for the morning of old Riley's murder, but Jacko wouldn't hear of it. Didn't want his precious Evie knowing he'd been doing the nasty with someone else. Why he cared what his slut of a wife thought, Daisy hadn't a clue, and maybe that's why she'd told the inspector's wife Evie was one of Riley's tarts. And maybe she was.

The sound of a motorcycle reached her.

Good. About time.

She pulled her skirt above her knees and eased her knickers down. Jacko would have to hurry if they were going to get some this morning.

Jacko put his head in the window. "Wot you think you're doin'? Already got your drawers down like a London tart."

Smack!

She shook her head and wiped a trickle of blood from the corner of her mouth. "What'd you do that for, you bloody bugger? It hurt."

"There's more where that came from if you don't keep your bloody mouth shut about my wife being one of Riley's whores. Don't think I didn't see you talking to your cousin wot's the fuzz."

"Not me. I didn't say a word to anyone." She eased back away from the window, but Jacko jerked open the door. "Now, Jacko. Calm down."

He unzipped his pants. "Wot's the matter, luv? Didn't you say you liked it rough?"

"That was rough enough. Go on, put that thing away. I'm not in the mood now. I'm gonna be late for work."

"You don't think I came all the way out here to not get off? Spread 'em."

She scooted back until she reached the opposite door, pulled her sweater up, exposed her breasts and then spread her legs. "Fine. Just make it quick. I ain't got all day."

Jacko fell on her and jammed his dick inside and started pumping for all he was worth without even so much as a nibble or a tweak on her tits. Pure waste of time for her it was.

"Oh, baby," she cooed and hoped he'd hurry up and get his rocks off.

Anytime now, Jacko.

He grunted and collapsed on her. If that was the best he could do, no wonder Evie screwed around on him.

She counted, one to ten. "All right. That's it then."

He pulled out and shoved his thing back in his pants. "Great, baby. You were great."

Guess it was all a matter of perspective. Any time a bloke got laid, it was great. "You bloody bugger, you didn't wear a condom."

She heard the roar of a car motor. "Bloody hell."

Jacko fell down on her again, ducked his head and waited until the car passed. "He didn't see anything."

"Go on with you. I'm gonna be late for work."

He backed out of the truck and swung his leg over his motorcycle. "See ya, Daisy," was all he said and roared off.

Bloody bugger. She sat for a minute then started up the motor, but she saw a figure approaching from the field. He waved at her. She shut off the engine and waited.

Now, what the devil did he want? They weren't supposed to meet until later.

David glanced in his review mirror. That looked like Jacko White's motorcycle parked beside the rusted green Land Rover. From his viewpoint, no one was visible in the truck, but he could just imagine the type of activity White was engaged in that early in the morning. Maybe that's what he was really up to the morning of the antiques dealer's death. Why not name his partner as an alibi?

The man was married to a woman who was certainly no better than she ought to be. Sauce for the goose was sauce for the gander.

David strode into the squad room only too aware of the late hour—nine-thirty. He eased into a chair and started going over the stack of forensics and interview reports on his erstwhile desk.

DCI Beecham leaned over David. "DCI French, there you are. I don't know what kind of hours DCIs keep in London, but here we turn up early."

David glanced up. Beecham was grinning from ear to ear. "Sorry, Beecham. I had a late start this morning."

Long drive was it?"

"Yes." He looked around the room. Everyone in the squad room was grinning from ear to ear.

So much for keeping a low profile. He shrugged. "My wife and I had family business to attend to."

"So that's what they're calling it now. Family business." Beecham roared with laughter as did the rest of the squad.

"All right. All right. Let's leave the honeymooner alone and get some work done."

After thirty minutes, a call came to David's phone in the squad room. "Inspector French."

"This is Millie Benson at the Shear Haven. Our Daisy Mellon is late for work. Very late. It's not like her, Inspector."

"Has anyone tried to call her at home or on her mobile?"

"Yes, no one's at home and her mobile just keeps going to voice mail."

He took down her address. "What kind of vehicle does she drive?"

"A rusty old Land Rover, green. Must be twenty-five years old at least."

"We'll check it out, Mrs. Benson." He set the phone back on the receiver. His gut twisted and yawed, his gut's way of saying it was too late.

*

A search party assembled quickly. First, two officers were sent to Daisy's flat where she lived with her mother, then David directed the majority of the force to the lay-by where he'd seen White's motorcycle and the old green Rover earlier that morning.

The officers started a grid search, while a SOCO went over the empty Rover. From the smell and dried body fluids, it appeared that someone had sexual relations and not too long ago. A pair of discarded woman's knickers were found in the front floorboard.

He turned from the vehicle. "Should be plenty of DNA evidence."

"Over here!" came the shout not fifteen minutes into the search.

David's gut was right...horrifyingly right. One of the constables had found Daisy Mellon's body in a thicket some twenty yards from the lay-by. Her killer hadn't even attempted to bury her. No, he'd displayed her in the worst possible way, arms and legs spread like the Vitruvian Man. Her nude body was covered in bruises and her throat slit. Her clothes lay nearby where they'd been ripped off her.

Multiple mutilations. Both breasts were amputated. One had been placed in her mouth and the other had been shoved into her private parts.

"Keep DS Tower away from the scene," Beecham said, shaking his head. "She was his cousin. He shouldn't have to see her like that."

David rubbed his eyes, wishing he could erase the visual images. "No one should have to see the poor girl like that."

"We've got us a serial killer on our hands, and it's Jacko White." Beecham rammed his hands in his pockets. "I mean to see him arrested before the hour is out."

"Well, his motorcycle was certainly here this morning when I passed." He glanced down at the ground. "Do you think we can match up his tread tracks?"

"Dunno. Ground was frozen this morning. Oy!" Beecham yelled at the white-clad SOCO. "Don't forget to check for tire tracks."

The tech nodded. "Soon as I finish going over the Rover."

"Here's the way I see it happening," Beecham said. "She and the perp were getting it on right there in the front seat, but it all went wrong. There's plenty of biologicals...what looks like blood on the dashboard. Then he drags her out of the Rover."

David pointed at the ground. "Drag marks. She breaks away, but he catches up with her and he kills her right where her body's found. Look at all the disturbed vegetation. She fought...and fought hard, too. But he was too strong. She was a tiny thing." About his Miranda's height and weight.

Beecham shook his head. "This is going to kill her mother. Tower says Daisy was an only child."

David nodded. A second death. Was it a lover's quarrel gone bad? Did they have a serial killer on their hands as he suspected? Someone who used terrible mutilations to right wrongs he'd fancied been done him. Or was it a copy cat?

Too many questions and not enough answers.

At any rate, he was doubly glad Miranda was forty kilometers away and would be busy with her—no, their—son. Out of harm's way, the two of them, and he meant to keep them that way.

The day dragged on like molasses in winter. After I showered and dressed, I didn't feel much like having breakfast, so Madison, the housekeeper, took me on a tour of the old house.

"The original house was built in 1617 and consisted of the central portion of the house; the ell wings were added later that century," Madison said as we toured. "The first Earl of Middlebury was Mortimer French, and he was awarded the estate for service to the crown. I don't know if you're very familiar with English history, but Charles I ascended to the throne in 1625. It was a turbulent time in England. The king dissolved Parliament in 1629, and there was a civil war. The Royalists were defeated in 1646. The house and all lands were awarded to one of Oliver Cromwell's cronies. Charles II restored Wyndswept House to the rightful family in 1663."

"I remember reading about the Restoration and Charles II," I said, not wanting to appear completely ignorant of English history. Of course, most of what I remembered about the restoration was from the historical novel, *Forever Amber*.

"The first earl, Mortimer, had died in the war, as had his son Richard. Richard's young son, Edmund, became the third Earl of Middlebury, and it is he who petitioned the Crown to have the lands returned and then commissioned the ells to be built in by the master architect of that era, Christopher Wren."

As I listened, I wandered along and marveled at Madison's grasp on the history of the house. I couldn't help but laugh, too. "In America, if a house is two hundred years old, it's considered something to treasure, but here I am in a house that's nearly four centuries old." I couldn't help but be awed by the history involved. Wars, life and death had been played out in this house and on this land.

"Yes, your ladyship. It's a proud heritage and a great old manor house. Originally it was a wooden structure, but after the Great Fire of London in, the young earl decided that it should be reinforced and built with stone."

"Since David and I will be living in London the majority of the time, how much staff is required to maintain this wonderful house?"

"The country house will be closed and the staff will move to London," Madison said.

"You will? The townhouse doesn't seem quite large enough to require a lot of house staff."

"The townhouse was David's—his lordship's—private residence, but now that he's assumed the title, there is another larger townhouse in which the previous earl lived and entertained."

Dumbass me, I'd always assumed we'd live in the townhouse where David had taken
Jamie and me when we first started our flight from my ex and where Stefan very nearly killed us.

She led me into the ballroom. At the far end was an enormous fireplace with a heavily carved wood mantle. "Grinling Gibbons?"

Madison smiled. "Yes. So you do know some of our masters."

"My mother is an antiques dealer in the States, and I've picked up quite a bit of design history from her."

"Then you have an appreciation for the finer things, old things."

"Yes. I do. In fact, I hoped I might buy a couple of antiques shops, one here in the area and one in London."

Madison nodded. "And I believe his lordship told us you're a musician as well? Perhaps you'd like to see the music room next. His lordship's mother was a fine pianist, but sadly she gave it up shortly after I came to work for the family."

We entered the music conservatory. It was a small jewel of a room with a grand piano and enough seating for a small gathering of music lovers. The tall French windows looked out onto a stone patio and the rear garden. "This is breathtaking," I said.

"It's a lovely sight in spring and summer, too."

"I'm sure it is. I hope my son's coming won't cause anyone any trouble."

"To the contrary, having your son here will be a thrill for us. I understand he's in France with Mina Griswold. I remember her as well."

"Yes, he's been staying with her and her husband, Jean-Luc, and she's bringing Jamie. It's been almost a week since I've seen him and I can hardly wait."

"Will you be requiring the services of a nanny until he goes off to school? I'll make inquires and schedule interviews for you."

Goes off to school? I hadn't thought about that practice. Would he have to leave home at the age of eight like other boys of his station? Like David did? That was something we would have to discuss in great depth.

"A nanny won't be necessary," I said with a shrug. "I've managed without one for six years."

"As you wish."

I looked at my watch. If Mina and Jamie left Aix-en-Provençe as scheduled on the 10:44 train, they'd get into Paris at 14:57. They would catch the Eurostar at 15:19 , and then they would be in Waterloo Station by around 17:54. Gracious, what a long trip for

Mina and Jamie, but another couple of hours after that and they'd be here.

"How long before your son will arrive?"

"They should arrive in Keyeston around nine or so. I'll go with Robbie to pick them up at the station."

"Then I'll have Cook arrange for a late dinner." "Yes, thank you."

The rest of the tour was a blur because all I could think about was Jamie and where he'd be at that particular time. And yet, I couldn't help but wonder how the case was going and if David was any closer to finding the killer.

Chapter Thirteen

Leaving the forensic tech to his work, David, DS Stafford and DCI Beecham returned to the village and found Jacko White hard at work at his motorcycle repair shop.

He scowled from the motorcycle where he was working and glared. "Wot you guys want now? Can't you see I'm a busy man and I got no time for answerin' more of your bloody stupid questions?"

Beecham started with, "Well, now, we need to talk about your whereabouts this morning, Jacko."

White set his wrench down with a clang. "Wot time?" "Nine o'clock," David said.

Jacko's face turned red, and his expression turned sarcastic. "Now, wot you be needin' to know where I was at that particular time?"

"We've a complaint. Daisy..." David deliberately hesitated revealing any additional information. Always best to get the suspect's reaction at the mention of her name.

"Wot did that bloody bitch say I did? We met in the lay-by for a little mutual gratification. She were in a hurry, she was, to get to work, so I grabbed some snatch and took off. That's about it. Nothin' illegal unless—"

"Daisy's dead, you sod," Beecham said. "From the looks of it, she resisted. You raped her and then killed her."

"'Old on. I know my rights. If you think I killed her, you're supposed to read me my rights. I didn't 'ear no caution from anyone of you."

DS Stafford raised an eyebrow. David nodded, and the sergeant read Jacko White his rights.

"Yeah, I want a solicitor. I ain't sayin' another word to the likes of you."

"Cuff him, Stafford," David said. "Jacko, if you didn't kill Daisy, you need to talk to us, instead of asking for a solicitor. You might've seen someone or something that will assist in our investigation."

"No." White began to breathe rapidly. "Where did it 'appen? Wot did 'e do to 'er?"

Beecham snorted. "Doesn't work, me boy. You already know the details. We just want to know if you killed Riley Stubbs, too, or were you trying to make it look like the same person did both?"

White's eyes grew red and he blinked furiously as if he might break down and cry. "Oh, God. No! Did he cut 'er up, too?"

"Enough!" Beecham yelled. "You won't talk to us. We don't have to talk to you. Get in the car."

White squared his shoulders and stood his ground. "'Old on, Beecham. You got to find out who's killing folks in this village. It ain't me. Killing an innocent girl like Daisy ain't right."

"Should've thought of that before you did her, Jacko." Beecham jerked open the car door. "Get in."

Beecham was convinced they had their man, and if it were up to him, he'd have White for the murder of Stubbs as well.

David wasn't so certain. A bit of rumpy-pumpy in a lay-by was one thing, but murder was another entirely. What was the motive for killing the Mellon girl? She'd talked freely to Miranda about who might've killed Stubbs. Had she more information than anyone suspected and talked to the wrong person? Had she tried to blackmail the killer or was she killed to throw off suspicion from the real killer?

And these questions needed an answer before he was ready to see Jacko White in the dock for trial.

*

White was placed in an interview room while he waited for his solicitor. David observed him through the two-way mirror. The man sat with shoulders slumped while his fingers drummed a tattoo against the table top.

A search warrant had been executed for White's house and shop. Whoever killed Daisy Mellon would've been covered in blood afterwards. The route from the lay-by to the village would be scoured as well, in case the killer discarded a weapon or his clothes.

Another wait for forensics to recover any trace evidence—all the shows on telly made it look so simple and quick. It bloody well wasn't either one. The Green was a small village with the majority of their forensics being sent to Keyeston.

A sound… Something made him turn toward the front of the stationhouse.

"I demand to see my husband!" A woman's voice grew louder and more insistent. Evie White.

He headed toward the commotion and found the desk sergeant restraining her. Her face and eyes were red from crying. "I'll speak with Mrs. White, Sergeant."

"Fine. You're welcome to 'er."

David led her to a separate interview room. "Coffee, tea?"

Ignoring his offer, she set her purse on the table and placed her hands on her hips. "What's this about my husband being arrested for murder? Search warrants at my house. It's an outrage."

"If you'll calm down and take a seat, I'll tell you what I can."

"Somebody better tell me something. We've rights." She hovered near the chair as if uncertain whether or not to sit or stand.

"Please. Sit down." He motioned toward the chair, and finally she sat.

"Your husband has been arrested for the murder of Daisy Mellon."

"Daisy? That little tart's been after my husband for six months. Now she's got herself killed, and you think he did it?"

David hated to tell her, but there wasn't any other way. "Your husband's motorcycle and Daisy's green Rover were seen parked side-by-side this morning in a lay-by. There's evidence sexual relations occurred in the Rover, and her body was discovered nearby later this morning."

Evie White's face grew redder with each syllable he uttered. "He were no good that man. Me mum warned me, but I wouldn't listen. No, not me. I knew better than me own mum. Smacks me around whenever he takes the notion, too. So now, he's killed one of his tarts." She banged the table with her fist. "Good enough for the both of them. Hanging—that's what he deserves."

"The death penalty was abolished some time ago, Mrs. White."

"Well, they needs to bring it back. That's what!"

"Do you still want to see your husband?"

She shook her head and grabbed her purse. "No, not unless you want another murder on your hands. Far as I'm concerned, he can rot."

"And your whereabouts this morning?"

She glared at him. "I was at me mum's from eight until ten. She getting on in years and pays me a few bob to clean for her. After that I opened the pub. And if you've any more questions, I'll be at me house, cleaning up the mess your officers made during the search."

"Thank you, Mrs. White." What else could he say? The woman had every right to her anger, but he still wasn't convinced Jacko White had murdered anyone.

David ran into Beecham in the hall. "Get anything from White?"

Beecham shook his head and smirked. "Still waiting on his solicitor. I had him put in lockup. What about the wife?"

"She has an alibi—supposedly at her mother's from eight until ten, then at the pub. It'll bear checking. As for her husband, she's decided to let him rot."

"You told her what he was up to in the lay-by?"

"Just that their vehicles were seen in the lay-by and that there was evidence of a sexual nature, and she offered that Jacko smacks her around."

"I'd let him rot, too," Beecham said.

David frowned. "It's too soon to know for sure, but..."

"You don't think he did it?"

"No. Like I said it's too soon."

"Didn't someone say, it if walks like a duck and quacks like a duck, it's a duck?"

"Probably, and there's if you hear hoof beats, think horses, not zebras," David added with a grin. "Still..."

"Then don't be looking for zebras, French. We're pretty far from a zoo."

David shoved his hands into his pockets. "You're probably right." But he didn't really believe it. Jacko White was a hotheaded bloke who acted first and thought later, if at all. The first murder was committed by an organized killer and likely the second as well.

At noon, in desperation for something to do, I resorted to listening to the local news and farm report. Frankly, since David wasn't going to feed me any info about the case, I didn't have any other choice. Stuck at the estate, I couldn't very well pop into town without involving Robbie, the chauffeur, who had strict orders from his lordship not to bring me anywhere near the Green.

And the news wasn't good. Details were sketchy at best, but another murder had taken place. The body of a young woman had been found five kilometers outside the village of Kinsey Green. Identification of the victim was being withheld until notification of kin. The announcer also stated the local authorities wouldn't comment on whether they thought the murder was related to the first, a serial killer or a copycat.

I shivered and rubbed the gooseflesh on my arms. Maybe being banished to the country like a misbehaving medieval wife wasn't so bad. Basically and at heart, I'm a big chicken. I hate flying in planes. I worry about my son all the time, and I don't know what I'd do if confronted by a genuine killer—serial or otherwise.

No. Hold on. That's not quite true. My ex was a genuine killer, although his modus operandi was more along the lines of ordering one of his henchmen to rig a car bomb. When Stefan came to the hospital in Aix to kidnap Jamie, I fought him like a tiger...okay, at least I managed to hold him off long enough for David to return to Jamie's hospital room and take over the fight.

Yes, I was safely out of the way for now, but there was an unsettling sensation in my gut. What else could I do but reach for my cell phone and hit the speed dial for David? I had a pretty good idea he wasn't going to tell me squat about the case, but somehow I just had to know who the new victim was.

He answered, "Miranda, is everything all right?"

Bummer. Never any surprises with caller I.D.

"Yes, but I just heard the news. About another murder...?"

"...and you thought you'd stick your pretty little nose in that one, too?"

I didn't exactly like his tone, but I knew the reason behind it was based on love and fear for my safety. "No, I do not want to do any such thing. Really, David, you have to give me credit for some sense."

"All right, then what is it?"

"I can't quite put a name to it, but I've had this weird feeling ever since I listened to the news. Maybe it's one of those gut feelings you detectives have."

I waited for him to say something, but there was at least a good thirty seconds of silence. "Are you still there?"

I heard him take a deep breath.

"What is it? What—?"

Finally he spoke. "I can't say who, except it was someone you've talked to in the last couple of days."

"Oh, no!" My stomach lurched, and for a minute, I thought I might throw up. What if my meddling had somehow led to someone's death? "Please, tell me who. I have to know."

"Can't. We haven't been able to locate her mother yet."

"Her *mother*? Not her husband?" I'd talked to a middle-aged waitress, the married former supermodel and tattooed Daisy. "Daisy. It was that poor little hairdresser, wasn't it? Omigod! Is it my fault? Did I do something to draw the killer's attention to her?

If I did I'll never forgive myself."

"Mi-ran-da," he chided, "you're jumping to conclusions. You weren't the only one to talk to her. The police talked to Daisy as well. It was her cousin, DS Tower, who interviewed her officially. So you see, her death isn't your fault."

I hiccupped and leaned back in the yellow and green chintz wingback. Tears sprang to my eyes. I bit my upper lip to keep from sobbing on the phone and making a general nuisance of myself.

"Gotta go." I didn't wait for a good-bye. I hit the Off button.

David was right. I had absolutely no business investigating a murder. I wasn't a professional. Instead, I was what the Brits call a nosy Parker. Daisy would never make it to the big city, and all her dreams would never be realized. Whoever killed that unique young woman ought to be hung. But they don't do that here anymore.

David put the phone back in his pocket. Bloody hell, but Miranda and her gut instincts were right on target with his. At least she was well out of it. Jamie would arrive sometime tonight, and that young man alone should keep her well occupied.

From the interview room, he heard a rising moan which crescendoed into a primal scream. No doubt, Daisy Mellon's mother had just learned of her only child's death. Somehow he'd never become accustomed to the raw and gutted expression of a new grief. It was too close to what he'd experienced when Cassie had been killed.

And he was doubly thankful he wasn't the one delivering the news. He couldn't imagine any worse news for a mother to receive: the death of her child...her only child.

He walked back to the interview rooms. Jacko White was in one conferring privately with his solicitor since there was no audio, and the Mellon girl's mother in the other.

DCI Beecham was handling the mother with more sensitivity than David would've ever imagined. He turned away, but a sensation of uselessness grew in his chest. He glanced down at his hands; they were balled in fists and, more than anything, he wanted five minutes alone with the real killer. He wanted to bash him...for taking the life of a young woman, whose only sin was nothing more than fornicating in a lay-by with a married man.

The humiliating way the killer had left her openly displayed as if saying to the police, "You don't know who I am. I can do whatever I want, and you can't stop me." The sickness of the mind behind the mutilations terrified him. What kind of person could carve another person like this one had? And was he through?

If the unsub was a true serial killer, he wasn't through. But what if the murders were personal issues being dealt with? One murder to right a wrong imagined or otherwise, and the second to silence someone who'd seen too much or a blackmailer?

Whether the unsub was through or not, he was one sick bastard.

Evie White straightened the last of her tossed house, a two bedroom, one bath Victorian terrace cottage. It was at the end of a row of similar houses and was the nicest place she'd ever lived, and she didn't appreciate those bloody coppers throwing her things about all higgledy-piggledy.

All afternoon she'd tried to figure out what was missing...mostly Jacko's stuff. His clothes and shoes. They'd probably torn up the storage shed in back, too, but she didn't care about that stuff. None of it was hers anyway. It was all his.

She sat down at the old desk and started going through the paperwork, but she had to stop and run her fingers over the scarred and pitted wood. In spite of its imperfections, she had fond thoughts of it. Six months ago, she'd wandered into Greenway Antiques and bought it. Riley told her it was a genuine George III walnut desk, but he only charged her five hundred quid for it. Said he gave her a deal because she had such pretty blue eyes.

And now he was dead. All her dreams were dead with him. He was going to sell the shop, take the money and move to the south of Portugal...and he was going to take her with him to the Algarve where Jacko could never smack her around again.

So, Jacko had killed Riley and her dreams, and that silly tart Daisy, too.

Who the devil was going to look after her now? With that blighter in jail for murder, she'd have to work two jobs just to keep up the mortgage payments on the cottage.

The brochures...the ones about the Algarve. They were missing. Had Jacko found them and somehow figured out what she was up to? Was that why he killed Riley? But why would he kill dingy Daisy? Or had the police found the brochures and taken them as evidence? Fine. Let them figure it out.

Nothing to do with her anymore. As soon as she could afford a solicitor, she'd start divorce proceedings.

Moira Delaney looked in the mirror and for the first time saw herself as Riley must've seen her: fifty-two, a trifle overweight and stupid enough to be his business partner. The night before he was murdered, she'd gone into the shop after hours and combed through his correspondence and his computer files.

Without telling her, the bastard was getting ready to sell the shop to someone in London and, no doubt, skip with all the money to the Algarve. Clearly the man was a crook and deserved to die. Someone had done her an immense favor. The shop was now all hers.

She smiled at her reflection. When she and Riley had formed their partnership, they'd also taken out survivor insurance policies in case either one of the partners died.

Those five hundred thousand pounds would come in handy. Indeed they would.

After a little cosmetic surgery, she wouldn't look fifty-two, overweight or stupid.

She blew a kiss to her reflection. "Thanks to you, whoever you are."

Sometimes a person got exactly what he deserved.

Chapter Fourteen

DS Stafford eased into the squad room and took a seat across from David. "Where the devil have you been?" David snapped.

Stafford's face flushed a dark pink. "Lunch, sir." "It's two o'clock."

At that moment DC Pettigrew came into the squad room and slid into her desk. "So that's how it is, is it?" Not that he blamed Stafford. Pettigrew was an attractive young woman with the fresh glow of a country girl.

"Well, sir." Stafford swallowed. "We were discussing the case and we lost track of the time."

"Really? And did you and DC Pettigrew come to any new conclusions over your two hour lunch? Do you perhaps have new insights which will assist us in this investigation?"

Stafford hung his head, but David could see a grin lurking on his sergeant's averted face. "No, sir. Nothing concrete."

"Then I suggest you take a shorter lunch break and come back here and make yourself useful by going over this stack of forensic results." David motioned to the foot-high stack of reports. "I was reluctant to take you on. Don't make me sorry, Stafford."

"No, sir. I'll tend to business from now on." The sergeant dragged half the stack over to his desk. "Nothing back on the DNA found at the scene?"

David shook his head. Stafford was obviously trying to make up for his tardiness. "Not yet. Too soon."

"Everyone involved been tested?" Stafford leafed through the files in a show of industriousness.

"As far as we know." David held the folder which contained Riley's business correspondence. One letter from Miranda inquiring about the shop, a rough draft of an agreement to sell the shop with no mention of his business partner, and confirmed airline reservations for two to Lisbon, Portugal, dated a week from the day Stubbs was murdered. And now evidence of an insurance policy for five hundred thousand pounds which named Moira Delaney as his beneficiary.

Without his partner's knowledge, Stubbs had planned to sell the shop and take off with one of his lovers to Portugal. Had Delaney discovered his plan? Had she killed him for the insurance money?

And who was going with him to Portugal?

"Stafford, I want you to pick up Moira Delaney at the shop, or wherever she is, and bring her in for additional questioning."

"Found something?"

"Possible motive. She's beneficiary of his life insurance to the tune of five hundred thousand pounds. People have been killed for less."

Stafford whistled. "That's a load of dosh, all right."

Thirty minutes later, David heard Moira Delaney as soon as she hit the stationhouse. From her outraged tone, she wasn't happy about being summoned for a second round of questioning.

She stomped into the squad room and plopped down her purse on David's desk. "I want to know the meaning of this. I was just getting a handle on the mess at the shop when your sergeant came and insisted I come right away."

David sent Stafford a "go along with me" expression. "I'm sure the sergeant didn't mean to upset you, but I do have a few additional questions. Why don't you come with me? Stafford, bring Ms. Delaney something to drink in the interview room. What would you prefer?"

"I'd prefer a G and T," she said with a flirtatious toss of her hair. "But I doubt you have my brand. Coffee will be fine."

David waited until Stafford handed Moira her cup of coffee. "I can't vouch for the
freshness, but it's hot," he said, knowing full well the stationhouse brew gave axel grease a bad name.

"That'll be all, Sergeant." He waited for Stafford to leave, then performed the date/time/who's present routine with the tape recorder. "Sorry about the formalities, but it has to be done."

"Of course, Chief Inspector," she said with a seductive smile. "I understand completely. Now, what is it you need to know?"

"In going over Mr. Stubbs's correspondence, I discovered a couple of interesting facts. First, it appears he was considering selling the antiques shop to an outsider. Were you aware of that?"

Moira's cheeks flushed a deep pink. "Sell the shop to an outsider? By our original contract, I had the right of first refusal. In other words, he had to sell to me and vice versa. In fact, I tried to get him to do that very thing, but he refused."

"Well, according to his correspondence, he was on the verge of such a sale. He makes no mention of his even having a business partner."

"The bastard. It would've been an illegal sale. I would've had to sue whomever he duped into purchasing the shop."

"Well, it would appear fortunate someone saw fit to murder Mr. Stubbs before the sale took place." He leveled his gaze on her and waited for her reaction.

Moira leaned forward, her eyes bright. "Perhaps the prospective buyer discovered Riley's double-dealing and killed him for it."

"Ahem... We've ruled out that situation."

"Well..." Moira shrugged. "...if you ask me, that's what happened."

David clenched his jaw to keep from revealing his relationship to the prospective buyer. "One other thing, we found an insurance policy for five hundred pounds which listed you as the beneficiary. Were you aware of that?"

"Of course," she said with a huff, "I also have an identical policy with Riley listed as beneficiary. It's common practice in professional partnerships."

"Makes sense in a business relationship." He nodded and paused, giving her time to relax. "It's also a good motive for murder."

Moira's face contorted into a mask of outrage. "Murder! You think I murdered Riley? How dare you...?" She postured and placed a hand to her forehead in a theatrical gesture straight from the days of silent movies. "I genuinely cared for the man. His betrayal by trying to sell the shop out from under me is hurtful, but I didn't kill him. No, I could never do something like that."

"What about the other women with whom he was having affairs? Didn't that make you angry? Jealousy makes a damned good motive for murder."

"Riley and I were business partners—that's all. As for affairs—rubbish. Simple village gossip."

"Surely you've heard the adage, 'where's there's smoke, there's fire'?"

"It's patently absurd. You should know what small villages are like, Inspector. Evil, small-minded people with nothing better to do than make up stories about their neighbors and spread them like God's own truth."

"Two facts remain. Riley Stubbs was murdered, and I intend to get to the bottom of
it."

Moira stood up with her purse firmly under her arm. "Here's a fact for you. Unless you're charging me, I'm leaving."

"Interview ended at 3:05 p.m." He turned off the recorder. "You're free to go...for now."

He watched Moira Delaney march from the interview room. He'd certainly managed to rattle her cage a bit, and he was more than glad Miranda's interest in Stubbs's shop hadn't come to fruition. She was well out of the mess.

David thumbed through another folder from Stubbs's desk. Nothing in that one—just invoices, sales receipts, purchase orders for office equipment and supplies.

"Earth to Inspector French." Beecham rapped on David's desk. "You're a million miles away. Finding something of interest or just thinking about your pretty little wife off in the country?"

"Stafford and I are going through Stubbs's business correspondence. Most of it's mind-numbing, but he was about to sell the shop out from under his partner, Moira Delaney, and she is the recipient of a five-hundred-thousand-pound insurance policy."

"Interesting, but my money's on White. He killed Stubbs for getting it on with his wife and killed Daisy Mellon because she found out and tried to blackmail him. Anyways, his solicitor says he's ready to talk to us."

"I'd like to observe." David stood, anxious to hear what White had to say. Beecham may have already made up his mind White was the killer, but David's gut said otherwise.

White was already in the interview room along with his solicitor, a no-nonsense woman in her middle years with short salt-and-pepper hair, wearing a gray wool suit, black blouse and comfortable low-heeled shoes. No jewelry except for an inexpensive watch with a leather band.

"Rosamund Mullins," she said, offering her hand to Beecham. "My client wishes to make a statement. He will not answer questions."

Beecham objected, "What good is that? He needs to answer our questions—all of them."

"He will cooperate as much as I feel appropriate to his defense."

"All right, then. Fine," Beecham said, although it was apparent to David it wasn't fine at all.

"Interview commenced at four p.m. Suspect Jacko White, his attorney, Rosamund Mullins, and DCI Beecham in attendance."

"Chief Inspector, I would appreciate if you would use my client's proper name, Jackson William White. Calling him by a nickname is disrespectful."

"Wouldn't want to appear disrespectful, now would I, Ms. Mullins? Amend the record to read 'Jackson William White'. Now, may we proceed?"

The attorney nodded. "Mr. White, go ahead with your statement."

White rubbed his nose with the back of his hand and sniffed. "I didn't murder no one. Not Riley Stubbs and not Daisy Mellon. I was wif Daisy the mornin' Riley Stubbs was killed…in the lay-by." White's gaze darted about the room before lighting on Beecham. More than likely he was lying.

"We met there most mornin's before she 'ad to be at work. I was wif Daisy this mornin' before she were murdered. I was late. She was 'uffy. I gave her a smack and then we got on wif it. After that, I left. And when I left 'er, she were alive. And that's the God's honest truf."

He glanced over at his attorney. She nodded. "That's it," he said. "That's all I got to say."

"That's it?" Beecham asked. "You call that cooperation? You'll have to do better than that, me boy."

White looked at Ms. Mullins, who shook her head. "That's it." He folded his arms across his chest.

"What time did you leave her?"

White smirked. "Wasn't wearin' me watch. Left it at 'ome this mornin'." He made the gesture of glancing at his left wrist. "They won't let me 'ave it 'ere, neither."

White's solicitor stood and picked up her briefcase. "You heard my client. He's cooperated by giving his statement. We're through here."

"Interview ended at 4:05 p.m." Beecham's back and neck were rigid. David could almost see wisps of steam spouting from his counterpart's ears. Damned inconvenient that White's alibi witness ended up dead. Dammit, they were missing something, but what?

If it weren't for the fact my son would be home by dinner time— okay, late dinnertime—I don't know what I would've done. All I could think about was that young girl Daisy. All sorts of images flitted through my mind. How had she been killed? Was it quick?

Or did she suffer and, even worse, know she was going to die? How horrible to know you were going to die and die horribly at that.

David had done his best to reassure me that I wasn't responsible, but I wasn't convinced. I wished there were something I could do.

Then I remembered—the phone call Daisy received while she was re-doing my hair. I picked up the phone and dialed David's cell.

"Yes." His tone was grim and not very encouraging. "Hi, don't be mad, but I just thought of something."

"Do I ever get mad at you?"

"Well, no, but—"

"However, your assumption that your call would anger me leaves me puzzled. What's up?"

"I just remembered something that happened the last time I saw Daisy."

"I'm listening."

"She received a weird phone call on her cell while she was doing my hair. I say *weird* because she acted nervous."

"Describe how she acted."

"First of all, she turned very pale, she gripped her cell like she was afraid it would get away from her and she was all hunched over in the chair. She was very subdued when she came back to finish my hair. That wasn't normal for her at all. She was very spontaneous and talkative before the call."

"All right, we'll check her mobile records. We would do anyway. Leave this investigation to us." He paused. "When will Jamie and Mina arrive?"

"In time for a late dinner," I answered. David was really determined to keep me out of the loop. I understood why, but I didn't have to like it.

"So just a few more hours then?"

"Yeah. Think you'll be able to make it home in time?"

"Yes. Unless something else happens."

"Okay. I really miss you." Then something else occurred to me.

"You know, I thought we'd live in your town house...the one on Fairway Crescent. But the housekeeper says—" I broke off because I heard a commotion in the background.

"We'll discuss it later," David said. "Something's come up. Have to ring off. Sorry."

And he was gone. Something had happened all right. And there I was, twenty-five miles from all the action.

I rang for Robbie. Maybe I could get him to take me to the Green for a shopping trip. Now I'm not a shopaholic or anything close to a fashionista. I don't have a closet of couture clothes or thirty pairs of Manolo Blahniks, and makeup from the average department store is good enough for me.

But I could pretend.

He answered quickly, "Robbie."

"Oh good. Robbie, this is—uh." I just couldn't get the words out. Sheesh.

"Your ladyship, yes. What may I do for you?"

"I wondered if we could breeze into the Green for a little shopping. I've run out of my favorite makeup."

"Keyeston would be a better bet than the Green."

Great. Keyeston was even farther from the Green than the estate. "No, I'd really like to just run in for a bit."

Silence.

Just as I'd thought. I'd bet a dozen Krispy Kreme doughnuts David had given him orders to keep me away from the village.

Robbie cleared his throat. "That might pose a problem, your ladyship. His lordship has...sort of given me strict orders about..."

"Never mind, Robbie. I had to try. You understand?"

"Yes, your ladyship."

After he hung up, I briefly considered throwing a temper tantrum, but restrained myself. I certainly couldn't hike the twenty-five miles to the Green. And Jamie would be home in about three hours. I could only hope I didn't go insane from frustration or inaction in the time between.

I picked myself up and dusted me off, figuratively speaking, and headed downstairs.

The housekeeper was in her small office off the kitchen knitting a bright red scarf. It really was almost like the old PBS show, *Upstairs, Downstairs*, and I still found it hard to believe that I was a "ladyship" instead of Rose the housemaid.

"Mrs. Madison, I need a pair of wellies. Do you think there might be a pair around here that would fit me? I have a mind to take a little hike around the estate."

Honestly, that's all I had in mind at the time.

She looked out the window and frowned. "Oh, now, your ladyship, I don't think you should be trekking out in the countryside. As you can see it's almost dark, and there's bogs and animals in the woods."

I wrinkled my nose. "I won't go far. Maybe just take a walk in the garden."

She pursed her mouth and scowled at me over her wire-rimmed reading glasses.

"Well, I guess you can't get into much trouble in the back garden, but you shouldn't go any farther than the back hedgerow. Otherwise, you'll be turning your ankle and falling, and we'll be forming a search party to find you. His lordship wouldn't like that one bit. No indeed."

No, I guess he wouldn't.

"I promise I won't go any farther, and I'm pretty sure-footed. In fact, I used to go hiking with my father and brothers, and they had trouble keeping up with me."

Madison raised her eyebrows and chuckled. "I imagine they did at that."

She pointed back at the kitchen. "There's a closet beside the back entrance. There should be a pair that'll fit you. Mind you, you wear a warm coat and something on that head of yours. You don't have enough hair to keep a kitten warm, if you don't mind my saying so."

I held back a giggle. I couldn't help but wonder what she would've thought if she'd see the black and green or the multicolored versions of my hair. "Thanks. I'll dress warmly, just for you."

"Forgive me, you ladyship. It's just you're so young and petite. I keep forgetting you're a mother yourself." Madison smiled. "And that young man will be here soon, won't he? It'll be so good to have a child in the house again."

"Yes, I miss him a lot, and it's only been five days since I saw him."

"He's a good boy, is he?" She glanced down at her knitting. "Oh dear, I've dropped a stitch."

"Yes, he really is. I know I'm prejudiced as his mother, but he's very bright and grownup."

"Only children have that tendency. I fancy you'll—" She stopped. "Sorry, your ladyship, I didn't mean to presume."

"Oh, I hope so. I have three brothers, so I wouldn't mind a house full of boys and girls."

Madison rubbed her eyes. "That's lovely to hear. None of my business, of course, but this house has seen too much sadness. It's time for a change of luck and I believe you've brought the luck with you." She ripped out a row of knitting. "Better get on before it's completely dark."

"I'd better do just that."

I quickly found the wellies, pulled them on, grabbed a scarf and stepped out into the crisp evening air. It was nearly dark, true enough. But I could still see well enough to navigate the back gardens. A tall row of hedges loomed in the back of the formal gardens. That was my boundary...for the time being, anyway.

Chapter Fifteen

David jammed his mobile back in his pocket. DCI Beecham sat down on the edge of the desk. He had a sheaf of papers in his hand and a decided frown on his face. "What is it, Beecham?"

"Damned DNA report. Says the hair roots from the crime scene match Nan Morgan. Must be some kind of mistake."

"Not Jacko White's?" No, and David hadn't expected it would either. "I still like him for Mellon's murder," Beecham insisted. "What about Nan Morgan? Are we bringing her in?"

David leaned back and fiddled with a pen. What a blunder. They were pretty far off track when they arrested a man and the DNA came back as belonging to one of their female suspects.

"Guess we have to. See what her explanation is for leaving hair at the crime scene." Beecham scowled, obviously displeased by this turn of events.

David shook his head. "I can't see Nan doing those mutilations. It's just not something a woman would do."

"Bollocks! Country women get up to all sorts of activities. My old granny used to wring the necks of chickens and help geld the livestock."

"Nan Morgan's a landscaper, not a farm hand."

"The evidence don't lie, French." Beecham's upper lip lifted in a sneer.

"No!" David jabbed the pen into the top of the desk, adding a new scar to the already pitted surface. "But evidence can be manipulated and planted."

"You think someone's trying to frame Nan Morgan?" That sneer again.

"Can't rule it out, and here's where we need to focus our efforts. Who has it in for Riley Stubbs, Nan and that poor Mellon girl?"

"Who indeed?" Beecham's head went back and forth as if he were watching a tennis match. "I still like Jacko White for the Mellon murder. You're not going to talk me out of that one. He did his best to make it look like a copy cat. Yeah, that's what he did all right."

"What about the weapon used? Was any found in either his shop or home?"

Beecham leaned across the desk right into David's face. "No, but it doesn't mean he didn't toss it somewhere."

"What about the angle of the blade, right or left-handed killer? Jacko's right-handed."

Beecham frowned. "Coroner said Stubbs's killer was a lefty. Nothing back yet on the Mellon girl."

"Rather than jump to conclusions, we need to wait until all the forensic evidence has been analyzed. Ballard hasn't even completed the autopsy on her yet."

"I'm not letting Jacko White out of here to kill anyone else." Beecham paced back and forth, his face growing redder by the second.

"I didn't suggest that." David smiled. "If anything else happens while he's in custody, it'll clear him."

"I don't get you, Inspector French. We have one perfectly good suspect, but you don't think he's the one. And you're the very one who pointed us in his direction, the one who saw him in the lay-by with the girl this very morning. Why don't you tell me who you like for this?"

"I don't know yet, but whoever he is, he's intelligent and organized. He's driven to protect himself, and he'll stop at nothing, even if it means another murder or two."

"So now you're a profiler—a bleeding Sherlock Holmes? What now—is he two point one meters in height, walks with a limp and drives a truck with a low right rear tire?"

Finally tired of Beecham's blathering, David stood and leaned into Beecham's space. "I'm bloody sorry my wife found Stubbs's body. I'm sorry I was drawn into your investigation, and I'm even sorrier I'm not enjoying my honeymoon, but I won't put up with your disrespect and your attitude, nor will I close a case just to get it off the books. Until I'm satisfied with the facts of the case, you're as stuck with me as I am you."

Beecham's face flushed, but he backed down. "Yeah, we're stuck all right. Guess things might work better if we kept to the case."

"And dropped the personal aspersions." David stuck out his hand in a gesture of good will.

Beecham nodded and shook David's hand. He opened his mouth as if to speak, but closed it.

"I'd feel the same way, Beecham, if someone horned in on what was my jurisdiction." And he would.

"Yeah. Sorry. I'll try to act like a grownup from now on."

"We're on the same side and it's normal for us to disagree occasionally."

"Yeah." Beecham scratched his head and shrugged. "Why don't we check on the Mellon autopsy?"

David grinned. "Why don't we?"

The morgue was a small room in the rear of the stationhouse. Most Middlebury villages sent their bodies for autopsy to the county seat in Keyeston, but Beecham explained, "Ballard lives in the Green proper, and he'd insisted on a space, any space, if he was going to be our coroner. Said he didn't fancy driving to Keyeston when he could stay in town."

"Can't say I blame him."

"Only has three cold drawers," Beecham said. "So he's two-thirds full today."

Ballard stood over the Mellon girl's body. Her chest had already been opened and he was carefully weighing her heart. He glanced up at their entrance. "To what do I owe this honor, gentlemen? I'm not nearly though with this poor child." He shook his head. "I can't imagine what kind of animal would commit such atrocities, but sadly I've seen worse."

"How much longer?" David asked.

"Another two hours for the gross autopsy, and many hours before the microscopic is done. I have to section her organs and all the rest, even though it's quite apparent what killed her."

"Exsanguination?" This from Beecham.

"Most assuredly, but she, too, was felled by a blow to the head. One or the other. Even without an intracranial injury, she would have bled to death." His gray eyes twinkled above his wire-rimmed glasses. "I'm about to examine the brain. Want to stick around?" He picked up the saw.

Beecham swallowed. "We'll wait for your report."

Ballard gave a wry smile. "I thought so."

David and Beecham headed back to the squad room. "Good thing you sent your wife home. This is a bad business."

"And I have a feeling he's not through," David said, wondering not for the first time if she and Jamie would be better off farther away in London.

From the small stone patio, I eased onto the lawn and headed toward the formal gardens. The grass was crisp from the freezing temperatures and it crunched under my boots. Still it was good to breathe the fresh air. In the distance beyond the hedges, a fine mist had started to gather and hover close to the ground. A shiver shook my body, so I pulled up my coat collar and settled into my walk.

On my left was a bed of dead stalks and herbs. Cook probably used them for seasonings, but there wasn't much left at this time of year. On my right was the glass-walled conservatory. In front of me were four large diamond shaped beds formed by boxwoods. In the spring and summer, I assumed, the centers would be filled with flowers.

In the middle of the four beds was a smaller diamond with a statue of a Grecian lady and fountain in its center. The water trickled, but was starting to freeze in a glistening pattern of icicles.

As I walked around the grounds, I tried to imagine what it would've been like growing up with a home like this. Don't get me wrong. I come from a pretty privileged background myself. My dad's a heart surgeon in Nashville, and people literally treat him like he's God. I grew up in a large home in West Meade, and now my parents live in Belle Meade—where the *old* money lives.

Old money is one thing, but David's family goes back for centuries, and that kind of heritage is something I'll get used to someday, I guess. My mother was a practical sort and did the minimal amount of socializing necessary. And when she wasn't on a buying trip to the UK or somewhere else in Europe, she ran an antique store every day from ten to six. So, I guess I come by my work ethic naturally. My brothers are all doctors or lawyers. I'm the renegade. A fiddle player—that's what I told my dad I wanted to be—just to aggravate him and watch his face turn red.

A twig snapped. I stopped to look behind me and the hair on my neck rose. The sensation that someone was watching me made me shiver again. I couldn't see anyone either behind or in front of me, but the sensation lingered.

Something was definitely giving me the creeps.

Madison was right. I didn't have any business outside in the cold, dark night. I pulled my coat tighter and beat it back to the house.

David stood in the front of the squad room. These locals were looking to him for direction. Beecham, too, whether he wanted to admit it or not. Graphic photos from both crime scenes were pinned to the bulletin board and served as a grotesque reminder of how far someone they likely all knew was willing to go.

"Mr. Ballard says both victims were mutilated with the same type knife—a large, smooth blade, most likely a hunting knife. Where the cut marks go deep, there is some sort of curve that stops the blade and marks the skin. It could even be a custom knife. The angle of the cuts indicates a left-handed killer or one who is ambidextrous.

"He also confirms that the victim in the second murder had unprotected sexual relations just prior to her murder. There's no bruising or tearing, so it could well have been consensual as Mr. White said in his statement. There is a bruise on her check which occurred shortly before death which also corroborates White's statement. Toxicology screens are pending. Examination of the Mellon girl's brain indicates she was rendered unconscious by a blow to the head, but it was insufficient to have killed her. We have in evidence a large rock from the crime scene which is positive for human blood."

"Does that mean she might've woken up while he was cutting on her?" DS Tower asked, his face pale as snow. After all, she was his cousin.

David hoped not, but said, "It's unsure. If she had, she would certainly have fought. There was no trace evidence under her nails. They were clean. Too clean, without a trace of Mr. White's skin cells, so it's conceivable our killer cleaned her nails after he killed her. We're dealing with someone who's intelligent and organized. Mr. White is admittedly hot-tempered and is likely to strike out from anger which doesn't fit the profile of this organized killer, and he is right-handed."

"Do we have a blood type on the rock?" From DS Stafford.

"Type A positive which is consistent with the victim's blood type, and a second trace of type O positive which means it's possible our killer was injured at some point in the attack. Approximately forty-six percent of the residents in this area have that O positive."

"Male or female on the Type O?"

"DNA's pending."

Evie White sat in a darkened room staring at the flickering light of the telly. She hadn't bothered to turn on the sound, and a BBC announcer was mouthing something. No doubt it was important, but what did it really matter to her?

Jacko was sitting in jail and good enough for him. Killing that silly little tart with the tattoo. Now why would he go and do something stupid like that? More than likely he'd killed Riley, too.

Her Riley. He was going to take her away from all this dark and dreary English countryside. She was going to live happily ever after in a part of the world she'd only heard about. What was it her brochures had said about the Algarve? South Portugal. The southwest tip of the continent and the sunniest spot in Europe with fine beaches and weather.

Bloody hell, but she could use some sunshine in her life. Now there was nothing but Kinsey Green and the rest of a long winter ahead of her.

She reached for the wine bottle. No point in pouring it into a glass. Straight from the bottle was lots quicker. She held it to her lips and took one long swallow after another until the bottle slipped from her hands and fell into her lap.

She giggled. What a mess. Who cared? She certainly didn't. She closed her eyes for just a second.

Chapter Sixteen

Once I was back inside the house—seems kind of silly to call it a house since it's more like a mansion. Okay, so it is a mansion. Anyway, once I was back inside the cozy warmth of the kitchen, I shrugged off the uneasy sensation that someone was watching me. I tugged off the wellies and slipped on my loafers. I glanced up at the clock on the wall, almost six? I must've stayed outside longer than I thought.

Cook and her two helpers were scurrying around preparing what would be my son's first dinner in his new home. Pots and pans of every imaginable size hung on hooks from a ceiling rack. And everything was spotless whether copper or stainless steel.

Does one ask Cook "What's for dinner?" or not? I had a long way to go before I felt comfortable with a houseful of servants.

I sniffed. Mm. Something savory like beef. And onions. What else could I figure out without being rude enough to start lifting the lids and peeking into the pots and pans.

As if Cook could read my mind, she smiled at me. "It's a simple supper, your ladyship. His lordship said fix his favorite dish from when he was a boy...said your boy would be bound to love it."

How sweet of him to think of Jamie and what he would like for dinner. David was a lovely, thoughtful man. "Really? What?" There was still so much to learn about my husband.

"Shepherd's pie." She picked up a large bowl of mashed potatoes and started spreading them on what looked like a meat loaf. "He and Master Terrence would fight each other for the last bit and gobble it down from the time they were in the nursery until they were sent off to school. Good boys with good appetites they were."

"Sounds wonderful. We used to have something like it at home. Especially if we weren't having guests. My brothers and I liked it, too."

"As for the rest of the menu, some salad greens from the greenhouse served with balsamic vinaigrette, home-baked bread and chocolate mousse for dessert."

"Except for the salad, Jamie will be in heaven. I don't know why boys are so slow to take to salads, do you?"

"No, your ladyship, I don't, but his lordship and Master Terrence were the same. It'll be a pure treat to have a young one around again." She opened a large hot oven and slid in the large dish of shepherd's pie.

The hands of the clock were creeping around. "I'd better get changed. It's almost time to go pick him up. I can hardly wait. And thank you for everything you do."

Cook wiped the perspiration from her forehead with a towel. "Bless you, your ladyship."

With friendly servants like Cook, I could get used to this kind of life. Oh yeah.

A bare two hours later, Robbie and I sat in the Rover waiting for the train from London. He kept the motor and defroster running to keep the windows from fogging up from our breath. The night sky was clear and stars stood out like pin holes in a velvet navy blanket.

"Just a few more minutes, your ladyship, and the little fellow should be here."

The floorboard of the Rover thrummed beneath my loafers. "It's coming. I can feel the vibrations."

"Yes, there's the light in the distance now. Won't be long."

"It's been too long already." My knees were jumping with excitement. It would be so wonderful to hold my boy in my arms again and to see the audacious Mina, too.

The train pulled into Keyeston station, brakes squealing. I jumped from the Rover and ran to the platform. The temperature was below freezing, but I didn't care. Numerous passengers disembarked and I kept bobbing up and down trying to see my son.

Finally I saw the silver head of a tall, elderly woman. Mina was waving at me, and my Jamie was at her side, holding firmly to her hand. "Jamie!"

Spectacle or not. I didn't care.

Jamie squealed, "Mummy!" and then took off running and launched into my arms. "Oh, my goodness. You've grown a foot since I saw you."

"Now, Mum, It's only been a few days, and I've grown a mere six centimeters."

I shook my head and hugged the stuffing out of that boy. "No, no, I'm sure you've been gone a month and you've grown a foot."

"How was your honeymoon? Did you and David have fun while I was with Mina and Jean-Luc?"

My face grew hot. It may have been nighttime, but the station was well lit. A couple of passersby glanced my way with smiles or smirks. I waited until they passed and said quietly, "Yes, we had a wonderful time. But David's on a case now, and my best-est boy's here, and I'm so happy."

Mina collected her bags, then she wrapped an arm around me for a big hug. "Jane Marple in blue jeans" is how I described her when we first met on the Pelletier farm in Ste-Thérèse in Provençe. She's tall, rangy and very spry. Today, under her bright red overcoat she wore a navy tweed suit with a powder blue silk blouse and looked every bit like the nanny she used to be for David and his older brother.

"How was your trip?"

"Long, but enjoyable. Master James is quite an accomplished traveler and conversationalist. Most amusing." Mina smiled and her eyes twinkled. I could almost imagine how she managed David and his brother when they were young. "I'm sure that's a typical

British understatement."

"He's an adorable child. You've done a wonderful job with him, Randi."

"Well, I think so, but I'm his mother and sort of prejudiced." I was so fond of Mina. We met only a few months ago in October, but I felt like I'd known her all my life.

Robbie took their luggage and hauled it into the back of the Rover, while I bundled

Jamie into his child safety seat. Then, Robbie assisted Mina into the front seat, and I hopped into the backseat next to Jamie. After fastening my seatbelt, I sighed. My heart was so full of love I could've cried on the spot. I was the luckiest woman in the world. I had a wonderful husband and a beautiful son...and I had a vague suspicion that soon we might have a new addition to our family.

David glared at the wall clock in the squad room. Almost seven and Jamie would be home soon. What would he think of the estate? Would he learn to love it as David did? His best childhood memories were tied to the old manor house. There his brother Terry, their friend Brinks, and he had pretended to be smugglers in the old caves on French property and on the neighboring lands of Lord Hutton.

Bloody hell, but they'd been chased off Hutton's land more than once by his old caretaker. What was his name? Smith, no Smite— Earl Smite. Old fellow who walked with a limp because he'd stepped into a trap of some kind in his youth, and blind in one eye from WWII. How he managed to catch them every time they ventured near Hutton's caves was still a mystery.

"Inspector French. Inspector French."

David looked up, a little startled. Jacko White's attorney was standing at his desk with a determined expression. "Yes, Ms. Mullins?"

"I insist that you either charge or release my client. It's come to my attention that my client is no longer a suspect in either murder."

"First of all," David pushed back in his chair and eyeballed the attorney. "I'd like to know how you came by that piece of information. And you well know we can hold him for forty-eight hours without charging. What's your rush?"

"My client cooperated with you—against my wishes I might add. He's innocent. I have it on good authority that you're looking for an individual who is intelligent, organized and left-handed. If you'll excuse me for saying so, Mr. White is none of those."

"Counselor, have you considered Mr. White might be better off in jail for the time being? If he's released and the killer strikes again—which could happen—your client would again be a suspect. Now if he remains in custody his forty-eight hours and another murder occurs, it would be to his advantage. Would it not?"

Rosamund Mullins smiled. "I hardly think you're that concerned about clearing my client. But even if you are, he's very anxious to return home and straighten things out with his wife."

"As he should do." David clasped his hands behind his head and smiled. "But the lady in question was pretty hot when she left here, and the only straightening he'll manage is being thrown straight out of the house."

"My client is also very worried about his wife's well-being."

She'd taken to batting her lashes at him. Did that old trick work on anyone anymore?

He leaned forward on the desk and smiled up at the attorney. "He wasn't worried enough to be faithful. Doubt he's worried now."

"Inspector, I—"

"No, Counselor. He stays here for his forty-eight, and then if there's nothing additional, we'll release him."

Leave please. Jamie will be in bed asleep before I get home.

"Hmph." She snatched her briefcase from his desk. "Is this how they do things in London? I don't think so."

"This is how I do things period. Go home, Ms. Mullins, and know that your client is in the tender care of the Kinsey Green constabulary." He dismissed her with a wave and stared until she whirled and left.

He was ready to pull out his mobile and call Miranda when another visitor was announced. "Guy Tanner from the pub needs to have a word, sir," DS Stafford said.

He restrained the groan building in his diaphragm. "What now?" He glanced around the squad room. He and Stafford were the only detectives left. How'd that happen?

"Fine, send him in."

Guy Tanner was a short, burly man with a barrel chest and a red face. His short ginger hair was streaked with gray. David remembered him from the pub as jolly and loquacious. But at the moment his demeanor was somber.

"What can I do for you, Mr. Tanner?"

"It's Evie White. She works at my pub. I went round to check on her after that business with her husband. I knocked but she didn't come to the door. The lights were off, except light flickering from her telly. I peeked in the window and I could see her in her chair, but she weren't moving. I knocked again, louder this time. But nothing."

Tanner wiped his forehead with his sleeve. "I'm worried. Could you just come and check on her?"

"She might just be asleep and would resent an intrusion. She has a right to her privacy."

"I got a bad feeling, Inspector."

"Is she a heavy drinker?"

"No, sir. That's just it. She doesn't usually touch the stuff. Always said Jacko drank enough for the both of them."

By this time, a bad feeling was nagging David as well. "All right, Mr. Tanner. My sergeant and I will check on Mrs. White." Behind Tanner, Stafford stood in the doorway of the squad room, making a face and shaking his head.

"Stafford, come on. You're with me."

Tanner didn't budge from his spot. "You'll let me know something? I live just over the pub. She's not a bad girl."

"We'll let you know."

Tanner nodded and left.

"Let's, go, Eric." He noted Stafford's eye rolls and grim

expression. "Unless you've something better to do tonight?"

Stafford swallowed. "No, sir."

"I didn't think so. Not like I do either. But if Mrs. White's just tapped out in front of her telly, we can both have a decent night, right?"

"Right, sir."

The night air was crisp and seared the lungs. David's breath hung in the air when he exhaled. He and Stafford parked next to the White cottage at the end of a row of identical cottages. As Tanner had described, the lights were off, except for the telly. "Check the back door. I'll check the front."

He touched the brass knob; it was almost cold enough for his fingers to stick. He tried turning it.

Locked.

He glanced into the window and could see a dark form lit by her telly. She wasn't moving and appeared very sound asleep...or dead drunk.

"Mrs. White!" he called and rapped on the window.

"Mrs. White! Inspector French here. Please wake up and open the door!"

Please.

"Sir!" Stafford called. "Back door's ajar."

"I'm coming." He strode around to the cottage's rear entrance. His gut was tight as were his lungs. He couldn't imagine why a woman would leave her back door open when there'd been two recent murders in the village.

"Carefully, Stafford." David pulled a pen light from his pocket to examine the door frame. Small splinters of wood appeared a fresh disturbance. "Looks to have been forced recently, too." He eased open the door with the blunt end of the pen light, then shone the light across the wood laminate kitchen floor.

No tracks. Evie White was a good housekeeper.

"Mrs. White!" he called again. He hoped she'd answer and give them the devil for disturbing her nap. He flipped on a kitchen light switch, again with the end of his flash.

The kitchen counters were crowded, but clean. No dirty dishes. No food on the stove.

"Hold on. Gloves." He pulled a pair from his pocket as did Stafford.

"I'm going to ease into the lounge. You stay here. No point in both our mucking up a possible crime scene."

"Right, sir."

David walked by a small dining table into the lounge. "Mrs. White?" He stopped at the arch of the lounge entrance and bathed the carpet with the light from his flash. No footprints in the medium-plush carpet. Only streaks made by a vacuum cleaner. Freshly vacuumed. Where were the footprints?

In the blue light from the telly, he identified the closest lamp. He could just reach it from his spot in the archway. Evie White sat in a recliner with her back to him. He couldn't see her face, but he could see one pale hand dangling over the side of the chair.

Not a good sign.

He tiptoed to a point where he could observe her face. Pale. Eyes open, pupils fixed and dilated. Frothy sputum at the corner of her mouth. A wine bottle on the floor in front of her chair.

Dead.

"Stafford, call the coroner."

"Dead, sir?"

David clenched his jaw and silently counted to ten. "That's the usual reason we need one, Sergeant."

"I know, sir. Sorry, I was being redundant, not stupid."

"And call in the SOCOs. They might as well miss dinner along with the rest of us." The questions in his mind remained. Suicide, accidental overdose, or murder?

The long case clock in the foyer chimed nine thirty. Gracious. It was later and later, and without a doubt, something had happened. David wasn't going to make it for Jamie's first dinner at Wyndswept. "Mina, I think we'd better go on and have dinner.

Jamie looks like he's all tuckered from the trip."

Mina nodded her agreement. And frankly she looked a little worn out herself. She'd changed in to a pale blue dinner gown. Her fluffy white hair was arranged in an elegant chignon at the base of her neck. I'd never seen her so regal and I wondered if her husband Jean-Luc had, either.

"Come on, buddy," I said to Jamie. "Let's have dinner. Do you know that David— your father—asked Cook to prepare his favorite dinner from when he was your age?" We walked into the family dining room—not the one with the table for twenty-four, but the smaller intimate one where the family would normally dine.

"That's very nice of him, Mummy. I wish he could be here, but I understand how his job is. He's an important detective. I bet he's solving a crime right now."

"I hope so, hon, because then we'll see a little more of him."

Jamie stopped and put his hands on his hips. "You look very pretty tonight, Mummy. I wish father could see *you*." He smiled as he said the word "father" with a sweet emphasis.

"Thank you. I do, too." In honor of our first real family dinner, I wore a long, silk skirt of red, green and gold tartan plaid with a glamorous—for me anyway—black V-necked top made of some kind of stretchy knit with gold thread interwoven. A less expensive version would've been itchy, but this one was lined in nude silk and was pure heaven against the skin.

"Yes, Randi, you look lovely." Mina smiled, then added, "Perhaps, I should say your ladyship looks lovely?"

I took Mina by the hand. "Oh, please don't. I've been 'your ladyshipped' to death in the last two days, and it's a blessed relief to just hear my name."

"As you wish, my dear. But you will have to become accustomed to the conventions. You mustn't disappoint the servants," she said with a smile and a twinkle.

I rolled my eyes. "It's David I worry about disappointing."

I settled Jamie in his chair on my left and gestured for Mina to my right. "I don't care how it's done. I just want the two of you right beside me."

My son reached over and patted the back of my hand. "I'm glad to be home, Mummy, but I had such a good time with at the farm with Jean-Luc and the kittens. They're almost big as real cats now. And Mina made me do my studies every day. Didn't miss a single thing, did we?"

Mina's eyes glittered with good humor. "No, Master James, we did not."

She turned to me. "I think you'll be quite proud of his progress, and whatever arrangements you make for his further schooling, he'll be caught up for his level."

I did another eye roll. "Ever since we returned from our road trip, David's had one high profile case after another. We had a hard time squeezing in time for the wedding and honeymoon, and now... We haven't had a spare minute to discuss schooling or where we'll live. I wanted to buy a couple of antiques shops once we were settled—one in London and one here in the country, and he found that out the hard way."

"I'm sure there's plenty of time to make those decisions." Mina took a thick slice of bread and buttered it.

The kitchen maids served the shepherd's pie, and Jamie dug in like it was the best he'd ever eaten. But as good as it smelled down in the kitchen earlier, now on my plate it smelled rich and heavy. My stomach grew queasy, and I picked at the meat dish with my fork.

"Why don't you just try the potatoes, dear?" Mina said. "They're seasoned very mildly and you might do better with those."

"It's good, Mummy. Try it. Father has good taste in food."

I picked a bite of the mashed potatoes with my fork. I opened my mouth and quickly swallowed them. I glanced at Mina. "My stomach's a little upset..."

"I see," she said with a knowing grin. "Try some of the bread. That might help, too. Starches are quite good for...upset stomachs."

"Thank you. I'll try that."

"So you two have found some time together?" Mina asked,

although she'd already guessed that pretty quickly.

"Well, yeah…" I giggled. "Just not to talk."

"Please, may I have more shepherd's pie?" This from Jamie.

"Certainly, you may have mine." We switched plates. "Now Cook won't know I didn't eat her perfectly wonderful dinner," I said with a grin. And she wouldn't guess as quickly as Mina had that I might be pregnant.

"Does David…?"

I shook my head. "Not 'til I know for sure. It's early yet." Here I was stuck out in the country and the nearest chemist was in the Green where David had made it pretty damn clear he didn't want me to go. And sending one of the servants for an OTC pregnancy test wasn't a good idea. Might as well make an announcement to the entire world.

My phone vibrated against my thigh.

"Maybe that's him now." I pulled the cell phone from my skirt pocket and checked at the caller I.D. "Excuse me," I said and got up from the table. "Hi, hon. I know you're going to be late for dinner."

"You are an excellent detective, darling. And if you weren't my wife, I'd be tempted to hire you for the force."

I giggled. "That's very nice of you to say so, and you know I'd take the job, too."

"You probably would at that. And yes, I'll be late. Something's come up. Would you put Jamie on? I hate I'm not there his first night."

"Believe me, he understands. But hold on." I handed the phone over to Jamie. "It's your dad. He wants to talk to you."

His dark brown eyes lit up. "Yes, please." He took the cell. "Hi, Father. Mum says you're working on a big case." His head nodded as he listened to his new dad. "Yes, dinner was super. And I haven't had dessert yet. Just what I wanted after our long trip. The Eurostar was terrific. I love trains, but I like flying even better." He looked up at me and winked because he knew all too well how much I hated flying. I wrinkled my nose and stuck out my tongue.

"All right, love you, too, Father." Jamie handed the phone back to me.

"I don't have any idea what time I'll be home," he said, "but I told him I'd look in on him before I looked in on you." His voice dropped into a low seductive range and reminded me of all the times we'd made love and never bothered with protection.

"It's all right. We both understand."

"Hearing him call me father..."

For a moment, I panicked. "Would you rather he not?"

"Don't be silly. It chokes me up. Never thought I'd hear those words from anyone...until I met you and your amazing son. I still can't believe how lucky I am. I love you both so much. Wait up for me?"

"Oh, yeah, you betcha."

He chuckled. "I have to ring off. I'm at a crime scene and the area is filling up with officers, and I've already amused them enough today."

We disconnected, and I gave a sigh. David thought he was the lucky one? Jamie and I might not be alive if it weren't for his being assigned to take us to a safe house. How or why he fell in love with me is one of life's sweetest mysteries. But I'll take it and treasure it and him forever.

The Whites' cottage had been thoroughly gone over by the SOCO. At David's insistence, the vacuum cleaner was taken in evidence as well. Before he allowed the techs inside, he asked them to photograph the carpet. "You'll see that the only visible prints in the carpet are mine. Even if she just vacuumed before retiring to her chair, there should've been her footprints present from where she put away the Hoover, at the very least."

For now, the coroner had just extracted the liver probe and looked at the readout. "Mr. Ballard, estimated time of death?"

"Taking into consideration the ambient room temperature and her liver temperature, I would say approximately two hours ago, give or take an hour either way."

"I know it's too soon for cause of death, but—"

Mr. Ballard frowned at David over his spectacles. "Way too soon."

"Best guess?"

"White froth on her lips. Drug overdose. Maybe accidental since there's also a wine bottle on the floor. Bad combination—drugs and alcohol. Possibly intentional."

"They've already dusted and didn't find any prints on the bottle. Wonder how she managed that?"

Ballard eyed David skeptically. "You think she was murdered, don't you?"

"I wouldn't rule it out until all the evidence is reviewed."

DS Stafford came down from upstairs. "Nothing much up there, sir. All neat and tidy."

"Stafford, make sure they bring the sheets in for trace testing and any medications from their medicine cabinet. I'm going back to the stationhouse. Someone needs to tell Mr. White his wife's dead."

"Not a welcome duty, sir."

"No, but a necessary one." One thing for certain, Jacko White couldn't have killed his wife from a cell.

Back at the stationhouse, it was quiet, nothing like the flurry of activity at White's cottage. A red-eyed Jacko White was waiting for David in the interview room, rubbing the sleep from his eyes. "Wot's up now, Inspector? Can't a fella get a night's sleep even in jail?"

"I'm afraid I've some bad news, Mr. White."

"Yeah? Like wot? You're gonna keep me 'erc 'til the cows come 'ome?"

"It's Evie. One of her coworkers went by to check on her, and she didn't answer. He was worried, so he called us. We found her, but it was too late to help her."

White's mouth dropped open, but his eyes appeared confused. "Wotcher saying? My Evie's dead? *Dead*?"

"Yes, Mr. White. I'm very sorry for your loss."

An expression of pure horror crossed his features. "Not like Daisy, not dead like the others? Oh, God, not like that."

"No, not like that. May've been an overdose. Did your wife take any medications?" Jacko shook his head. "'Ealthy as an 'orse, she was. Rarely took an aspirin."

"Was she in the habit of drinking to excess?"

"Occasional glass of wine after supper, sometimes before supper to unwind after a busy day at the pub."

"Any particular brand?"

"It's all the same to me," Jacko said with a shrug. "I likes havin' me a beer. That's it for drinkin' in our 'ouse."

"Thank you, Mr. White. Again, I'm sorry for your loss."

"You gotta let me out to make arrangements. Gotta do right by Evie, even if she did trash me right proper for having it off wif poor Daisy."

"Tomorrow morning. They're still busy at your place. In fact, you'd better find another place to stay for a couple of days."

Jacko nodded. "Yeah, I can stay wif me mum. She won't turn 'gainst me like the rest of the town 'as."

David signaled for an officer to take White back to his cell. He considered whether Jacko could've spiked the bottle of wine with something and gotten rid of his wife from the cell after all. But no, that wouldn't explain the absence of footprints in the carpet and lack of fingerprints on the wine bottle. One thing for certain, the lab reports would tell the story on what drugs were in her system and any remaining residue in the wine bottle.

He sat down at his desk and rubbed his eyes. Half past eleven. He'd promised Jamie he'd check on him when he came in. Time to keep that promise, store away all thoughts of death and murder in another compartment and lock the door.

It was a little after twelve when I saw the car lights and heard David's car pull into the driveway in front of the house...mansion...whatever. Jamie slept soundly in our bedroom on the cozy sofa in front of the fireplace, and I was on the chaise.

His first night in his new home shouldn't be spent tucked away on another floor in the nursery. The bedroom was warm and comfortable from the toasty fire, and a candle by the bed provided more than enough light.

Mina and I talked briefly after dinner, but I could tell from her heavy eyelids that their journey from Provençe had been a long one for her, too. I sent her off to bed in a pretty blue and white guest room.

I think I was the only one still awake in the entire place, and I finally heard David's footsteps in the hall.

He opened the door and poked his head inside. "I can't believe you waited up for me. Where's our little guy?"

"Asleep on the settee in front of the fire. I hope you don't mind—just for tonight."

He walked over to the settee and pulled the blanket up over Jamie's shoulder. "Sleep well, little one."

Then he pulled me from the chaise longue where I was curled under an afghan and wrapped his arms around me. "This is so perfect. I'm a stereotype. This, my very first time I'm home from the office and greeted by my wife and son."

He gave me a very long kiss, which curled my toes and sent warm tingles a little higher. "I love you."

"Love you, too." He sat on the chaise longue and pulled me onto his lap. "I'm so sorry I couldn't be home earlier...for his first night."

"It's all right. He understands." I snuggled in the comfort and warmth of his arms. "I have something to tell you."

He reared back, a scowl on his handsome face. "What've you done now? Please no more investigating."

"No, not that." I put my arms around his neck and whispered, "I'm not quite sure yet, but I think I might be pregnant."

His scowl changed instantly. His eyes lit up and his chin dropped. "Really? When will you know for sure?"

"Another couple of weeks at the most. But I had symptoms early with Jamie and my breasts are already tender—and no, I don't think it's from anything you did—I was queasy at dinner. I know it's really vague, but we haven't bothered with protection for the last month or so. Are you happy? I know you want a family, but is it too soon?"

"Darling Miranda, I'm ecstatic. Are you happy?" A smile wreathed his face and his eyes shone warm in the firelight.

"Me? I'm thrilled. But I just want to keep it between us until I know for sure. Although Mina already guessed at dinner."

David let out a soft chuckle. "No doubt she and Jean-Luc already have a wager riding on the sex and the birth date."

"Probably so."

He cupped my face in his hands. "I've said this before, but I'm the luckiest man in the world. You've given me everything I thought I'd never have...a home...a son...and now a new life created from our love."

Tears sprang to my eyes—okay, I'm just an old softy, but I loved this man so much. "I'm the lucky one, but you just go on and keep thinking you're the lucky one. Because I know the truth." I blinked back the tears and David carried me to our bed where we snuggled like spoons for a long time.

Yes, snuggled. After all, there was a six-year-old boy sleeping on the settee just a few feet away.

Chapter Seventeen

Thursday

The next morning over breakfast, Mr. Nice Guy was gone and in his place was a stern Mr. I Mean Business. He quietly laid down the law. "Now, it's even more important that you take care of yourself. No caffeine, no alcohol and no horseback riding."

"As if... Yes, hon. I've done this before."

"I know you have. And there's one more: no private detecting. I'll send you straight to London so fast your head will spin if I so much as catch you speaking, calling or writing a bloody e-mail to anyone concerned in this case."

I snorted orange juice. "And you, my dear husband, are being bloody ridiculous," I said, imitating his plummy British accent. "I promise I'll behave. I have enough to do riding herd on Jamie. I won't have time for any of that other stuff." I grinned. "But if it would make you feel better, leave me a list and I'll be sure to refer to it every now and then."

David, Mr. Nice Guy, grinned and glanced down at his plate. "I am being bloody ridiculous, aren't I?"

"Yes." I dabbed the napkin to my mouth.

"One more thing," he said. "Which should we employ? A nanny or a governess for Jamie?"

I stopped the inner groan and said, "Just let me handle him for the time being. I'm already experienced."

David's eyes darkened to slate and the corner of his mouth

kicked up. "Yes, I can vouch for your ability to handle *me*," he said in an undertone.

"Yeah, and I'm getting more experienced at it, all the time." I fluttered my lashes.

Flirting with my husband over breakfast was a treat I intended to enjoy as often as possible.

"Your plans for today?" he asked.

"Oh, back to business. I see. Well, Mina and I will take Jamie on a tour of the house and grounds. She's going to stay a few days to rest up after the trip. I should've had them fly. It would've been easier on her. I don't know what I was thinking."

"Make flight reservations for her return trip then."

I spread some jam on my toast. "Mm. Cook's homemade jam is wonderful," I said.

"Watch your calories," he said.

"One more word, your lordship, and I'll bounce the next piece of toast off your noggin like a Frisbee."

"You're feeling very smart this morning, aren't you?" He grinned over his cuppa, excitement shining in his eyes.

"Not queasy at all... Maybe I'm not—"

"Not what, Mum?"

I jumped. Jamie stood at my elbow, all scrubbed and shining. Mina's doing, of course. "Uh, not going to eat all the toast before you get to the table."

"Better not. I'm hungry as a bear." He growled and let out a roar.

"I believe that's the point. Anyway, one slice is enough for me." I gave David a wide toothy smile. The smarty—he was right about the calories. With Jamie, I gained about fourteen extra pounds, which was a good thing. Before I got pregnant with him, I was built like a stick, and now I have a few curves in the right places. But another fourteen pounds and I'll look like a Pillsbury dough boy with more dimples in more places than any one person needs. Let's face it, I'm a short-statured person and watching my weight is a fact of life.

"Fella, don't I get a hug in the morning?" David asked and

stretched out his arms.

"Of course." Jamie promptly jumped into David's lap. "I really enjoyed the shepherd's pie last night. Cook said it used to be your favorite, so it's going to be my favorite, too."

"Good. I'm glad you liked it."

"Mum didn't eat much. I think she was excited because it was my first night home. Can Mina live with us? No, I guess not because then Jean-Luc would be ever so lonesome, wouldn't he?"

"Yes, he would. And Mina is retired. She's enjoying her golden years."

"Oh, yes, she is. I heard strange noises one night, and when I asked her the next morning what happened, she said it was just she and Jean-Luc enjoying their golden years. Sounded like fun anyway."

I nearly choked on my last bite of toast and jam. David handed me a glass of water and I managed to catch my breath without laughing. Of course the images of a very rotund Jean-Luc and the slender Mina engaged in their golden years' activities were already burned on my brain.

I wasn't sure if therapy would help or not.

I looked over at David. His eyes were bright with amusement. "Way to go, Jean-Luc," he said.

"Honestly... Men, you're all the same."

"Me, too, Mum?"

"Yes, eventually."

David set Jamie on his feet and stood, giving me a sorry smile. "I have to go to the stationhouse."

"Will you take me to the stationhouse sometime, Father? I want to be a detective like you."

David grinned. He loved hearing "father" from Jamie as much as Jamie loved saying it. "One day when we're back in the city, I'll take you to the stationhouse in London."

"Scotland Yard?"

"New Scotland Yard, yes. And if you go to school, get your education and still want to join the force..." David paused and glanced across the table at me as if to say "Okay?"

The idea of my precious little boy being in danger every day wasn't exactly a thought to warm this mother's heart. But I nodded. What else could I do?

"...then you may apply just like everyone else."

"I'll be a DCI like you, too. I'll put the criminals and killers away in prison for life. Yes, I'll catch them all."

Oh dear, my son was certainly optimistic. Little did he know his biological father was in one of those prisons and would likely remain there for the rest of his unnatural life.

At least I hoped so.

How I would ever manage to tell him about Stefan wasn't anything I was ready to tackle for another decade anyway.

David collected his briefcase and Jamie ran after him. "I'm going to walk you to your car, and I'll take good care of mummy while you're at work."

I was right behind the duo. David looked over his shoulder and winked at me. "See that you do, young man."

I walked up behind David and gave him a surreptitious pat on his butt. "See that you behave at work today, because I'll be busy corralling this young man."

He hugged and kissed us both. What a revelation such a simple gesture can be. I didn't mind being a stereotype. All I needed was to take off my shoes and I'd be your barefoot and pregnant bride straight from the hills of Tennessee.

On the other hand, the marble floor of the foyer would be a tad cold on the bare tootsies.

Still elated by Miranda's news, David entered the squad room and realized ruefully he was the last to arrive. DS Stafford, DS Tower, DCI Beecham were all there, along with pretty DC Pettigrew.

Beecham made a big show of checking his watch. "I guess his lordship is on London time. Come rolling in at nine at the Yard, do you?"

"No, but go on. I can take it. In my defense, it was my son's first morning in the house and so I stayed and had breakfast with him...and my wife."

"Nice little domestic scene at the estate. How touching," Beecham said with a wide smirk. "Of course, we've all been here since seven and working."

"I was on duty until quite late last night."

Beecham nodded knowingly. "Yeah, poor Evie White. She offed herself. At least we don't have to bring in the entire village on that one."

"Wouldn't be too sure about that. There were some troubling anomalies at the scene." David sat and glanced through the stack of reports on his desk. "Is there a toxicology report back on her yet?"

"You don't think she did herself in?" Beecham's brows drew together in a frown. "This one's nothing like the others."

"No, but how do you explain the plush carpet was freshly vacuumed with no footprints leading to her chair and a wine bottle wiped clean of prints?"

"Bloody hell, French. Maybe she flew to the bloomin' chair and being the tidy sort wiped her bottle."

"Three murders in four days, gentleman. That's not a coincidence. Evie White's connected to the murderer in some manner, and he took care of her, but took great pains not to leave any evidence behind. As for the vacuum, I want an analysis of the contents, too."

"You're barking up the wrong tree on this one, French. We've only two SOCOs and one M.E. We can't turn the evidence around as fast as London—that's the sad truth."

"I don't want anyone else to die." David leaned back and rubbed his eyes.

His desk phone rang, and it was the desk sergeant. "Mrs. Denton to see you, sir." Denton. Nicola Denton. Right. The former supermodel. "Send her back."

He stood when the tall slender woman entered the squad room. Long dark hair and arched eyebrows and very blue eyes. For a moment, he faltered. His mouth dried like cotton. He swallowed.

Cassie.

Or enough like her to be a sister.

After a moment, he recovered his powers of speech. "Mrs. Denton, I'm Inspector French. How may I help you?"

She glanced around the room. "Could we speak privately?"

"Y-yes, of course." He motioned toward the interview rooms. "This way."

Once she was settled and had a cup of tea in hand, he asked again, "How may I help you?"

She smiled. "I believe I met your wife the other day. She invited me for tea. Charming."

"Yes, she mentioned meeting you."

But not that you looked like my dead fiancée.

He couldn't keep his gaze off Nicola Denton's face. The resemblance was uncanny and why hadn't Miranda mentioned it? Another mystery?

"I wish to amend my statement...the one I gave to the detective sergeant and his partner."

"Indeed?" *Now what was this?*

"It's about my relationship with Riley Stubbs. I may've glossed over a few details."

"I need to record this." He turned on the recorder which activated the video as well.

"Interview commenced at 9:45 a.m. with Nicola Denton and DCI French in attendance. Mrs. Denton has indicated she wishes to amend her previous statement taken by DS Stafford and DC Pettigrew."

The Cassie lookalike glanced up at him with a plea in her eyes. "Now?"

Barely able to think clearly, he nodded. "Yes."

She took a delicate sip of her tea. "I wasn't as forthcoming as I should've been. I'm terrified, Inspector French. Two people have died, and I'm afraid I might be next." She took a deep breath. "I had a brief...very brief affair with Riley."

"Why didn't you mention this previously?"

She wrung her hands, those long slender fingers so like

Cassie's. Her diamond caught the light and glistened. The stone was nearly the size of Ireland.

"I didn't want my husband to know. It was only a couple of times, and I realized I'd made a mistake...out of loneliness, you see. My husband's very successful and works all the time. You understand, don't you?"

"I'm not here to judge you, Mrs. Denton. Go on."

"I broke it off when it became clear that Riley had gone off the deep end—calling me all hours of the day and night. I told Philip about the calls, but I couldn't imagine why he was stalking me. I'm sorry for lying to your subordinates."

"Are you afraid your husband had something do to with Mr. Stubbs's death?"

Her eyes grew wide. "I don't know. He said it was the kind of thing a man would do...a jealous husband. I got to thinking, maybe...he did. He even mentioned he watched all those forensics shows." Her fingers went to her mouth. "What have I done?"

"Do you have any reason to believe your husband would've killed Daisy Mellon? Both were undoubtedly killed by the same person."

"Daisy Mellon? The girl from the beauty shop?" Her gaze darted around. "No, I doubt he even knew her." Then she smiled. "Well, then, my Phil couldn't have done Riley then?" She lifted her shoulders in a deep sigh. "What a relief. Thank you so much. I knew talking to you would solve everything." She reached over and patted the back of his hand.

Reflexively he jerked away from her touch. "Thank you for coming in."

"It was such a pleasure meeting you." Away she went, swaying her hips and arms as if she were still on the catwalk.

The woman was like Cassie in appearance only. There was none of Cassie's humanity and warmth. This selfish woman could've cared less about the murder of two people, only that her husband not discover her infidelity. All was right in her superficial and self-indulgent little world.

What a contrast to his Miranda, who felt responsible for Daisy

Mellon's death because she'd merely talked to the young woman. His wife would never be unfaithful simply because she was lonely or bored.

He emerged from the interview room to see the males fanning.

"Hot. Hot. Hot," said DCI Beecham, shaking his hand as if he'd been burned. "All the hot ones want to spill their secrets to the inspector from the Yard. What's your secret, French? Why do the women all love you?"

"I treat women with respect, Beecham." David sat down and made a note on Denton's file. "Maybe you should try it sometime."

"Ouch!" Beecham leaned back. "I'll bet a ten pound note the next pretty woman in here asks for Chief Inspector French," he mimicked in a falsetto.

"I'll take that bet," came from DS Tower.

David glared at Stafford and dared him to speak a word. The sergeant wisely refrained from jumping on the bet, but he was the lone holdout. David relented and grinned. "Go ahead. You know you want to."

Stafford dug a note from his pocket. "I'm in."

"Now if you're sufficiently amused, might I have an update on everything related to Evie White's death?"

"Yeah." Beecham shrugged and grinned. "'Bout the same time I win the National Lottery."

"Please, Mum. I want to go out." Jamie looked up at me with his most pitiful expression. "I've seen enough of the house. I want to play in the woods where there's fresh air."

How could I refuse a request obviously based on health reasons?

Even though the day was a typical gloomy and damp one, Mina, Jamie and I bundled up in our warmest coats, pulled on our wellies and set out to explore the estate with Mina as our guide. We headed out through the kitchen. A fine mist hung in the air, and I couldn't help but remember the previous evening when I'd sensed someone watching me. I shivered, but with Mina along, I felt somewhat safer, however nonsensical that was.

As we walked past the formal gardens, Mina said, "I used to take your father and his brother on what I called daily constitutionals."

"Did they like the fresh air, too?"

Mina smiled down at my son. "Yes indeed, but I believe it was more a matter of running and romping around the estate and the woods in particular. The estate was much larger then, but there are still dangers of which you should be aware, young man."

"Super." He ran ahead of us, but was still in sight.

"Dangers?" My heart sped up a bit. I glanced at Mina. "Like what?"

"There's a protected bog which extends from Hutton estate lands to your estate, and it's quite treacherous. One step you're on solid ground and the next you're trapped." She smiled, perhaps amused by my concern. "The bog is quite far from where we are. I wouldn't recommend going into the woods at all, but boys will be boys. It was difficult to keep his father and Master Terrence out of the woods or away from Lord Hutton's land as well. There are caves. I've heard, mind you, that some boys played smugglers and pirates from those caves along the beach. But it's been a long time. The current Lord Hutton may've had them filled or blocked."

"I believe David mentioned their playing in the caves. Where are they exactly? How close?"

"You have newly-built dwellings on either side of the estate, but Middlebury lands abut Hutton lands along the line of the woods in the rear of the estate. There's a stony outcrop which rises smartly beyond the woods. The caves are located in the outcrop which falls sharply to a small beach which floods at high tide, as do some of the caves."

I took a nervous glance at my son who was already fifty yards ahead of us. "Slow down, kiddo. Don't get too far from us."

He stopped for a second and then turned around and waved.

My heart gave a jump. In my mind's eye, I could just see him sinking in a bog or falling in a cave and never being found until too late. "I don't know what I'd do if…"

"Bless you, girl." Mina patted my forearm. "He's a sturdy young boy, but they will tempt fate from time to time."

"He's already had one close call..."

Mina shivered and rubbed her arms. "You don't have to remind me. I'm not likely to forget that incident."

"I never blamed you or your stepson Pierre. It was an accident. Just one of those things. I know I'm an absolute nervous Nellie and afraid of everything, especially where Jamie's concerned, but I don't want him to be afraid..." I threw up my hands in exasperation.

"I know. But you want him to learn caution. It's a fine line we walk when children are given to our care."

I stopped and turned to Mina. "I'm so scared of disappointing David. I'm still not sure I'm the right person for him."

Mina laughed, a deep hearty laugh, surprising for one so slender. "You are *perfect* for him, and I'd be very surprised if he doesn't tell you so daily."

I shrugged. "Don't they say love is blind"?

"Indeed they do, but aphorisms don't mean much when it's so obvious to me and everyone who knows him how happy his lordship is since he met you. You must work on your self image. Learn to rely on your inner strength, my girl. You're worth a hundred women in this village, in the entire UK"

I hung my head. "Not a hundred of Cassie. She was wonderful."

"You'll never be Cassie, and sadly she's gone from us, but that doesn't mean you're any less wonderful than she. She chose you for her best friend, and she wouldn't have done for anyone who wasn't worthy of her friendship."

"But I repaid her by getting her killed."

"Ah, so we're back to that, are we? You still haven't forgiven yourself. It was a tragedy, but it was Stefan Kristoforus who killed her, not you. *His* choice. Not *yours*."

"I'm living her life." I twirled around with my arms spread widely. "All this should be hers. David should—"

"Hush! I've heard enough self-pitying remarks for one day. The best way to honor Cassie's friendship is living your life to the fullest. Besides, you're simply hormonal because of the baby."

She hugged me and I began to calm down. "Is that it?" A wave of relief flooded through me.

"Of course, it is. Now, let's corral that young man—"

We both scanned the area. No Jamie. "Jamie! Jamie!" Panic grew in my chest and threatened to explode my heart. How could I have let him get out of my sight after all Mina's warnings about the dangers on the estate lands?

"Boo!" He jumped up from behind a large boulder. "You didn't see me sneaking up on you. I'm a spy for the Queen, and you..." He pointed at us with a stick. "...are terrorists. I'm taking you to the authorities at MI-5."

Terrorists and MI-5—where had he gotten such notions? I grabbed him and hugged him tightly. "What have you been watching on the telly?"

"It's my fault," Mina said. "I caught Jean-Luc and Jamie watching *Spook* one night and I had to punish them both, especially that husband of mine," she said, then chuckled.

I thought it better not to explore that. "I think it's time we went back inside for a hot lunch," I said.

"Do we have to?" That came from my son naturally.

Between us, Mina and I herded him back inside and I warned him about the bog and caves and staying out of both.

Chapter Eighteen

Lady Jane Hutton set a vase of cut flowers down on the Sheraton sideboard. It was so handy having a special friend who grew such magnificent flowers in her nursery greenhouse. She leaned over and inhaled the glorious scent of her favorite pale pink Kalinka roses. Today was her birthday and Nan had already delivered them along with the large order of green plants for the conservatory.

It was time for another trip to the summerhouse where she and Nan could truly be themselves. Nan's body was firm and well-muscled, almost like a man's but without the odious appendage with which the male gender was so obsessed.

"Jane."

She jumped. Damn. He had no right to sneak up on her. She slid the note from Nan into her slacks pocket, then turned and faced him. "Yes, Edward, dear?"

He shut the pocket doors behind him, leaving them quite alone. "Flowers for your birthday already? But they can't be mine. I ordered red."

How like him not to know after all these years that her favorites were the delicately shaded pinks, not the common red. "Nan sent them. She knows what I prefer."

He smiled, but it was pale effort. "That's what I hear." He set his pipe down on a table. "But that's not all I hear."

"Whatever do you mean? Don't be tiresome."

"Tiresome. I'll show you tiresome." He grabbed her wrist and twisted it behind her back.

Pain, excruciating pain shot up her wrist and into her shoulder. "Stop it. What's the matter with you?" Tears sprang to her eyes. "You're hurting me."

"Which one of you is the butch dyke? You don't have to answer that question. I can figure that out easily enough. Your hard-bodied, darling Nan sent you those flowers, didn't she?"

"I already said so, but—" Her arm was going to break if he didn't stop, but he kept jerking it higher behind her back. "You're hurting me," she said, panting with pain.

"Shut up," he said quietly. "And keep your voice down. I've put up with your coldness over the years. I attributed it to having the children and our busy social life. But now I know you've been tipping the velvet all along, and that's how you really get off."

"Please, stop!"

"If I'd only known your true leanings, darling, I would've brought her in and watched the two of you at it. Then we could've all had a good time."

He released her wrist and shoved her roughly to the floor. She fell on her knees and rolled to her side. "You've broken my wrist, you bloody bastard." She clutched her wrist to her abdomen. Sharp pain, yet a certain deep-down numbness. How could he have hurt her so? She tried to move her fingers, but except for the involuntary trembling of her thumb, she couldn't.

"Stop your sniveling." He bent down and shrugged. "So 'tis." He stepped over her and went to the door, opened it and called the butler. "Call my physician. I'm afraid her ladyship's taken a tumble and broken her wrist." He turned back and held out his hand. "Here, let me help you to your feet."

She jerked away from him. "Don't touch me. I'm in enough pain as it is. I can manage." Once settled on the sofa, she glared at him. "How did you find out? Who told you?" she asked, keeping her voice low.

He sat on the chair across from her, casually crossed one leg over his knee and relit his bloody pipe.

"At least you don't bother denying it." He puffed on his pipe and said from the corner of his mouth. "I've known quite some time. Someone saw fit to repeat something she observed at the pub. I didn't believe it at first, until I saw with my own eyes. The old summerhouse makes a private trysting place, doesn't it dear?"

"You watched? Of course, you did." Her spirit was returning. Actually she'd feared more than a broken wrist if he ever found out. A broken wrist would heal, but a broken neck would not.

In spite of the pain, she raised her chin a notch. "Where do we go from here? Do you want a divorce?"

He shrugged, as if he could care less. "No. Nothing will change."

"Nothing? Then I'll continue to see Nan as before and you won't do anything? No more temper tantrums like just now?" The next tantrum would be hers, and he wouldn't see it coming.

"Carry on as before, but more discreetly. I won't have our names and photos dragged through the tabloids. The children must never know."

"Stiff upper lip and all that. Do as you wish, just don't do it in the streets and frighten the horses. Lovely British sentiment." Who did the bastard think he was kidding? He had to have a plan. Blindside her with divorce proceedings at the worst possible moment—more like him.

Bastard. Before he humiliated her before the entire world, she'd see him dead.

David studied the DNA results on the gray-blond hair recovered from the first crime scene. To a percentage of 99.98, the DNA matched Nan Morgan's sample. A sample she'd provided freely and without showing the least sign of resistance. Could she have actually killed Stubbs and the Mellon girl? Hacking them, mutilating them almost beyond recognition?

"Well?" DCI Beecham leaned over on David's desk. "You've seen the results?"

"We have to bring her back in for more questioning," David said. "But I still don't like her for these murders."

"Not just bring her in." Beecham's face grew red. "We've

enough evidence to charge her with murder."

David rubbed his chin. "It's still circumstantial." And his gut didn't agree with the obvious.

"Her hair was in Stubbs's fist, matted in blood. That's a little more than circumstantial." Beecham's tone grew exasperated, and David couldn't blame him. It was just too tidy.

"Ordinarily I'd agree. But would a killer who wiped his or her prints from the immediate scene forget to check the victim's hands. The killer certainly cleaned the Mellon girl's nails."

"You think it was a plant?"

"I'm leaning in that direction. I'd like to know who might have a motive for framing Nan Morgan."

"You're still thinking zebras instead of horses, French."

"Perhaps." David shrugged and raised his hands in surrender. "Let's bring her in and charge her if the Chief Crown Prosecutor agrees with your evidence." He grinned up at Beecham. "And you're releasing Jacko White?"

"Guess we have to. I'll send DS Tower to pick up Nan Morgan."

David leaned back. Let Beecham spin his wheels by arresting Nan. Conviction the murders were committed by a highly intelligent, organized male only grew stronger with each piece of the puzzle. He was of a mind to interrogate three of the four husbands again, if necessary. Poor Jacko White was ready for release and had funeral arrangements to make at the mortuary, but the others were worth another turn of the key.

"Why don't I send along Stafford to bring in her husband too," David said. "I'd like another go at him. He may've been lying about something or they're in it together."

Beecham smiled and nodded. "Now you're thinking horses."

Another go at Lord Hutton and Phil Denton would round out this day nicely. Nicola Denton might be reassured her husband hadn't done it, but he was still a suspect. And while Lord Hutton had no visible connection to either victim...one never knew. When all was said and done, a small rural village could hide as many secrets as there were inhabitants.

*

It might be a dreary winter afternoon outside, but the sun always shone in Nan Morgan's heart when she worked in her greenhouse. Plants never betrayed or whined if their dinner wasn't ready on time. She should've never married Freddie. He wasn't much of a man. She snickered. If truth be told, she was more of a man than her wimpy husband. She brought in the family income and kept the nursery afloat. She went out and did the hard work necessary. While that bugger Freddie...

What kind of man played on his computer all day, pretending he was a big shot accounting consultant? If he was bringing in any income, he certainly wasn't putting it in their joint bank account.

Her mobile chimed. Better not be her lazy-arsed husband. She checked the caller I.D. No, it was Janie. Darling Janie.

"Hi," she said brightly because that was how hearing from Janie affected her. "Y-you have to be careful, Nan. He knows." The sound of sobs reached her. "What? Tell me what's happened. What did he do to you?"

"The bastard. He broke my wrist. Someone tipped him. He's seen us in the summerhouse."

"Broke your wrist? Have you seen a doctor?"

"I'm up in my room. He's downstairs sucking on that bloody pipe of his like nothing's wrong. Had the butler call for the doctor. Couldn't be bothered himself." More sobs.

The sound of those racking sobs ate at Nan, filling her with hate. "We have to do something about him. He's gone too far."

"Y-yes, I agree. But how? He's vicious. I had no idea how cruel he could be. 'Carry on as before,' he said. Can you believe that? Said if he'd known sooner, he would've had you come round and we could've all had a good time."

"No. He said that? Bloody sod."

A bitter laugh. "No, he doesn't want the world to know his wife would rather shag her landscaper than him."

"Make a police report. When the doctor comes, tell him what happened."

"No, no. Edward's personal physician will come. He won't do anything. If I say anything, I'll be packed off to a sanitarium for a long rest."

"Then we have to kill him. We can make it look like these other murders."

"You'd do that...for me? I don't think I could bear..."

"Darling, leave it to me. You know I would do anything for you." And if it meant slicing off a few body parts, so be it. She'd rather enjoy taking care of him that way. Janie said a quick good-bye, then disconnected.

Her mobile rang again. Damn. This time, 'twas Freddie.

"DS Tower and DS Stafford are here, Nan."

"What of it? I don't have time for more silly questions."

Silence.

"Well?"

"They want to have another word and take us down to the station."

An hour later, David watched a visibly shaken Nan Morgan sit hunched over in one interview room biting her nails, while husband Freddie relaxed in another room, swilling down cup after cup of tea. While Nan appeared to be worried about something, Freddie didn't appear to have enough sense to be concerned about anything.

"Let them sweat for a while," he suggested. The more nervous they were, the more likely one of them would make a mistake.

"Enjoy the view," Beecham said. "Mrs. Morgan's not too happy about being here." "Have they been cautioned?"

"DS Tower cautioned both of them once we got them in the stationhouse."

David nodded toward the squad room. "Let's go over everything we have on them before we have a go."

He led the way with Beecham right behind. The man was too anxious to arrest someone, anyone. While David was anxious to clear the case, he wanted the real murderer and not a convenient substitute.

He sat and reread his notes. "We interviewed Freddie Morgan first in an attempt to substantiate Jacko White's alibi about riding out that far. Of course, we know that was a lie and he said he was up to no-good with Daisy Mellon. Morgan said he was up at six-thirty and Nan came in from her nursery at seven and left at half-past. He spent the rest of the morning working on his accounting business, trying to set up a deal with a car dealership in Yorkshire. He mentioned his bad business deal with Stubbs, but tried to downplay it."

"That's a good area to focus on," Beecham said.

"When I approached Nan about being involved with Stubbs, she was irate. Said he'd gypped her on a deal—sold her some fake Staffordshire dogs. Says he closed his shop when she came in to keep other customers from hearing her trash him. Says after she left home, she went over to Lord Hutton's to work on the winter veg beds and check the mulch. Only verification we have that she was actually there is Lady Hutton says she waved at Nan from the window but Nan didn't see her."

"Hmph. Might've been trying to give herself an alibi."

"I agree. At the time, I was dubious about Lady Jane's flimsy time-line, so whether or not she actually saw Nan Morgan is anyone's guess."

"That Freddie's a weird one. He's not local originally. Doesn't have a lot of men friends, but I've heard him in the pub boast about keeping that wife of his in line. Now, I'd guess it's the other way round."

David nodded. "Muscle mass alone, I'd say she outweighs him a stone or two."

"And we have DNA proof that Nan's connected to the scene. You can't get round that." Beecham added with a triumphant air. "And she's a lefty, too."

"Maybe that's a coincidence. We also must consider who might have a reason to implicate Nan. Her husband for one, if she truly were having an affair with Stubbs and not just angry about his selling her the fake dogs."

Beecham rubbed his eyes. "Sorry, but the image of Stubbs getting it on with Nan Morgan isn't pretty, and her Freddie ought to be glad of a rest."

"Unkind to think, much less say." David shook his head. Marriage was a complicated business and one could never know what went on between a couple. "Are you married?"

Beecham frowned. "Damned personal inquiry that."

"Huh." David laughed. "This from one who's ragged me unmercifully about my honeymooner status."

"Aw-right. I guess I was a little hard on you in that respect." He shrugged and shook his head. "My wife and I are separated. She didn't fancy moving to the Green. I suspect we'll make it a more formal separation if either one of us ever sees the need. No kids, so not a big deal."

"Sorry, old man." David glanced at his watch. "Think they've sweated enough?" "Let's do it. I'd like a go at Nan. You take Freddie?"

David nodded and stood. Maybe he had overlooked something Beecham could find. In the past, he'd misjudged someone once with tragic results, and he couldn't afford to let his arrogance stand in the way of this investigation.

Will Beecham was happy to let French take old Freddie Morgan. Nan was the one whose hair was found clutched in Riley Stubbs's fist, therefore as far as Will was concerned, Nan Morgan was the culprit. She certainly had the body strength to knock Stubbs in the head and rearrange his nasty bits with her handy hunting knife. She was country woman born and bred, not some delicate flower from London. When he was first on the force in Suffolk County, he'd seen what a country-bred woman was capable of and it had given him nightmares for at least a fortnight.

He walked into the interview room, nodded at his suspect, sat down and made the entry note for recording purposes.

"You bloody pillock!" Nan banged her fist on the table. "What on earth are you thinking?"

"*I'll* ask the questions, Mrs. Morgan. You'll do the answering." Now here was a woman with a bloody bad temper.

"Hmph." She settled back in her chair with her arms folded across her chest. "If you say so. I've already answered the other inspector's questions. Polite he was. I don't appreciate being dragged away from my work in the nursery."

"Unfortunate, but necessary. In fact, you're looking like our prime suspect in Riley Stubbs's murder. Are you certain you don't want to call a solicitor?"

"What? You're a blooming lunatic. I don't need a solicitor." Her gaze darted from side to side as if reckoning her chances for escape. "And my Freddie...why'd you bring him in, too? And am I supposed to have killed that girl, too—what's her name—Daisy?"

"You tell us. Did you kill Daisy? We already have evidence connecting you to the Stubbs's death." He shook his head. "You've been a busy girl, haven't you?"

Nan shook her head. "Can't say as I ever met the girl."

"As small a village as this one?" He leaned into her face. "You don't expect me to believe a porky pie like that."

"Not a lie!" She stood with her fists clenched.

"Sit down!" he ordered.

She obeyed, but her weathered face grew red. "Do I look like I spend my days in the bleeding beauty parlor?"

She spread her large, weather- and work-roughened hands for his view. Was there blood on those hands? He believed there was.

"Never had a manicure. I cut my own hair once a year in the spring when the weather starts to warm up. And I never had any use for fancy facials. The sun and rain are all the facials I have time for."

"So was the Mellon girl just handy?"

"Why're you harping about the Mellon girl? Where's your evidence on that one?" She leaned back and nodded. "Yeah, you don't have any to connect me to that one. Well, I'd like to know what evidence you have connecting me to Stubbs?"

"DNA...your DNA was found at the scene."

"Never denied I were in his shop. Lots of traffic in that shop."

"What if I told you that your hair was found gripped in his hand and matted with his blood? The hair roots tested within 99.98 percent as being compatible with your DNA. What would you say?"

She ran her fingers through her hair. "My hair?"

"Yes, yours."

She shook her head. "I can't explain it. Someone's set me up. I'm not saying another word until I speak with my solicitor. Call him. Roy Peters. Call him."

Damn it all. Maybe he could change her mind. "Now Nan," he said softly, "you're doing yourself a disservice by not being completely cooperative."

She squared her broad shoulders and raised her chin. "I know my rights. Call my solicitor and call him now. I'm through talking."

"Interview ended at quarter past seven," he said. More than mightily pissed off, he stood and glared at her. "Stupid cow, I'll see you in the dock yet." He just hoped French could get something out of Freddie. He motioned for the constable to enter. "Let her make a call to her solicitor, then put her in a cell."

Next door, David nodded as he entered the interrogation room. "Mr. Morgan."

Morgan leaned back and cocked his head to the side. "What's this all about, Inspector? I was in the middle of an important business deal."

"Sorry. We have more questions concerning your whereabouts around the times of the murders of Riley Stubbs and Daisy Mellon. I know I've asked questions regarding Stubbs, but Miss Mellon hadn't been murdered then."

The coffee cup in Morgan's hand shook and sloshed on the table top. His face turned pale. "Y-you think I might've had something to do with their deaths?"

"It's all a part of our enquiry. We appreciate your speaking to us without presence of counsel."

Morgan set his cup down and put his hands in his lap. "I'm

rethinking that. Perhaps I should have a solicitor here."

"All we need to know is where you were at ten in the morning the day Daisy Mellon was murdered—yesterday? And where was your wife?"

"Yesterday?" Morgan ran his hands through his thinning hair. "I was online with the car dealership in Yorkshire finalizing the details of our contract."

"I'll need the names of your contacts there who can verify your alibi."

"Take my computer, Inspector. Do whatever you need to do. Your computer people will be able to confirm I was online from…" He paused. "…from nine thirty until ten thirty. I'm not your killer."

"What about your wife?"

He shrugged. "I'm sure she was about the place. When I'm involved with a business deal, I don't waste time keeping track of her. I can't see my wife killing anyone, but she would speak quite harshly to someone who over-watered a plant."

David hid the smile which threatened to break through and cleared his throat. "I'm afraid the situation is rather more serious than over-watering a plant."

"Bad analogy." Freddie shrugged. "I know she was very ticked off at Stubbs, but I can't see her killing him. Calling a solicitor and suing the bugger in court, yes, but not murder."

Obviously the man believed in his wife, even if he couldn't give her a decent alibi.

"Can you think of anyone who would want to frame your wife for murder?"

"Frame her? Bloody hell! Do you have evidence against my wife?"

"Her DNA has been retrieved from a hair sample at the murder scene."

Freddie's eyes bugged wide at the news. "I-I don't know what to say. Nan's a good person at heart. No enemies I know of. May not be the best housewife around, but who is nowadays?"

"Let's go back to the day of Stubbs's murder. Take me through your morning again."

Morgan reached for his cup of coffee, took a long swallow and grimaced. "I was up early, six thirty; Nan came in from the greenhouse about seven. We had some breakfast, then she left after doing the dishes around seven thirty to run errands, and..." He paused.

"Now I remember, she said she might go over to Lord Hutton's. Said Lady Jane had called earlier."

"She does some work for the Huttons?"

"Oh, yes. She and Lady Hutton are old friends. Quite an odd pair, I've always thought, but they attended the village school when they were quite young. Of course, Jane Manley, that was her name then, was the daughter of a businessman and went off to school, but their friendship lasted in spite of their different stations in life."

"Interesting," David said.

And very uncommon.

Lady Jane Hutton didn't strike him as someone who'd hobnob with those she considered beneath her station. On the other hand, the majority of his friends were coppers and ordinary people and he liked it that way.

"It's not like we're invited to dinner, but the Hutton estate provides a lot of business for the nursery. I'm not into rubbing shoulders with the titled anyway. Nan and I, we live a quiet life. Comfortable house. And it suits us both."

"Do you consider that you and your wife are happy then?"

"Yeah, happy enough. Like I said, she's not much of a housekeeper or that good a cook, but she hasn't poisoned me yet." Morgan laughed at his own joke.

"And you're certain your wife wasn't involved in an intimate relationship with Riley Stubbs?"

"Lord, no. I know how it sounds, him being dead and all, but after he stiffed her on those damned dogs, she was set to sue his arse in court."

"Thank you, Mr. Morgan. I appreciate your candid responses. You may go."

Morgan nodded, rose quickly and headed for the door without a moment's hesitation. David didn't blame the man for his hasty retreat, either.

"Interview ended at twenty past seven." And how did Nan's interview go? Guess he'd find out soon enough. He walked from the room into the observation hallway and found no sign of Beecham or his suspect. And that fact could mean one of two things: she'd asked for a solicitor or Beecham had released her.

Chapter Nineteen

The squad room had every desk full. The smell of stale coffee and sweat made breathing difficult. The overheated squad room was hot enough to roast a Christmas goose. Everyone on duty? David arched his brow at Beecham. "What's going on?"

"Called them in 'cause I felt like it." Beecham laughed, then shook his head. "We're all getting anxious now that we've identified Stubbs's killer and most likely the Mellon girl's, too."

"Nan Morgan confessed?" He didn't believe it for a second.

"No. Demanded her solicitor. We're waiting now, but I tell you, French, we've got this one tied up. Many thanks for your assistance, but you can go back to your honeymoon."

The detectives erupted in laughter. David darted a glance at Stafford. Good man. At least his sergeant knew better than to laugh. This case was anything but tied up.

"What about Evie White? Anything back on her yet? Tox screen?"

"Read it and weep. Mrs. White died of a drug overdose, booze and a massive dose of diazepam, and with a massive overdose it can't be accidental, so says Mr. Ballard." Beecham shrugged. "Poor girl. She must've been upset over her Jacko being arrested and over his seeing the Mellon girl. He's back home now, and they might've worked it out. Too bad she couldn't have waited."

"Doesn't rule out murder," David insisted.

"Only person what had a motive to kill Evie was her husband and he was in our nick."

"Yes, and you were just as certain that he was the killer. Now his wife's dead and he's free. You've rushed to judgment, and you've made another mistake while the killer still remains free to kill again."

"Go on." Beecham's brows drew together in a frown. "What's the matter? Don't you want to go home to that pretty little wife of yours?"

Enough with the personal references. He clenched his jaw and his fists. "The next person who mentions my wife, my marriage, my honeymoon or lack thereof can bloody well step outside and we'll discuss it like gentlemen."

Beecham's hands came up in a gesture of surrender. "Sorry, mate."

David scowled around the room. "Anyone else?" No one so much as met his gaze; each seemed to find something more interesting on his or her desk. "Fine. I'm positive Evie White was murdered. There were no tracks in the freshly vacuumed floor and no fingerprints on the wine bottle. That's what we know for sure."

David paced as he continued. "Was she a loose end that needed to be tied up? That's where our inquiries need to focus. And who has it in for Nan Morgan? There's a connection to all these murders. We just haven't dug deep enough to find it yet."

"You think the three are connected?" DS Tower asked.

"Tower, how long's it been since there was a murder in the Green?" "Five years. And it was a domestic thing."

"Now all of a sudden you have three—they have to be connected."

He gauged their reactions. Beecham was quiet but his expression was clearly skeptical. Tower was making notes, same as Stafford.

DC Pettigrew's expression was puzzled. "Question, guv?"

"Sure."

"If Daisy Mellon knew something she oughtn't, she might have mentioned it to someone—maybe even the killer. Maybe she mentioned what she knew to Evie White or someone else." She shook her head. "I know I'm reaching, but..."

David nodded his approval. "We need to get into these women's lives for the last week. We need to find out who they talked to, if they ever talked to each other." He pointed at Stafford. "You and Pettigrew look into Daisy Mellon's life from the time of the first murder. I'll do the same with Evie White's. Those women ran across our killer with the worst possible results."

DC Pettigrew raised her hand. "Do you really think he'll strike again?"

"I wish I knew. He's gotten a taste for it, refined his modus operandi. The first two murders strike me as personal revenge, while Evie White's wasn't as personal and therefore neater. If he's tied up all his loose ends, he may be through. He may just sit back and take his chance we'll never catch him."

"Or he may find he likes it and continue?" she suggested.

"Yes, that, or he may still have loose threads or something to prove."

"Want to know what I think? You're the one with something to prove," Beecham said with a growl. "The highly touted Detective Chief Inspector French from New Scotland Yard wants to prove his gut is better than my hard evidence. Go ahead. Waste your time. I've got the killer in custody, and you've nothing but a bunch of hot air in that gut of yours."

David appreciated Beecham's play on words and bit the inside of his mouth to hold back the laugh. No doubt Beecham would take the laughter wrongly.

He stuck his hands in his pockets. "I do have something to prove. Nothing to do with ego or turf, but until I'm convinced we have the right person, I'm not backing down."

DCI Beecham shrugged as if he could care less what David did. "It's your time you're wasting. You can have Pettigrew, but no more of my crew are going to waste their time chasing fairy stories."

Pettigrew glanced up and gave Beecham a sharp look. "It's okay for me to waste time with Inspector French's team? Why is that, Inspector? Aren't I a valuable member of your crew?"

Beecham snickered. "Of course you are, DC Pettigrew, but

you're already shagging his sergeant. I thought I'd use you for a spy to keep tabs on what they're up to, and now you've gone and spoiled that plan."

The other detectives laughed, and Pettigrew's face grew pink. "As if..." David laughed. "Bloody hell, but that was my plan as well."

Beecham looked up from beneath his sandy brows, his lips twitching with a near smile.

"Come on, Beecham. We're on the same side, but we're never going to agree until we're both satisfied who the killer is."

"Got that right."

"We've had some long days and nights." David surveyed the room, daring anyone to snicker. No one did.

"Let's go home at a decent hour tonight and get a fresh start tomorrow...unless you have any objections, DCI Beecham?"

"Could use a bite myself," Beecham responded with a shrug.

David watched the murder squad members trickle out. The air became a little easier to breathe. Tomorrow he would hit the pub. Talking to Evie's co-workers might tell him something he didn't already know about her last days.

Lady Jane winced as Edward's personal physician, Doctor Jacobi, applied a half splint to her wrist and secured it with an elastic wrap. "It's got pretty good alignment. Luckily you won't need any additional reduction. After a week, the risk of edema will be over, so come to my surgery. One of my assistants will x-ray it and then cast it for you."

"A cast? How long?"

"Total of six weeks should see it healed."

"Terribly clumsy of me. Tripping over the carpet like that," she murmured. Yes, her bastard husband should be relieved by the lie.

"You're not getting any younger, Jane. Osteoporosis has probably already set in. You've the body type for it."

"Wonderful." She adjusted her sling for more comfort. "You've just impugned my age and condemned me to a life of broken bones, hips and such."

"Fact of life my dear. Aging happens to us all. Take your calcium tablets and this other prescription. It'll help regenerate the bone loss, but follow the directions exactly. And here are some pain tablets as well. If it's not already hurting, it will certainly worsen during the night. Never fails."

"Thank you for coming all the way out here."

"Anytime, Jane. You know I'm almost always available, and when I'm not my associate Reynolds is."

"Very comforting to know." Now, if the old goat would just leave her in peace. She couldn't help but wonder about Nan. She'd tried to call her again just before the doctor arrived, but there'd been no answer at the nursery or the house. Nan hadn't answered her mobile either. Where could she be?

Jacobi let himself out and Jane reached for her mobile again. Still no answer. She tried the house, then Freddie answered. Drat.

"Lady Hutton here. Where's Nan?"

"Nan's been arrested for the murder of Riley Stubbs. They had us both down there and questioned us. They let me go, but they've still got her in the nick."

"What! Have you called a solicitor?" Dreary man needed a swift kick.

"Yes, as soon as I was released."

"Why would they arrest her of all people?"

"Said they had DNA evidence, but I can't imagine my Nan killing anyone, much less that berk."

His Nan?

"Well, it appears you have everything in order. Let me know if there's anything I can do to help. Of course, she's innocent."

"Thank you, Lady Jane. You're a good friend to her. Most find it odd, you two being so different."

Not so different, but Freddie had no need to know the truth.

"We've known each other since we were children. It's as simple as that. I must ring off now."

She hung up without waiting for whatever inane response he might have.

Her wrist definitely ached. What a bastard Edward was. She reached for the bottle of pain tablets, then stopped. Perhaps, there was a better use for them.

No, killing him was too good for him. She'd have to think of something more appropriate for his punishment.

Chapter Twenty

David drove slowly with his headlights on low beam. The road in front of his motor was shrouded deep with a heavy evening mist. He rounded a curve and didn't see the buck until too late.

He slammed on the brakes; the seat belt held and nearly choked him. Head pounded against the headrest. The front bumper hit the buck. It bounced up and onto the bonnet, then crashed into the window screen on the passenger side.

Glass cracked and made a web of fractures. Tiny slivers of safety glass stung his face and cheeks. The car careened from the impact into a dry stone fence. The head and antlers intruded through the broken window and dangled over the dashboard.

Dazed, he shook his head to clear it.

Bloody hell, why hadn't he been more careful?

He tried the accelerator. The wheels spun, but the car wouldn't budge. Nothing to do but call for a tow...as soon as he called Miranda first.

It was almost eight and I figured David would be late for dinner again. Being stuck in the country wasn't all that bad now Jamie was home, but not knowing what was going on with the investigation was the pits.

My cell phone rang—actually it didn't ring, it vibrated. Had to be David calling to tell me he was going to be late. Nothing new there.

I answered, "I know. You'll be late."

"I'm all right, but—"

"But what?" I asked, cutting him off.

"On the way home, I hit a deer. I'm all right, a few scratches, but the deer isn't. I mean the car isn't moving, so I'm calling for a tow."

"Okay. Where are you? Should Robbie and I pick you up?" "Yes, if you would, please."

"Are you sure you're all right?"

"Yes, I'm fine. I'm about five klicks from the estate. You can't miss me. I'm the only one with a dead deer on the bonnet."

"Very funny. We're on the way."

I called Robbie and quickly gave him the details and asked him to pick me up at the front entrance. My hand shook as I stuffed the cell phone inside my pocket. While I was on the phone with him, I pretended I was cool and collected, but inside I was hysterical. One of my older brothers had a close friend who was killed when his car struck a deer. At the time, everyone was devastated, including me. Ronnie was an intelligent, funny guy who treated me like a little sister instead of an annoyance.

That could've been my David. I glanced down at my hands. Still shaking. I slid them into my pockets.

Mina came into the room attired in a lovely gray silk gown. In dismay, I looked down at my jeans and running shoes. "Mina, you should be her ladyship and I should be the nanny. Am I making sense at all? And David's hit a deer."

"Oh, my. Is he all right?"

"Yes, Robbie and I are going to pick him up, David—not the deer." I collapsed on the sofa and buried my face in my hands and cried. "He could've died. My brother had a friend..." I said between sobs.

She sat down beside me and hugged me. "Now, now. You said his lordship's all right."

"Mm-hm."

"Then his motor will need a fix, but your husband will come home with all his limbs intact and everything will be fine."

"I know. I'm hormonal. What can I say?"

"Now dry your tears and wash your face, dear. The driver will be out front and you won't be ready."

I nodded and did as she ordered. Just in time too, because Fields announced Robbie was outside and waiting for me. Somewhat in control of my emotions, I ran down the front steps and hopped into the Rover.

Ahead of us the evening mist was heavy and hovered low to the ground. No wonder he hit a deer. He couldn't have seen it until he was right on it. I checked my seatbelt.

"Don't worry, your ladyship. I'll take it slowly."

Robbie kept his gaze on the road, something for which I was grateful. Hormones or not, the hovering fog and the thicket of trees lining the road all made for an eerie ride, as if he and I were the only people on a mysterious and empty planet.

"He said he's about five klicks from the estate," I said, peering into the fog which had now become so heavy it seemed to float and waver in a ghostly fashion.

"That's a rough area for deer. There are a lot of them. We'll have to organize a hunt next year...just so they don't starve in the winter. There are fewer places for them to forage with all the building going on."

I nodded. David's father had contributed to that by selling off such a large portion of the estate. "Intellectually I know it's necessary, but I don't want Jamie around during the hunt."

"Pardon me for saying so, but you don't want to coddle the boy. Hunting is a fact of life on estates like this one."

"What about the meat? Does it go for food?"

"The estate will keep some of the venison, and the hunters will keep what they kill. A properly seasoned venison stew's a treat."

"At home, my father and brothers hunt, but it's more for the sport than for food."

Okay, so I sounded like a namby-pamby girlie girl, but actually I am. My father insisted on my knowing how to handle a gun, but that was the extent of the testosterone influence in my life. As the only girl, I hung around with my mom. I did my music thing, attended all my brothers' sports events. Honestly I don't know how she handled it all.

"Hunting for sport isn't a bad thing when the animal populations need controlling."

"I can't help it. I just don't like the idea of grown men out with guns going after helpless wildlife."

He shot a quick glance in my direction. I imagined I could see disapproval in his eyes, but then he smiled. "My wife Laura's the same way." His gaze back on the road, he said, "Ah, here we are. I see his lordship waving."

I squinted and could just make out a large dark object which grew clearer the closer we came. Finally I saw David. Relief shot through me and tension drained from my body like water from the shower and left me almost giddy.

Robbie pulled up and stopped on the side of the road. I opened the door and jumped out into the damp mist. I ran over and hugged him. "Are you all right?"

"Said I was, didn't I?"

I got a closer look. "You're not fine. Your face is bleeding."

"Just some nicks from the safety glass," he reassured me. "I'm fine."

I put my hands on my hips. "Buddy boy, we're taking you to the nearest E.R." "An emergency visit isn't necessary."

"You have glass imbedded in your face. It needs attention and you're going to get it."

"Miranda, I'm fine. All I need is a wash up, a pair of tweezers, and then some dinner."

"Did you hit your head or lose consciousness? Are you hurting anywhere else? I'm a doctor's daughter, remember?"

"Not likely to forget, am I? You're turning all medical on me. No, I didn't lose consciousness, so no concussion. My only injuries are nicks on my face and hands. They sting, that's all."

Clearly he was determined he wasn't going to the E.R. "All right, but I'm taking care of your injuries myself. Mina and I will decide if you need further attention."

He smiled down at me. "All right, if Mina agrees I need medical attention, I'll call a local fellow by the name of Jacobi, but a visit to Emergency is out of the question."

"You are so stubborn, but I'll go along with that scenario."

"Robbie," David said, "I've already called the garage for a tow. They said they'd take care of the buck."

A nod from the taciturn Robbie.

I shivered, and David pulled me closer. "Let's get you out of the damp, or you'll be the one heading to Emergency."

I nodded and snuggled into the warmth of his arms. He bundled me into the Rover, then we set off through the fog for home.

Yes, I'd already come to consider Wyndswept "home".

Once they reached the estate, David allowed Miranda and Mina to guide him into the bedroom, and then wash the abrasions on his face and hands with anti-bacterial soap. "Gently, please. I'm already a veritable pin cushion. No need to make my injuries worse."

Miranda frowned and turned to her partner in crime. "Was he always this big of a baby when he was a kid?"

Mina dabbed a cotton ball in the liquid anti-infective soap and then on his face. "To be sure. The boy thought he was invincible, but if he was injured, we had to chase him around the house and then hold him down whilst I or the doctor treated his injuries."

"I'm right here, I'll have you know," he said with a grimace. "Ouch!" He winced as Miranda attacked the backs of his hands with something akin to a scouring pad.

"You're worse than Jamie. He's very brave. Why can't you be half as brave as your son?"

David looked around. "Where is he anyway? I don't want him to see me before my face is tended. He might be frightened."

"He's in his new bedroom across the hall from ours. I hope you don't mind my putting him there. It's just that I'm used to being able to hear him if he has a bad dream or needs a glass of water."

"Of course not," he said, followed with, "Easy on the knuckles.

You never know when I might need to bust someone in the chops with those."

"Who busted your face?" Jamie stood at David's side and tugged on his sleeve. So much for not scaring the boy.

"Hello, there. I'm afraid a big old deer got in the way of my motor. He crashed into the windscreen and it shattered. These are just little splinters of glass that your mom and Mina are removing."

"Does it hurt?"

"Sometimes...just a twinge, you understand." "I heard you yell 'ouch'."

David glanced up at Miranda and forced a grin. "Your mum can be quite relentless when it comes to her nursing care."

"She always takes care of me when I'm sick. She's good at that."

"Enough talking," Miranda said. "I've picked all the fragments from your knuckles—they were worse than the backs of your hands—and I'm going to apply an ointment and wrap them with gauze. How are you coming on his face, Mina?"

"I believe the scars will only add character to his face," Mina said primly, but with a decided glint in her eyes.

David levered up on his elbows. "Scars? I'm scarred?"

"For life," Mina said, deadpan. "Now lie down, my boy."

What a sad state of affairs when a man's wife and his old nanny felt they had to take charge. Perfectly ridiculous. "Hold on. I give the orders around here. You're not my nanny anymore."

His sweet wife spoke next. "No, but you agreed to our tending to your wounds, so lie still and pretend to be a grownup."

He lay back and folded his arms across his chest and then winced because his knuckles were raw. "Ridiculous." The protest was pro forma. "Fine. Do with me what you will." He turned to a wide-eyed Jamie. "Son, take note. Women will take over if you give them the least bit of latitude."

For his feeble attempt at humor, he received a poke in the ribs from his wife. "David! What a thing to say."

"It's the truth."

Jamie cocked his head to one side, his dark eyes sparkling with mischief. "You're so funny, sir. He's joking, Mum. Can't you tell?"

"Of course I can, but I wasn't sure you could."

The bright tyke sighed. "Oh, Mum. I've known David—I mean, father—ever so long and I know when he's teasing us. I really like that about him."

"Hah!" David said in triumph. "See there, my son is brilliant."

"Smarter than we are," muttered the good Mina under her breath. "And you'll need to keep an eye on him because anyone who's as smart as he is bound to get into trouble once in a while."

"Not if I can help it," Miranda said. She wrapped gauze around his last knuckle.

Thank heaven, for he was ready to explode with all the devoted attention he'd received.

Mina stood back and admired her handiwork. "I think you're only going to need a sticking plaster on a couple of spots. There's one over your eyebrow and your left cheek. The rest should heal on their own with careful washing."

"You look much better, sir."

"Thank you, son." He leaned down to Jamie's level. "So what about the scars? Am I going to be a monster? Will I scare all the other little children away?"

Jamie shrugged and grinned. "Hm, not this one anyway."

The little devil. "Fine son you are," he teased, then sat up and swung his feet off the bed. "I'll have to see for myself since I can't depend on even you to tell me the truth."

"I was teasing, too, sir. Couldn't you tell?"

David picked up his son and swung him around. "Yes, I could. You're a great kid. I couldn't ask for a better son."

With Jamie still in his arms, David walked over to the large ornate mirror on the wall. "See here and here." He pointed at the red abrasions. "That's where Mina's going to put little bandages. Do you think your mum will still love me even if I'm scarred for life?" He winked at Miranda's reflection in the mirror.

"I'm pretty sure she will, sir. After all, she took you for better or worse, didn't she?"

David grinned. "I believe you must've been listening to that marriage ceremony. I thought the fellow would never cease talking."

"I was the ring bearer and I always listen," he said solemnly. "And well you should."

"Here, let me have him." Miranda held out her arms. "Let's get your hands and face washed for dinner."

"Goody, father's having dinner with us tonight."

Miranda led his son from the room, and he looked to Mina. "I've never been happier," he told her.

"You're well and truly blessed, David. I'm thrilled for you and I know your lady mother is smiling from Heaven on this family." She wiped her eyes. "I just wish she could've lived to know Randi and her son."

"Me, too." On one hand, he couldn't help but wonder how or if his life would've been different if his mother hadn't found solace at the bottom of a wine bottle. Still, his life was rich and full and about to become even fuller if Miranda's feelings were correct. The past couldn't be changed, but the present and the future were ever-changing. He would never let his children down as his father had him. He would go to the ends of the earth to protect and support them.

Chapter Twenty-one

We'd just finished dinner when Fields announced the doctor. Okay, I'm a total worry wart and I called him without David's knowledge—just the sort of thing a sneaky and worried wife like me would do.

"Miranda?" David looked at me with a pained expression which clearly said "what have you done now?"

"Hm." I bit my bottom lip and put on my most innocent expression. "I got his number from Madison. I thought he should see you...just in case." Then I grinned and batted my lashes. "And since he's already here, you can't turn the man away after he's come all the way out here through the fog and all."

His gaze softened and a tender smile played about his mouth. "I could get used to being taken care of by you."

Well, that made me go all mushy inside. I reached over and touched his forearm, which I could do because we dined informally and I preferred to sit close to my new husband. I suppose if we do any formal entertaining, I'll have to sit at the opposite end of the table, but for now—no way.

"Show Doctor Jacobi to the morning room, Fields. I'll join him in a moment."

Mina rose from her chair. "Master Jamie, why don't you and I check out the telly in your room? I'm sure we'll find some suitable programming while your mother and father entertain the good doctor."

"Thanks, Mina," I said. After a bear hug from my son, he and

Mina left the room.

David stood and pulled out my chair. "I'm glad you're not angry because I called the doctor."

He smiled down at me. "No. Strangely I'm not. I'm getting used to your way of doing what you think is best, even if I don't always agree."

Arm in arm we went to the morning room where Dr. Jacobi waited. The morning room was a comfortable sitting area with pale yellow walls. Blue and white chintz draperies hung at the tall windows. A cushy sofa was covered in the same chintz. Two yellow wingback chairs faced the sofa with comfy pillows in the same chintz. A fire had been set in the fireplace. It flamed and popped pleasantly while the smell of hickory invited one in to have a seat. Over the mantle hung an oil painting of a hunting scene. Inside the house, the entire effect was one of comfort and warmth. Outside was another matter as the mist hung and shifted in ghostly patterns.

Dr. Jacobi rose as we entered, the obligatory introductions were made and I proceeded to describe David's injuries along with our first aid treatments.

He inspected David's hands and face. "Hm. Done quite a nice job of it. Don't think anything else will be required, except daily cleansing with an anti-bacterial soap. The hands should heal quickly—dispense with the dressings completely in three days." He peered at David's forehead and cheek. "Hm. Couple of sutures wouldn't be amiss. Good idea for the butterfly plasters, your ladyship."

I smiled. "My father's a heart surgeon in the States."

Then he smiled. "A doctor's daughter. That explains it."

"Sutures?" David said with raised brows and a tone I thought amusingly nervous.

"You can come to my surgery in the morning or I can glue them now."

"Glue?"

"Yes, quite common and less time-consuming than sutures. I usually carry some for injuries such as this."

"Glue it is then," said my not-so-brave husband, obviously anxious to avoid the needle.

"All right." Jacobi dug around in his medical bag for the glue.

"We really appreciate your coming all the way out here in the fog. You were surprisingly quick," I said.

"Quite all right," he said. "Already in the general area. Called earlier over to Lord Hutton's. Silly household accident, you know."

I was dying to know what happened, but the doc would never reveal more than he already had because of patient confidentiality.

"I hope everything's all right," David said. My husband certainly wasn't above an attempt to pump the doc for info. Nothing ventured, nothing gained—right?

I cut my gaze to David. He wore an intent expression, and I could just imagine the wheels spinning in his head.

"Well, at least you didn't use all the Super Glue," I said. After all, I wasn't above a little doc pumping either.

"No. Wasn't needed."

And that was it. The doc wasn't volunteering anything else. I felt a little deflated after that.

Once the glue was applied to David's forehead and cheek, the doc closed his bag and bid us a pleasant evening.

As soon as he was out of earshot, I turned to David. "What do you think happened over at Lord Hutton's?"

He frowned. "Damned if I know, but I'll find out one way or another." He lifted his shoulders in a casual shrug. "Still could've been one of the household staff."

"Maybe not. Maybe Lord Hutton smacks his wife around?"

"Now you're being melodramatic."

I made a face at my husband's condescending tone. "Hmph. Then why are you so curious about a simple household accident?"

He smiled, and I melted. "It's my job to be curious about anything that happens to anyone under suspicion in a murder investigation."

"Ah ha! So Lord Hutton is a suspect?"

"Only one of entirely too many suspects."

I inspected the doc's gluing. "He did a good job. You shouldn't be too scarred." I winked.

"Why are you changing the subject?" he asked with a puzzled frown.

"Because I'm not supposed to be involved, so I thought... Unless you need a good ear or a sounding board, then I don't mind taking the time to listen."

David laughed, and it was a marvelous sound. Unfortunately it didn't happen often enough to suit me. My husband is a serious man. I suppose it's the nature of his disposition and his job.

"You are a devious and sneaky woman, and I love you," he declared and patted his knee. "Why don't you come here and soothe my injuries with your soft wifely touch."

Like the good wife I am, I sat on his lap and traced his boo-boos with the tip of my finger. "How's that? Feel better now?"

"Much better," he said with a sensual growl. "And there's something else you can touch and make it all better, too."

I grinned and crossed my eyes. David had no idea but...

Fields cleared his throat. "Coffee, your lordship?"

David jumped a bit and turned around. "Yes, that'll be fine."

After the ever-so-discreet Fields shut the pocket doors and made his retreat, David shook his head and laughed. "Why didn't you warn me?"

"I didn't have time, and the doors were already open."

He gave me a swat on the behind and I planted a kiss on his nose. Obviously as newlyweds we were always in danger of providing a little risqué entertainment for the household staff...or would be if we weren't a little more careful.

We drank our coffee while he told me about Evie White's death and his grave doubts about her having committed suicide. "Three deaths in four days sound like an awfully big coincidence to me," I said, then took a tiny sip of my coffee. I'd speak to the housekeeper tomorrow about having decaf. That should pretty much seal the deal, and I hadn't even peed on a stick yet.

"Now DCI Beecham has Nan Morgan under arrest for the antiques dealer and Mellon girl's murders. Yesterday he was just as certain Jacko White was the killer."

"One thing's for sure: Jacko didn't kill his wife. Has he been released?"

David nodded. "We released him so that he could attend to her funeral arrangements." He shifted in the chair, but I let him keep talking.

"It appears that she was involved with Stubbs. We found brochures for the Algarve at the scene. That fits with his partner's story he was planning to sell the shop to you and take off with someone to the Algarve. Funny thing is one of the other women, Nicola Denton— By the way, you might've mentioned her resemblance to Cassie. She quite took me by surprise."

Oops. "She came in?"

"Yes. Said Stubbs asked her to run off with him, too."

I snuggled closer to David. "He was a real player, wasn't he?"

"An equal opportunity player, if you ask me." He drained his coffee cup, and I refilled it.

"Well, he wasn't in the best of shape when I first saw him," I said. "I can't help but wonder what he was really? Why were all these women drawn to him? Granted they must've been unhappy, but what was it that drew them to him?"

"First of all, only one of the women has admitted an involvement with him. Nan Morgan admittedly hates him because he gypped her on some collectibles. Nicola Denton denied it several times, but came forward and finally admitted a brief affair, then said he stalked her. His partner denied involvement, but the Mellon girl's testimony, if she were still alive, would refute that. Lady Hutton denied it as well, said he closed the shop as a courtesy so she could have his undivided attention."

"But he must've had something? Charisma, charm?"

"Damned if I know. Whatever it was, it wasn't apparent from his remains."

I ran my fingers through the auburn waves of David's hair. "I appreciate your catching me up on things...now that you know I'm not going off investigating on my own."

He smiled at me warmly. "I'm trusting you to take care of yourself and our baby."

I grinned. He had to know I'd never do anything to endanger the new life inside me. "So this debrief is my reward?"

"If you like," he said with a warm grin. "Another oddity. Freddie Morgan went on and on about how his wife and Lady Hutton were such close friends."

"Odd because they were friends, or because he went on and on about it?"

"Because they'd remained friends from the time they were in the local village school. Quite unusual, really. Jane went away to school, married up and snagged herself a titled husband while Nan remained working class. Say what you will about the class situation in the UK, it still exists."

"Maybe they're more than friends?" I suggested. Even though I hadn't met either one, I couldn't help but wonder.

"Gay? Is that what you mean?"

"Yes, that's exactly what I mean."

"Hmm." David rubbed his chin. "That brings some other possibilities to mind." I brightened. "Like what?"

"Like I might just take you up to bed and..." he whispered in my ear, "kiss you all the way from your head to your toes, with a stop for a snack midway."

"Omigod, did you just say..." I looked around. Luckily the doors were still shut. "...you were going to eat me?"

He positively leered at me. "Yes, that's it, luv. And I'd do it right here if we were alone."

I shook my finger in his face. "You are so busted. Why do you men get so turned on by the thought of two women together?"

"Bloody hell." He shook his head. "I don't know why, but it's a known fact."

"I can't believe you're admitting this to me. Would you want me to be with another woman? Would you watch or join in?"

Not that I ever would be with another woman, but it was fun teasing my husband.

He gave me a long look, rubbed his chin and took his time answering. "I don't know. It's all I can do to handle the feisty woman I've married."

I wrinkled my nose and shot him a quick smile. "As long as you keep your fantasies and your reality separate, I'll allow you to live another day." I licked my lips, because it never fails to turn him on, and tucked a curl behind his ear.

"Miranda, stop teasing. Let's go to bed," he whispered in my ear. Who was I to deny him his—and my—pleasure?

Chapter Twenty-two

Friday

The next morning dawned with clouds low in the sky. David stepped outside and recognized the smell of more snow coming. The mist hadn't begun to abate, and driving conditions weren't much better than they were the night before. He'd commandeered Robbie's Rover because he needed a dependable vehicle. Doubtful his own motor would be ready in less than two weeks.

He flexed his hands, the fingers somewhat stiff. The knuckle abrasions stung, but he was none the worse for wear. After a somewhat tedious drive, he reached the village stationhouse without incident. Still, thoughts of the new life Miranda carried sent an unknown thrill though his mind and heart. A son or a daughter.

What a gift.

DCI Beecham greeted him with a wide smile. "What the bloody hell happened to you? Did your..." The man paused, apparently deciding to err on the side of caution.

David smiled back and shrugged. "Hit a buck on the way home last night. Damned fog. Had some glass slivers in my hands and face. Save your sympathy for the buck. He didn't make it."

"I say, that's too bad. Could've been bloody worse."

David nodded. "Don't I know it. The garage says it'll be two weeks or more before my Roller's ready."

"What are you driving?"

"The old Rover used on the estate."

"Still, handy you have an extra motor or two."

"Yes. Wish I'd been driving it instead of the Roller. Be damned less expensive to repair."

Beecham snorted. "You toffs are all alike. Moaning when you have insurance."

"Yes, but there's a damned large deductible, and you have some mistaken idea that I'm rolling in pound notes at night when I go to sleep. The Inland Revenuc takes a large chunk of my income."

"I'm going to cry, French. I'm so sorry for you."

"There's no doubt about it, Beecham. I'm privileged. Even so, I'm still a copper with a wife and new son and now—" He stopped before he blurted it out.

Beecham's eyebrows arched. "What?"

"Nothing." David smiled on the inside. A new baby, a new start for all of them. He wanted to shout it everywhere, but it was entirely too soon. Too much could go wrong.

"Hmph. I could guess, but I wouldn't want to step outside for a gentlemanly discussion."

"Wise of you." David checked his watch. "I'm off to the pub to interview Evie White's workmates."

"You're not letting up on the idea she was murdered, are you?" Beecham shook his head.

"No, I'm not." David checked his pocket for his notepad. "Stafford and Pettigrew are already out, I hope, interviewing Daisy Mellon's workmates. Hopefully they'll turn up something useful."

"Good luck, French."

"What's on your agenda today?"

"Firming up my case on Nan Morgan," Beecham said with a satisfied smile.

"Good luck with that," David replied with a broad smile. He turned and left Beecham standing there with his mouth open. What was it his old mentor'd said? "Evidence doesn't lie."

This time it had.

*

David hit the pub at opening time. He headed for the bar and the publican. He was tall and broad-shouldered with a belly running to fat. "Chief Inspector French," he said, showing his warrant card. "Mr. Tanner?"

The publican wiped the bar with a white cloth. "What can I do for you, Chief Inspector? This about Evie?"

"Yes. I'd like a word with you and your employees as well. I'll make it brief. You're all working."

Tanner shrugged. "Not too busy yet. Ask yer questions. "Bout Evie, are they?"

"Yes. Just tell me what you know about her. Anything out of the ordinary the last week or so?"

Tanner kept swabbing down the bar top as he talked. "Hard worker, came to work in a timely fashion and got on well with her mates. She had a rotter for a husband. Had to warn him 'bout bothering her when she was working."

"That's it?"

"Busy place here. Don't have a lot of time for personal conversations. Her mates Belinda and Carrie over there could tell you more...maybe." He nodded at the two waitresses standing at the end of the bar. One was tall, thin and had dark hair. She cast him a suspicious glare, while the other was short and plump, a redhead with an infectious laugh.

"Thank you for your cooperation."

The pub owner nodded and turned to drying tankards.

"Which one of you is Belinda?" he asked.

The redhead cocked her head to the side and grinned. "I might be." "I'm DCI French and I'd like a word with you."

"Sure." She led the way to a corner table and plopped down in a chair. She leaned forward on her elbows. "Damned shame about her committing suicide. I blame that husband of hers. He smacked her around more than he should. She couldn't always hide the bruises."

"I don't believe she killed herself," he said quietly.

"You don't? Fancy that. You think she was done in by him what killed Riley Stubbs and Daisy?"

"Perhaps." He pulled out his notebook. "Besides her husband, did she get along well with everyone else?"

"Yeah. She was a good workmate. We enjoyed many a good gossip session...after work usually, not during work hours 'cause Guy can be a bugger when he wants." She took a quick glance over her shoulder in Tanner's direction.

"What did you gossip about...recently I mean?"

Belinda twisted her mouth to one side as she considered his question, then she leaned forward and said in a low tone, "There was this one deal we figured out. Nothing for sure, mind you, but what we suspected."

"Go on."

"A very odd couple was in here one afternoon when business was slow, or I might not've noticed at all."

"Yes?" Dammit, woman, tell me.

"The woman with the nursery, Nan Richmond—forget her married name—she came in and five minutes later Lady Hutton joined her at the back table. An odd couple, indeed. Nan, she came to the bar, ordered, and took their drinks to the table where the lady waited all prissy like. They had their heads together for a while, couldn't hear a word, but then I saw them holding hands underneath the bloody table! I couldn't believe my eyes." She shivered.

"Anything else?"

"No, but I called Evie over and gave her the nudge. Neither of us could believe it, but there they were—big as life—if you had eyes to see."

"Ever see them together again?"

Belinda shook her head. "Nah. Hope I don't ever again."

"Thank you. Will you send Carrie over?"

Belinda nodded and motioned for Carrie to take her place.

Carrie marched over and sat down. "So, you're a copper and you're going to waste time asking honest working folk stupid questions while there's a killer running loose." Her tone was as argumentative as her words.

"I take it you don't have much use for us coppers?"

She leaned back, frowning at him. "I'd have more if you found the bloody bastard what killed our Evie."

"You don't think she committed suicide? Everyone else does."

"You don't or you wouldn't be here."

Astute woman. Did she know something or was it her woman's intuition? "Tell me what makes you think she was murdered."

"I overheard something she said to a customer."

"Go on."

"He must've made a pass at her. I heard her make a smart remark about him taking care of his wife at home and she wouldn't be running to a woman for comfort."

"Who was the customer?"

"Didn't get a look at him. I was in the kitchen chewing Rafe's ear off about a problem with one of my orders. I guess they call that multi-tasking. By the time, I got out of the kitchen, they were both gone. She came back, said she'd gone for a quick smoke, but she wouldn't tell me who she was talking to. Said it was a need-to-know situation, and I didn't need to know."

"Evie have any other run-ins with customers?"

Carrie shook her head. "None as I know of."

"Thank you. Don't mention this incident to anyone else."

Her eyes widened. "You think she said the wrong thing to the wrong person?" "Very possibly."

"I can keep my lip zipped for sure." She made the gesture of zipping her mouth.

Evie'd been killed to keep her quiet about certain things. He could guess who the unknowing husband was. Another interview was in order and it was one he dreaded. Belligerent, arrogant and nearly untouchable Lord Hutton.

DS Stafford and DC Pettigrew greeted David on his return from the pub. "We think you should talk to Millie Benson, guv," Stafford said. "She was Daisy Mellon's boss and the owner of the Shear Haven. Thinks she might've overheard Daisy talking to someone not long before her death. Said she'd talk to the boss and no one else."

"Good. Bring her in."

Pettigrew tripped out and quickly brought the woman to an interview room. David observed her before entering. A large and flamboyant woman dressed in a smock so pink it almost glowed, she sat hunched over and rocked back and forth. Her hair was arranged in curls and drawn back in some kind of...deal. Women's hairstyles left him amused at best and confused at their worst. Millie Benson's was somewhere on the amused end of the continuum.

No matter. If the woman had information, he aimed to hear it.

He entered the room and sat across the table from her. "Ms. Benson, I'm DCI French. My detectives tell me you've information which might assist us in this enquiry."

Her gaze darted around the room. "Are we being recorded?"

"Do you wish this off the record? I must warn you that should this information lead to an arrest, there's every possibility you will be called to testify."

Her substantial bosom heaved and she fanned her cheeks with her hand. "Oh, dearie me, I don't know wot to do."

"Are you afraid of someone?"

She nodded, her head nearly vibrating with the intensity of her nods. "I'm bloody afraid of being *killed* like poor Daisy."

David leaned forward and spoke quietly. "I assure you your identity and the information you provide won't leave the murder squad. But make no mistake. If you have knowledge which will help us bring this killer to justice, you're obligated to assist us."

The hairdresser leaned back and took a deep breath. "You're saying I owe it to the women of the village to tell wot I know?"

"Yes." He held back his anger and the urge to throttle the woman until she gave it up. The women of the village included his wife, even if she was forty klicks away at the estate.

"Daisy made a phone call using the shop's phone. Normally she uses 'er cell, but for some reason she was yakking on our business phone. I nudged 'er to make it snappy for that reason."

"Go on."

"All I 'eard 'er say was, 'Saw your Rover turn in to the back alley that day.' She listened for a second or two like and then said, 'I want more.' That was the day before she was murdered. At the time I didn't think too much, but now with everything that's 'appened…" She gave her cheeks another good fanning. "You understand why I'm afraid, don't you?"

"Indeed. But we'll do everything we can to protect you. My sergeant will see you back to your shop and take you out by the rear exit."

"Thank you, Inspector. I appreciate it."

"Do you live alone?"

"No, sir. Thank goodness. My man is retired and is always about the place."

"Good. Don't go off anywhere with anyone, whether you know them or not. Stick to your shop and home."

"Right."

Her eyes were wide with fear and her hands shook. He'd scared her, as he'd meant to do. Three deaths were three too many, and he didn't want any more on his watch.

Stafford escorted the woman from the interview room, and David headed back to his desk. Phil Denton and Lord Hutton—they were next on his list to interview.

David sat at his desk and read through his notes as a refresher. Phil Denton, husband of the Cassie look-alike, was a property developer. Had he discovered his wife had an affair with Stubbs? Had Stubbs confronted Denton who took matters into his own hands?

Wouldn't be the first or last time a jealous husband lost his temper with his wife's lover.

Lord Edward Norris Hutton—what would make a man turn homicidal at his stage in life? Mid-fifties, wealthy, with an elegant if somewhat flawed wife. Was there something to the notion that Lady Hutton and her childhood friend were lovers? Someone had certainly gone to a lot of trouble to implicate Nan Morgan in the

Stubbs murder.

It was a well-planned and well-executed murder. The Mellon girl's was more hurried, but still well-executed. The lack of evidence from underneath her nails bespoke of a careful, well-informed killer, but one with less time to plan since it was very possible she was blackmailing him.

He quickly made two telephone calls. The one to Denton was quickly resolved when the property developer grudgingly agreed to come in between business calls.

To say his call to Hutton hadn't gone as well was an understatement.

"You've already interviewed my wife and me once. I don't see the need for a repeat of your insulting charges."

"New information has come to light, and I have additional questions." On impulse, he added, "For both of you."

"You can't seriously expect to drag my wife down to the police station for more questioning of the most impertinent kind?"

"That's exactly what I expect."

"We'll see about that. Our solicitor will arrange a time."

Ah ha.

"As you wish, Lord Hutton," He said obsequiously, then added with a bite in his tone, "as long as you make it today."

"I expected better from one of my own class."

"Haven't you heard? Justice is blind." David rang off, leaving Hutton to sputter and fume to dead air.

"Stafford!"

The sergeant and DC Pettigrew both came running. "Yes, sir."

"Phil Denton will be coming in around four for an interview. And sometime Lord Hutton, his wife and their solicitor are also coming in at my request."

Stafford's eyes widened. "Sounds like the Huttons have something to hide, guv."

"Yes." David smiled and nodded. "It does indeed. And if we can manage it, I want them interviewed separately. Pettigrew, I want you to wait with Lady Hutton. Offer her tea, make her comfortable while I rattle Lord Hutton's cage."

Pettigrew's cheeks pinked with excitement. "You think she'll trust me with some womanly confidence?"

"It's possible, but mainly it'll upset his lordship to have her out of his line of sight where he can't be sure she's not spilling something she shouldn't."

"Divide and conquer, eh?" Stafford asked.

"Exactly. One of the oldest interrogatory methods in the book."

Chapter Twenty-three

After David left for work, I looked out the bedroom window and contemplated going back to bed and pulling the down-filled duvet over my head. The fog surrounded the manor house and it was so cold I could almost imagine the fog had turned to a bank of movable snow. But instead I heard a robust shout from Jamie's room.

"Mummy!" Then a rush of feet.

"The floor's cold," I said. "Where are your shoes?"

"You aren't wearing any." Hands on hips, his entire attitude was that he was the grownup and I the child.

"That's how I knew the floor was cold, kiddo." "I'll get dressed. I want to play outside."

"You're not going anywhere, buster. Not until the fog burns off...and then we'll have to see what it's like outside."

His bottom lip pushed out. "When am I going back to school?"

"When we get settled again in London."

"But I'll be behind in my studies."

"Master James." Mina's welcome voice rang out. "Did I hear you ask about your studies?"

A smile played about his mouth as he gauged our responses. "Yes. I can't play outside and I can't go to school. What's a boy supposed to do all day?"

"Never fear." Mina bent down to his level. "I can find ways to occupy a boy. First, I suggest you dress, wash your hands and face and brush your teeth and come down to breakfast. Afterwards, we'll go to the schoolroom for your lessons."

Jamie cut his dark olive brown eyes at me and gave a world-weary shrug. "I had to ask."

"The schoolroom?" I asked. "It was dark and shrouded on my tour the other day."

"I spoke with Madison yesterday, and we deemed it time the schoolroom was aired and had a proper scrub."

"I hadn't even thought about it. I don't know what I'm going to do when you go back to Provençe and Jean-Luc."

"If you wish, I can check on schools in the area, or you could hire a tutor."

"That's just it. I don't know how long we'll be here."

"If you hire a private tutor, he can return with your family to London whenever the time comes. Jamie's mid-term in his studies and perhaps you want him to start at a new school in the fall, but for now a tutor, since returning to his day school in Oxford isn't feasible."

"A tutor sounds great, but I'll speak to David tonight for a final decision."

After all, it was David's money we'd be spending on the tutor. I could make decisions all by myself, but I was already overwhelmed by the same fatigue I remembered having early in my previous pregnancy.

"If you don't mind," Mina said, "I'm going to find a nice thick romance novel for you to read. You look like you could afford to take it easy for a change."

"Oh do. I'll finish dressing and head down to the morning room for coffee—no, it should be decaf—I need to instruct the staff about that."

"Already taken care of, Randi. Very discreetly I might add."

"Okay then, I'll curl up in front of the fire and read all day."

"And don't you worry, I'll keep young Jamie occupied with his studies."

"Thank you, Mina." Full of gratitude, I gave her a big hug and let her go off to corral my son into some studying.

*

The telephone rang. Anxious for the interviews to begin, David snatched it, answering, "French."

"Philip Denton to see you, guv," the desk sergeant said.

"Send him back, but have him escorted to interview two."

As usual, he waited until the man was seated and observed him through the two-way glass. Denton was of medium height and well-built, with bright red hair, cut short. His skin tone was florid which fit with the red hair. His suit was Savile Row tailored and the cut flattered his muscular body.

For a while, Denton sat calmly, with only an occasional glance at his watch. After ten minutes, the glances became more frequent, and the irritation of being kept waiting began to show on Denton as the man drummed his finger tips on the table.

David opened the door and entered the interview room.

Denton rose and held out his hand. "Chief Inspector French?"

He ignored the proffered hand and gave a quick nod. "Yes, Mr. Denton. Sorry about the wait. I appreciate your taking time from your busy schedule to come down here." He gestured for Denton to have a seat and then turned on the recorder.

Denton flicked a speck of something off his suit and eased back into the chair. "I understand you've already spoken with my wife."

"Yes, twice."

"Twice?" An expression of shock crossed Denton's face. His posture grew tense.

"Yes, she made an amendment to an earlier statement." David shrugged. "You can discuss that with her at home, but I have some questions about your whereabouts on Monday and Wednesday mornings, as well as Wednesday evening."

"You think I had something to do with the murders?" Denton partially rose, but David motioned him down. "But why Wednesday evening? Has someone else been murdered?"

"A hairdresser by the name of Evie White died under unusual circumstances Wednesday evening. We can't rule out her death as a homicide."

A hint of irritation flashed over his face. "I don't even know an Evie White, but hold on. I'll check my mobile." He pulled out the gadget and tapped on the screen with a stylus. "Monday, I was on the road to Keyeston checking out several properties from eight until eleven."

"Anyone who can verify that?"

"I was alone. Typically I check out properties on my own. Occasionally I meet an owner or estate agent at the property."

"So which was it on Monday?"

"I checked four residential and two commercial properties, all alone, then met with the representative of an auction house—Reston's."

Basically the man had no alibi for the time of Stubbs's murder. "What about Wednesday morning?"

More tapping on the mobile. "Attended an auction in Essex county. I picked up my paddle at ten and turned it in at two. I was seen by several people and picked up five new properties in Essex. And I don't know that hairdresser girl. No dealings with her. Nor has my wife. Has her hair done in Keyeston."

"Wednesday evening?"

"Dinner meeting with my business partner at the White Goose in Keyeston. He arrived rather late, though. Don't remember his excuse."

"His name?"

Denton took a deep breath.

Why was he hesitating?

"All right. It isn't generally known that I have a partner. He's of the silent variety and doesn't want his involvement in the business known."

Tamping down his impatience, David said, "If he's your only alibi, I need his name."

"All right. Lord Hutton. He's my partner." Denton leaned back in the chair.

"Satisfied?"

Lord Hutton, again. "Specifics. What time did he arrive?"

"We were to meet at eight, but he didn't show up until eight forty-five. I was right put out, but he paid for dinner, so I figured we were even. The maitre d' can verify the time I arrived."

"That's it then," David said. "Interview ended at three forty-five." He shut off the recorder. What would Denton say off record?

"I'd like to know about my wife's amended testimony."

David pulled out his notes as if he couldn't quite remember. "Ah, yes. Here we go. She was particularly concerned she might be in danger and gave me a reason why."

Denton's face grew red. He banged his fist on the table. "Bloody hell! She had an affair with that bastard, didn't she? That's what she came to tell you. I'd wager a Victorian townhouse on it."

"She also needed reassurance you weren't guilty of Stubbs's murder."

Denton's mouth formed a thin hard line. "So that's what this interview is about? Needed to reassure my wife I wasn't a murderer. Oh yeah, gotta love that."

"No, it's to reassure me."

"And are you reassured?"

"Not completely. Thank you for your cooperation."

"You never cautioned me." Obvious alarm constricted the man's throat until his voice sounded worse than a fingernail scratched along a windowpane.

"You weren't cautioned because you haven't been charged with any crime."

"I'm free to go?"

"Yes. Good idea if you remained within the county."

Denton glared. "My business takes me out of the bloody county. How do you expect me to earn a living?"

"Perhaps you could at least confine yourself to East Anglia?"

"Yeah, whatever!" Denton stomped out without further argument. Now, if only Lord Hutton would be so forthcoming. But chances of that were slim to nonexistent.

David rubbed his chin while he considered the new information: the business partnership between Denton and Lord Hutton. There was the suspicious matter of Hutton's being late for dinner the same evening Evie White met her death. And now both

Lord and Lady Hutton and their no-doubt London solicitor were on the way to the station.

He reached for his coffee and drained the cup down to the bitter dregs.

Too soon, Lord Hutton and his solicitor swept into the stationhouse. Wearing some sort of sling and wrapping on her left wrist, Lady Hutton quietly trailed behind the two men.

The small household accident?

The ever-so-solicitous DC Pettigrew cut Lady Hutton from the group as neatly as a Border Collie cutting sheep from the flock by offering her tea and a place to sit quietly, which just happened to be in interview one.

Stafford showed Lord Hutton and his solicitor into interview two. The Keyeston solicitor was a dapper little man, with a bit of a barrel chest. He carried a briefcase which appeared to weigh almost as much as he.

"Thomas E. Smythe, Esquire," he said, setting the case on the desk. David nodded. "Chief Inspector French."

"Lord and Lady Hutton have agreed to your request to come in and assist with your enquiry. And I've come along to protect their interests."

"I have a few questions for Lord Hutton."

A silent Hutton sat down and crossed his leg over his other knee. Smythe peered over his glasses. "And questions for Lady Hutton? It was my understanding that you requested her presence as well."

"Lady Hutton—a couple of questions for clarification. Nothing for her solicitor to worry about."

"I'll be the judge of that."

"Of course. Mr. Smythe." He turned on the recorder. Gave the date and time. "Interview with Lord Edward Hutton. In attendance, Lord Hutton's solicitor Edward Smythe, Esquire and DCI David French."

He hoped Pettigrew was off to a better start with Lady Hutton.

＊

Detective Constable Alice Pettigrew was thrilled DCI French had entrusted her with interviewing—more like babysitting really—Lady Hutton. The woman was everything Alice would never be: rich, titled, privileged.

"I'm DC Pettigrew, Lady Hutton, why don't you wait in here." Alice showed her the way into interview one. "Have a seat. What about a pillow for your poor arm? How about a cup of tea or coffee?"

Her ladyship glanced down at her arm and lifted her shoulders in a graceful shrug. "Thank you, but the sling is sufficient. And a cup of tea would be lovely."

Alice started from the room, but stopped. "Cream or lemon or sugar?"

"Artificial sweetener if you have it."

"I keep some at my desk. Can't afford to pack on the weight in this job."

Her ladyship smiled politely. Okay, so the lady could care less, but a little female small talk would make her more at ease in the long run.

She returned quickly with the tea and one for herself as well. Just two women sharing a cuppa. That was the atmosphere she was going for.

"Now then. Aren't these murders just awful? Makes me afraid and I'm on the force. I'm trained to take care of myself, but this fellow must be someone in the village, someone we all know and maybe trust. That's what really scares me."

"Yes." Her ladyship nodded, took a small sip of her tea and swallowed. "One never truly knows what evil lurks in another's mind...or what someone is capable of doing."

Her gaze went to her arm, but remained averted from Alice's. Had someone broken her arm?

"How did you break your poor wrist?" Alice asked in the most solicitous manner she could manage. After all, if the husband had broken it, she'd enjoy a session with him and teach him some manners.

"At home. I stumbled over the edge of a rug and my wrist hit a side table. Stupid accident really."

Oh, yeah? Then why did her ladyship's head shake ever so slightly as if denying the words as she spoke them?

The mouth might lie, but body language didn't.

"My dad used to knock my mum around. Broke her wrist once…among other parts." Alice shrugged as if it were a common occurrence, when in truth her dad and mum would've been horrified by her lying at their expense.

"How terrible." Her ladyship's eyes widened, but her gaze went to her wrist. "I can't understand why a man would treat a woman like that. They're supposed to be our protectors." Her tone rose in pitch as she uttered those words.

Alice considered for a moment, then said, "Your husband—he didn't hurt you, did he?"

"Oh, no! Of course he didn't." Lady Hutton held her arm protectively.

"Because there are places—women's shelters—where you can be protected."

"You're confused, DC Pettigrew. This…" She held up her wrist. "…was an accident."

"I'm sorry. I just had to make sure. Because of my family history, I'm very protective toward the women who come to me. I take our mission to protect and serve as the truest part of my job. I didn't mean to offend you or Lord Hutton."

For the first time since coming into the interview room, Lady Hutton met Alice's gaze straight on. "I appreciate your concern, DC Pettigrew. Truly I do."

Lady Hutton rubbed the sling and averted her eyes again. "Do you know what they want with us? My husband especially? He wasn't very happy about being called down here. After all, we were interviewed by Chief Inspector French earlier this week."

Alice shrugged. "I'm not sure. DCI French doesn't share all his thoughts on a case with someone at my level, but I think it might have something to do with new evidence."

"We want to cooperate," Lady Hutton said with a smile, drifting into a more relaxed mode. "But it's a bit off-putting to be summoned in such a manner."

Alice shook her head. "Oh, no. It's not all that unusual. In murder investigations multiple interviews are often necessary. It's easier to rule out a person or persons if their alibis can be verified."

"But I don't understand why my husband and I are considered suspects. Oh, some village tittle-tattle actually had me having an affair with the antiques dealer. I suppose it might make someone like the inspector consider a jealous husband angle, but nothing could be farther from the truth."

Alice nodded. "I can see why you'd be upset. Gossip is a fact of village life, though. I don't see that changing anytime soon."

"No, I don't suppose it will." Lady Hutton started drumming her fingers against the table top. "How much longer do you think they'll be with my husband?"

"I don't know, your ladyship," Alice said with a shake of her head. She dug in her pocket. "I'm going to give you my card." She handed it to Lady Hutton who took it with a polite smile. "And if you think of anything, even the smallest detail during the times of the murders that might help us, I'd appreciate a call."

Lady Hutton pursed her mouth, then asked, "What were the times of the murders?"

Hm. Was the lady suspicious of her husband?

"Let's see here." Alice pulled out her notepad and riffled through the pages. "The Stubbs murder took place between seven and nine on Monday morning. The Mellon girl's Wednesday between eight and ten. Evie White's TOD—that's time of death—is a little more fluid, but somewhere between five and ten."

"Well, I can help with my husband's alibis for those times. He always walks the dogs in the mornings...quite long walks for several hours."

"Always? Every single day?" Bloody man had nothing better to do than take his pooches for a long walk every blooming day?

"Yes. Never fails."

"There you have it." Alice smiled. "The Mellon girl's murder actually occurred very near your estate. They must want to ask him if he saw anything." She closed her notepad and left it on the table between them. Lady Hutton's gaze was riveted to the pad.

"What about Wednesday evening? Was he home?"

"That's a little more difficult. I know he had a dinner meeting with his business partner. Those are always so tedious I never attend, but he left the estate around four—said he had errands to attend to before the dinner at eight—and didn't return until after eleven." She smiled at Alice. "I'm sure he'll have his entire itinerary in his mobile diary and then his business partner can verify his time at the meeting."

Alice hoped she could keep all the details straight in her head long enough to get them recorded in her notepad. Writing them down now might halt her ladyship's talkative mood. "Would you like another cup of tea?"

"That depends," Lady Hutton said with a tired sigh. "Do you think they'll be much longer?"

"Honestly I don't know, your ladyship. It takes as long as it takes." "Then yes, thank you. I would like another cup."

Alice picked up her notepad and strode from the interview room. For a second she stopped and observed her interviewee who glanced around the room, patted her well-coifed hair, then adjusted her sling strap.

In the guise of providing her husband with alibis for the times of the murders, the lady was really giving the police large pockets of time where her husband could've committed them.

And why would she do that?

He'd broken her wrist for some reason. It would pay to see her x-rays to see if they could determine just how the bone was broken.

Satisfied, Alice then went to her desk and quickly sketched out the details on her notepad and noted questions she still had. She poured another cup of tea, but before taking it in, she stopped at interview two. DCI French was leaned back in his chair. Lord Hutton had a bored expression on his patrician face and the fancy

London solicitor was shaking his head back and forth.

Alice entered the interview room. Lady Hutton jumped. "Oh, you startled me." She reached for the cuppa. "Thank you. This is so thoughtful."

"One more thing. Did you have your wrist x-rayed?"

"No, Jacobi—our physician—tugged on it and pronounced the alignment was good enough. No pins needed. I'm to go to his surgery in a week to have it x-rayed and then his nurse will apply a hard cast. It's just sort of splinted now."

Bugger, no x-ray films. No way to tell if it was a clean break or more of a twist. That's where she'd put her money. An avulsion break.

"By the way, your ladyship, I checked on DCI French and it appears like things won't go much longer."

Not if the solicitor had anything to say about it, it wouldn't.

David intended to take his time with this interrogation. He leaned back in the chair and pulled out his notepad and made a show of reading his notes.

"Chief Inspector, ask your questions and allow my client and his wife to go on their way."

"Lord Hutton, first of all, where were you on the mornings of Monday and Wednesday?"

Hutton took a deep breath. "I've already given you a statement regarding my whereabouts."

"On Monday morning you were walking the estate lands with your dogs, but I need the same information for Wednesday morning and Wednesday evening."

"I walk the dogs every day—long walks, Chief Inspector. If I'd known some little tart was going to be murdered, surely I would be able to come up with a better alibi for my Wednesday morning perambulation."

"Yes, it would've made this much simpler. What about Wednesday afternoon and evening?" Smythe held up his hand. "Enough of this fishing expedition. Do you have evidence connecting my client with the murders or not? It's my understanding a woman has already been arrested for the murder of the antiques dealer. Am I mistaken?"

"No."

"Then I must insist you stop harassing my client."

"Why don't you want your client to answer my questions concerning his whereabouts on Wednesday?"

Hutton took a deep breath. "I'll answer your bloody nosy questions."

"Lord Hutton," the solicitor interjected. "I'm advising you to remain silent."

"I was with my mistress from four-thirty until half past seven. I left her to meet with my business partner at eight in Keyeston. He was late, didn't arrive until around eight forty-five."

So who was lying? Denton or Hutton?

"The name of your mistress and your business partner?"

"Must I name her? That's a caddish thing to do. I freely admit I'm guilty of adultery—not murder."

"I have to verify your alibi."

"My business partner—or rather I'm his silent partner—is Philip Denton. He's a local property developer."

"Quit beating around the bush. The name of your mistress?"

"Nicola Denton," Hutton said in a low tone. "And I would appreciate your discretion in this matter. I love my wife, but…"

Hutton had balls of steel. Having an affair with his business partner's wife.

"We'll keep it quiet," David said, "as long as it doesn't impede our investigation, but we'll need to interview both of them." No need for Hutton to know they'd both already been interviewed, but indeed they would be again.

Smythe picked up his briefcase. "Good. We're through then. My client has cooperated with you. Good day."

"What about my wife?"

"I don't think we have anything else to ask her after all," David said. "Sorry for dragging her down here. I had no idea she'd been injured."

Hutton gave a dismissive wave. "Silly household stumble over a carpet or some such thing."

When Lord and Lady Hutton left, David noticed a backward glance from her ladyship which held his gaze for a moment. Was there something she wanted to tell him? Something she was afraid to say in the presence of her husband?

As soon as the Huttons had cleared the stationhouse, David called his team together. First, Pettigrew gave him a quick rundown on her interview with Lady Hutton.

"Now then, Stafford, I want you to interview the maitre d'. Place called the White Goose in Keyeston. Find out what times Denton and Lord Hutton arrived, specifically who was late and who was on time."

Stafford nodded. "Get right on it, guv."

David turned to Pettigrew. "Hutton says he was out with his dogs on both Monday and Wednesday mornings. Talk to anyone in the area who might've seen him walking the estate. Find out if there's any spot he might've tied the dogs and taken off on his own. Daisy Mellon's murder scene was actually on the periphery of his lands. I want you to take a forensics tech out there and see if there's any trace evidence from the dogs anywhere near that crime scene."

"Yes, sir." Then she frowned. "It's a big estate, guv."

David smiled. "You want some help? Of course you do. All right. I'll have another go at Nicola Denton and then I'll check out the maitre d' in Keyeston."

"Tonight, sir?" Stafford looked over his shoulder at the window.

"Bloody hell," David said. "Look at the time. It's already dark. No, tomorrow." He smiled. "But I could call my wife and see if she'd like to have dinner in Keyeston."

"Yes, sir." Stafford executed a sharp salute. "You set a sterling example, sir."

"Out of here before I change my mind."

Chapter Twenty-four

Out of the blue David called and asked if I'd like to have dinner in Keyeston. Since I'd done nothing all day but read a very spicy romance novel, the idea of a dinner date with my husband pleased me very much.

After I let Cook know we wouldn't be dining at home, I rushed to tell Mina our plans.

"Excellent idea. Now aren't you glad you rested today. Master James and I will have a simple dinner and I'll find some appropriate programming to occupy him after dinner, and I'll have him read me a story and see that he's in bed by eight."

"You're wonderful, as always." I gave her a hug and headed to my bedroom for a quick wardrobe inspection, then a shower. I settled on a pair of navy light wool slacks, a white wool sweater with a cowl collar, and a pale blue wool blazer. The effect was warm and feminine and definitely not too dressy.

I didn't want to appear to be trying too hard. Classy and comfortable were my goals as far as my budget allowed. I added a navy purse and shoes, then pulled out a gold charm bracelet that Jamie, with input from David, gave me for Christmas. It already had a Christmas tree, a baby boy and the Eiffel Tower on it. At the time, Jamie informed me each birthday and holiday would result in an additional charm.

How wonderful of David to come up with such a sweet idea for Jamie's gift, since mothers are notoriously difficult to buy for. The charm would always give my son a head start and, of course, stress the importance of how much women love jewelry as presents. This vital knowledge will serve him well in his adult life, and his future wife will thank me—of that I'm sure.

By the time I finished my shower, hair, and makeup, I heard David coming up the stairs.

He poked his head into the bedroom. "About ready?"

I need another thirty minutes," I replied from the bathroom.

"Really? I need a quick shave," he said, rubbing his strong chin, but his tone was a little on the grouchy side.

I stepped from the bathroom into the bedroom and twirled around for his approval. "Just kidding," I said. "How do I look?"

His gaze softened; his soft gray eyes warmed the longer he looked at me. "You're lovely. So lovely it hurts." He pulled me into his arms.

I melted, but then I always do when David pays me a compliment.

During our drive to Keyeston, I reached across and placed my hand on David's knee. He'd changed into a fresh white shirt, burgundy silk tie and a very fine gray wool suit. "I'm so glad you thought of this," I said.

He frowned for a second and chewed his bottom lip. "What's wrong?"

"It's partially business," he admitted. "Do you mind?"

"Not unless you think there's going to be a shootout of some kind."

"Nothing like that." He flashed me a quick smile. "I need to question the maitre d'...briefly."

Frankly I was glad he was taking me along for a small part of the investigation. "This must mean you're beginning to trust I won't get involved."

"Yes." He smiled over at me and covered my hand with his large one. Our fingers twined together. This affectionate and loving man was so different from my first—I shook my head to erase the memories. I didn't want anything to spoil our evening.

I started cautiously. "How does a maitre d' fit into your investigation?" He grinned. "You're still curious, though. Aren't you?"

"I never promised I wouldn't ask questions." I poked his thigh with my thumb for emphasis.

"All right. On the evening of Evie White's murder, two suspects both say they had dinner at the White Goose, but that the other was late."

"Maybe they should've gotten their alibis straight before they talked to you."

"They're business partners and they had dinner reservations for eight, but one of them showed up at eight forty-five. I need to know which one of them was late for dinner."

"Because he'd be the one who probably murdered Evie White?" "Correct, and the others as well."

"What if they were both late, but one showed up, say, ten minutes before the other?"

He drummed his fingers on the steering wheel, and his brows went together in a frown that creased his forehead. "Should that occur, it'll bear further investigation into their alibis."

"And tonight would be a wasted trip."

"Not at all. I'm having dinner with my favorite girl." He reached over and patted my knee. "And that could never be considered wasted time."

Aw, how sweet.

"How do you always know the right thing to say? Is that something you learned at Oxford?"

"No, my dear. You may thank Mina Griswold Pelletier for that particular gift."

"I have so many things to thank her for, but she's going home tomorrow. We have Jamie in a routine now, and I've booked her flight from Heathrow to Aix. Jean-Luc will pick her up there."

David nodded. "Easier for her."

I nodded. Yes, easier for her, but terrifying if it were for me. I hate flying.

*

The White Goose in Keyeston was originally built in Elizabethan times, and as a coaching inn it served travelers in the East Anglia area since then. Covered in ivy and built in typical Tudor half-timbered architectural style, it was charming and picturesque.

I have to admit my imagination ran away with me. I could almost see myself alighting from a carriage, stiff and sore from the jostling, seeking food and rest in such a place. Never mind in that time the beds would likely have been infested with six-legged critters and I would've had to share my bed with another guest whether I knew her or not.

And the quality of the food wouldn't be what any of us are used to eating nowadays.

We followed the maitre d' into a lovely wood-paneled dining room. Darkened to nearly black by time but gleaming with a beeswax shine, two of the walls still had the original linen-fold paneling. The room was lit by candlelight alone and the atmosphere was romantic. Small vases of fragrant nursery-grown winter roses adorned each table.

The maitre d' was a slender, elegant man with the superior attitude one comes to expect with a French accent. "I am Armand at your service, Lord and Lady Middlebury. Your table ees zees way."

He led us to a table next to the old fireplace. At one time they would have used it to cook the food, but now it served its purpose of providing the most romantic ambience I'd experienced in a long time.

After we were seated and we had our menus, David discretely produced his warrant card and asked the maitre d' if he'd been on duty Wednesday night.

The maitre d' blinked rapidly, then stuttered, "Y-yes. Wot's this 'bout?"

"A small investigation, Armand," David said, downplaying the truth.

Initially Armand might've sounded French, but when startled, his accent came across as pure London East End.

Keeping his tone low, David said. "Two men had dinner reservations Wednesday night. I need to know what time each of them arrived."

"*Certainement*. I must check ze reservation file. If you will give me ze names."

David looked at me, obviously considering whether to let me in on who his suspects were, but then he relented. "Lord Hutton and a Mr. Philip Denton," he said quietly.

The maitre d' nodded. "I will check and get back to you with ze information you desire."

"*Merci*, Armand."

Armand checked the reservation file. He remembered the evening quite well and the one-hundred pound note one of the gentlemen had slipped him to call if anyone asked questions.

He called the number.

"Yes?"

"Armand 'ere at the White Goose Inn. You asked me to call if..."

"Who's asking questions? Spit it out. I don't have time for foolishness."

"A Detective Chief Inspector French and 'is wife are 'ere having dinner. He asked if you or the other gentleman were late."

"What have you told him?"

"Nothing yet and I won't if you could see your way..."

"You want more money? What for?"

"I'm not a bloody fool. I've read about the murders over in Kinsey Green. Maybe you're involved and your alibi's about to fall through. I want ten thousand quid to keep my mouth shut."

"Ten thousand pounds? Are you crazy? I don't have that kind of money."

"Can't fool me. You and that partner of yours 'ave the dosh to spare."

"You'll have to meet me."

"Broad daylight. Somewhere there are plenty of people around. I'm not interested in being one of your victims."

"I'll make it simple for you. Market Street tomorrow at ten in front of the Inn."

"See that you do or I might have to tell the Bill who was really late that night."

The warmth from the fire and the dim lighting made me drowsy, and more than anything I wanted a good cup of coffee, but it was decaf for me, at least until I was absolutely sure whether I was preggers or not.

"You really think the maitre d' holds the answer to all these killings?" I asked.

"If only it were that simple. At best he'll narrow down the field of suspects." A waiter came and poured coffee for David and decaf for me.

David reached for his coffee, took a sip, then set it back on the saucer. "It seems as if we've interviewed half the village at least twice. I could do with a lucky break right now."

"Poor baby." I patted the back of his hand. I'd spent the entire day lolling on the sofa in the morning room, but the stress was telling on David. His handsome face was drawn, and his color wasn't healthy. "You look tired. Too much coffee and not enough fresh air."

David opened his mouth to say something when the maitre d' appeared.

He leaned over David's shoulder. "Lord Hutton arrived at five minutes past eight and Mr. Denton at eight forty-five. Hees lordship was quite irritated wit hees business partner's late arrival."

David frowned then looked up at the maitre d'. "Thank you, Armand. You're sure it was Mr. Denton who was late?"

"*Oui, m'sieur.*"

"I'll need you to come to Kinsey Green police station for a formal statement in the next day or two, so stay available."

"You can reach me on zee cell phone anytime." The maitre d' produced a business card from his inner pocket and gave it to David. "I hope you and your ladyship weel enjoy your dinner," he said, then bowed and left our table.

The waiter took our dinner orders and, once he'd headed to the kitchen, I focused on David with my evil eye. "When he said it was Philip Denton who arrived late, you seemed surprised."

"Can't fool you, can I?" David smiled wryly. "I must confess it did." "What reason would Armand have to lie?"

"I can think of several."

I sat up straight and leaned closer to my husband. "You can?"

"Money. Filthy lucre."

"But still. He'd have to know he was implicating someone for something he didn't do."

"I'll run a background check on M'sieur Armand in the morning. In the meantime, let's enjoy our time together alone and focus on the fantastic food."

"You know how I love to eat. But I have to be careful this time. I can't afford to balloon up like I did with Jamie. Did I ever tell you I was in labor for twenty hours with him?"

David's eyebrows rose an inch and his face tightened into a mask of slight horror. "No, you never did, but you're not going to tell me all about it now at dinner, are you?"

I giggled. "Gotcha. No, I was lucky. Spit Jamie out like a watermelon seed. That's what the midwife said."

"Lovely imagery, darling," he said in a tone that clearly belied his words.

I held up my hands and said, "That's it. I'm through. No more details over dinner."

He awarded me with a half smile. "For which I shall remain ever grateful."

I did the eye roll thing. I loved shocking his aristocratic sensibilities ever so often.

Personally I thought it was good for him.

Chapter Twenty-five

Saturday

The day dawned cold and clear. Armand stood in front of the inn, checked his watch, then looked up and down Market Street...and there was no sign of his nice little paycheck. It was a quarter past ten already. The street was filling up with village shoppers and ghastly tourists in big puffy jackets which made the buggers look like they might shoot up in the air like helium-filled balloons.

He stomped his feet. Bloody toes were going numb from the cold. Cross the street and get out of the shadows. Yes, that's what he'd do.

He looked both ways and started into the thoroughfare. A car motor gunned. Someone was in a damned hurry. He looked left, then right and then left again.

Tires squealed with sudden acceleration.

Bloody hell!

A beige small coupe was headed directly for—

He screamed. The coupe struck his knees and he screamed again. Flipped into the air, flying...then nothing.

His anxiety level growing, David glanced at his watch. Stafford, Pettigrew and a forensics tech were already out going over the Mellon girl's crime scene and Philip Denton was on his way in for another interview. The rest of the squad worked quietly at their desks. As far as they were concerned, DCI Beecham had pegged Nan Morgan as the doer in both Stubbs's and Daisy Mellon's murders and considered Evie White a sad victim of suicide.

As for David's line of inquiry, everyone thought he was a fool chasing a red herring.

All right. This time the interview would be an interrogation. The maitre d' had reported Denton was the one late to dinner, and procedure said he must follow up on the information. He couldn't ignore it just because his gut said otherwise.

He picked up the telephone again and called the White Goose Inn and left a message for the maitre d' Armand to call him as soon as he reported for work. Better to get his official statement for the record, no matter what it was.

No matter how many times David went over his notes, Lord Hutton crept into his thoughts. Could his lordship have murdered the antiques dealer and framed his wife's lover for the murder. Where would he have obtained the hair with Nan's DNA? Did the two women meet somewhere on Hutton's estate...somewhere he could've obtained the sample and planted it at the scene? Why pick on the antiques dealer? Had the dealer done something to piss off his lordship? He made a note to check on any prior relationship between the dealer and Hutton.

Conversely had Philip Denton learned of his wife's affair with Hutton and... But how would Denton know of Nan and Lady Jane's affair? Could he have possibly set up the murder to frame Nan which would lead them back to Lord Hutton?

No, that was entirely too convoluted.

His phone rang. The desk sergeant notified him of Denton's arrival. "Send him back."

A minute later, Denton arrived, attired in a navy workout togs. "I was on my way to the gym when you called. I hope you don't mind."

David motioned him back to interview one. "Your wardrobe is of no concern, Denton. Have a seat."

Denton flushed a tomato red, but he complied with a huff.

"Your attitude leaves a bit to be desired, Chief Inspector. What's this about? I've cooperated, told you my business secrets. What else could you possibly want to know?"

David held up his hand. "One moment for the record, interview with Philip Denton commenced at twenty-five minutes past ten with DCI French in attendance."

"In your statement of yesterday, you said you arrived at the White Goose for dinner at eight?"

"That's right. Didn't you bother to check it with the maitre d'? Armand, his name is."

"Yes, Armand remembers your arrival as sometime later. Would you like to alter your statement?"

"No! I bloody well know when my reservation was and when I arrived. Eight o'clock or a few—very few—minutes afterward." Denton hit the desk with his fist.

"Armand says you arrived at eight forty-five and Lord Hutton was the one who came at five past eight."

"Then he's got his facts mixed or he's lying outright!" Denton jumped up from his seat. "I don't know what's going on here, but if you think I had something to do with these murders or have evidence, say so."

"I'm required to follow up on any alibis that don't check out. Have to wonder what you're hiding, Denton. That time period is crucial to my investigation."

"How's that? The papers say someone's been arrested for the two murders, and that the last death was a suicide. What are you investigating?"

"I don't believe Evie White's death was suicide. That's what I'm investigating."

"And you think Lord Hutton or I have something to do with these murders. You're way off track. You've not even left the stable, Chief Inspector. His lordship and I are businessmen and property developers, not bloodthirsty killers who go round the countryside hacking off body parts from people who've never done us harm."

"The fact remains. Your alibi doesn't check out." Even so,

Denton's outburst had the outraged ring of truth.

"The maitre d' made a mistake. Call him. Talk to him again."

A knock on the door halted David's response. One of Beecham's men stuck his head inside. "Sorry to interrupt—urgent phone call."

Miranda came to his mind first, then Jamie. "Excuse me, Denton." David rushed to his desk and grabbed the receiver. "French."

"This is James Taylor from the White Goose Inn."

A surge of relief flashed through him. Not a family emergency then.

"You left a message for our maitre d' Armand Dillehay to call you, but he can't. He was run over—I can barely believe it—hit-and-run right in front of the inn...just now."

David glanced at his watch: half past ten. "Just now?"

"Fifteen minutes ago."

He took a deep breath, dreading the answer to his next question. "His condition?"

"Dead, Chief Inspector. He's dead."

Dead. Frustration and anger twisted in his gut and vied for control. A damned good lead and now he was as dead as the others. Reining his emotions, he managed, "Thank you for calling. One more thing. Will you give the inspector in charge of the case my name and number and ask him to call me?"

Taylor agreed. David hung up the receiver and leaned back. He didn't like coincidences and this smelled of their killer in full panic mode. He'd killed Armand to keep him from recanting his statement.

Bloody hell, but he needed to see that reservation file for himself.

Denton ruled out on this one, but he could've hired someone. No, it didn't fit the M.O. of their killer. Have to let Denton go for now.

Fifteen minutes later David's phone rang again. This time it was the Keyeston detective who'd caught the hit and run, DI Erin

Santella.

Her manner of speaking was clipped and to the point. "What connection do you have to this case, Chief Inspector?"

"Armand Dillehay was giving evidence in an investigation here in Kinsey Green."

"Yes. You have a bloody mess over there, but I was under the impression you had your killer."

"Let's say I'm not convinced. It's routine follow up, but now he's dead, I feel there's more to it. I'd appreciate if you'd keep me in the loop about the car, where it came from, et cetera."

"Can do that now. Beige coupe, stolen thirty minutes before the hit and run, found abandoned on the edge of the city."

"Very efficient, Inspector."

"Anything else?"

"If anyone saw the driver, a description would just about make my day." "We're still canvassing the area for witnesses."

Bloody hell, but he needed a copy of the reservation file. "Later today, I'll be in Keyeston...on a different matter," he explained quickly. "May I call you for an update?"

She hesitated for a moment, then agreed and rattled off her mobile number.

He thanked her and rang off.

DS Eric Stafford shouldered into the thicket, pulled his coat tighter around him, and stepped carefully. "Bloody hell, I can't believe we're freezing our asses off looking for dog poo."

Assisting him, DC Pettigrew, giggled and rattled her evidence case. "Evidence. We're looking for evidence, Eric."

"I notice you're taking care not to step in it."

"See here, mate," the forensics tech Michael said. "I think we need to look farther afield. Stands to reason the dogs would set up a right howl if the killer was hacking the girl right in front of them."

"You're right. They'd go nuts at the scent of blood," Eric said. "We need to check for outbuildings where he might've stashed them so he could do his dirty business."

"Michaels, you keep checking around the site for anything you missed earlier."

White-clad, Michaels glared. "I didn't miss anything the first time. No sign of dog feces. If there is now, then it's newly dumped."

"We'll do a grid search. The sergeant and I'll take the north sector and you can take the south."

Michaels curled his lip, but headed to the southern portion of the field. Eric and Alice started stomping through the underbrush in the direction of an outbuilding visible in the far distance.

"You weren't very nice to him. He's an all right bloke," Alice muttered while they trudged along.

"I wanted to get you alone." Eric smiled down at his new playmate.

"That was obvious." She sniffed. "I'll hear all about it when we get back to the squad. Don't you think I won't."

"So?"

"So, I have to work here all the time. You're a temp."

"I'm your temporary man on the side?" He wasn't too sure he cared for the designation.

"Yeah, that's what you are," she said with a shrug which was a shade too casual for his liking.

After a fifteen minute trek, he and Alice finally reached the clearing and outbuilding.

They started thirty meters from the ramshackle building, making careful circumnavigations—each one smaller in diameter as they surveyed the ground for trace evidence.

Eric pointed. "There's a disturbance of the undergrowth."

"Yeah. Looks like someone came in from the north to the back of the building. I can't see any footprints or paw prints, as the case may be. The ground's too rocky." Alice peered closely.

He glanced around. The forensics tech wasn't in sight.

Good. He put his arm around Alice and nudged her up against the rickety building. "What you said before—did you mean it?"

"What?"

"About my being your temp? Is that all I am?"

She gazed up at him, her expression stony. No way to gauge her mood.

"What do you think? As soon as this case is cleared, you and the inspector will head back to the rarified air of London, and I'll be stuck here in the Green."

"Then let's take advantage of every moment." He wiggled his eyebrows.

She glared at him as if he were mad as a hatter. "Are you nuts? Out here in the open field, in the cold, you want me to get starkers so you can have a go?"

"Something like that. Is that a no then?"

She giggled. "Had you going for a bit, didn't I?" "That's a yes?"

"No, you're nuts, but you're a sweet nut. Keep that bad boy in your pants, and I'll be extra-special nice to you tonight. Okay?" She kissed him, which only made his bad boy want some fresh air.

"We've a job to do and we'd better come up with something for your chief inspector or he might send me right back to Beecham's squad."

"We don't want that, do we?" He went for a nibble on her neck, but she deftly dodged him.

"No, we don't." She frowned. "You know I don't think this building is long for the world. One good push..."

If she wasn't going to give him a ride, then she wasn't. He held back the sigh. "Let's check inside."

He eased open the door and shone his flashlight along the floor. The pong of dog feces reached out and grabbed him. "Get a whiff of that."

Alice wrinkled her nose. "Think I'll pass." Still she bent down and opened her evidence case, pulled on a pair of gloves, and smiled. "Dog poo isn't my favorite type of evidence to collect. I don't suppose you...?"

"No, I'm pulling rank. Be my guest. Collect all you want."

Alice grimaced, then grabbed her comm unit. "Michaels, we've found some evidence. What about you?"

"Nothing so far. Heading your way," came the reply.

"After I collect all this evidence," she said, "we should take a good look around this building. We might find something else."

"Thank you, Sergeant. I'm so glad I brought you along."

"Don't be testy. After all, I'm the one collecting piles of dog poo."

"At least the guv'll be happy."

Alice grinned. "And when the guv is happy…"

"…everybody's happy," he added.

As soon as Alice was through bagging the evidence, they shone their flashlights across the floor of the shed. "Far corner," Eric said. "Looks like the earth's disturbed."

"Right. Like something's been dug up there."

"Or buried."

He walked gingerly to the far corner where the earth was loosely packed. "Get an evidence bag ready, just in case."

"What the hell have you done now?" Michaels demanded from the doorway.

"We've collected a shit load of dog poo, and now we're checking to see what else we have," Alice snarked. "Care to join us?"

Michaels sniggered.

"The soil appears blood-stained." Eric kept digging by hand. "Bloody hell. We've hit the mother lode."

He pulled out a blood-stained shirt, a pair of pants and socks, and a knife with a curved blade. "Looks like a murder weapon to me." Excitement made his heart beat faster. The chief knew what he was up to, no doubt about it.

Michaels quickly placed them into paper bags to preserve the blood evidence. "Must've thought he'd get back here and retrieve them."

"Guess he waited a little too long." Alice looked from Eric to Michaels. "The boss'll really be happy with this day's work. This is the first evidence that's without a doubt from our killer."

Eric smiled back. "With all the blood, there's bound to be DNA from the victim and more importantly this shirt is bound to have the killer's DNA as well. He was probably in a flop sweat by the time he finished."

"Who wouldn't be," Alice said with a grim expression. "Poor Daisy, she never had a chance."

David was on the road to Keyeston when Stafford called.

"We've found a shack full of dog feces and the killer's bloody clothes, guv. And a knife, guv. We found a curved blade knife."

"Where?" A burst of adrenaline hit and his heart rate surged in response.

"Buried. About half a mile from the crime scene in an old shed on Lord Hutton's land. Looks like that's where he kept his dogs tied while he did the dirty work."

"Good show! I'm on my way to Keyeston. One of my leads was the victim of a hit and run earlier this morning. Our killer's getting desperate. He's trying to wipe away all traces which might lead back to him."

"We're on our way in, sir."

Stafford rang off. David was more convinced now than ever of Hutton's guilt. The bastard had killed four people and heaven help anyone else in his way.

Chapter Twenty-six

After David left for work, I rubbed away an area of frost from our bedroom window. Though the opening, the sun was shining, and the threat of snow had missed us. I shivered, but without a doubt Jamie would be anxious to get some fresh air. My son simply wouldn't care that it was colder than a witch's tit in a brass brassiere. We'd dress warmly and it wouldn't be too bad. He'd get his fresh air and I'd get some sorely needed exercise.

This morning Robbie would take one of the estate cars and drive Mina to Heathrow for her flight home, leaving Jamie and me all alone.

At a tap on the bedroom door, I drew the heavy draperies and answered, "Come in."

It was Mina, darling Mina. I rushed to hug her. "I'm going to miss you so much."

"And I, you." She shivered. "I'd forgotten just how cold it is here and how these old bones of mine are used to the warmth of the south. Perhaps you can visit us for a while. We'd love to have you."

"We'll see how things go." As appealing as the south of France was at this moment, somehow I just couldn't bear the thought of leaving David behind.

"You can't fool me, my girl. You're still a honeymooner and don't want to leave his lordship."

I grinned. "Busted. So when are you taking your psychic powers show on the road?"

She hugged me back. "No need for psychic powers when your

emotions are written so clearly on your face, Randi. All the same, my invitation is a permanent one. Your entire family is welcome at any time."

"Are you packed and ready to go?"

"Of course. Now what I would suggest is hiring a tutor for Master James...at least until the fall term. That will give you and his lordship time to map out a plan and choose a school. By that time, your new child will either have arrived or be on the verge of it."

Pure reflex. My hand went to my lower belly. I still couldn't believe I already carried a new life. A baby made from our love.

"Any sickness in the morning?" Mina asked.

"No," I shook my head. "Just a little queasiness with certain odors."

"Excellent, my girl. Now then, what will you do today?"

"This afternoon I'll bundle up Jamie and we'll go for a walk. I need the exercise and you know how he is about 'fresh air'."

Mina smiled. "My only caveat is that you stay in sight of the manor house. I can see you twisting your ankle and falling."

"You're a darling and a worry wart. We'll be fine."

Jamie and I stood in the foyer and waved good-bye to Mina. Already I missed her soothing presence. As soon as the car drove away, I shut the door, then rubbed my hands together. "Let's get warm, have lunch, then I'll bundle you up and we'll go out for our daily constitutional."

Jamie looked up at me with his big brown eyes and giggled. "You sound like Mina."

"Well, just because she's on her way home to Jean-Luc, doesn't mean we're not going to stick to her routine." I ruffled my son's black hair and hugged him.

Jamie's response was to run into the morning room and stand in front of the fire rubbing his hands. "I'm warm now," my cheeky son said, his dark eyes filled with anticipation.

"All right, you." I shook my head. "We're going to wait until after lunch. It might actually be a couple of degrees warmer then. Don't want my boy to freeze himself to death."

"Oh, Mum," he whined.

"Cook is already making soup for lunch, and you don't want to miss that, now do you?"

He did the eye roll thing. One of my tricks—guess I'll have to watch it.

After lunch, I scrounged around and found our coats, hats, gloves, and wellies for the two of us. Once I was certain my son and I wouldn't freeze our butts and other important parts off in the cold, we trooped out through the kitchen.

Cook looked up from chopping away at a large cut of beef, which I fervently hoped would make a savory stew for our dinner. "It's mighty fresh outside, your ladyship. I'm more than happy to spend the day in here where it's nice and warm."

"Young boys need fresh air," my son said.

"That they do." Cook nodded and grinned. "And there'll be some hot cocoa waiting for you when you've had enough of that fresh air," she said with a wink.

"Will you have some for mummy, too? I'm sure she'll need it."

"Never fear, Master James. We'll take care of your mum, too."

"Let's go, kiddo." I nudged Jamie in the behind with my knee.

We stepped out into the fresh air, so cold it burned my lungs whenever I took a deep breath. The grass crunched under our feet as we walked along toward the gardens.

"Race you to the trees, Mummy." And off the little bugger went, flying as fast has his legs could carry him. I set off after him, and about halfway there I noticed a tall man standing at the edge of the trees along with five yapping dogs—four spaniels and a small Jack Russell Terrier.

"Jamie, wait!" I called, hoping to stop him from rushing headlong into a stranger. I ran after him, but a cramp in my side stopped me. I bent over and struggled to catch my breath. Still I never took my eyes off them.

"Jamie, come back here *now*!"

He stopped and glanced back in my direction. "Mum, I want to see the dogs," he yelled.

"I said no!" I yelled back.

He started walking toward me, his head hanging down in disappointment. I finally caught a second wind and started running toward him again.

This time the man also started walking in our direction. "Hello," he hollered. "I'm your neighbor. Our lands converge in the woods." He continued his approach.

That meant he was...Lord Hutton, one of David's suspects. A shiver zapped up my spine. I couldn't be sure if it was the weather or one of those feelings we're not supposed to ignore.

Of course, his being a suspect didn't mean he was the killer, and I didn't want to be rude to a neighbor, but my son and I weren't about to play nicey-nice with a possible murderer, either.

Just to be semi-sociable, I waved, but stood my ground. "Come on, Jamie, it's time to go back inside." I willed him to obey me and not show a rare display of temper.

"Aw, Mum." His bottom lip protruded in a pout.

Okay, pouting is fine with me. "Now," I said through gritted teeth. By now, he'd reached my grabbing distance and I took his hand firmly and we headed back to the house.

"I wanted to see the dogs." Still pouting, Jamie glared up at me.

"We've gone over this before. You must not talk to strangers, even if they have dogs or say their dog is lost and they need your help to find him. Do you understand me?"

He kicked a rock as we walked. "Yes, ma'am."

Ten minutes later we were back in the house, divested of our coats and sitting in the kitchen drinking hot cocoa when Fields came to tell me Lord Hutton had called and wondered if I were "at home."

My throat closed. "He's here?"

"Yes, your ladyship."

"No, I'm not at home to him or anyone else. Say I'm indisposed, whatever. Frankly I don't care what you tell him."

Fields eyebrows rose an inch, but he merely nodded and left us in the kitchen. A little unsteady, I looked down at my cocoa. There was already a skim on the top. A sudden wave of nausea hit me. I covered my mouth with my hand and looked around in desperation for the nearest loo.

Cook pointed and I ran.

After losing both my lunch and cocoa, I settled on the cold tile floor, leaned against the wall, and tried to sort out my emotions. Was I just being a paranoid nervous Nellie or was Lord Hutton actually stalking me?

A little tap-tap-tap on the lavatory door. "Mum? Are you all right?"

"Yes, baby. I'm all right. Just a minute." I pulled to my feet, rinsed my mouth and washed my face.

I opened the door. My son looked up at me with concern written across his face. "My tummy was just a little upset," I explained. "I'm okay now."

He hugged me around the waist. I couldn't believe he was getting so tall. It seemed only last year he was hugging me around my thighs. "Let's go find a book for you to read. Mina says you're supposed to read to me."

"I read to you at night. You read to me in the daytime. That's how it's supposed to be."

My son is so bright. He can keep track of our routine a lot better than I can. I winked. "Okay, I'll get it straight. Where are we on old Harry, anyway?"

"Chapter four."

"Okay, you go find your book, and while you're doing that I'm going to check in with your father."

A quick nod and off he ran. I took a deep breath. My stomach had settled. I emerged from the loo and into a host of concerned faces—Cook, the kitchen maid and Fields. "I'm fine," I announced for their benefit.

I eyeballed Fields. "Did Lord Hutton leave?"

Fields nodded. "Yes. He said he hoped to see you sometime soon." A touch of queasiness shook me, but it passed quickly.

"Thank you, Fields." I held my head high, as if I weren't really shaking in my boots from what I perceived as a threat in Lord Hutton's words. I headed to the morning room which was rapidly becoming my favorite room in the house—not counting the bedroom.

I pulled out my cell phone and punched the speed dial for David's cell.

He answered quickly. The sound of classical music in the background told me he was driving. "Hello, darling."

"Where are you?" I asked.

"On my way to Keyeston."

"Something odd happened this afternoon."

"Tell me."

As quickly as I could, I related Lord Hutton's suspicious behavior and his impromptu visit. "I don't know if I'm imagining things or..."

"Listen to me. Whatever you do, don't leave the house. And keep Jamie inside, as well. Who's there with you now? Call Robbie and—"

"Robbie's driving Mina to Heathrow. He won't be back for hours, but Fields, Madison and the rest of the staff are here."

"Damn."

"You're scaring me, and I was already scared."

"Your instincts are good, Miranda. I'm certain Hutton's our man." "Is that the gut or the evidence talking?"

"We may have both very soon. Stafford and Pettigrew made a discovery this morning. It's all come together very quickly. He's decompensating. Desperate and making mistakes."

"I'm sure as long as we stay inside we'll be okay."

"Tell Fields I want him to keep the shotgun handy. Tell him whatever you need to tell him so he'll understand the situation."

By this time, I was shaking in my boots. "All right."

"I'm ringing off now. I'll have Hutton brought in for questioning. That should help."

I took a deep breath. "All right." I absolutely could not lose it. I had no choice. I had to keep calm and protect my son—not for the first time. His father Stefan was bad enough when he tried to take Jamie from the hospital. But this Lord Hutton, if he was the killer, was a step beyond with his carving up people and rearranging their body parts.

I closed the cell phone and rang for Fields. He came quickly—thank Heavens. "Your ladyship?"

"We have a situation."

David punched in Stafford's number. He answered after a single ring.

"Stafford, don't talk. Just listen. Pick up Lord Hutton, bring him in for questioning. Hold him until I get back to the Green. He was walking on my estate today and even asked to see my wife. I don't want him anywhere near my family. Understand?"

"Yes, guv. Got it."

"Good. I'll be back as quickly as I can."

"What if we can't find him?"

"Then put out a bloody BOLO. Not for murder. 'Sought as material witness.' Anything to get that bastard off the streets."

"Done."

David wiped the perspiration from his brow. His heart pounded rapidly; the thought of Hutton showing up uninvited at the estate sent a rush of nausea. He swallowed back the fear. For once, he was sorry he was a copper. He bloody well wanted to rip Hutton's head from his shoulders and use it for a football.

Chapter Twenty-seven

David floored the accelerator and careened around a sharp curve in the road. The
Range Rover acted as if it would fishtail, but he corrected quickly. The drive would smooth out as soon as he reached the A-146, then he could shoot straight into Keyeston.

The longer he was on the road, the greater the sense of panic pervaded his entire being. Didn't have a choice. He must retrieve the reservation file before it disappeared. And if DI Santella could come up with an eyewitness or two, so much the better.

Once he was on the A-146, he accelerated to a rate just over the legal speed limit. Miranda's phone call about Hutton's impromptu visit had shaken him more than he'd admitted.

After about ten minutes, the flow of traffic slowed. He eased over to see around the truck in front of him. Up ahead of him, brake lights were lighting. Was it a wreck?

Bloody hell. He pounded the steering wheel. As far ahead as he could see, vehicles were lined up ahead for at least two miles.

Count to ten. Then to twenty. He pounded the steering wheel again. Obviously his self-advice wasn't worth much.

Lord Hutton leaned over his office computer. Thank heaven for the Internet. One could find anything...simply anything. One just had to pick one's poison, so to speak.

What luck. All the components for his preferred device were

already on his estate. What was Brazil like this time of year? Warm, most likely. Anyway, the weather had to be better than East Anglia's.

Quite methodically he made a plane reservation in his own name, leaving from Heathrow late that evening for Rio de Janeiro. Then he pulled out a cloned mobile phone and called one of his silent business partners.

Berger Schoenfeld was an international arms dealer who had managed to fly below the radars of MI5 and MI6...thus far anyway. With Schoenfeld he arranged a circuitous route of escape starting in France, hop-scotching across Europe and Africa, eventually ending in Rio. An arduous trip, no doubt, but his survival depended on it. His funds were in untraceable numbered accounts in Switzerland, as well as in the Cayman Islands. And through Schoenfeld, he also obtained a few specialty items which would be delivered personally by one of his partner's henchmen.

He had just one thing left to do.

Get even with DCI French. Oh, yes. That he would do.

After an interminable two hours on the road and four phone calls to check on Miranda, David finally reached Market Street in Keyeston. He pulled up in front of the White Goose and parked in the no parking zone.

He jumped from the Rover and was met by a valet from the inn. "Sir, you can't—"

David whipped out his warrant card, flashed it, then brushed by the valet. Once inside, he stopped at the front desk and introduced himself. "It's urgent. I need to speak with the manager."

The desk clerk nodded and called the manager who came promptly. The manager was a short portly man with a shiny pate. "Bailey Sweeney, at your service, Chief Inspector."

"I need to see the dinner reservation records for Wednesday evening."

The manager pursed his lips. "We prefer to keep our patrons records private. May I ask what this is in reference to?"

"It's in reference to murder and your former maitre d', Armand Dillehay."

"Oh, dear." He patted his pudgy fingers together. "I was afraid of that. So shocking, and it happened on our very doorstep—well, not on the doorstep, but right out front in the street."

"It's a simple request. Are you going to produce the records, or do I have to call for a warrant? I might add you're about to piss me off in a major way."

"Right away, Chief Inspector." He spun around like an off-balance child's top.

A minute later, he returned with the reservation book in his hand, but his face was flushed and small beads of perspiration dotted his shiny brow. He dabbed his brow with a navy handkerchief.

Not a good sign.

David held out his hand. "Well?"

"I'm sorry. I don't know how it happened. Nothing like this has—"

"What? Spit it out, man. I don't have time—"

"The p-pages for Wednesday evening have been removed."

"Let me see." David grabbed the book from the manager's shaking hands and started riffling through the pages. "Perhaps you overlooked it."

Please let him have overlooked it.

"Monday. Tuesday. Thursday. Damn." He handed the reservation book back to Sweeney. "Do you have any idea who might've torn out those pages?"

"I c-can only assume Armand removed them." Sweeney's double chin quivered.

"He's the only maitre d' on duty all this week. We only have a maitre d' for dinner. No reservations for luncheon."

David agreed. The maitre d' was the likely culprit, but had he removed the pages to protect the identity of the late-arriving partner or as backup for future blackmail?

Whatever the reason he removed them, where were they now?

*

After leaving the White Goose, David called DI Santella's mobile number. She answered quickly and gave him the address of the new headquarters building at Wymondham. It turned out to be a large modern, brick and glass affair. He strode inside and asked for her at the desk.

DI Santella appeared to be about his age, slender, with light brown hair cut short and piercing blue eyes. She authorized a visitor's pass for him and he followed the detective inspector back to her desk. She nodded for him to sit. "Now what's your interest in my hit and run?"

David sat and said, "It's a long story."

Her brows went together in a frown. "I don't have time for a long story. Why don't you give me the short version?" Her short-clipped nails tapped on the desk.

"Triple murder in Kinsey Green. This Armand Dillehay may be his latest victim. I interviewed him Friday evening about two men who met for dinner the evening of the third murder. Both individuals say the other was late. Dillehay told me which one was late, but the man Dillehay implicated was in my office at the time of your hit and run, therefore—"

"—you think it was the other who was late?"

"Yes. Dillehay might've called the real culprit and tried to extort money from him to keep quiet."

"Plausible." DI Santella nodded and pulled out her notebook. "I want to get all this," she said and began taking notes.

"I left a message for Armand to call me as soon as he came to work. I wanted a copy of the reservation file from the night in question. His superior called me back to inform me Armand had been involved in a hit and run."

"And he was dead."

"Exactly. I came to Keyeston to obtain the file myself, but pages had been removed." "Suspicious." Her gaze narrowed.

"Yes. How was your canvass? Anyone get a good look at the driver?"

"The closest thing to a description we received was from a seven-year-old boy. He said the driver looked like Sherlock Holmes on the telly. He even described a deerstalker cap and a pipe."

"A pipe?" Elation fizzled through David like champagne bubbles.

"Yes, does your suspect smoke one?"

"Indeed, he does. Thank you, Santella. I'll need a copy of his statement faxed to me...here." He threw down his business card and turned to leave.

She held up a hand. "Hold on. Not so fast." She picked up the phone and punched in a number. "Campbell, in the Dillehay case, we found some folded papers in his pocket. I need those up here in my office...now."

David took a deep breath. Please God, he needed a break. "Papers on the victim?"

Santella nodded. "At the time, they didn't seem significant, but they were preserved and catalogued according to procedure just the same."

David sat back down, his heart racing. "I know I can't have your original evidence, but I'd like copies of them—if they're significant."

"Certainly. I'll prepare a signed statement to go with them." She turned to her computer and quickly keyed her statement, printed and signed it while they waited.

"You're pretty certain they're of value?"

Santella leaned forward and smiled. "I think we might have what you missed at the inn."

"Here you are, Erin." Campbell from forensics laid the plastic envelope on Santella's desk. "We're not through testing it yet. Prints belong to the maitre d', though."

"Thanks, Campbell." Santella handed the plastic envelope to David. "This looks good."

He stared at the note by the Hutton/Denton reservation: *Lord Hutton called. Won't arrive until 8:45 p.m.*

"This is it. I've got the bugger now. He was the one who was late and had the opportunity to kill my third victim. Thank you."

"Thank you. Now we know who had a motive to run down Mr. Dillehay."

She pursed her mouth. "We need copies of this document, Campbell. Okay to photocopy through the plastic?"

"And copies of the photos pertaining to this piece of evidence," David said. Campbell nodded. "Will do. ASAP."

Finally. The case was coming together. He had Lord Hutton's lie regarding his whereabouts on tape and now he had the evidence to refute him.

"I need to make a call. I had a BOLO put out on his lordship as I was coming over here."

He called the stationhouse and was quickly put through to his sergeant. "Eric? Has Hutton been brought in yet?"

"No, sir. Beecham canceled the BOLO. Said you were full of it and we couldn't waste time when we already had our killer in the nick."

"Damn it! You work for me. Get out to the estate. Lord Hutton showed up there and tried to see my wife this afternoon. They're on guard, but I'd feel better if someone were there under the age of fifty, besides my wife."

"Will do."

"Reissue that BOLO. I'm on my way home, and I have documentation the maitre d' lied. Lord Hutton was the one who called ahead he'd be late—not Philip Denton." He closed the mobile with a snap. He had to get home.

He turned to DI Santella. "Something's come up. I'll take the copy of the reservation file now, but I can't wait for the photos. Will you messenger or fax the copies to me at Kinsey Green constabulary? I'll reimburse your expenses."

"No problem. We may have our case cleared because of your cooperation."

"Thanks." He ran for his car. Hutton was a stone-cold killer without a conscience. All he cared about was tying up his loose ends. And because David had taken Miranda to dinner the night he interviewed the maitre d', she might be a loose end, too.

Dear God. What had he done?

Chapter Twenty-eight

As the afternoon passed, I wasn't any more comfortable about the situation with Lord Hutton. David called at least four times on his way to Keyeston. There was supposed to be what he called a BOLO—be on the lookout—for Lord Hutton. I expected to hear from David anytime the creep had been brought in for questioning.

But nothing.

I supposed he was at the White Goose Inn and would check with the Keyeston local LEOs. That took time...

As the sun went down, I wandered from room to room. The doors were bolted and the windows locked as if we were in a medieval castle and expected a siege from the nearest warlord.

Come to think of it, we were.

In the States some of the wealthy actually have safe rooms with separate systems for air and electricity which can't be penetrated from outside. Well, I sure wished we had one of those and one big enough for the household staff. Mentally I counted: Fields, Madison, Cook, one house maid and one kitchen maid. Thankfully Mina was already on her way home.

One less person to worry about. And of course, Jamie. He was in the lounge watching a kid show on the TV. He'd been very good all day long, but his eyes held unasked questions. What was he worried about? Poor little guy, he'd already been through so much, playing hop-scotch all over Europe and then falling in the pool in Provençe and nearly dying from pneumonia.

And a new life as well. Instinctively my hand went to my belly. I knocked on Fields's door.

"Yes?"

"Are we armed? I mean, is there a gun I can use, if need be?"

The butler's response was a grim smile. He opened a drawer and pulled out a six-shot revolver. "If it has to be used, and if questioned about it, you've never seen it before. It's loaded and ready. Do you shoot, your ladyship?"

I smiled back. "As a matter of fact, my father taught all of us kids how to handle a gun, even girlie me."

Fields nodded. "Thoughtful of him. Excellent."

"What about a semi-automatic? I can handle one of those as well."

"Your ladyship, the revolver won't misfire like a semi. Six shots dead center should suffice."

"I like the way you think, Fields." I chewed the inside of my lip, wondering how much more to tell him. After all, the man was putting his life at risk to protect us. "Do you think it odd...all this? I know I haven't told you much."

He frowned. "I thought it odd when Lord Hutton showed up as he did with his dogs in tow. He's not been a guest in this house for at least fifteen years. I don't need to know the details. It's enough that his lordship doesn't want the man near his family."

My cell vibrated. David on the caller ID.

"Thank heavens. I've been so worried. Have they picked up Lord Hutton yet?"

"No, Beecham wouldn't authorize the BOLO. I'm leaving Keyeston now. Sergeant

Stafford is on his way to you. Beecham can't do a bloody thing about it. But I have to return to the stationhouse to convince him and the Chief Crown Prosecutor of Hutton's guilt in all this."

"We're okay so far. The house is locked down and the alarms are set. And if it's any consolation, Fields and I are packing heat."

"What?"

"Fields has the shotgun and I have a revolver. If Lord Hutton shows up, we're ready."

"Good. I don't want to know where the revolver came from."

"What revolver?" I asked with the most innocent tone I could muster.

"Just take care," he said softly. "You and Jamie are the most important people in my life, and I can't have anything happen to you. Try not to shoot anyone but Lord Hutton. But don't hesitate if he comes near you."

"Right." I had no doubts that Lord Hutton was a stone cold killer, and I definitely wouldn't hesitate to protect my son and myself.

"Call me if anything happens, but Eric should be there soon." I heard him take a deep breath, then, "I love you, Miranda."

"Love you, too."

We disconnected, and I felt a great big sigh building up inside me. "Jamie," I called. "Where are you?"

I found Jamie and Fields, shotgun and all, in the entry hall engaged in a deep conversation about gun safety.

"DS Stafford's on his way," I told Fields.

The muscles relaxed a bit in his grim face. "Excellent. I was just telling Master James he mustn't touch this gun for any reason. And that when the weather improves I'll teach him how to use it...if that's not overstepping."

"He should learn," I said. If our lives were going to be one crisis after another, it might not be such a bad idea. The family that shoots together stays together? Oh dear heavens. What a gruesome thought.

The trip from Keyeston to Kinsey Green passed in a blur. David made the trip in record time, and it was a bloody good thing no one got in his way. He strode into the squad room past the bulletin board with the crime scene photos, past DC Pettigrew who flashed him a quick smile and over to Beecham's desk where he apparently had nothing better to do than fiddle with a pencil.

"I have it," David said. "Proof that connects Lord Hutton to the murders here in the Green and another this morning in Keyeston."

Beecham stopped his pencil fiddling and glared back. "You're out of your bleeding mind, mate. Nan Morgan's our killer."

"Listen! Lord Hutton lied regarding his whereabouts on Wednesday night, the night he killed Evie White. I have a copy of the reservation file where the maitre d' made a notation of Hutton's late arrival which gave him time to murder Evie and eradicate any evidence he might've left behind."

"Evie committed suicide, you berk!" Beecham's face grew red. "Where's your maitre d'? Why didn't you bring him instead of a copy of a so-called file?"

"He's dead. Killed by a hit-and-run driver this morning before he could come in and

make an official statement. My evidence is a copy..." He waved it under Beecham's nose, "...because it's also evidence in the hit and run. DI Santella in Keyeston found it folded in Armand Dillehay's pocket. I have Santella's signed statement verifying its authenticity."

"But what about the other two murders? How does this piece of evidence tie in to make Lord Hutton guilty of them all?" Beecham leaned back in his chair and snapped the pencil in two.

"All right. Bear with me. From the pub, I have a witness to prove Lady Hutton and Nan Morgan were lovers."

Beecham sat up straight, his face a mask of disbelief. "What?"

"Yes, then Evie White was overheard making a remark to an unseen man about Nan and her ladyship. My witness was in the kitchen and overheard everything. By the time she came from the kitchen, he'd already left the pub. It has to be Lord Hutton. He killed Stubbs to frame Nan for murder to punish his wife. Somehow, maybe from a trysting place, he obtained Nan Morgan's hair and used it to frame her."

Beecham leaned forward, his expression intense. "Go on. Keep building your case."

"Why in particular he chose to kill Stubbs we need to look into. Perhaps there's an old connection we don't know about, or maybe Stubbs discovered Hutton's affair with Nicola Denton and was blackmailing him. She said Stubbs was stalking her. He might've followed her to one of her assignations with Hutton."

"But what about Daisy Mellon?"

"The owner of the shop overheard a call which sounded as if she were trying to extort money from someone. He killed Daisy to shut her up and made it look like a signature killer was at work in the Green. One loose end tied up, and then Evie White stepped in and sealed her own death."

"His alibi was he was with Nicola Denton."

"Let's call her back in—right now. See if it's true or not. But from his statement we know he lied about being late to dinner Wednesday night, because he said Denton was late. That's what we can refute with the reservation file.

"To top it off, Hutton has no alibi for the time of either of the first two murders, other than he was out walking his estate with his dogs. We've located bloody clothes buried on his land a half mile from the Mellon girl's murder scene, and a ton of dog feces where his dogs were stashed while he committed the murder. My God, man. What more do you want?"

Beecham eyed him. "I'll call the Chief Crown Prosecutor and see if he agrees we have enough evidence to arrest Hutton." Beecham's movements were slow, as if he really didn't want to make the call.

"You're still reluctant. What's the problem?"

"The CCP is going to require a great deal of proof to arrest someone of Hutton's station."

"No one is above the law. Check with forensics. By now they'll have a blood type on those clothes Stafford and Pettigrew recovered."

Beecham reached for the phone, spoke with forensics and set down the phone. "Two types on the clothes. Majority was A positive, like the Mellon girl's, along with a small amount of O positive."

"We need to get Hutton in here and tested for DNA before he kills someone else. I've already sent Stafford to the house to protect my wife. She was with me at dinner when I interviewed Dillehay. I'm afraid he might've mentioned her to Hutton. The man actually showed up at my estate this afternoon and tried to see her."

Beecham scowled and shook his head. "Think he might try something with your wife? No, we can't have that."

"He's shown no remorse and killed four people already. I don't think he'd give a second thought to another body or two."

"We'll get Nicola Denton in here. I'll put out the BOLO to pick him up for questioning." He grabbed the phone, ordered one of his officers to bring in the Denton woman and instituted the BOLO order on Lord Hutton.

David took a deep breath. Finally Beecham had begun to see reason. "The CCP," he prompted.

"Right." Beecham grabbed the phone again and called the CCP.

David's fingers drummed against the desk top. Twenty minutes since two police constables were dispatched to bring in Nicola Denton. Twenty *long* minutes.

His desk phone rang. Snatched the receiver. "French."

"Nicola Denton's here."

"Bring her back. Interview room two."

Finally. One last thread to tie off.

He waited until she'd been placed in the interrogation room, then for a moment he stood outside and watched through the glass. She paced back and forth. Even in a measure of disarray she was beautiful, but like the cliché, hers was only skin deep. Anxious to get it over with, he jerked open the door. "Have a seat."

She whirled on his entrance, her face contorted in a mask of rage. "I bloody well won't have a seat. I hope you like being sued, Chief Inspector. The constable literally pulled me from the shower. He barely gave me time to dress. No makeup. My bloody hair's still wet. If I don't die from pneumonia, my husband and I will certainly sue you and the entire local constabulary!"

With the life of his wife and son in the balance, the niceties of conversation wouldn't do. "Sit down and shut up!" He turned on the recorder and quickly entered the date, time and their names.

She sat and clenched her fists in front of her on the metal table.

David got in her face. "Time's of the essence. Here's what I know. Lord Hutton says he's having an affair with you and you're his alibi for Wednesday afternoon."

"Absurd." She drew up and jutted her chin at him. "I don't know what he's talking about."

"Stop lying. Was he or was he not with you Wednesday afternoon?"

She turned away, but not quickly enough to hide the red flush already spreading from her neck to her face.

"Dammit! Lord Hutton has stalked my wife and son. He's a cold-blooded murderer. He's killed four people in the last week."

She turned back and replied archly, "Have you lost your mind? Lord Hutton's no killer. He's not my lover. He's my husband's business partner. That's all."

"Maybe I wasn't clear. Now you're either his bed partner or his accomplice. Which is it? I've enough evidence to arrest him when I find him. And when I do, I can always let him know how cooperative you were. His solicitor might get him released on bond and you might just end up victim number five. We can protect you until he's caught. Otherwise, he's more than welcome to you."

"Evidence? What evidence?" What little composure the woman had, it was crumbling if her trembling hands were any indication.

"If you're convicted of being his accomplice either before or after the fact, you'll spend another ten to twenty years in prison. When you get out of nick, you'll be old, worn, haggard. There won't be much left of the supermodel. Or if he gets hold of you, he won't leave much of your pretty face by the time he carves off your breasts and stuffs them where the sun doesn't shine. That's what he did to Daisy Mellon."

The bitch had the decency to turn pale and gag. David waited a moment until she was partially composed before hammering at her again. "Were you with Lord Hutton on Wednesday afternoon or evening?"

"All right!" Anger flashed in her eyes. "I never saw Edward at all. He stood me up. Left me cooling my heels for two hours in a motel outside Keyeston." She began wringing her hands as she spoke. "Edward said Riley approached him and tried to extort money from him. Stubbs was stalking me. That's how he found out about my seeing Edward. He said he'd take care of Riley. I didn't know he'd kill him!" Tears streamed down her face. "You have to believe me."

Finally. The truth. "That's it?"

"That's all I know. He never said anything about the other murders. I assumed he only took care of Riley to protect me. I didn't know he was connected to the others."

"Interview terminated..." He gave the time and nodded to the constable outside. "Put her in a cell. We're holding her as a material witness."

"But..."

David strode from the interrogation room. No time to waste.

David rejoined Beecham in the squad room. "She confirms Hutton stood her up and Stubbs was blackmailing Hutton about their relationship. There's our link."

DS Tower nodded. "Good. 'Cause I haven't come across anything else to link Stubbs and his lordship."

The fax rang and David rushed for the machine. "Here it is. Crime scene photos of Dillehay and the evidence." The documents kept rolling off the fax.

"Here's a description by the only eyewitness who saw the driver." He tossed it at Beecham. "Kid said he looked like Sherlock Holmes with a deerstalker cap and pipe. There you go. Lord Hutton smokes a pipe."

One of the constables knocked on the squad room door. "Delivery at the front desk for Chief Inspector French. You'll have to sign for it, sir."

Expecting it was possibly more evidence from DI Santella, David nodded.

David signed for the package and returned to the squad room a minute later. "Hm. It's small, flat, like a CD or DVD," he said with growing unease. He check the return address. "And the return address is Lord Hutton's estate."

"Should we check it for anthrax?" Pettigrew asked from the corner.

"You may clear out if you want. This is specifically for me...a message of some sort." His gut twisted as if a boa constrictor had taken up residence. The package couldn't be good news.

He ripped open the pull tab and gingerly glanced inside. "No powder. Just a DVD." He glanced around.

"My computer will play a DVD," Beecham offered. "Careful, we'll play it then dust it for prints." Touching only the edges, he slid it into the computer, and David walked around behind Beecham and watched with growing fascination.

The image of Lord Hutton leaning back comfortably in a chair in his study, smoking his pipe, came up on the monitor screen.

"Chief Inspector French, you've come a little too close for comfort. By the time you receive this, I'll be on my way to Rio. It wasn't very nice of your subordinates, digging up those bloody clothes from my outbuilding, now was it?

"I have to say that this is a situation which got away with me entirely. I only set out to kill an extortionist antiques dealer—who would miss him anyway—and to frame his murder on that disgusting woman who debauched my wife." He puffed on his pipe, then continued.

"That's all I did. And then that bloody Mellon girl called and said she'd seen me turn in to the alley behind the antiques shop. She had the nerve to attempt to extort money from me. So..." He shrugged. "...she had to go.

"And then, the barmaid. Imagine hearing one's most private secrets bandied about in the pub by the likes of her. You must understand. I couldn't allow it, could I? Arranging her suicide was a little trickier. I did my research and let myself into her tiny little place. Neat housekeeper she was, though. Have to give her that."

He set his pipe aside on a table. "I spiked her wine with my wife's Valium," he said with a smile. "I'm afraid I used quite a bit of the stuff. If I'd had any left, I might've taken time to use it on my wife as well. A missed opportunity that. Oh well...one can't have everything."

From Hutton's self-righteous smiles and smirks, he obviously enjoyed playing before the camera.

"And then we come to the maitre d' at the White Goose. I really didn't have much time to plan as I would've liked. I prefer to do things at my own pace. I was rather late for dinner Wednesday night, so I slipped him a hundred and asked for a heads-up in case anyone inquired about my dinner appointment with my business partner Denton." He turned the pipe upside down and emptied the remaining tobacco, then set the pipe aside.

"Consider my consternation when he reported you and your wife were having dinner—you'll probably regret taking her along that night—and you'd inquired about my arrival time. I don't know what the world is coming to when extortion has become a valid career choice, but that bloody fellow tried to blackmail me into paying him more money. Obviously he had to go as well."

"So there you have it, Chief Inspector." He picked up his pipe and slid it into his jacket pocket. "Oh yes, one more thing. At an appointed time, you'll receive another DVD with a very important message. I'd stay tuned if I were you."

The monitor went black.

"Bloody hell!" David shook his head. "I don't believe he's slipped away like this. Check the flights from Heathrow to Rio. See what time he left."

Ten minutes later he had an answer. "Lord Hutton has a reservation for a flight at eleven tonight," the reservation clerk told him.

"He's still in country. We can get to him," he told Beecham. "I'll call the Met. They can pick him up for us."

David pulled his mobile from his pocket, jammed the ear bud in his ear, and called Miranda. "Status report, darling?"

"So far so good, but my stomach is dancing like a pair of elephants doing the *lambada*."

"We have him on the run. He messengered me a DVD with his confession for all the killings, then he said he's already gone, but we found a reservation for eleven tonight to Rio."

"Could it be a decoy?" she asked. "While he sneaks out of the country some other way?"

"Possibly. Whatever you do, don't let down your guard. Is Stafford there yet?" "Someone's coming up the lane now. That's probably him."

"Make sure before the door is opened." He paused, unsure of what to say next and not desiring to alarm her anymore than she already was. "He made an oblique threat concerning you."

"I'm not surprised, David. I'm sure he was stalking me today."

"He's promised the delivery of one more DVD, especially for me, but I'm afraid it's to keep me occupied and away from you."

The sick realization hit him like a sledge in the stomach. "Dammit. I know it is." He banged the desktop with his fist. "I'm coming home. Someone else can wait for the disc and call me with what he says."

"Good. Hurry. I'll feel so much safer once you're here." "How's Jamie taking all this?"

"His eyes are big with questions, but he's not asking any. By the way, he and Fields have bonded over the shotgun. But don't worry. He knows he's not to lay a finger on the thing."

"Great." The sound of a commotion reached him and his heart stuttered. "What's going on?"

"It's all right, hon. I think it's the sergeant."

"Tell him everything I've told you. I'm on my way."

He rang off and jammed the phone back in his pocket. "I'm heading out," he announced to Beecham, who was already on the phone with the Met. "I'll be on my mobile." Beecham nodded and waved him on.

A sense of time running out swamped and almost overwhelmed him. If anything happened to Miranda or Jamie... If he lost either one of them, he'd lose his reason for living.

Chapter Twenty-nine

Edward Hutton stepped around the corner of the manor house. Headlights glimmered through the grove of trees approaching the front of the estate.

Bugger. Someone was coming. He darted back. Who the bloody hell could it be? According to the exact hours he'd specified the DVDs be delivered, there hadn't been time for French to view both and be here. He'd planned everything carefully, if hurriedly, given the time constraints necessitated by the elimination of a pesky maitre d'.

He reached into his pocket and pulled out the silencer-equipped revolver his arms dealer associate Schoenfeld had provided. He waited until the vehicle stopped and its occupant started to emerge. He sighted and fired. The occupant collapsed backward.

He waited. No response from inside the manor.

Excellent.

He turned and retraced his steps until he found the convenient entry point he'd scouted that morning.

After I hung up from David, I stared out the window. DS Stafford had pulled up and parked, but he hadn't come in yet. Perhaps he was checking the perimeter of the house. It was already dark and something was nagging at me. I knew the estate had a security system, but just how good was it? "Fields?" I called.

"Yes, your ladyship?"

"Tell me about the security system. What all's covered?"

He frowned. "The estate has never been under attack before, and there's never been any reason to think we would be..." He paused.

"What are you trying so hard not to say?"

"His lordship's properties in London are wired up the ying-yang, if you pardon my using such an expression, but I'm afraid the system here isn't quite up to the same standard."

Uh-oh. If the situation was causing Fields to drop into using slang like ying-yang, then the situation was grave indeed.

"Just how much security do we have?"

"All entry points, both ground and first level are wired. Internal motion detectors which are only turned on at night after everyone has retired. No motion detectors outside.

We also have fire alarm service which connects directly with the nearest fire station."

"So Lord Hutton could be right outside and conceivably enter from the second floor if he had the proper equipment." Like a big-ass ladder or grappling hook, or was my imagination running away with me?

Fields sighed and cast his gaze toward the floor. "Yes, I'm afraid so, but I'm patrolling the second and third floors at hourly intervals, except for the north turret which is always kept locked."

"Does the rest of the staff understand the situation?"

"Yes. Only Mrs. Madison, Cook and I remain. I thought it best the daily cleaner and the kitchen maid be sent home."

I nodded. "Good idea. Should've thought of it myself."

"No, need. Staffing falls under my purview." He smiled and gave me a discreet bow.

"What's keeping the sergeant? Once he's inside, I'm sure we'll all feel safer."

Honestly Fields was a fifty-year-old man whose slender physique didn't exactly inspire confidence. I couldn't help but wonder if he ever got any exercise other than answering the door and announcing visitors and meals.

Fields must've read my mind, or perhaps the expression on my face, because he gave me a tight smile. "Your ladyship, in my youth I was a member of the SAS in the security division. Now, I know many individuals who claim such an association, but I assure you that I remain well-equipped physically and mentally to protect you and your son."

"The SAS? I've heard of it, but what is it exactly?"

"It's our military equivalent of your Delta Force or Special Forces. In recent years, there was a popular show on ITV called *Ultimate Force*. Quite a good one, actually."

"Until the sergeant comes inside, maybe I should patrol with you?" I suggested.

Fields scowled. "I'd rather you didn't. You should remain with the boy and keep him from being more concerned than he already is."

I nodded and watched my son who was now sitting quietly on the sofa and pretending to read his latest Harry Potter book. I sat down beside him and gave him a hug. "Sergeant Stafford's right outside, checking things out."

Jamie smiled up at me, but I could still see the concern in his dark eyes.

"We're going to be okay. Your father is on his way home too. Are you all right?"

A series of quick nods told me he was more upset than he was willing to admit.

"Let me see what's taking the sergeant." I stood up and walked into the entry hall, but I couldn't see anything. "Fields, do you think we should check on the sergeant?"

"No. I'm not opening that door until I hear the sergeant or his lordship's voice."

"Do you think he's surveilling outside?"

"Possibly," Fields said with a frown, "but I would've thought he'd check in with us first."

"Maybe he's just being cautious."

At least, that's what I hoped.

*

After Fields nixed my reconnaissance offer, I sat in the morning room with Jamie and read aloud from the latest Harry Potter. Trying to concentrate on the words was a total bitch. My gaze kept drifting to the front hall, and my ears were pricked for any untoward sounds. Fields stood next to a window and peered through the drawn draperies.

Jamie tugged on my sleeve. "With expression, Mummy. You're supposed to read with expression."

Thump.

"Fields," I called, "did you hear that?"

"Yes," he said. "I shall investigate." He and the shotgun headed back through the hallway.

The next thing I heard was, "Argh!" quickly followed by a heavy thud. I threw down the book and pulled Jamie to the floor. "Hide behind the other sofa," I whispered. He scurried out of sight.

I drew the revolver from my jacket pocket. Easing from the morning room into the entry hall, I found Fields crumpled in a heap. The shotgun was nowhere in sight. I jiggled his shoulder. "Fields?"

Without warning two strong hands grabbed my upper arms and shook me. My revolver clattered to the floor and slid across the black and white marble tile. I relaxed my body and allowed it to go limp. I slipped out of his grasp and scrambled for the gun. I had it—

"Not so fast, you bloody bitch." Lord Hutton fell on me and wrested the gun from my hands. "Where's the boy?"

I glared up at him. This was the same face that all his victims saw. The hatred. The pure evil. "You're too late. He went back to Provençe with his nanny so David and I could finish our honeymoon." I'm afraid I babbled this out without thinking.

"You're lying. Don't forget I saw you both this morning after your driver left with the nanny. Come on. You're going with me." He got to his feet and jerked me up as well.

"No!" I screamed and stomped on his foot, aiming for his

instep. Dammit. Missed.

At that moment, Jamie ran from behind sofa and attacked Hutton, pummeling his back with his small fists. The bastard kicked my son back into the sofa.

I reached up and clawed at Hutton's face, and yelled, "You won't get away with this. My husband—"

"To hell with your bloody husband. He's useless or he'd be here protecting you."

"He's on his way. I just spoke with him. You don't have a chance."

"That's what you think. Now, come on! We're going on a little nature walk."

Biding for time, I said, "Wait. Jamie needs his coat."

"No."

"No! He'll freeze." Empowered by a mother's fury, I doubled my fists and beat on Hutton's chest like a base drum. Out of nowhere his fist came at me. I found myself on the floor with my head ringing like Big Ben at midnight.

Jamie ran over to me. "I'm all right, Mum."

"Me, too," I managed to say.

"That bad man hit you." He stood with his hands on his hips. "My father says a gentleman never hits a woman." He glared at Hutton. "You're no gentleman."

"You might be right at that," Hutton said with a grim smile. He jerked my hands behind my back and tied them with cord he removed from his jacket pocket, then fastened dog collars around our necks.

Once the collars were fastened, fear and desperation hit me like a storm surge and washed me overboard. "Fields! Madison!"

And where was DS Stafford? Perhaps he waited outside to surprise Lord Hutton. I had to believe he was.

"I believe your butler remains somewhat indisposed. As for your housekeeper and cook—" Hutton broke off without finishing.

Ugly images filled my mind and my heart felt like it was falling to my feet. "What've you done?"

"They've come to no harm...not yet."

"You'll never get away with this." I had to stall for time.

"Come on. Clichés are of no use, your ladyship." He yanked me to my feet. My head still rung like an out of tune gong. He tugged on the leashes. "Time for our walk. I'm sure you'll enjoy it at least as much as my dogs."

As he led us outside, I glanced over my shoulder to check on Fields who still hadn't moved.

"Don't dilly-dally. Time is short."

Outside, it was dark, cold—oh, so cold. At least, Jamie had on a sweater and shirt, if no coat. It was below freezing. How long could Jamie last?

He led us past DS Stafford's car.

Oh, God. I could just make out the sergeant's body inside. His feet were on the ground, but he'd fallen back. He'd never made it out of the car for any kind of reconnaissance. Chalk up another kill for Hutton.

My legs grew rubbery and my stomach threatened to rebel. I stumbled over a rock. He jerked on my leash. "Come on. Move it."

"I can't move that fast. Please slow down." I stopped, gasped for air. The frigid cold seared its way to the bottom of my lungs.

"You'd like that, wouldn't you? Slow down so your stupid husband can catch me. Don't worry. By now, he thinks I'm on the way to Rio."

"Too bad you're not," I muttered. I wouldn't cry, no matter how much I wanted to dissolve in tears. Crying wouldn't help anyone.

One good thing—he hadn't bothered to check my pockets. I still had my cell phone and it was turned to vibrate, as always. Maybe David would be able to pinpoint our location…before it was too late.

Chapter Thirty

The Rover careened around an icy curve but held traction. David's mobile chimed. He pulled it from his pocket with one hand and answered. "French."

"Beecham here. We just received word that the Metropolitan Police have taken Lord Hutton into custody at Heathrow. DS Tower and I are heading to New Scotland Yard now, so you can relax."

Could he really?

"Thanks," he said guardedly. "I'll call my wife and let her know." Let her know what? That he was still worried? That Hutton's apprehension seemed a touch too easy?

He rang off from Beecham and hit the speed dial for Miranda's mobile.

No answer. He called the estate number.

No answer. Someone should bloody well be answering the estate number. Where was Fields? In the pit of his stomach, a sense of dread grew like a mushrooming cloud. Disbelief. Horror.

Again his mobile rang.

"Miranda?"

"Beecham, here. We just played the second DVD."

His counterpart's tone was leaden. What could it mean? "And?"

"I'll play it for you. First, pull over to the side of the road."

"I can't. No one's answering at home. I'm almost there."

"Bloody hell, mate," Beecham yelled in his ear. "Pull over. You need to hear every bleeding word of this."

"Right." David braked and pulled to the side of the road, but left the motor running.

"I'm listening." Dread collected and coiled in his gut like a cobra ready to strike.

"Now here we are again." Hutton's arrogant tone couldn't be mistaken for anyone else's. "I hope you're glued to a computer or DVD player because you're not going to want to miss this message. By the time you receive this, I'll have taken your wife and step-son to different locations. Both are in imminent danger of death. You must choose which one you'll rescue, because rescuing both is impossible. I've seen to it."

The bloody bastard sounded as if he were smiling. Did Hutton really have Miranda and Jamie? David had no choice. He must proceed as if he did.

"I'll offer you two clues. What time is high tide and how well does your wife swim? That would be the first. And how long can a small boy without a coat to keep him warm remain alive when the temperature is below freezing? In case you've lost count, that was the second clue."

High tide? Little Jamie outside without even a coat? Dear God. Panic nipped at the edges of his mind—no, he couldn't give into it.

"Oh, and they are miles apart. Make your choice wisely, Chief Inspector."

A choice? Between his son and his wife? What manner of monster would ask such a choice of anyone?

His breathing grew ragged. His vision blurred. The gathering cloud of dread expanded into a fiery rage. He floored the accelerator and roared away toward home.

"French? Are you there?"

Snapped back to reality by the sound of Beecham's voice in his ear, David answered,

"Yes."

"Do you really think he's got 'em?"

"Yes. I'll know in ten minutes." As clearly as a sun at daybreak, Hutton's treachery was laid before him. "Let the Met hold Hutton. Verify he really is Hutton. He could've hired a decoy and be leaving the country through another venue. If he's managed to get hold of my wife and son, we'll need every available man in the county to search for them.

There are a series of caves on the eastern portion of his estate. My friends and I used to play smuggler in them. Some of them flood completely at high tide. Check the tide tables."

"Tower's just pulled up the tide table info. Low tide is at zero point eight meters; high tide crests at two point six meters."

"Where could he have left your son?"

"In the woods somewhere; my estate lands join Hutton's to the rear." "Think the 'miles apart' was BS?"

"Possibly. Time's an issue for him. He's a careful planner, so he'd have a place in mind, already prepared. Plus, he has to control my wife and son both. He's not a team player, so no one's helping him."

"We're ready. Just give the word."

David drove around the fountain and pulled to a squealing stop right behind Stafford's motor. "Stafford's here, but I—wait—"

He kept the phone connection live, jumped from his car and glanced inside Stafford's. "Stafford's slumped in the front seat." Dead?

He felt for Stafford's carotid where he found the faintest of pulses. "Officer down!" he shouted into the mobile. We need an ambulance. He's alive...barely. Going to check the house."

David flew up the steps. The door unlocked. He entered and in his haste, nearly stumbled over Fields lying in the entry hall. He knelt beside him and checked him for injuries. The unconscious servant had a bruised temporal area but his pulse was steady and strong.

The acrid odor of smoke reached his nostrils. God. Bloody place was on fire. He ran to the morning room. Signs of a scuffle were everywhere. A chair, two tables and a lamp overturned.

Bloody bastard.

"Miranda!" he called, but the knowledge flooded through him, more bitter than the greenest fruit.

He was too late.

But where were the rest of the staff? "Madison! Cook!" Where could they be? He flew downstairs. Smell of smoke heavier. His eyes burned. His head pounded. No one. "Cook?" he called again. Had they managed to escape?

And leave an injured Fields behind? No.

The pantry?

He banged his fist on the massive oak door. "Anyone there?" A feeble cry. "Help us!"

He tugged on the handle.

Locked. Bloody hell!

"Hold on." The key? He remembered it from childhood, but no time to look for the bloody thing. The air grew heavier with smoke. His lungs burned with each breath.

He grabbed a large iron skillet and bashed the lock over and over.

Nothing. He started to choke. His breath came in gasps. He grabbed a towel and soaked it in the sink, then wrung out the excess and held the towel to his mouth and nose.

Think, man. Think.

Then it came to him. The storage room off the kitchen. An old ax used to chop wood. He grabbed the ax and ran back to the kitchen. "Stand back," he ordered, gasping for air. He raised the ax high over his head and bashed the lock with all his strength.

Again and again. The heavy door and lock resisted, but finally it splintered and bits of wood flew back and stung his face. No matter. The lock was history.

He jerked open the door. Cook, with Madison close behind her, tumbled out. "Oh, my word, your lordship. That horrible man. He took them." She started coughing and gagging for air. "He set a fire?"

David nodded and handed her the wet towel. "Breathe through this. Fields is down in the hall. We have to drag him out. My sergeant's wounded in his car. One of you, see if you can do anything for him." He glanced around desperately. Where was the fire? "The extinguisher? Where?"

Cook bent over and pulled it from a lower cabinet and handed it over to David. "Now, get out of here," he said.

"I'm sorry, your lordship." A somewhat unsteady Fields stood in the kitchen doorway. "He took me by surprise. You have to go after them, sir. I'll find the fire."

"You're hurt. Concussed."

"My head is harder than one might think." Fields coughed. "I believe it's coming from the wine cellar." He took the extinguisher from David.

"Careful." Aware of Fields' background and training, he didn't doubt his ability to contain the fire.

Fields nodded, then stumbled toward the wine cellar.

Desperation clawed his gut to ragged ribbons of fear. "Madison and Cook, get out of the house now!"

He guided the women upstairs and out to the front. Once in the cold fresh air, he gasped and set to coughing up what felt like his very lungs.

"Stafford—see if he's still alive. Do what you can for him. I've got to think."

Madison knelt beside Stafford's unmoving body and felt for the sergeant's pulse. "Barely, sir."

"Check the boot. See if there's anything to cover him with. We're all going to bloody well freeze to death. Keep moving."

Cook coughed and took a ragged breath. "Never mind us, sir. That poor little tyke doesn't even have a coat. Horrible man wouldn't let her ladyship put one on him, no matter how hard she begged and cried. We heard her screaming through the ventilation ducts. Everything. We heard it all."

David sucked in a deep breath. He paced, trying to wipe away the frightening images of Miranda and Jamie freezing to death. The temperature was below freezing and plummeting. Winter storms were wreaking havoc with Europe and were headed this way. He had to find Jamie...and then Miranda.

"What about Miranda?" he asked.

"Wouldn't let her wear a coat, neither, sir. Not that she cared. She kicked and screamed over the boy until..."

"Until what?"

"He must've hit her, your lordship, 'cause there was a loud crash." Cook stopped and wiped her eyes.

Madison took up the horrifying narrative at that point. "He made us go down to the pantry and he locked us inside. We would've died in the fire if you hadn't come when you did." She shivered and collapsed weakly against the sergeant's car.

In the distance he heard the claxon of an ambulance.

From behind him, he heard Fields' footsteps. "The fire in the cellar's out. Would've had Armageddon if it had spread to the stores. He set the fire in the middle of the wine cellar with paper."

"Madison, you and Cook back in the house before you freeze to death."

Freeze to death?

Was that what Miranda and Jamie were experiencing now? Not just a clichéd phrase, but the cold hard reality. "How'd Hutton get in?" David asked in a whisper. Desperation drained him until he could barely speak.

"Tunneled into the wine cellar and ambushed me as I came down from checking the upper floors."

"Through solid stone?"

"Somehow he accessed the house through the abandoned drainage system."

The claxon grew louder. David jumped up and strained to see the blue flashing lights now visible through the grove of trees leading to the manor house, as well as the tactical van following. Two EMTs emerged from the ambulance with Beecham and DS Tower hopping out of the van.

Like clockwork, the EMTs set to working on Stafford. They checked his wound, took his vital signs, and started an intravenous in the space of what seemed like seconds.

"Will he make it?" he asked of a fresh-faced young man who didn't look old enough to have graduated from his local comprehensive.

"It'll be close, sir. The cold helped. Reduced his oxygen needs."

They bundled Stafford up and took him away. David turned to Beecham. "It's a bloody mess. He's got them."

"I heard. Your mobile's still active. Didn't shut it off until we got here."

"Oh, right." David pulled the ear bud from his ear and stared at it for a moment. "Wait. Miranda always has her mobile with her. She never turns it off. We can track her with the GPS and all that, right?"

Beecham rolled his eyes. "Be a lot simpler if we were in London. Hold on. I've some calls to make."

Now that he could breathe easier, David paced back and forth, growing more and more anxious with each passing minute. His wife and son were out in this weather which was worsening by the second.

While Beecham made his calls requesting authorization for GPS tracking on Miranda's mobile, six more vehicles from Kinsey Green constabulary pulled up and at least four men emerged from each.

The search party.

Twenty-four men to search acres and acres of heavily forested land and a warren of caves.

David itched to run shouting into the woods and what would that accomplish?

Nothing.

The best use of resources deemed thorough organization was the key.

Beecham rang off. "The county has one unit capable of tracking GPS and they're on the way from Keyeston constabulary. Should be here in fifteen minutes. I've also requested helicopter coverage with thermal imaging. They're going to try to take off, but the severity of the storm's a problem. Might be easier to pick up their traces that way."

If the storm would allow the helo to take to the air. If his wife and son weren't already dead. Two very big "ifs".

David nodded. He'd never experienced the victim's side of a kidnapping; not many of the force had. It took every ounce of self-control to keep from collapsing and being useless. But rolling around on the ground and surrendering to his fear wouldn't help anyone.

"You've got to make a choice, sir. Until the GPS unit and the helo support arrive, where do you want the search focused? We've twenty-four men for a foot search of the woods between here and the caves."

"Make a choice? Between my wife and my son?" David shook his head. "Do you know my wife thinks she's pregnant? How can I choose between them?"

"Think logically, sir."

"Logically? This situation defies logic, Beecham."

Beecham tried to place a hand on his shoulder, but David shoved him away. "Give me a minute. I have to think." He walked toward the front steps, sat down and hung his head between his hands.

Images of Miranda and Jamie playing on the beaches at San Remo. Jamie running up with a colorful shell, his dark eyes alight with joy.

Miranda's soft green gaze smiling up at him after making love. A new child coming—boy or girl—no matter. And now to lose any one of them?

Unthinkable. What man could choose one over the other?

Allow one son to die in order to save his wife and another child. Make no bones about it, Jamie was as much his child as the child to come would be. Blood or not.

How could he ever explain to Miranda that he'd chosen her over her firstborn? She would never understand his decision, no matter his explanation, and she'd blame him for her son's death for as long as she lived.

Time. A matter of time. Jamie without a coat abandoned somewhere in the woods in below freezing weather. His wife, pregnant, stranded in a place where the high tide would take her life. High tide was just after midnight, but she might not have even that long before where she was flooded. She had to be in that vast warren of caves on Hutton's land.

"David."

He looked up. Beecham stood with his hat in hand, brushing

away the flakes of snow beginning to fall. "The men. Tell us where to focus our efforts."

"The woods. Search the woods first. Hutton's statement about placing them "miles apart" was a bluff. He didn't have time."

"Still a lot of territory for only twenty-four men. Any areas of focus?" He spread out a topographical map. "Can you think of any possible route he might take?"

David stood. "Yes, there's a shortcut through the woods. If he took Miranda to the caves, he wouldn't go too far out of his way. For his own safety, he had to get her there during low tide."

"We'll search along that route then."

"All right. I'll lead. I know the shortcut. Been that way many times when I was a lad," David said.

"All right, men. You heard the Chief Inspector. We're to follow his lead through the woods. Tower, you man the tactical van and notify me the moment the helo's in the air and when the GPS tracker unit arrives."

"Will do."

"Will you let me know if there's any word on DS Stafford's condition?" David asked.

Tower nodded.

"Let's go." David didn't wait for anything or anyone else. He tore off in all-out run toward back of the estate property and the iced over frozen woods. Driven by desperation. Driven by love for his family. And driven by the realization...time was running out.

Chapter Thirty-one

"Come on. Come on." Lord Hutton yanked on the tether around my neck. Even with a heavy knapsack strapped over his shoulder, he moved so quickly over the slippery and uneven terrain I could barely keep up with him. He'd tied my hands behind my back, and it was all I could do to stay on my feet. Yet all I could think about was my son freezing to death.

"You've got to let me go back. He's just a little boy. It's too cold. You can't just leave him like that. He'll die!" I screamed and cried, but Lord Hutton just smiled.

"That's the point, Lady Middlebury. He'll die. You'll die, and DCI French will have learned a valuable lesson. He shouldn't have nosed into my affairs."

"You're heartless. What did you expect David would do? That he'd overlook how many murders over some "old school tie" bull shit?"

"So common."

"Great. I'm being lectured on social niceties by a serial killer."

"Shut up, woman, or I'll cut out your tongue. I'm sure that would make a lovely scene for your husband to stumble across."

I shivered and shut my mouth. Far better to use my energies to pray for Jamie's rescue. I had no idea where the bastard was taking me. It would've been bad enough if he'd left me with Jamie. At least I'd have been able to keep his little body warm and give David time to find us. I knew he was bound to be searching frantically by now. I'd felt my cell phone vibrate at least twice.

Wherever the fruitcake was taking me, I had a better chance for survival than a little six-year-old boy left outside sealed in a wooden box...unless he intended to kill me outright.

Inside the wooden box, Jamie shivered. The bad man had hit Fields and then his mother and dragged the two of them outside into the cold. And it was *dark*.

"Your father will find you. Don't worry. He'll come." Those were the last words he'd heard his mum say before the bad man shut him in the box and took off in the woods with her.

His father would come because he was a very smart detective. An important one, too. But he wished his father would hurry. Terribly cold. He rubbed his arms and flexed his fingers. He couldn't even feel his feet. His whole body was growing numb.

Maybe it wouldn't be so bad. All he had to do was go to sleep. But it was too cold to sleep.

What would Harry Potter do? Of course Harry was a wizard and could perform spells. Too bad it was just a story. He could use a spell or two right now. First he'd cast a spell for a fire to keep him warm, and then he'd cast a mean spell on the bad man who'd hurt mum. That would be just what the bugger deserved.

But he wasn't supposed to use words like bugger. As long as he didn't say it out loud, no one would know. In spite of his constant shivering, he grinned.

He'd tell himself a story until his father came to rescue him—that's what he'd do.

But what story? And so aloud, he began to tell himself the story of wizard Harry Potter from the very beginning.

Numbing cold. The darkest night David's soul had ever known. But he wouldn't give up. Jamie and Miranda weren't lost to him forever. No.

Desperation—no other word came close to the misery threatening to overwhelm him every second of his trek through the woods.

How long had it been? No bloody idea.

How long could a child survive in near blizzard conditions? The fury of the storm, which had already devastated Europe had descended full upon the search party and increased the difficulty in finding any kind of trail Hutton might've left in his one last mad hurrah.

A dog handler had been called, but he'd yet to catch up with the rest of their team. "Branch out twenty paces on either side," David called. "Slowly and carefully. And for God's sake, listen for the slightest sound."

Onward they forged. In spite of the snow and wind, not one man of them complained. David would forever be grateful...no matter the outcome.

And Miranda—where was she? Would she understand his reason for searching for Jamie first? Of course she would. And she would fight for her life and that of their unborn child. In spite of her many fears, she wasn't a pushover. Far from it.

Hold on, darling. I'll find Jamie, then I'll come for you.

Was he lying to himself and to her? No. One way or another he would find his family and keep them safe and sound. No other outcome was conceivable.

Hold on.

"Come on!" Lord Fruitcake yelled and jerked on my leash for the umpteenth time. "Bloody stupid woman."

"You're going too fast. Lost my footing." I slipped and fell— okay, it was on purpose. I'd already decided I'd do whatever I could to slow him down.

He grabbed me by the shoulders and hoisted me to my feet. "One more fall, and I'll end your misery right here and now." He glared down at me. The rage poured off him in waves.

"I can't help it. It's slippery."

"Shut up!" He backhanded me, but I saw it coming and went with the blow. "I can't stand your whining."

"Then you should've left me at home, your lordship. It's bad enough you've left my child to freeze to death. And you can't stand my whining? Screw you!"

He turned and faced me. I saw death in his cold blue gaze

"One more bloody word from your trashy mouth and I will break your neck and leave you on the trail—a present for your interfering husband."

I bit back the rush of trash talk threatening to spill out. The longer I stayed alive the better the chance David would find me. He couldn't be far behind.

Finally we came out of the woods onto the cliffs, the ones Mina had warned us about. Hutton walked over to the edge and looked down. Since I was on a short leash, I was right behind him and could see below to the swirling black water. The brunt of a horrible winter storm was whipping snow and ice all around us. The rocks below were icy, and my breath almost froze in my throat whenever I inhaled.

"Now what?" Was he going to shove me over? God, I hated heights.

"Low tide was at six seventeen," he said not answering my question. "Keep going." I looked at Lord Fruitcake. "Where?"

"Down the cliff."

"How?" My hands and fingers were stiff from the icy conditions and quickly turning into frozen lumps of meat.

He set his shoulder knapsack down and opened it. He pulled out what looked like mountain climbing equipment—ropes, a hammer-like instrument with a curved spike at the head and some kind of harness contraption.

I shook my head. "I'm not good with heights."

He snatched me by the arm and leaned me over the edge of the cliff. "I'll bet you're not good with falls either."

A rush of vertigo made my head swim, and I nearly passed out from the sight of the rocks and imagining my broken body lying on them. He jerked me back from the edge, untied my hands from behind my back, then retied them in front of me.

"I'm going first," he said, "then you'll follow."

"Unh-uh." I tried to back up.

He jerked on the leash. "If you don't follow willingly, I'll pull you over and you'll end up down there. Do you understand?"

Man, did I ever. I nodded.

He set about tying one rope to the leash, then he took another and secured it to one of the rocks with a spike, using the spiked hammer to drive it in. He lowered himself over the side of the cliffs. I leaned over and made out a small ledge in the darkness. I sat and tried to wiggle my hands and fingers from their bindings, but they were useless from the freezing cold. I might never play the violin again. Funny how something so relatively unimportant could pop into my mind at such a time.

Too soon, I felt a tug at my neck.

"Your turn."

"I can't do it. I'm a musician not a frigging mountain goat. You tied my hands."

Silence. Then he uttered a long string of colorful British expletives.

"Yes, you can. That's why your hands are in front of you. Put yourself in the other harness."

"I can't. I'll fall."

"One way or another, you're coming down," he growled. "Don't make me come up there, because if I do, I'll throw you down. I have an appointment and your dilly-dallying is making me late."

"But—"

"Listen to me. Put yourself into the harness, fasten it and secure the end over the head of the spike. Drop the long line. I'll catch it, and you'll repel down to me."

I hurried to follow his directions. Nothing was more important than staying alive. I worked at the harness. Finally I dropped the long line to Lord Fruitcake and said a quick prayer and ended with, *I love you, Jamie. Daddy will find you. David, I love you.*

I eased over the edge and dangled there for a moment, terrified to go any farther and terrified not to. I don't know how long it took—at least a year and a day—but my feet eventually touched the ledge. I gasped for air. I must've held it all the way down.

"See what you can do when you try," Lord Fruitcake said.

From the narrow ledge I saw an opening about two feet in circumference and no higher than knee level.

"Now what?"

"Get down and crawl." He shoved me to my knees. With no other choice, I crawled through the cave entrance and found I was able to stand.

Inside the cave and out of the blowing icy wind, it seemed almost warm in comparison.

He threw something at my feet. "Here."

I bent down and picked it up. He'd given me his watch. "Why?" I was pretty damn sure I already knew the answer.

"These caves flood with the high tide. High tide tonight is three minutes past twelve. I want you to know exactly how long you have left to live."

I had to ask? Sheesh.

The LED dial read three minutes before eight.

He grunted. I got back down on my knees to see what the hell he was doing just in time to see him roll a boulder in place over the cave entrance.

He'd sealed me inside the cave—a cave that would flood in four hours and six minutes.

Okay, I was out of the wind and snow, but it was dark, blacker than anything I'd ever experienced...oppressively so. The darkness seemed to enter my mind and grow like a smothering cloud.

Carefully I eased a foot to my left, running my hands over the cave's walls. Smooth. I reached as high as I could, still smooth. That bore out what Lord Hutton said about the caves flooding.

I moved gingerly back to my original spot and tried moving to the right. Still smooth as high and as far as I could reach. Terrified of stepping into a drop-off and falling, I moved with caution.

I pulled out my cell phone. The screen provided a second or two worth of light. No signal. Of course not. At least I'd left it on. If they thought to use a GPS locator, they could follow my movements from the cell towers.

I edged to the front of the cave. Maybe if I was close enough to the opening...?

The cold draft increased the closer I moved toward the boulder which sealed me inside. Fearing I'd stumble and drop the cell, I put it back in my pocket. I felt around the edges of the cave opening. At one spot, I was able to wiggle my fingers through to the outside...barely.

I snatched them back before they turned into freezer pops. I looked at the cell phone screen. Still no signal from inside the cave even at the entrance, but if I slid it out through the opening, maybe...just maybe someone would find me before midnight.

I pulled Lord Fruitcake's watch from my other pocket. The LED dial read: ten minutes after eight.

From somewhere in the cave, the sound of water...coming and going. The tide had turned.

Edward Hutton, Lord Hutton, made a quick climb back up the cliffs. He attributed his physical prowess and strength to his daily long walks with his dogs. Too bad he had to leave them behind, but someone would care for the little buggers.

He hauled his body over the edge and glanced down. The tide was turning and soon his vengeance would be complete. He untied the repelling equipment from the piton and looped it over his shoulder. He tugged on the piton, but it held firm so would have to remain. Snow would soon bury it anyway.

He glanced at his wrist, then smiled as he remembered he'd given his watch to the soon-to-be late Lady Middlebury.

Never mind.

He still had time to reach his exit point and money to last a lifetime.

Slogging through the bitter cold and whipping snow was nothing compared to the despair eating at David's heart. A child couldn't last this long. Already too late.

Then the faintest sound...

"And...then...Harry...took..." The tiny voice grew fainter with each word.

"Quiet! I hear something." David strained to hear in the sudden silence. "Jamie! Jamie! Where are you?"

Dear heaven, let him answer.

Nothing. David swallowed his disappointment. Drops of sleet were freezing on his face. He swiped them with his gloved hand, but the knowledge his son didn't even have a pair of gloves hurt him more than the stinging nettles of sleet hitting his face.

"Jamie!" Silence again as they all stopped and listened.

Finally a faint cry. "Fa...ther?"

I was cold. Never been so deep down, bone-chilling cold. Keep moving. At least I was out of the wind. I'd always been told caves had a constant temperature, and so they may, but this one was damn near close to freezing. Tears had already frozen to my cheeks in our trek through the woods to the caves.

My son was freezing to death in a wooden box. Maybe he was already... No.

David, find Jamie first.

Over and over in my head I sent the message to him. It only made sense. A small child couldn't last long in the below freezing temperatures. It might be close, but if David didn't find Jamie, I wasn't sure I wanted to survive. For the most part, I'd had a wonderful life, but Jamie's was still in front of him.

If I didn't make it... Poor David. So many losses: his mother, brother, Cassie and then me.

But I *had* to survive. More than likely, I was carrying our first child together. This baby had a right to be born and grow up with both his parents and his older brother.

Get off your ass.

All right, I was at the point of talking to myself. At least I didn't have to face the smirking bastard who sealed me in here.

The sound of rushing water intensified. Would there be any kind of air pocket at high tide?

No. The icy water would sap my strength and energy long

before the tide ebbed.

Chapter Thirty-two

"Did you hear?" David glanced around, afraid he'd imagined hearing Jamie's voice.

The members of the search party stood stock still. The snow whirled and eddied with the wind.

DS Tower nodded. "Aye."

"Jamie! Jamie!" David called. He hadn't imagined it. His son was still alive. "Where are you?"

Silence. The blowing snow even made more noise. In the distance, the sharp crack of a falling tree.

"Call out, son. We're here. We'll find you!" David collapsed on his knees and dug furiously at the snow. So close, but so far. Where was he?

"Spread out, men. He can't be far."

The men tromped and trudged along both sides of the trail. They stopped intermittently to listen for any sound.

"Jamie!" David called, his throat raspy from screaming.

"Sir!" came a shout from David's left. "Here's a box or something."

David, along with every man of them, converged on the spot. They dug through the snow with their bare hands. They uncovered the box. David ripped off the side wooden slats and inside...

"Jamie. Oh, my God." His son was pale, nearly frozen and shivering. David jerked off his overcoat and wrapped his son in it.

"He's freezing." He rubbed Jamie's hands and arms. His eyes were shut and his little body was limp, but there was a weak pulse in his throat. "We've got to warm him up."

An EMT had remained behind to assist with the search party. He stepped forward.

"Sir. It's only a few minutes back to the 'ouse. Let me 'ave 'im. I'll get the little fellow warmed up. You need to find your wife."

"Is he going to be all right?" David didn't want to let his son go. But—

"The sooner I get him inside, the better his chances. He was in good health before— right?"

David nodded. "Yes, excellent."

The EMT held out his arms. "Come on. Let me 'ave 'im. I'll run like 'ell."

"All right. Go!"

The EMT opened his coat and covered Jamie's body with it. The EMT took off, and the rest of the party gathered round David. "What now, sir?" Tower asked.

"The caves. I'm sure that's where he's taken her." He pointed. "This way."

He headed in a northeasterly direction through the woods. The blizzard winds had died down somewhat. The actual trail was obscured by mounding drifts of snow but the lack of tall growth made the way easier to follow. Now the party had better direction, they moved at a rapid pace through the woods.

With the sound of water coming closer and closer with each surge of the tide, I wondered how long I could tread water. What a cruel joke. I'd already tried to find handholds along the cave walls, but no luck.

No handy ledges either.

I kept moving in a small safe path, back and forth. If I stopped moving, it would mean I'd given up.

And I would never give up. My son needed his mother, and I had a baby to bring into the world. My hands went to my belly. I hoped he or she wasn't as cold as I was. I pulled Lord Fruitcake's watch from my pocket.

Nine. Three hours was plenty of time for David to find me. I played a scenario in my head. He'd already found Jamie who was back at the estate being warmed in front of the fire and being spoon-fed hot soup personally by Cook.

David was on his way. In my mind's eye I saw him crashing through the woods, stumbling upon Lord Fruitcake's equipment.

Damn. He'd better have left it.

What about the cell phone? Was the battery holding out? I inched my way back to the entrance and wiggled my fingers through the opening.

Damn thing was frozen to the rock. Would it still work in the extreme cold?

David was coming. David was coming. All I had to do was stay alive.

What if old Fruitcake was lying? What if this cave didn't flood? Maybe he just said that to torture her.

No. With a sickening lurch, I remembered the smoothness of the cave walls. No such luck.

Huddled inside the tactical van, DS Tower listened to the squawk box. The helo was in the air and running systematic sweeps over the woods behind French's estate.

"Rapidly moving heat signature, heading southwest. Multiples moving northeast," the helo pilot said. "Storm's dying down. We've a better chance of staying in the air."

"They must've found the boy." Tower let out a sigh of relief. "They're headed to the coast and the caves. Follow and sweep the cave area."

What chance the child was still alive? Still, someone was running toward the estate for a reason.

Tower punched in the number for the estate. "They may've located the boy. The helo pilot reports a rapidly moving heat signature coming back to the estate. We're going to need hot blankets, hot water bottle, whatever you have," he told the butler. "There's another ambulance on the way, but with the storm there's no way to know the ETA.

A pause, then, "We'll be ready."

David and the search party emerged from the woods into a small clearing before the sheer drop of the cliffs. There was little to remind him of the days when he'd played smuggler on those same cliffs. The snow drifts ranged from knee to waist high. He stopped long enough to catch his breath.

Beecham, too, was bent at the waist gasping for air. "Have to lose some weight once this is over. Can't do many more forced marches like this."

"What about the GPS locator?" David asked Beecham.

"I'll check with Sergeant Tower." Beecham grabbed the walkie-talkie from his shoulder. "Tower, GPS unit here yet?"

"On line now, guv. Last location noted is at the coast." Tower gave the latitude and longitude readings.

Beecham listened, then said, "Signal's weak and growing weaker. Stationary. Hasn't moved in ten minutes. Looks like we're right on top of her."

David eased to the edge of the cliffs. "I have to go down. There's a ledge with a cave entrance partway down this cliff." He had to believe Hutton came prepared. Miranda couldn't have managed without help. He peered down at the rocks below, fearing what he might find. No—the craggy boulders below were barely visible above the rushing waves where the tide was moving in rapidly.

Beecham walked over to David's side. "Careful. Cliff face is solid ice. You won't make it."

"Hutton and my wife made it." Had to believe she had. Any other outcome— inconceivable. "I can make it." He knelt in the snow. "They had to have some kind of equipment to get down there. Maybe..." He found a protuberance and brushed away the snow. "Here's a piton. All we need is a rope."

"You're nuts, but it's your wife. I'd do the same." Beecham turned and called, "Rope!"

One of the searchers ran forward with a thick coil of rope

looped over his shoulder. "Thank you," David said, then bent down and tied the rope though the eye of the piton.

"Set up the lights," Beecham ordered while he braced the piton as David slid over the cliff's edge. "We're going to be here for a while."

David's boots weren't meant for mountain climbing or repelling. They scrabbled and slid against the cliff face. He couldn't imagine Miranda making the trip downwards...if indeed she made it.

How far was the ledge? He chanced a downward glance and wished he hadn't. It was a lot farther than he remembered. As boys, they'd approached from the beach and climbed like monkeys all over the cliffs. But that was in summer—not the dead of winter in a storm.

The rope was wet and freezing. The further he journeyed downward, the more slippery it was. Once, he slipped a scary three feet and only his feet hitting the ledge stopped his dizzying descent.

The ledge. He'd made it. Now where was the bloody cave?

Fields paced back and forth in the kitchen but made periodic trips to the rear entrance. No sign of anyone with the boy or the ambulance, either.

Bugger.

"We've woolen blankets in the oven, and Cook is stirring up a pot of chicken soup to feed him if he's able to swallow," the housekeeper said. "We'll warm that child up quick as a wink." She rubbed her upper arms. "I can't imagine the two of them out in this weather. Lord Hutton is an absolute fiend and Sir David must be out of his mind with worry."

"Certainly not his best day," Fields muttered. Not anyone's idea of a best day. In fact, he couldn't imagine a worse one. He strode to the rear door and opened it for what had to be the tenth time in the last hour.

The blowing snow and biting wind had died down and the full

moon had risen. In the distance he made out a half-running, half-stumbling, dark figure emerging from the woods. "He's carrying the boy! Quick, a blanket."

Cook opened the oven, jerked out the blanket and thrust it at him. "Here. Now move it."

Any other time Fields would've resented her tone, but not tonight. He grabbed the blanket and raced out the door without taking time for a pair of wellies.

Outside he stumbled through the drifts, some of them waist high.

Drat. He might get wet, but the boy needed the hot blanket more. Onward he trudged until he met the shivering EMT holding the small, still boy.

"Good man. You've brought a heated blanket. He's almost a goner. Got to get the little tyke inside."

Chapter Thirty-three

I looked at Lord Fruitcake's watch. Eleven.

All right, David. If you're going to rescue me, now would be a good time.

The sound of the water surging and slapping against the cave walls was closer and closer. I couldn't be sure, but it sounded as if it was already in my part of the cave. Would I even know how close until my feet got wet?

A new desperation seized my imagination. I could swim and I could tread water, but how long would it take for hypothermia to set in and weaken my resolve. I couldn't just give up.

"Randi..."

It was a woman's voice, and I heard it in my head over the sound of rushing water. "What?"

"Don't give up. You're strong. You always were."

"Gran?"

Dammit. Gran was right. I had to get out of that hell hole somehow. If David wasn't coming... Of course he was coming. But would he be in time?

I felt my way back to the small cave entrance. I lay down, drew up my knees and kicked at the stone Fruitcake had used to seal me inside the cave.

Nothing. I kicked again and again. Lying on the cave floor chilled me more deeply than if I was outside. I kicked again. Nothing, but I kept it up. If anything the physical activity increased my heart rate and made me feel as if I were actually doing something—as opposed to lying down and waiting for rescue like some damsel in distress and too stupid to live.

Gran was right. I was strong. I kept kicking. Something had to give. Might as well be a boulder. And if Fruitcake took the climbing gear with him—well, I'd worry about that once I kicked the boulder to bits.

Lord Hutton emerged from the woods on his estate lands. There it was: a hired Rover. Hired with a false identity. He unlocked the door and slid inside. The authorities would be looking for him at Heathrow. Good enough for the fools. All he needed now was to drive to Dover, normally a four-hour journey, but who knew how long it would take in this weather. Not even a winter storm would keep him from reaching Dover. There he would reconnoiter with the contact who would provide him with a new identity. He would cross into Europe through the Chunnel, drive south through France, then farther south to Italy. From there, he would then fly to Brazil. Through his contacts he'd already arranged the purchase of a lavish villa on the sunny coast near Rio de Janeiro. After all, Brazil was renowned for its beautiful women.

Yes, Rio... He could hardly wait. It was summer there, and with all the money a man would ever need and no nagging wife to spend it, he would live out his years in comfort and enjoy every moment.

By the time he reached Dover, it would be all over for the common Lady Middlebury. Without a doubt, her son was already dead. If French had just stayed out of his business, only one person need have died. His wife's lesbian lover would've been found guilty of Stubb's murder and imprisoned for years. All the other tidying up wouldn't have been necessary.

Indeed, it was all French's fault and the nosy little Yank he'd married.

*

David yelled to Beecham at the top of the cliffs. "I've hit the ledge. The cave entrance I remembered is covered by a large stone." He brushed away the ice and snow as best he could. The ledge was only a foot wide. It'd seemed much wider when he was a boy. Below the ledge was a sheer drop to the rocks and swirling tide waters, but he put his shoulder to the stone.

His feet slipped on the ice. Down to his knees. He swallowed back the wave of terror. "It's slippery. I'm tying the rope around my waist," he yelled.

"I'm coming down," Beecham yelled back.

"No! The ledge might give way under both our weights."

"Thanks a lot, French. Should I send someone who's built like you?"

David gave the rock another nudge. "No!" He pulled the Swiss Army knife from his pocket. Maybe he could chip away the ice at the top and free the stone blocking the cave entrance.

His fingers felt something, an anomaly. Something rather more regular than usual for the surface of a rock...and a rhythmic vibration emanating not from the phone, but from the stone itself. "Light! Lower me a torch."

Beecham quickly lowered a torch. David turned it on and shone it on the anomaly.

A mobile phone was frozen to the rock. Miranda's mobile phone.

"It's my wife's mobile," he yelled. "Miranda! Can you hear me?"

The rhythmic vibrations increased in frequency and intensity. "Miranda!"

Desperation seized him. He hacked at the periphery of the stone, finally freeing the edges of ice.

"Dammit, Miranda. You'd better answer me. You'd better not die on me now. I will never forgive you if you do. We found Jamie. He's going to be all right." He wasn't lying. His son had to survive. "An EMT took him and ran back to the estate."

"Da-vid..."

Alive. By God, she was alive. "Keep kicking. It's moving. We almost have it."

He nudged the stone, then put his back into it. The boulder rolled a half meter revealing the entrance and a pair of size six shoes which thankfully were still attached to his wife.

"David!"

"Yes, yes. I'm here. Hold on just a second longer."

"That's about all I have. Water's lapping at my hair line."

He gave another heave and the entire cave entrance was free. "Come on."

"Hold on. I have to crawl out."

A grunt or two later, Miranda's blonde head poked from the opening. "I'm so freaking glad to see you. Did you find Jamie? Is he all right?"

"He's all right." He pulled her carefully to her feet. "Easy. It's icy. Don't look down."

"No surprise there. I will *not* look down." She threw her arms around his waist.

"No, I wouldn't either if I were you." He removed the rope from his waist. "Put this on. Raise your arms. That's a good girl." He tied it under her arms as she shivered and her teeth chattered. Her face was pale. So pale. "Beecham! Pull her up. And carefully, mate."

He watched from the ledge at Miranda's slow ascent. He let out a sigh of relief when the last of her sweet body disappeared over the cliff top. She was safe. Thank God.

A second or two later, Beecham let the rope snake down to David's waiting hands.

He grasped it and tied it around his chest. "All right."

A smiling Beecham leaned over the edge. "Good mind to leave you down there, mate. You've been nothing but trouble since we met."

"Most humorous. And here I was positive you had no sense of humor." David glanced down and took a deep breath. The tide waters were even with the ledge.

"If you don't hurry, my feet are going to get wet. Now haul me up."

"You wife's backside is all wet. I don't think having wet tootsies will hurt *you*."

Beecham laughed at his joke. "Come on, mates. Let's haul the Chief Inspector up, so we can get back and have our cuppa."

Whether it was David's weight, the surging tide or a combination of both, the ledge gave a sickening shift and gave way. He grabbed the rope and held the lifeline while the icy water licked at his ankles. "Anytime. I've no interest in a swim tonight!"

"Do something!" That was a squeal from his darling wife. Good to know she had that much energy left after her ordeal.

"By all means, mates," he yelled. "Do something."

"Well, since you insist." Beecham stepped back from the cliff edge and disappeared.

Beecham's cheerful mug was replaced by two members of the search party— constables who obviously spent a lot of time in the gym. Bruisers they were with thick necks and forearms. No doubt they'd pull him to safety quick enough.

The trip back was even more difficult than the one he'd taken down, but the bruiser constables hoisted him steadily. When they finally dragged him to the top of the cliff and over the side, he was greeted by the dearest sight in the world—Miranda.

Her heart-shaped face was still pale and pinched with the cold, but someone had covered her head with a bulky fisherman's sweater. And who gave that up for her? He'd thank them all later, but getting her out of the cold was imperative.

"Thank you." He pulled to his feet and leaned on Beecham. He held out his arm for Miranda and she snuggled close. Her small frame was shaking with a hard chill. "Let's get my wife out of the cold," David gasped. "Everyone, back to the estate. There'll be tea and food for everyone."

Beecham grinned. "Sure of that, are you? Must be handy having servants and all."

David grinned back. "Times like these—damned straight." He pulled the mobile from his pocket. "I'll let them know we found Miranda." He stopped to catch a breath.

By the time he'd completed his call to Fields, the search party had gathered their equipment and were ready to head back to the estate. David picked Miranda up in his arms.

She struggled somewhat ineffectively. "You don't have to carry me. I can walk."

"We'll make better time. I'm not taking any more chances with you. And that's all there is to it." He'd come too close to losing them. And Jamie's current condition was unknown. The quicker they made it back to the estate the sooner they would know.

She settled in his arms and must've read his mind. Her next question was, "Tell me again. Are you sure Jamie's going to be all right?"

David swallowed and stalled for time. Their son was near death from hypothermia— how could he tell her that? "He was cold and barely conscious, but still alive. He's strong. An EMT ran with him back to the estate."

"Lord Fruitcake gave you a terrible choice. You made the right one."

"Fruitcake?" He shook his head and smiled.

"Yes, that's what I came to call him throughout all the mess. He was clearly unhinged at some point. Killing all those people. Did you ever find out why?"

"Why don't you save your breath for breathing?" he gasped. Trudging through the snow with his wife in his arms was more than he'd bargained for—even though her weight was a bare forty-eight kilos.

Now he thought about it, his own breathing wasn't too good. More and more difficult to move air through his lungs. "Agh..." he groaned and collapsed, taking Miranda with him.

Chapter Thirty-four

Sunday

When David's legs gave way and he fell on top of me, Had he had a heart attack? Had I killed him? "David? What's wrong?"

"Can't breathe..."

Two police constables—the Schwarzenegger wannabes—stepped forward and pulled David to his feet. "Agh."

The sound of his groans knifed through me as if I were the one in pain. "Where does it hurt? Is it a crushing pain?" I wasn't a heart surgeon's daughter for nothing.

"Right...chest," he gasped again.

"Did you break a rib?"

He shook his head. "Not rib."

"Might be a spontaneous pneumothorax. We've got to get him back to the estate," I said.

"What?" from David.

"That's doctor talk for collapsed lung, hon. You need a chest tube inserted PDQ Then you'll be able to breathe just fine."

"Agh..." His eyes widened.

"Well, don't worry. I can't do anything like that."

"Good."

The two constables managed to half-walk, half-carry David back to the estate. It was a hell of a trip—cold, damp, and dark—

and it seemed to take forever.

Luckily Fields had already called the doctor to attend to Jamie, who I discovered had been in worse shape than David, but the administration of warmed intravenous fluids had perked him up immensely. I found my son lying on one of the sofas in the morning room. I knelt beside him. "Mama's here." I brushed back a lock of damp black hair from his forehead and kissed him.

His dark lashes fluttered and he smiled up at me. "Hi, Mum," he said, then drifted back to sleep.

Behind me, David was on the other sofa. The rest of the search party I sent to the kitchen. Fields informed me on our arrival Cook had prepared a feast of sandwiches and gallons of fresh tea and coffee.

I quickly described the events leading up to David's collapse.

Dr. Jacobi listened to David's chest. "No lung sounds on the right, Sir David. Spontaneous pneumothorax is the diagnosis. No time to waste."

The doctor turned to Fields. "I've a suction apparatus in my vehicle. Be a good man and bring it."

Fields nodded and rushed out. If he hadn't been unconscious the last time I saw him, I would've never known he'd been injured.

As soon as Fields returned with the suction machine, the doctor removed a sterile packet which contained a long plastic tube from his bag. "Latex allergy?"

David shook his head, but his eyes widened while he watched the doctor's preparations.

"Good thing. I don't normally carry latex-free equipment in my bag." He proceeded to cleanse David's right chest wall. "I'll inject some numbing medicine, but this is still going to hurt. You *will* feel much better once it's done."

"That's somewhat reassuring," David muttered.

The doctor injected, waited for the Xylocaine to take effect, then positioned his fingers on two adjacent ribs. He opened another packet containing a scalpel and proceeded to cut between the ribs.

"Exhale as deeply and as long as you can," he said. He jammed the plastic tubing into the bleeding space.

"Careful!" David let out a groan.

"Sorry, but I warned you." Dr. Jacobi connected the tubing to a suction machine containing sterile water, then switched it on. A small amount of bloody fluid spurted into the container. "We'll keep this tubing in place and connected to suction until his chest x-ray shows his lung is completely re-expanded. Normally a day or two. I want him at hospital."

I nodded my agreement. I glanced down at my husband. His face was pale and sweaty. "Are you breathing any better?"

"A bit."

I sat down on the floor beside the sofa. "Are you really all right?"

He tried to shrug off my concern but winced in pain. "Felt better. Felt worse."

"Cute."

"Jamie all right?"

I nodded. "He's asleep. His color's good. He's tough." It'd been a close call for both of us.

"I love you," he said.

"You, too, pardner." I rubbed my coming-back-to-life fingers across his forehead. He grinned up at me and promptly went to sleep.

Must've been my magnetic personality.

After the ambulance took David off to the hospital, I had the rocker brought from the nursery and placed before the roaring fire. I held Jamie in my arms and rocked him. When he finally opened his big brown eyes again, a huge rush of relief swept through me. "Hey, there, little guy. How're you feeling?"

His gaze darted around the room. He gave me a sweet little smile when he realized where he was. "Where's the man with the box?"

"He's run away, darlin'. Far away." I hoped my words were the truth.

"He might come back."

I shook my head. "No, no. He's not coming back. He knows he's done some bad, bad things, so the police will be looking for him."

"Where's father? I thought I saw him in the woods. But my eyes were all fuzzy."

"You did see him, but he's had a little medical problem and he's on his way to the hospital...for a chest x-ray. Yes, they're going to take a picture of his lungs." That much was certainly the truth.

"Did the bad man hurt him?"

"No, no. He's going to be all right." Jamie's eyelids fluttered at half-mast. "Go on back to sleep. You don't have to worry. We'll go see your father this afternoon."

"Can he come home with us then?"

"Maybe or the day after. Now, go back to sleep." I kept holding and rocking him and glanced at the long case clock beside the fireplace. Three in the morning.

Saturday was a damn long day, but knowing Sunday had arrived and my family—my world—was still intact was all I needed.

Fields came into the morning room.

"Do I smell smoke?" I asked. I'd been so focused on my husband and son, I hadn't noticed the acrid smell of smoke until then.

"Yes, your ladyship. Hutton set a fire in the cellar, but it was quickly extinguished."

Fields was his normal neat and tidy self. "Would you like me to carry Master Jamie to his room?"

"No." I shook my head. "I'll think I'll just move to the sofa and we'll sleep here. The fire is so warm. I hate to leave it." In spite of our being safe and warm, there was still a chill deep in my soul. It wouldn't go away until old Fruitcake was caught.

Fields nodded. He helped me move Jamie from the chair to the sofa, then covered us both with a coverlet. He set about dimming the lights. "Thank you," I murmured and dozed off.

"That's my girl."

I opened my eyes and glanced around the room. Except for

Jamie, I was alone.

Think what you like. As long as I lived, I'd know I heard my Gran's voice in the cave. She spoke my name and told me not to give up. That's my story and I'm sticking to it.

Sunday afternoon

By the time we saw David at the hospital, everything was resolved. His lung had re-expanded, the tube was removed, but he was to stay another day for a repeat x-ray. Then, if it was normal, he could come home. He'd be barred from duty for another week and the honeymoon would still have to wait a little longer.

Lord Hutton would never pay for his crimes by going to prison; however, he hadn't escaped a higher form of justice. He'd crashed in a hired Land Rover and flipped it on the M-11. A semi-truck was unable to stop and slammed into Fruitcake's vehicle, jack-knifed and landed on top of it.

Lord Fruitcake deserved to die. Can't say I'm sorry or that I'll ever forgive him. I'm not that highly evolved yet. He killed four people, tried to kill my son and me and the tiny life I carried.

And yes, I finally peed on the stick.

The End

About the Author

Marie-Nicole Ryan was born in a small western Kentucky town, but after college and marriage, she said "Good bye" to small town life. After spending three years as an army wife, she landed in Nashville, TN, where she spent several decades working as an R.N. and case manager. Finally in 2002, she achieved her lifelong dream of becoming a published author.

She loves all lawmen and detectives and writes erotic historical western romance and contemporary romantic suspense. TOO GOOD TO BE TRUE, won a 2008 EPPIE for erotic romantic suspense. In addition, her mystery/suspense novel, ONE TOO MANY, was a 2009 EPPIE Finalist.

She returned to her old hometown in western Kentucky in 2010. When she's not slaving away at her current work in progress, you might find her walking her dog Cassie, a Sheltie rescue, or at the Y. But you won't ever find her in an airplane. No, not ever.

She's a former long-time member of Romance Writers of America® To learn more about Marie-Nicole Ryan, please visit her web site at https://marienicoleryan.com. To keep up with her latest releases, new, and contests, send an email to Marie-NicoleRyanNews-subscribe@yahoo.com_Or you may follow her on:
Facebook: https://facebook.com/marienicoleryan.author
Twitter: @MarieNicoleRyan

www.ingramcontent.com/pod-product-compliance
Lightning Source LLC
Chambersburg PA
CBHW020223260626
47156CB00002B/511